Dismounting awkward
ping jaws with a stro
staggered away from t

The simple act of walking a few steps brought on fresh weakness. His head started swimming, and he could not seem to hold himself upright. Gritting his teeth, he struggled to keep planting one foot in front of the other, and splashed his way across the stream that, ordinarily, he could have easily jumped over.

Climbing the hillside was nearly impossible, even when he grabbed onto the shtac saplings to pull himself forward. He could manage only one or two steps at a time without resting, breathing heavily all the while. Then his knees buckled despite his resistance, and he sank down.

The mouth of the shrine where he hoped—and prayed— he would find the Chalice was only a few feet distant, but it looked far away. He could feel himself sinking into unconsciousness, and desperately fought to stay awake. If he stopped now, he would likely die, and so would his friends, and all the Netherans fighting in his name.

"I . . . will not . . . let Gavril kill . . . me!" he vowed through gritted teeth . . .

Ace Books by Deborah Chester

THE SWORD
THE RING
THE CHALICE
REIGN OF SHADOWS
SHADOW WAR

Lucasfilm's Alien Chronicles™

THE GOLDEN ONE
THE CRIMSON CLAW

The Sword, the Ring, and the Chalice

---- BOOK 3 ----

THE CHALICE

DEBORAH CHESTER

ACE BOOKS, NEW YORK

THE CHALICE

An Ace Book / published by arrangement with
the author

PRINTING HISTORY
Ace edition / January 2001

All rights reserved.
Copyright © 2000 by Deborah Chester.
Cover art by Jean Pierre Targete.

This book, or parts thereof, may not be reproduced
in any form without permission.
For information address: The Berkley Publishing Group,
a division of Penguin Putnam Inc.,
375 Hudson Street, New York, New York 10014.

The Penguin Putnam Inc. World Wide Web site address is
http://www.penguinputnam.com

ISBN: 0-441-00796-1

ACE®
Ace Books are published
by The Berkley Publishing Group,
a division of Penguin Putnam Inc.,
375 Hudson Street, New York, New York 10014.
ACE and the "A" design are trademarks
belonging to Penguin Putnam Inc.

PRINTED IN THE UNITED STATES OF AMERICA

10 9 8 7 6 5 4

PART ONE

1

IN UPLAND MANDRIA, pewter-gray clouds scudded low over woods and marshland alike. A light but steady drizzle—the kind that rusted mail and weapons faster than squires could polish them clean again—had been falling all day. The road was muddy and rutted, hindering the already slow progress of the expedition. Dain and Prince Gavril, united in their quest to save Lady Pheresa's life, were traveling northward with a large force of church soldiers and priests.

Clad in a quilted wool undertunic, a fine hauberk of triple-linked mail, a green surcoat, and a heavy cloak of dark wool, Dain was riding along, lost in his own thoughts, when he sensed something unusual. At once he spurred his horse, Soleil, off the road and into the woods that lay eastward.

His protector, Sir Terent, cantered after him, crashing through the undergrowth and slinging mud as he came.

Reining up, Dain gestured for Sir Terent to turn back, but he was too late. The hind that had been frozen with fright in the bushes leaped from cover and bounded away with a white flash of her tail.

Swiftly Dain tried to capture what might lie in her dim mind, but all he found there was a frantic *run/run/run/run*.

Disappointed, he let the contact fade and stayed a moment beneath the shelter of the trees. Ah, it felt good to inhale the fragrances of damp soil, mossy tree bark, the rotting leaves underfoot, and the marshland in the distance. The frosty bite to the air stung his cheeks and numbed his fingers, but he welcomed the cold. Foliage blazed in hues of scarlet and gold, and leaves drifted down around them, cartwheeling across the ground wherever the wind gusted.

Sir Terent rode up beside him. Muscular and ruddy-faced, the knight protector was rough-hewn and unpolished. But his gruff exterior belied a heart both true and loyal. Right now, he was looking puzzled. "What set you this way, sire? Were you thinking to course game?"

"Nay," Dain said with scorn. "Unlike Gavril, I need no sport to amuse me. I thought I sensed something."

"Nonkind?"

"Nay . . ." Frowning, Dain turned his face eastward again. He listened, but all he could hear was the clanking, creaking progress of the wagons and the steady plod of the church soldiers' horses. They'd been eight days on the road thus far, since disembarking from the royal barges at the river town of Tuisons, and at this slow rate of travel they'd be at least that many days more—if not longer—before they reached the Netheran border. Since yesterday, Dain had been troubled by an uneasy feeling of being followed. It came and went, as light and elusive as the breeze.

"Anything?" Sir Terent asked quietly, watching him.

Dain shook his head in frustration. He didn't want to tell his protector that of late his eld senses seemed sometimes clouded and uncertain. If he opened himself too much, there came an assault of men-minds all jumbled with thoughts of piety, war, jealousy, worry, and vengeance. Added to that was the odd spell woven by the priest guardians keeping Lady Pheresa alive. It wasn't magic exactly, but something mysterious and unexplained. Although Dain felt no serious harm in it, it made him uneasy and restless.

He longed to get away from all of them, longed to lose himself deep in the forests, to find peace and quiet for a time. But such a wish was only self-indulgence; he could not afford it now.

"Nothing," he said to Sir Terent with a shrug. "I thought we might be followed."

"If not by Nonkind, who?"

Dain frowned. He could not help but glance at the trees once more, although there was nothing to be seen among them.

Sir Terent grunted. "Bandits, mayhap. We travel rich enough to tempt anyone."

"If they attack, they'll rue the exercise."

Exchanging grins, they let their horses amble back toward the road. The company was still moving at a steady pace. Church soldiers, wearing their distinctive white surcoats with the black circles on both breast and back, trotted past. Their helmets were tied to their saddlecloths. They rode with spurs and bridles jingling. Yet for all their noise and chatter, they stayed watchful and alert.

Although Dain had no liking for these knights and their rigid set of pious beliefs, they were well-trained warriors, stalwart enough to ward off most trouble. No bandit with any sense would dare confront a hundred armed knights, no matter how tempting the contents of these many wagons.

It was not bandits, however, that worried Dain. There was much unrest across these uplands. The common folk who emerged from small villages to watch their progress cheered little and seemed relieved to see them go. Now and then they came across an isolated homestead that had been burned out or else stood deserted.

As for this sense of being watched, Dain wished he could determine what was bothering his instincts. All he knew was that it was hostile.

A shout rang out, rousing him from his thoughts. Dain saw four knights galloping toward him, with a familiar, red-haired figure in their midst. Feeling exasperated beyond measure, Dain scowled at them.

"Lord Faldain, hold there!" called one of the knights.

But Dain had already reined up.

Beside him, Sir Terent scowled. "Damne, they do insult you without fail."

Since the first day of this journey, the church soldiers had steadfastly refused to address Dain by any rank higher than chevard. Despite King Verence's public acknowledgment of Dain as a prince of Nether, Mandrian prejudice against the eldin grew from deep roots, fostered by the Reformed Church. Although these knights were required to treat Dain as nobly born, they expressed their disapproval in myriad ways. Calling him by his lesser rank was but one of them. Coming here now, with his squire Thum in tow, was no doubt yet another.

Sir Terent's hand went to his sword hilt. "Time they had a bit of courtesy stuffed down their gullets."

"Nay," Dain said sharply to him. "You know my wishes in this matter."

Growling, Sir Terent subsided, but his green eyes were afire with resentment as the soldiers came up.

Their officer, Sir Wiltem, was a burly man of middle years whose nose had been broken often in past conflicts. He stopped his horse directly in front of Dain's and glared at him. "Is this your man?" he asked curtly, gesturing at Thum.

Dain looked his friend over swiftly. Although pale enough to make his freckles stand out like spots, Thum showed no bruise marks. He sat upright in his saddle, his gloved hands clenching the reins, his breath steaming about his set face. He looked furious, but unharmed.

"My lord," the officer repeated, "is this your man?"

"You know him to be Thum du Maltie, my squire," Dain replied with equal brusqueness. "What do you with him?"

"We were on scout patrol, and caught him sneaking away—"

"I was not!" Thum said indignantly, glaring at the knight. "Morde a day, but this is the basest slander. I was riding on my business in plain view."

The man ignored Thum's protest completely and went on scowling at Dain. "Your squire has no leave to depart the company. He can produce no writ of authority from Lord Barthomew. Nor would he tell us his destination."

"Release him, Sir Wiltem," Dain said in rising annoyance. "He rides to Thirst Hold, by my order."

"And has your lordship permission from his highness to dispatch this rider?"

Dain's fists clenched hard on the reins. "Sir Wiltem," he said in a voice like iron, "we ride across Thirst land today. If anyone's permission is required to come and go here, it is *mine*. Or have you forgotten I am chevard of Thirst, and by the king's own warrant?"

For a moment Sir Wiltem looked as though he'd swallowed a wasp, then he bowed over his saddle. "Your pardon, my lord. It did not occur to me—"

"Plainly," Dain snapped, cutting short his apology. His gray eyes—eld eyes—blazed at the officer, who shifted his gaze away uneasily.

Sir Wiltem cleared his throat. "We, er, have our commander's orders to keep all in the company close. For the safety of—"

"And do your orders tell you to interfere with my affairs?" Dain broke in sharply.

Anger flashed in Sir Wiltem's eyes, but Dain's gaze never wavered. Once again Sir Wiltem was the first to look away.

"The safety of this company is—"

"Thod's bones, will you say that my squire's departure threatens us?"

Sir Wiltem's face reddened. "I follow orders, my lord," he said stiffly.

"Then perhaps you are too zealous, sir," Dain told him. "Be sure your orders do not again interfere with what I tell my men to do."

Sir Wiltem's eyes were stony, his face impassive. The offense he'd given was serious, but clearly he'd offered all the apology he meant to.

Without another word, he wheeled his horse around and rode away with his men, cutting through the line of wagons lurching ponderously along the road.

Glaring after them, Thum spat eloquently.

Sir Terent flung back a fold of his cloak. "Hah, sire! That told 'em! 'Tis good to see Wiltem put in his place; aye, and well-whipped with reprimand. He'll think twice ere he crosses your majesty's will again."

Dain was less sure. The church soldiers' allegiance belonged to Gavril and Noncire; Dain's authority in this expedition was slight indeed. Although the plan was for him to enter Nether disguised and unnoticed, he now wished he'd accepted Prince Spirin's offer to send an entourage of exiles with him. Aside from a few servants provided by King Verence, Dain had only his few loyal companions from Thirst to stand by him. At times like these, he felt himself to be teetering on a political precipice.

"Did they harm you?" he asked Thum.

"Nay, I'm well," his friend replied. Lanky, tall, and still growing, Thum du Maltie had of late grown a small brown chin-beard and narrow mustache which made him look more mature than his actual years. A well-born, quiet-spoken young man, Thum seldom lost his temper. But right now, his ire was hot, and his hazel-green eyes were snapping.

"I tried to outrun them, but they cut me off," he said. "I had a bad moment or two when I thought they might run me through. Thod's bones, they acted like I was a dire enemy instead of a mere messenger."

"Those knights weren't scouting," Sir Terent said scornfully. "They acted with direct intent, or I'm a—"

"And did they search you?" Dain asked, interrupting him.

Thum shook his head. "Their saying I refused to tell them my business is a lie! They never asked, just rounded me up and forced me to come back with them." He frowned at Dain. "It's wondrous strange."

"No stranger than refusing to spend the night at any hold we've passed thus far," Dain said thoughtfully. He looked ahead at the wagons rolling up the muddy road. "There's need for haste, but this goes too far. The lady cannot keep up such a pace."

Thum sighed. "We're crawling. Mud or not, these kine could pull faster if—"

"For *her*, it's fast enough," Dain said sharply, then softened his tone. "Well, no matter now. My message must still go to the hold."

Thum gathered his reins at once. "Then I'm to ride again?"

Dain nodded. "Let's hope you reach it unhindered this time."

"I'll ride like the wind to make up for lost time." Thum wheeled his horse around, then spurred away in a gallop, his cloak billowing out behind him. In three huge bounds, horse and rider reached the trees and vanished from sight.

"I can send Polquin to follow him in case he's set upon again," Sir Terent offered.

Dain frowned. "Nay. If I know Thum, he won't be caught a second time."

"He'll be lucky to reach Thirst's gates before eventide, delayed like this. If they won't open for him—"

"He'll get there," Dain said, refusing to think of Thum being left stranded for the night outside the hold walls, shivering with cold and prey to whatever evil might lurk in the darkness. "He'll think of that, and he'll take no chances."

"Aye, he's a smart lad." Sir Terent inhaled deeply and glanced overhead at the drizzling sky. "It's good indeed to be back on Thirst soil, sire."

Dain smiled at him. "We've been away too long."

"That we have."

"Before tomorrow's nightfall," Dain promised him, "we'll be in our Hall, drinking Thirst cider."

"With roast pig in our trenchers?"

Dain laughed. "Perhaps so. But now it's time to talk to his highness about his meddling."

Sir Terent sobered at once. "Now, Dain—uh, I mean, sire," he said uneasily. "It ain't wise to go picking a quarrel. Could be this was all Lord Barthomew's idea."

"Barthomew cannot scratch himself without Gavril's suggestion."

Sir Terent grinned. "Aye, 'tis true enough. Still, it ain't wise to fuss with his highness—"

"This is my land," Dain said grimly. "And I owe Gavril no oath of fealty for it. He should not interfere with me here."

Sir Terent looked alarmed. "His highness will do whatever he chooses. You know that."

"I know that tomorrow night Lady Pheresa will rest inside Thirst's walls as long as she needs to."

Not giving Sir Terent time to think up any more objections, Dain kicked Soleil forward and rode to the front of the column.

He passed the numerous wagons piled high with provisions,

tents, clothes chests, and countless gifts of great cost which Gavril intended to give to King Muncel for his assistance in their quest to save Pheresa.

The lady herself traveled in the foremost wagon, lying in her glass encasement with a blanket spread over it to shield her from curious eyes. Next to her sat Megala, her serving woman, today a cold huddled figure in her damp cloak. On either side of Pheresa's wagon rode the thirteen guardians on donkeys. These priests were entrusted with the difficult task of sustaining the spell of faith which kept her alive. Cowled and silent, each guardian was attended by a monk assigned to lead the donkeys and bring food and drink when needed. It was paramount that the guardians never be distracted, never be required to perform the most mundane task, never even be spoken to directly. All their attention and energy had to remain focused on their difficult task.

And that it was difficult Dain had no doubt. Several times he'd heard some of the guardians moan aloud whenever Pheresa suffered most.

Dain could not bear to look at her encasement, traveling well-secured with ropes to keep it from shifting. Each time he thought of her, afflicted with poison and paralyzed inside this mysterious Mandrian spell that kept her alive, he wanted to cry aloud with anguish. She was so beautiful and good. She had never done anyone harm. She deserved nothing as terrible as this affliction. Every morn when he awoke, he renewed his vow to find a way to save this sweet maid who'd stolen his heart.

As he trotted past her wagon, he glanced at the servant woman. "How does the lady?" he called out.

Megala, clutching her cloak beneath her chin, bowed to him nervously and would not directly meet his eld eyes. "Well enough, sir," she replied. "The pains trouble her, I think. She cries a little in her sleep, poor lamb."

Fresh worry filled Dain. The spell holding Pheresa safe sometimes grew weak and allowed the poison to progress further through her body. That's when her pain came back.

Unhappy to hear that the lady was failing again, Dain spurred Soleil onward and rode past the flag bearers. Gavril's blue and gold pennon hung slack in today's rain, as did the cardinal's yellow one and the black and white banner of the church soldiers. Yet another man carried the brown flag of pilgrimage, although its display was unnecessary until they reached the Netheran border.

At the very front of the column, Gavril rode astride a magnificent black horse caprisoned in silver. Surrounded by his personal guards, lord protector, noble-born squires, Lord Barthomew and two other church knight officers, a minstrel, and various advisers, Gavril glowed with proud self-importance. Although he remained as handsome as ever, of late he'd begun to look thin and sometimes haggard. It was rumored he did not sleep well. Among the men it was said that the prince's worry for his betrothed affected him. Dain, however, believed that Gavril was pining for Tanengard. Against all common sense, the tainted sword had been brought with them, locked away in a box among the baggage. Dain had silenced its terrible song for a while, but he knew eventually its power would begin to stir anew. When it did, Gavril would not be able to resist its call.

Still, however hard his personal demons might drive him, Gavril had not lost his taste for finery. Today, his gold-colored chain mail shone brightly despite dreary rain and mud. A vivid blue cloak lined with pale, exquisite lyng fur protected him from the elements. His gauntlets were stitched of costly blue leather, with his crest embroidered on the cuffs.

At his side rode Cardinal Noncire, whose obese bulk flowed over the saddle in all directions. Robed in black wool with a yellow sash of office beneath his fur-lined cloak, the cardinal looked like an immense pillow balanced precariously atop his stout, slow-moving horse. Hooded against the rain, Noncire appeared grim and miserable as he conversed with the prince.

As Dain rode up, Gavril's guards glanced his way, instantly alert, and his protector wheeled about to put himself between Dain and the prince.

"Lord Kress, who is that?" Gavril called out, pretending he could not see Dain clearly.

"It is I," Dain said impatiently.

"Ah, Faldain," Gavril said in his mocking way. "Move aside, Kress, and let our visitor approach."

The protector reined back his horse, and Dain rode up between Gavril and Noncire.

The cardinal stared at Dain through his small, beady eyes, and instinctively Dain stiffened in his saddle. He did not trust this cunning schemer, who spoke so softly and kindly, yet had a heart of flint. Noncire was neither friend nor ally to Dain, and never would be. After giving Dain a cold stare, he bowed his head slightly in a token gesture of courtesy.

Dain nodded back to him and turned his attention to Gavril. He had his temper in hand. He intended to start with diplomacy. "My thanks for your reception," he said politely.

The prince, his handsome face looking tired beneath a thin, light brown mustache, eyed Dain with even more coldness than had the cardinal. "What do you want?"

"I offer invitation and hospitality," Dain said. "On the morrow, let us stop at Thirst Hold and bide there."

A twisted smile appeared fleetingly on Gavril's face. He glanced across Dain at Noncire. "It seems that our kingly companion wishes to play host."

Noncire stroked his gray goatee. "The offer is well-intentioned, your highness. A rest in some comfort would be most welcome to all, I'm sure."

"There is no comfort to be had at Thirst, lord cardinal. 'Tis a dour, drafty, inhospitable place, fit only for uplander barbarians."

"'Tis better than pitching tents on the mud," Dain said mildly. "Why not avail ourselves of what the hold can offer? I will not forbid your highness wine, if it's Thirst cider you fear."

His small joke made Noncire smile, but Gavril seemed unamused by the reference to their foster days, when Chevard Odfrey had kept Gavril's wines locked in the cellars and insisted all hold folk stay sober.

"No," Gavril said. "We will not stop there."

Dain sighed. "Why is my offer not pleasing? I have sent a rider ahead to tell them we draw near. All will be prepared for our arrival."

Gavril frowned. "Damne, I gave orders against such—"

"So I learned," Dain said grimly. "But my rider has been dispatched all the same."

Fire sparked in Gavril's dark blue eyes. "Do you dare defy me?"

"Thirst is mine, by your father's generosity," Dain said, knowing the reminder would twist Gavril's guts. "'Tis not defiance to order my men to meet certain responsibilities."

"You—"

"Please," Dain said, wanting to keep Gavril from working up his notorious temper. "I offer this for Lady Pheresa's sake. She grows worse. She needs rest."

"We'll camp early today," Gavril said.

"Sleeping in a tent in the midst of a forest, with rain, mud, and inconvenience, is hardly the rest she needs," Dain said, trying to stay patient. "At Thirst she can be made comfortable for a few days until she—"

"A few days! Thod's grace, are you mad?" Gavril shouted. "There is no time for lolling at our ease while you play host."

"This is a hard journey we make. Surely—"

"You have done nothing but urge us forward since we left Savroix. When we were on the royal barge, you complained about how slowly the rowmen took us upriver against the current. When I would have taken Lord Ardelon's recommendation to follow the king's road north, you insisted we take this one instead. No doubt because it runs past Thirst Hold."

Dain frowned. "This road is the shortest route—"

Gavril's lip twisted. "Yet how convenient for you. And how remarkable that now, after all your urgency and fretting, it seems you are no longer in such a hurry. Let us dally at Thirst, you say. Let us feast and take our ease and make merry."

"I only—"

"It is not Pheresa you think about, but rather yourself."

"Nay!" Dain said angrily.

Gavril's eyes flashed. "You want time at Thirst to foment more unrest among the divisionists. You want to busy yourself raising an army among men inclined to forget they are loyal Mandrians first. You—"

"Have done," Dain snapped. "Let it be Thirst or any other hold in the land. I care not. Only deliver the lady to a place of comfort. She suffers, and I seek only to alleviate that."

Gavril's eyes grew hot and jealous. He glared at Dain. "You

would do well to remember that Pheresa's welfare is *my* responsibility. Not yours. She is under excellent care. The physicians who attend her have assured me not an hour past that she remains strong."

"Her servant woman says otherwise."

"Morde!" Gavril said as though driven to the limits of his patience. "What care I for the opinion of an ignorant servant? Shall I listen to *her* instead of learned men?"

"She—"

"And why should I listen to *you*?" Gavril went on furiously. "What knowledge of science do *you* possess?"

Dain's mouth clamped tight. He sat there, feeling his pulse thud in his throat and temples.

Noncire cleared his throat. "Perhaps, your highness—"

"Perhaps what?" Gavril interrupted rudely. "Do you intend that I should listen to the advice of this pagan who would be a king?"

Dain's eyes narrowed at the insult. Behind him, Sir Terent inhaled sharply. For a moment, as Dain glared at Gavril, he saw only haze and fire. Then came a vision of himself, clad in rags, with a leather collar buckled around his neck and a chain leading from it like a dog's leash.

This, Dain realized, stunned by his first direct glimpse into Gavril's mind, must be what Gavril really thought of him. *This* was what Gavril actually wanted from him. To the prince, Dain would always remain a pagan dog, fit only to sniff out the whereabouts of the missing Chalice.

Rage burned inside Dain, rekindling his hatred of Gavril, which he'd banked low on this expedition for Pheresa's sake. Now it came up inside him like the spew of a volcano, hot and violent, and it was all he could do not to draw his weapon and challenge the prince then and there.

Somehow, his good sense held him silent, though it took a severe struggle with himself to control his ire. His chest felt on fire, and his voice was hoarse when at last he said, "Tomorrow I shall ride to Thirst, and deal with matters there as are needed. I am sorry your highness does not feel the lady merits its hospitality. No more will be said."

"Your time would be better spent searching for these mysterious eld-folk you claim can cure her!" Gavril said. "At Savroix, you boasted you could find them. Yet where are they? Why do you not produce them? Instead of causing trouble among my father's subjects, why don't you confine yourself to accomplishing your sole task on this quest?"

Dain glared at him, stiff with frustration. It was futile to keep arguing, he realized.

Just as he started to back Soleil away, however, Megala stood up in the front wagon and screamed. "My lady!" she cried out. "My lady! Help her!"

2

THE DRIVER OF Pheresa's wagon yanked his team to a lurching halt. Gripping the encasement to keep her balance, Megala screamed again.

Horrified, Dain cried out, "Pheresa!"

As Dain spurred Soleil in that direction, one of the guardians groaned loudly, clutched his head, and fell off his donkey. Church soldiers, frozen till then, rushed to his aid.

Dain reached the wagon and flung himself off Soleil just as the guardian priest was lifted from the mud. The man's hood fell back to reveal his face, withered and drawn as though he'd aged a century. Dain stared at him with astonishment, for to his knowledge none of the guardians were old. This man's eyes were open and staring fixedly, and his head lolled as though he were dead.

Others crowded around, everyone talking at once. Dain elbowed and pushed his way through the confusion and climbed into Pheresa's wagon just as Megala screamed again.

She reached out her hands to Dain. "Help her," she pleaded. "Help my sweet lady!"

When Dain twitched aside a corner of the blanket, he saw Pheresa writhing inside the encasement. Her eyes were shut, but she was red-faced and clawing the glass with her fingernails.

Flinging aside all caution, he reached for the lid, but strong hands seized him from behind and pulled him back. Furious, Dain struggled, but Sir Terent had him clamped in a stout hug and would not release him.

"Let me go!" Dain shouted. "Damne! Let me go!"

"I won't let you kill yourself. Come away!" Sir Terent shouted back.

Cursing, Dain twisted to get free. As he did so, the blanket slid off the glass entirely, revealing Pheresa in her agony to everyone.

"Cover her!" Gavril commanded, riding up on his black horse. "In Thod's name, cover her now!"

Megala bent to pick up the blanket. A knight swung himself into the wagon and helped her spread the cloth over the encasement.

Meanwhile, Dain was hauled bodily out of the wagon by Sir Terent. As soon as Dain's feet hit the ground, he struggled and cursed with all his might, but Sir Terent's hold was an expert one, and Dain could not break it.

Sir Polquin arrived at a run, took one look at them, and helped Sir Terent manhandle Dain over to one side, well out of the way.

Sputtering and fuming, Dain cursed them both. The royal physicians came hurrying past him, and someone shouted for the men crowding round to let them through. Men and horses milled all around, and the servants came crowding up to whisper and gawk.

When he felt Sir Terent's hold slacken, Dain wrenched free. "How dare you pull me off that wagon!"

"I'm sworn to keep yer grace alive," Sir Terent said simply. "If you touch her, you'll die."

That wasn't strictly true. Dain would be in danger only if he tried to draw the poison afflicting her into himself. But he did not have the healing gifts, and he knew he lacked sufficient skill to withstand the eld-poison in her veins. He started to explain all this yet again to Sir Terent, then told himself it was of no use.

Frowning, he turned and headed back in Pheresa's direction, where men were still shouting and hurrying to and fro. "I must know what—"

"No, sire!" Sir Terent called out in alarm. He ran to block Dain's path, and there was fear in his face. "In Thod's name, don't risk it!"

Amazed, Dain stopped in his tracks. He had never seen Sir Terent like this before.

"Please," Sir Terent pleaded.

"She will not harm me. You need not—"

"She will, sire. She *will*," Sir Terent insisted. "I know you have a generous heart and you would gladly risk yourself on her behalf, but you must not."

Sighing, Dain gave up the argument. By then Sulein had come squelching through the mud, looking alarmed. "Sulein," Dain said to him, "make haste, and tell me what can be done for her?"

"As I told your majesty before, the spell they have cast over her is weaker than they believe," Sulein said, steepling his long fingers together. "If one of the guardians has collapsed, the spell is now out of balance. It may fail completely."

"Morde!" Dain said in fresh alarm. He gripped Sulein's sleeve. "Come! We must help her."

"Your majesty forgets I am forbidden to attend the lady."

"But you know what to do. You can help her, can't you?"

Not giving Sulein a chance to answer, Dain stepped around Sir Terent and headed grimly toward the spot where Gavril was now standing, asking a question of one of the physicians.

"The spell cannot hold long without thirteen guardians, your highness," the physician replied loudly. "The potion my colleague is giving her will ease her only if the spell can be rebalanced—"

"Agreed," Sulein said as he and Dain halted beside the prince's group.

Gavril's face clouded over, and the physician turned to look at Dain and Sulein with raised eyebrows.

Silence fell over Gavril and his small group. The hauteur on their faces angered Dain, for their pride and bigotry put Pheresa at more risk.

Cardinal Noncire gave Dain a very slight inclination of his head. "I fear your majesty's creature has no place here," he said quietly, with a hostile glance at Sulein. "His opinion is not requested."

"Hear him," Dain said with equal coldness. "For once, put aside your prejudice against all who are foreign. Master Sulein's knowledge is more useful than you suppose."

Gavril sniffed and swung his gaze back to the royal physician. "And what is necessary to rebalance the—the means by which she is kept alive?"

"Another guardian must be substituted or the spell will fail completely," Sulein said before the other physician could answer.

"Silence him!" Gavril shouted at Dain. "He has not my leave to speak."

Ignoring the prince, Dain turned to Sulein. "Could you take the fallen guardian's place?" he asked. "Truthfully," he added in warning before Sulein answered. "This is no time for ambition or vanity."

Sulein's dark eyes flashed in umbrage. "Your majesty maligns me," he complained. "But, yes, I possess the power *and* the skills for this kind of spell."

Gavril stepped up to them, his dark blue eyes snapping with fury. "He is dismissed, I said! This blasphemer will not go near my lady."

"Then she'll die," Dain said harshly. At that moment, he'd never despised Gavril more. "Or is that what you really want?"

A white ring appeared around Gavril's mouth. He reached for his sword. Dain did the same.

Before either of them could draw, Sir Terent and Lord Kress jumped between them.

"Please, please, excellencies!" Cardinal Noncire called out. "Consider the lady. This is no time for fighting."

Dain took his hand off his sword hilt and stood there hotcheeked and fuming while Gavril's face grew paler and paler until his eyes were like burning coals.

Noncire turned to Sulein, and although a look of distaste crossed his fleshy face, his small black eyes never wavered. "Give me the truth, Master Sulein. Can you contribute to the weavings of faith emanating from the guardians?"

"Yes, I can," Sulein replied.

"You are not of the Circle," Noncire continued. "Are you foe to it? If I permit you to join your skills with theirs, will you destroy what has been wrought or assist it?"

Sulein bowed to him. "I will assist. This, I swear on all that is held most sacred."

"Don't let him near her!" Gavril shouted. He would have rushed at Sulein, but his protector blocked his path. Gavril swore and struck the man with his fist, but Lord Kress grimly held firm. "Keep him away from her!" Gavril said. "I command it!"

Dain started to protest, but instead stretched out his hand in appeal to the cardinal. "Does it break the laws of Writ to let a nonbeliever give assistance?"

Noncire frowned, but before he could reply, Sulein pulled a Circle from his pocket and held it up. "But I *am* a believer in the Circle," he announced. "Because I am not Mandrian-born does not mean I have not heard the message of Tomias the Prophet."

Dain's head jerked around, and he stared at the physician with astonishment before he swiftly lowered his gaze. He felt certain that Sulein was lying. The physician seemed to accept any art or magic that would advance his greedy ambitions, but he was no member of the Reformed Church.

Noncire seemed taken aback. Finally, however, he extended his hand in benediction to Sulein, who bowed low.

"Your highness, this changes everything," the cardinal said to Gavril.

"No!" the prince shouted. "No!"

"Your highness, if this man can help keep the lady alive, then surely we must permit him to do so."

"I do not trust him."

"Does it matter, if he can help?"

While Gavril stared openmouthed at his former tutor, Dain stepped close to Sulein and glared at him.

"You play a dangerous game, Sulein," he said very softly, for their ears alone.

The physician's eyes were glowing. "I will never fathom the hidden secrets of these priests' power unless I partake of it," he murmured back.

Angrily Dain gripped his arm. "Do not put her life at risk—"

"I won't." Sulein put his hand atop Dain's, and the Ring of Solder that he wore on his finger—concealed by a small spell of invisibility—flickered momentarily into sight before vanishing again.

The sight of it, as always, had the power to distract Dain, to tempt him, to tantalize and exasperate him. He realized Sulein had let him glimpse it now to silence his protests. And although he fell silent, Dain burned inside with resentment. He'd tried every persuasion he could think of to get the Ring from Sulein, for by right it belonged to him, as it had been his father's before him. Without the Ring he believed he had little chance of finding the Chalice. But Sulein kept it as a guarantee that Dain would someday grant him a high position in Nether's future court, as well as give him part of that kingdom's treasury.

"You must trust me, sire," Sulein said softly. "I know exactly what I am doing."

Noncire came over to them. "His highness has agreed. On his behalf do I thank you, Master Sulein, for your willingness to serve."

Sulein glided away in the cardinal's wake. While Pheresa's encasement was unloaded from the wagon and carried a short distance off the road, wattle panels were unloaded from another wagon and hastily assembled around her tent for privacy. The guardians were led by their attendant monks into the small enclosure, with Sulein following. Soon Dain heard them all chanting in unison.

Aching with worry, he had the feeling that he might never see Sulein or Pheresa alive again.

Church soldiers dispersed the gawkers and issued orders for camp to be made. Soon the whole company was abustle with chores and tasks. The fallen guardian was buried, and laments for the dead rose across the camp in eerie counterpoint to the chanting on Pheresa's behalf.

Sir Polquin directed Dain's servants to put up his tent, and soon they had their own small enclave in place, with a fire crackling and kettles of water aboil.

Restless and unable to occupy himself, Dain started to walk over to Pheresa's enclosure to keep watch there, but he saw Gavril and his minions go by on the same errand.

Frowning, Dain abandoned the intention. Some of Gavril's words had scorched themselves across his mind earlier that day, and he could not forget them. Pheresa was indeed Gavril's lady, not his. No matter how much he still loved her, he could not rightfully intrude.

Instead he paced back and forth, and wisely Sir Polquin and Sir Terent left him alone.

At twilight there came the sound of hoofbeats on the road, and a lone horseman was halted by the sentries.

Watching, Dain saw the silhouette of a thin, upright figure and for a second thought it was Thum returning against orders. But he sensed none of Thum's warm, kindhearted spirit. This was a stranger, no doubt a courier bringing fresh dispatches to Gavril.

The sentries permitted the man to enter camp, and he rode through the tents slowly, his gaze scanning the faces around him.

"The lazy knaves," Sir Terent said, squinting. "You'd think they'd escort him straight to the prince."

"These church soldiers were born in sloth and idleness," Sir Polquin said critically.

Ever since that black day on the banks of the Charva River, when Nonkind had attacked Lord Odfrey's forces while they were escorting Gavril home to Savroix, Sir Polquin's contempt for the church soldiers' cowardice had grown rather than abated. These knights were not the same men, but all were judged by Thirst men under the shadow cast by the infamy of the soldiers who'd chosen to surround Gavril, staying out of danger, while the Thirst knights fought to their deaths.

Dain lost interest in the newcomer and started for his tent

to collect one of the scrolls he'd been studying on this journey. He'd set himself to learn Netheran, and tried to work on his lessons daily.

Just then, however, the courier rode up to their fire and drew rein. "Faldain of Nether?" he asked in a heavily accented voice.

Jumping up, Sir Terent set his hand on his sword hilt, even as Dain turned around in astonishment.

"We are all Mandrians here," the knight protector said in a growl, but the courier was looking at Dain.

With an audible gasp, he dismounted and took two steps before Sir Terent blocked his path. The courier dropped to his knees in the mud and bowed low.

"Your majesty," he said. *"Da venetne skekse? Skekse van yt Thod!"*

Dain stared at him in curiosity. The courier had the look of a man who'd ridden long and hard. He was young, hardly older than Dain himself, with prominent cheekbones and slightly tilted eyes that told of some eld blood. His hair, which was black and straight, was divided into innumerable plaits knotted with carved wooden beads at their ends. Swinging with every movement of his head, these beads clacked softly together. Both of his ears were pierced and sported multiple small gold rings that glinted in the firelight. His skin had a tawny cast to it, his beard was sparse and very black, and his eyes were dark brown. They shone at Dain with a degree of reverence and awe that made him uncomfortable, for he felt he had done nothing as yet to deserve either.

"Rise," Dain said. "Come near the fire and get warm."

The courier obeyed with visible gratitude, and looked around curiously at Dain's modest trappings. Dain wondered if he'd expected to see someone attired in fine velvets and furs, wearing more jewels than a single ruby ring, and waited on hand and foot by liveried servants. Still, he sensed no criticism in the young man, and no doubt.

Although pale with exhaustion, the courier refused offers of food and drink. "My duty, sire, is to give you these letters."

Opening the pouch he kept concealed beneath his fur cloak, the Netheran produced three scrolls of parchment, and dropped to one knee as he handed them to Dain.

Dain accepted them with mixed feelings. No one at Savroix, save King Verence, was supposed to know that he was a member of Gavril's expedition north. Officially Dain remained an invalid at Savroix, gravely ill from a wound and allowed no visitors. The ploy, thin indeed for a place as riddled with spies and gossip-mongers as Savroix, had not been expected to hold long, but Dain had hoped he would at least be able to cross the border into Nether before his true whereabouts were discovered.

"Did Prince Spirin send these missives to me?" he asked.

The courier blinked. "Nay, your majesty. I have ridden from Lubeck. As soon as word reached us that you were found, my father—that is, the rebel leaders met and drew up these pledges of support. I was dispatched to Savroix, but when I arrived there you had gone."

Behind him, Sir Terent swore softly.

The courier cast him a nervous look before returning his gaze to Dain. "From there, I was sent along this road, so back have I ridden."

"Who at Savroix directed you?" Dain asked. "Spirin?"

The courier flushed and hesitated, but at last he gave Dain a nod that made his braid beads clack together. "We spoke in private, I assure your majesty."

Oh, yes, Dain thought with exasperation. And how did Spirin himself know that Dain was gone? Before his departure, Dain had had a long talk with the elderly exile, but he hadn't taken the man completely into his confidence. He knew not yet who among the Netherans he could trust. Spies and paid informants were everywhere, and the Mandrian courtiers and their servants were readily bought. Besides, who might have overheard Spirin's conversation with this courier? And, more important, who, if anyone, had followed the courier here to this camp?

Dain remembered his earlier feeling of being watched this afternoon, and a cold chill went up his spine. He hoped the courier had not brought him additional trouble. "What is your name?" he asked.

The courier pulled himself to attention. "Chesil Matkevskiet, your majesty."

Dain nodded absently, and beckoned to his servants. "Give him food and see to his horse."

Bowing, they hurried to comply. Dain, with Sir Terent at his heels, ducked into his tent. The small lamps inside it had been lit, and they cast a ruddy glow over the narrow cot where Dain's hauberk—freshly cleaned and oiled—now lay spread out, its links reflecting the light softly.

He sat down on a stool while Sir Terent stood guard at the tent flap, and one by one broke the red-wax seals on his letters. He hoped they were not written in Netheran, for his studies had not yet made him proficient in that language.

The first letter was not, much to his relief. Instead, he saw the angular lines of runes. Dain could read these fluently, but he doubted if many others in Mandria could. As a code, it served excellently.

Once he'd gotten past all the florid and excessive salutations, Dain saw that the letter came from Prince Ingor Matkevskiet, leader of the Agya forces in southwest Nether. Matkevskiet pledged his army to Dain's service, all four thousand Agya warriors, legendary even in other lands. Dain had heard many tales of respect among the dwarves for the Agya warriors' bravery and fighting prowess. It was said, however, that they did not always serve the kings of Nether. Even some of King Tobeszijian's battles were reputedly fought without the Agyas. King Muncel had never commanded them.

But now, with the stroke of a few words on this simple piece of parchment, they were offered to Dain . . . all four thousand of them.

It was said that one Agya warrior was worth three men.

A leap of excitement made Dain grin. He laid the letter on his knee and smoothed it with his hand. This was a tremendous honor. The Agyas had not even measured the muscle in his sword arm, as was their custom before swearing allegiance. Yet they were accepting him sight unseen, willing to follow him against Muncel.

Go to Nether, Tobeszijian's ghost had whispered to him, *and the army will come to you.*

So it was true. Dain swallowed the sudden lump in his throat. Opening the second letter, he found it also written in runes.

In it, Count Romsalkin pledged two hundred men to Dain's service.

The third letter was much stained and creased, almost illegible and scratched out in a combination of rune and Netheran that told Dain the writer was hardly more literate than himself. He puzzled over the short sentences for a long while before he finally deciphered their meaning.

Feeling stunned, he looked up and the letter dropped from his hand.

"Sire?" Sir Terent asked in concern. "Are you well?"

"What?" Dain blinked at him without really seeing him, then the tent came back into focus. He bent over and picked up the letter with shaking fingers.

"Bad news?" Sir Terent asked.

"Nay." Dain read the note again, but its message was plain. "It's a pledge from someone named Samderaudin. I know not the name, but I think he must be no lord."

"What does he offer?"

Dain lifted his gaze to meet Sir Terent's. "He offers a cache of weapons and armor that he's concealed in the mountains. I cannot make out everything he writes, but . . . have Chesil Matkevskiet come inside. I wish to talk to him in private."

"Aye, sire."

Sir Terent went outside, and Dain heard his voice calling the courier. Moments later, Chesil entered the tent.

He bowed low to Dain. "Sire?"

Dain swallowed a couple of times to be sure of his voice. "Do you know a man called Samderaudin?"

Chesil's dark eyes widened, and he flung back his head. *"Aychi!"* he exclaimed, and made a quick gesture with his hands that Dain did not understand. "This name I have heard, sire."

All too conscious of Sir Terent's listening ears, Dain leaned forward on the stool and said in his awkward, far-from-fluent Netheran, "And is he a *sorcerel*? Does he command such creatures?"

Chesil looked distinctly uneasy. He stared at the letter in Dain's hand, hesitating, before he nodded with a clack of his beads. "Aye," he replied in Netheran, speaking slowly for Dain's benefit. "He trains them, and is considered a very powerful *sorcerel* himself. He went to the wars when Runtha fought."

"Runtha," Dain said slowly. "My grandfather."

"And great-grandfather," Chesil said. "Two Runthas were there. Both powerful kings."

Dain stared. "Samderaudin served *both*?"

"Aye. Long-lived, are these *sorcerels*. Unless they are hit too often with the death-fire. Then they die young. That Samderaudin himself has written to you is a great honor indeed, your majesty."

"Yes." Dain swallowed. His dwarf upbringing had taught him to fear and avoid *sorcerels* at all costs. Capable of commanding great, magical power, the *sorcerels* supposedly could open the gates between the worlds. It was whispered that there once had been a *sorcerelle*, a female whose name no one dared speak, who had even opened the gates to the gods themselves, and had then perished because she could not withstand the sight of their greatness.

Dain frowned. "It is the custom, I've heard, for Netheran kings to use *sorcerels* in battle."

"Always," Chesil said without hesitation. "Especially when Nonkind are the foes."

"Have you ridden in such battles?"

"No. But my father has, many times."

Dain eyed him with curiosity. "And you do not fear their powers?"

Chesil blinked at him. "I would fear, your majesty, to go to war without them. I would fear to face any Nonkind without their spells of protection."

Dain frowned, thinking of his own encounters with Nonkind demons. Both times he'd fought with the aid of a magic-endowed sword, Truthseeker first and later Tanengard. He wondered what it must be like to face the Nonkind armed with magicked sword and magicked armor as well.

"Prince Volvn," Chesil said, "fought last summer without *sorcerels* and died. He and all five hundred of his men. It was a great loss, for he was the most favored of your father's generals. We Agya admired him much. Since then, the rebel forces of Nether have almost given up. Even we Agya were packing our tents to exile ourselves in the uncharted lands. But when word came that your majesty was found, my father saw new hope. We will fight to the death and beyond for you."

"Thank you," Dain said, and his words seemed inadequate to convey what he was feeling. He held out his hand, and at once Chesil knelt and pressed his lips to the fine ruby on Dain's finger.

When he stood up again, he asked, "Have you a message for my father?"

"Yes," Dain said. "But first, I want to ask another question about Samderaudin. He writes of weapons and armor. I—"

"Does he offer such?" Chesil exclaimed.

"Aye, he does."

"*Aychi!* This is a gift indeed," Chesil said in excitement. "Magicked armor and—"

"Swords?" Dain asked, his own excitement kindling. "Magicked swords?"

Chesil nodded.

Dain rose to his feet with a grin. "Wait outside while I write my responses."

With a bow, Chesil hurried out. Sir Terent came forward, curiosity written all over his ruddy face.

"Aught I can do, sire?"

"I must write something," Dain said, searching through his clothes chest for the small box that held his lesson scrolls, a few scraps of parchment, and his inks. He couldn't help but think of Gavril, who traveled with his exquisite writing desk, an ingenious contraption that looked like an ordinary box made of beautiful woods and inlays. Inside, however, it was a series of clever hinges, drawers, and compartments that held his glass pens and his finely embellished writing papers.

Dain tore off a piece from where he'd been practicing his letters and began scratching out a reply to Prince Matkevskiet in runes, thanking him for the generous pledge of men. He wrote similar notes to Count Romsalkin and Samderaudin.

As he sanded the letters to dry the ink, disbelief tingled through him.

He now had an army to command. Unable to hold his news any longer, he glanced up at Sir Terent, gripped his arm, and whispered, "We must keep this secret for a while, but over four thousand men are pledged to me!"

Sir Terent blinked at him, and slow comprehension dawned in his green eyes. "Great Thod!" he said in astonishment. "That foreign boy has brought you this news?"

"Aye," Dain said. "But voice it not. Secrecy gives me some advantage over King Muncel."

"Of course. I'll say nothing," Sir Terent promised at once. Then he shot Dain a sly grin. "But may I tell Sir Polquin? He frets something awful about how you're to cope without men."

"Let him fret a while longer," Dain said with caution. "I trust him with my life, but too many secrets have escaped us already. Let this bide until I am free to act on it."

"Better yer grace should act on it now," Sir Terent said bluntly. "Leave the lady and her poor fate in the hands of those responsible for her, and get on to—"

"No!" Dain shouted. He slammed his fist down so hard he snapped his pen in half. "I have sworn that I shall see her cured. That comes first."

"But, sire—"

"The people of Nether have waited this many years for deliverance," Dain said harshly, refusing to yield. "They can wait a few months more."

Disappointment crossed Sir Terent's face. He bowed and argued no more. "As yer majesty judges best," he said, but in disapproval.

Annoyed, Dain said no more. From the first day they'd set out on this quest to save Pheresa, Sir Terent and Sir Polquin had been against it. They didn't understand, Dain told himself as he sealed his letters. If they'd ever known what it was like to love a maid as fair as Pheresa, then obviously they'd forgotten. Besides, finding the Chalice would not only save her but also help him regain his kingdom. Dain set his mouth and called Chesil back inside the tent.

He handed over the letters and bade the Agya courier a swift journey. "Will you wait until daybreak to ride?"

"Nay, your majesty. There is a strong moon tonight. I do not fear the darkness."

"Then Thodspeed," Dain said. "My compliments to your

father. Tell him I look forward to the day when he and I shall meet."

"Let it be soon, majesty," Chesil said, and departed.

Dain rose to his feet and secured the pledges in a safe place among his possessions.

"Yer majesty's supper is ready," Sir Terent said. "Give the word and I'll tell 'em to bring it in."

"Nay," Dain said. He felt distracted and restless. He picked up his cloak and wrapped its heavy folds around his shoulders. "I want to walk a bit first."

"You want to go stand over the lady," Sir Terent grumbled. He pulled on his gloves and followed Dain outside into the frosty night air. "'Tis not kingly to moon over her like—"

Dain stopped short in his tracks and glared at his protector. "Take care, sir," he said in a low, furious voice. "I decide what is and is not 'kingly' for me to do."

Over by the campfire, Sir Polquin was standing with a trencher of food in his hands. He stared at them worriedly.

Dain and Sir Terent, busy glaring at each other, ignored him.

Although Sir Terent's face reddened, he didn't back down. "Aye, sire," he said at last. "Seems I've got a bit more to learn about serving a king, even if he ain't got his kingdom yet."

Stung by that, Dain frowned. Before he could speak, however, Sir Terent went on: "Remember this, sire. 'Tis said that King Tobeszijian was a man who liked to do things his way, in his own good time. 'Tis said that he wouldn't pay enough mind to his duties, and that's how his brother took the throne away from him."

The fire that kindled in Dain's chest burned its way up into his face. He felt as though he were being strangled. "Who— who told you that?" he asked hoarsely, his fists clenched at his sides.

"We common knights hear a lot, here and there."

"Did the Netherans at Savroix tell you that? Or is it just a Mandrian lie?"

Sir Terent's eyes flashed at Dain's deliberate insult, but he kept his temper. "I couldn't say, sire."

Dain glared at him a moment longer, then he turned on his heel and strode off into the darkness. Sir Terent followed, his big feet crunching on the frozen mud. As Dain picked his way through the camp toward Pheresa's enclosure, his anger slowly dissipated. He knew, in his heart, that what Sir Terent had said was true.

Yet how could he be expected to turn his back on Pheresa's plight? She had drunk the poison meant for him. Did he not owe her something for that?

He loved her, no matter what Sir Terent said. And stubbornly he kept walking toward her tent.

3

THE MORNING DAWNED bright and fair, with no hint of the previous day's rain. Sunlight sparkled on frosty leaves and grass. Dain, Sir Terent, and Sir Polquin left the road and cut first across marshland, then fields harvested and gleaned, to take the shortest route to Thirst Hold.

Behind them, Gavril's expedition was still camped on the roadside. Like a band of nomads, Dain thought scornfully. Despite Sulein's being successfully substituted for the dead guardian, the royal physicians said that Lady Pheresa should not be moved as yet. Not even to nearby Thirst. In the meantime, Dain seized the opportunity to visit his hold. Much business awaited him there, and it was long past time that he attended to it.

Having galloped across an empty field, Dain reined up inside a small wood to give the horses a breather. Woodcutters had been at work in this grove, leaving stumps in their wake. *Thirst land,* Dain thought, inhaling the mingled scents of woods and autumn with pleasure. It felt good to come back, and Sir Terent and Sir Polquin were grinning like boys.

Soleil tossed his proud head, flinging his golden mane and pulling on the reins. "Steady," Dain crooned to him, laughing at the chestnut stallion's fiery spirit. "You can't race the wind all day."

Sir Terent pointed northeast. "Just over the next rise past these trees, and we'll—"

An arrow sang past Dain's face, so close the fletchings brushed his skin, and thudded into Sir Terent's shoulder. The protector reeled in his saddle with a hoarse cry of pain.

Sir Polquin drew his sword. "Get out of this! Ride, sire. Ride! I'll hold them."

More arrows came raining down on them, but Dain knew they had to stick together if they were to survive. Rearing Soleil to make himself less of a target, he shouted, "Sir Terent, can you ride?"

The protector's knight was pale with strain, and he was barely keeping himself in the saddle. Ignoring Dain's question, he glared at Sir Polquin. "Get him out of here!"

Sir Polquin wheeled his horse toward Dain.

"Ride, Terent!" Dain commanded. Leaning forward, he pulled his sagging protector upright. "Ride to the field!"

An arrow sliced across the top of Dain's hand, cutting his heavy glove and bringing pain like fire. Ignoring it, he kicked Soleil hard, but as the three of them retreated from the grove, another volley of arrows came at them. One hit Sir Polquin's horse in the flank.

Squealing in pain, the animal shied violently, and Sir Polquin came off. He thudded hard against the ground and lay there unmoving.

Cursing in alarm, Dain drew up and wheeled his horse around to go racing back for him. By then Sir Polquin was sitting up, trying to wave him away.

"See to yourself, sire!" he shouted gruffly. "I'll do."

"No, you will not," Dain replied grimly.

The sporadic hail of arrows stopped, and just as Dain noticed this, a half-dozen riders emerged from the trees to surround them. Several of these men wore red mail. Helmeted with their visors closed, they wore no surcoats to identify themselves.

"Bandits, damne!" Sir Polquin said, scrambling to his feet. "Get away! I'll hold them as long as I can."

Dain flung back his cloak to free his arms and drew his sword. "It's too late for that," he said grimly.

Beside him, Sir Terent snapped off the arrow still sticking out of his shoulder, swore with shrill vehemence, and drew his sword. "For Thirst and Dain," he said, pasty-faced and sweating.

"Aye, for Thirst and Dain!" Sir Polquin echoed grimly.

Dain swallowed hard. "For Thirst!"

At that moment their attackers charged, yelling in a language Dain did not understand. From that point forward, there was no chance to think, but only to fight.

In seconds, Dain found himself flanked by two foes. Desperately wheeling his horse around to get out from between them, Dain swung his sword at the closest man. His blow was parried with a resounding clang of steel. For a split second he stared deep into foreign eyes glittering behind the slits in the man's visor.

Right then, Dain felt the force of his opponent's thoughts: *Catch/catch/catch.*

Twisting his wrists, Dain broke free, reversed his swing, and struck again. His sword tip raked across the man's midsection, slicing through links of chain mail and spilling a gush of blood. But as that attacker tumbled from his horse, a blow across the back of Dain's shoulders came from his second opponent. He wheezed for air, the world nearly going black on him, and fought to keep gripping his sword.

Strong hands grabbed him, yanking him upright in the saddle. Through blurred eyes, Dain looked around for Sir Terent, assuming his protector was steadying him.

Instead, he found himself staring at another helmet, painted blood red with strange symbols on the sides. This man laughed, the sound echoing low from inside his helmet, and gave Dain's arm a powerful yank that nearly pulled him from the saddle.

Twisting desperately, Dain brought his sword up and around, but it was impossible to land a blow at this angle. He turned Soleil and swung again, but just then a third foe came galloping up and gave him a shove.

Dain went tumbling out of his saddle. He hit the ground swearing, and rolled as he'd been taught, coming up on his feet immediately. With a yell, he ran straight at the closest attacker, whose horse reared with deadly forefeet.

Ducking those dangerous hooves, Dain cut the horse's saddle girth. Horse blood splattered across his arms. The animal screamed, and the saddle—along with rider—went flying off. Dain gave the man no time to gain his feet. Rushing at him hard, Dain kicked him as he tried to rise, and swung with all his might. His sword took off the man's head, and it went rolling beneath the feet of another horse, which bucked and kicked in alarm.

Sir Polquin plunged his dagger into the guts of an opponent, then came running to Dain's side. Standing shoulder to shoulder, they fought two more, while Sir Terent—still mounted—exchanged blows with the last man. The woods rang with the clash of combat.

Sweating inside his mail, his heart pounding hard, Dain sized up his remaining opponent. Already he'd realized these men weren't trying to kill him; they could have done that at the start with a well-aimed arrow. But if they were trying to capture him alive, that gave Dain the advantage. Recklessly he charged his opponent with a rapid, two-step attack. His sword bit deep at the point where the man's neck met his shoulder and nearly cleaved him.

Screaming, the man fell, and Dain finished him with a swift thrust.

Panting, blood dripping from his blade, Dain turned around in time to see Sir Polquin finish his man with a triumphant yell. Sir Terent's opponent screamed foreign curses at them and abruptly galloped away.

Silence fell over the small, trampled clearing, a silence broken only by the snorting horses and the harsh panting of Dain and his friends.

Gulping in air, Dain shoved back his mail coif to let the cold air bathe his sweat-soaked hair. Aside from the shallow arrow cut across the back of his hand, he'd taken no harm. The others were less fortunate. Sir Terent's surcoat was stained with blood from his wound. The side of Sir Polquin's face was scraped raw; he'd have a tremendous bruise there by eventide.

Sir Polquin gave one of the corpses a kick. "I'll have Bosquecel's hide for this," he muttered. "What's he thinking of, letting road bandits run free on Thirst land?"

"They weren't bandits," Dain said. Bending over one of the dead men, he tugged off his helmet.

"Careful, sire!" Sir Terent gasped out.

But Dain was busy studying the hatchet-thin features and distinctive bone structure. He even peeled up the man's lip to reveal a small set of pointed fangs.

"Morde a day!" Sir Polquin exclaimed, coming over to take a look. "What in Thod's name is he?"

"Gantese," Dain said grimly. "The red mail was an indication that they might be so."

Visibly alarmed, Sir Polquin took a quick step back from the corpse. "How long before these devils come alive again and start at us anew?"

"Nay," Dain said in reassurance. "They're Believers, not Nonkind."

"Is there a difference?"

"Yes." Dain frowned in the direction the lone survivor had fled, and wondered if he would return with more men. "At least now I understand why I've felt watched the last few days."

"Watched, eh? And why didn't your grace speak of this?" Sir Polquin complained.

"There was nothing to say. I had no certainty. Would you have me share every uneasiness I feel?"

"You? Aye, I would," Sir Polquin said pointedly. "Your senses are our best warnings of Nonkind attack."

"This was not Nonkind business." Dain sighed. "They intended to capture me alive, I think."

"Aye," Sir Terent said unsteadily. "'Twas plain. No one could shoot that many arrows at you and miss."

"Didn't miss *you,* did they?" Sir Polquin retorted.

Sir Terent looked terrible, and fresh blood was still seeping into his surcoat, but he mustered a glare for his fellow knight. "That first arrow was intended to put me out of the action. The next arrow brought you down. If you'd stayed on your horse, his grace would have escaped this ambush."

Instead of arguing, Sir Polquin grew thoughtful. The fire died in his eyes, and a strange look appeared on his face. "Our lad should have been dead in the first minute the way they surrounded him."

"Aye," Dain agreed. "That's why I think they meant to take me alive."

Sir Polquin scowled. "Damned, pagan devils. What did they want with you? What?"

"I suspect they were paid agents of my uncle's. Which means he knows I have left Savroix."

"Aye, and where you've gone to," Sir Terent said. "Once they learned the first, the second wasn't hard to guess."

Sir Polquin swore. "And us so careful about smuggling you out of the palace and keeping you out of sight on that barge. I knew those Savroix court daisies would never keep the secret."

"Many at court are easily bribed," Dain agreed. Inside, he felt more relief than annoyance, however. "At least I no longer have to keep myself confined. The secret is out. I might as well make use of it."

"Best we get you to Thirst at once," Sir Polquin said worriedly. "Where there's one Gantese agent, it's said there are always more. They won't give up capturing you this easily."

Dain nodded in agreement. It was beginning, he thought. This attack of his uncle's would be only the first. From now on, he would have to take stronger precautions.

Riding slowly for Sir Terent's sake, they reached Thirst Hold a good hour later than Dain had intended. Although the knight did not complain, he rode with gritted teeth and a set face. Dain permitted Sir Polquin to ride pillion behind him, for Sir Polquin's injured horse had fled into the forest and could not be found.

Although they expected a second attack, none came. The sight of the hold, standing square and dark against the sunlight, brought grins of relief to all their faces. Dain could feel his tense muscles relaxing.

Sir Polquin grunted at his shoulder. "Put me off, sire."

"Nay," Dain protested. "I am not ashamed to let you ride."

"Put me off. 'Tis unseemly for a king to share his mount with a master-at-arms. Not in front of the men."

"But—"

"I'll serve better by leading Sir Terent's horse."

"Hah!" the protector said at once, but his voice was weak. "Lead me like a babe on a training rein, will you?"

"Aye, I will." Sir Polquin slid off Soleil's hindquarters, and dodged the stallion's ill-tempered kick. "Go ahead, sire. Let 'em see you plainly."

As they all drew near the hold gates, Dain squeezed Soleil with his legs and coaxed the horse into prancing sideways so that his mane and long tail streamed in the wind. "Ho!" he shouted. "Thirst Hold!"

A sentry's head appeared atop the ramparts.

Dain lifted his arm. "Ho!"

More heads appeared. "It's Lord Dain!" someone shouted. "He's here at last!"

A commotion of voices broke out, and with an ear-splitting squeal the ancient winch turned ponderously to open gates and portcullis. Dain had instructed Thum to answer the men's questions about his royal status—if questions they had—with honesty, but not to proclaim it at large. He would have preferred to come here simply as their chevard. For Thirst folk to accept an eld as their new lord and master was surely challenge enough. He realized he should have arrived with an entourage of guards sworn to his service, aye, with pages, servants, dogs, and minstrels. Who would ever take him for a lord, or even a king, if he did not act the part? His plain ways had to end; that, he knew.

"You'd think," Sir Terent grumbled, squinting up at the crenellations, "that they'd have had these gates open ere now. What's the hour? And them not ready, for all Thum's warning a day ahead."

"They've seen trouble here," Sir Polquin said. "Like as not, they're expecting more." He craned his neck to do an inspection of his own. "That crack above the left arrow slit has widened. Ought to be fixed properly this time, and before winter ice widens it more."

From inside the hold, the chapel bell began to peal joyously, even as the groan of the winch stopped with the gates barely shifted.

"Damne, what's amiss with these louts?" Sir Terent muttered. "Bosquecel!" he roared out. "What in Thod's name are you doing up there?"

The captain of the guard appeared atop the gate and peered down at them. Even from that angle, he looked ruffled.

"I beg pardon, your grace," he said to Dain, ignoring Sir Terent completely. "How far behind you comes the rest of the company?"

"They do not come today," Dain replied.

"Do not come?" Sir Bosquecel repeated in astonishment. "But—"

"Your chevard is here," Sir Polquin broke in gruffly. "That's honor enough. Stop yammering and open the blighted gate. We have a wounded man in need of attention."

Sir Bosquecel started to retort, obviously thought better of it, and vanished. Within a few minutes, the petit-porte swung open.

Dain rode through it, ducking his head as he passed beneath the massive timbers supporting the weight of the wall and ramparts overhead. Sir Terent and Sir Polquin followed him, grumbling between themselves at Sir Bosquecel's unusual laxity.

Meanwhile, from across the fields came serfs and villagers at a run, answering the summons of the bell. Dain rode into the stableyard, to the ragged cheers and shouted greetings of his servants. Yet not all looked happy to see him. Many gawked and pointed. Some of the maidservants held up their aprons to shield their faces from his gaze.

Dain sighed to himself. Three months gone, and already he'd become a stranger to them again.

Although the Thirst folk gawked at him with more curiosity than love, Dain held his head high, reminding himself that this mixed reception was what he'd expected. While he'd lived here he'd won the affection of many, the tolerance of some, and the avoidance of others. He'd come to them first as a ragged waif, as ill-mannered as he was hungry. Through Lord Odfrey's kindness and the generous acceptance of the knights, who proclaimed him their mascot, he'd been put through a foster's training. Later Lord Odfrey had adopted him as his heir. The inheritance was secure, guaranteed by King Verence himself, and if these people feared to serve an eld they would have to soon grow used to it.

As he rode through the rambling complex of the hold, his keen eyes noted with approval the stacks of fodder and other signs of a bountiful harvest. During his time away he'd received regular reports from Sir Bosquecel and less frequent ones from Julth Rondel, the steward. From their accounts, the hold was running smoothly, but now as he looked about, Dain saw signs of neglect and slackness. Here at mid-morning, the stableyard was not yet swept. One of the doors to the barn was broken and splintered as though a horse had kicked through it. What appeared to be a new barracks was half-constructed, and boards and timbers lay scattered about in disarray.

Sir Bosquecel, down from the ramparts, came hurrying up to Dain in the stableyard and bowed hastily. "Welcome home, your grace," he said, looking nervous and flustered. "We are not as prepared as we ought to be to give you a good and proper welcome. I mean, a proper welcome for a—a king."

As he stammered and turned red, Dain realized what the problem was. It was not that he was eld, but rather than his rank had grown too high. A tremendous gulf yawned between him and these plain folk, a gulf that could not be crossed.

Sir Bosquecel cleared his throat. "The men have been sore bedeviled this month, holding off raids from across the river."

He paused, frowning up at the three of them, and his gaze widened at the sight of bloodstained Sir Terent. "Morde! What's gone amiss here? I'd have sworn no raiders were afoot this day, else we'd have been patrolling the road. Did dwarves attack you?"

"Nay," Dain said grimly. "I'll explain later. Have Sir Terent's wound seen to, if you please."

As Sir Bosquecel issued orders and servants came forward to gently assist Sir Terent from his horse, Dain glanced around with a deepening frown and wondered where the knights themselves were. He'd expected them to issue forth from the guardhouse as he rode across the keep, but there'd been no sight of them. Had they grown so sullen, then? Did they resent his good fortune? Had they turned against him, when once they were mostly his champions?

"And the men?" he asked. "Are they on patrol now?"

Sir Bosquecel glanced up and turned redder than ever. "Uh, no, your grace. They're here. Gently, man!" he snapped at one of the servants assisting Sir Terent.

Dain held back more questions. The men's failure to greet him hurt deeply.

Dismounting, Dain handed his reins to a sullen-faced stableboy who used to pelt him with dried manure. In the past, Dain would have left the boy alone, feeling it best to avoid confrontation. But his time spent with King Verence had taught him how to deal with men, both common and high.

He paused a moment, gazing at this former tormentor until the stableboy turned bright red and would not meet his eyes.

"How fare you these days, Zeld?" he asked.

"Well enough, sir," the boy mumbled.

"Say your grace," Sir Polquin barked at him. "Stand up straight when you do it. And don't mumble."

Zeld stiffened as though he'd been stung. His face turned even redder as he looked up, met Dain's eyes, then shifted his own away again. "Uh, yer grace," he mumbled.

"As I recall, you never had much use for me, but you've a good hand with horses," Dain said to him. "I would ask you now to treat my horse kindly. He was a gift from King Verence, you see, and I value him highly."

Zeld's mouth fell open. "A gift from the *king*? Our king? Damne, not true!"

"Aye, true," Sir Polquin told him sternly. "And don't you insult your master by disbelieving him. Oaf that you are, surely you can see there's no horse in Thirst as fine as this. Saelutian bloodlines, bred in the royal stables. See that you take care with the steed, as his grace bids you."

Zeld clutched the reins. His eyes were shining now, and they flashed up to meet Dain's with none of their former resentment. "And does he run like the wind? I hear tell—"

"He's a fine courser," Dain said. "Keep him in good trim."

"Aye, sir . . . m'lord . . . uh, yer grace. Aye! That I'll do!"

With a smile, Dain moved on, aware that Zeld's loyalty was

now fiercely his. He heard murmurs among the others, but he ignored them as Sir Polquin and Sir Bosquecel broke apart from a brief, private conversation to flank him on either side.

When he neared the innermost courtyard, he heard a gruff command beyond the wall. As Dain strode through the gate he saw all the knights of Thirst standing rowed up in a double line between him and the steps of the Hall. Shined and polished, their helmets casting blinding reflections in the sunlight, they stood shoulder to shoulder in their green surcoats, holding their freshly painted shields in front of them.

Dain checked at the sight, and realized now why they hadn't met him at the guardhouse. All this time they'd been waiting quietly to surprise him. A lump filled his throat, and he wondered how he could have ever doubted them. Somehow, bursting with emotion, he managed to keep his stride steady.

Sir Bosquecel stepped away to issue a low command, and the sergeant-at-arms bawled it to the men: "Arms to Thirst!"

In response, they shouted the Thirst war cry and drew their broadswords in unison.

"High salute!" the sergeant bellowed.

Down the line, the broadswords swung aloft, and were held point-to-point in a shining arch of steel.

Walking proud and tall, honored beyond words, Dain went down the row beneath their swords, keeping his shoulders erect and his chin high.

He reached the foot of the stone steps, emerged from beneath the steel arch, and started to ascend. As he did so, another command roared forth, and the swords came down in a flashing arc and thudded against the knights' shields.

Dain turned to face them and drew his own bloodstained sword in brief salute, holding it up until they sheathed their weapons. Only then did he slide his back into its scabbard. He stared at them a moment, reacquainting himself with their honest, rough-hewn faces. He seemed to have lived through two lifetimes since last he'd seen them. But yes, there was Sir Alard and old, sour-faced Sir Blait. He saw Sir Bowin and Sir Deloit, his single eye shining bright with joy. Dain caught himself looking for faces he knew he would never see again. So many he remembered were missing, and in their place stood new men, recruits he did not know, to replace those who had died that black day on the banks of the Charva. *Would they serve him with the same loyalty as the others?* Dain wondered.

Today's honor gave him hope that the answer would be yes. He saw no hostility in their faces, no prejudice, no sullenness. They looked thrilled with how they'd surprised him.

"Welcome, your grace. Welcome!"

It was Julth Rondel, steward of Thirst, who came hastening down the steps to meet Dain. Thum, grinning beneath his thatch of red hair, followed on the steward's heels.

"Well met, sire," he said with a bow.

"I see you got here in one piece this time," Dain replied.

"Aye." Thum's grin sobered. "But I hear you met with trouble this morn. How many were there in the attack?"

"A handful plus one," Dain replied. "Who's seeing to Sir Terent?"

"He's been taken to the infirmary. And yourself? No harm to you?"

"I'm well," Dain said impatiently, and turned to the steward.

Spreading wide his pudgy hands, Rondel bowed low. He was a short, plump man with a ring of straight blond hair encircling his bald pate. Garbed in Thirst green, he wore his steward's collar of silver with pride, and had served ably in his post for many years.

"Come inside, Lord Dain—er, your grace—and welcome to you!" he said warmly, although his gaze seemed shy and unsettled behind the good cheer. "There's a fire built on the hearth to warm your bones, and some spiced cider waiting in your cup."

"That is a fine welcome indeed, Steward Rondel," Dain said, and gripped the man's shoulder briefly as he walked inside.

Barking broke out, and Lord Odfrey's dogs came bounding to meet him. But at the first sniff, they dropped their fine heads and slunk away in poignant disappointment.

"They still wait for his return, every day," Rondel said sadly, and made the sign of the Circle. "Such a terrible pity."

"Aye," Dain agreed. His heart turned momentarily to lead

inside his chest, and he was grateful when Rondel said nothing more about Lord Odfrey.

The Hall smelled musty from disuse, but a good fire burned on the hearth. As he stood by it to warm himself, Dain stripped off his gloves, then flexed his cut hand gingerly while Thum hastened to take his cloak and mail coif. A servant brought Dain a cup of spiced cider.

Accustomed by now to some of the finest Mandrian wines, Dain nearly gasped at the astringent taste. He'd forgotten how fresh-pressed cider could pucker the mouth.

"Not our best harvest this year, I'm afraid," Rondel said, watching him anxiously. "So I have ordered Lord Odfrey's private supply brought out especially for your grace's use."

Dain concealed his expression by taking another sip. This time the cider went down more easily, although he disliked the heavy spices that had been used to mask the fact that this was last year's press, and gone vinegary to boot.

"Very well," he said. "That is all for now, steward. I'll be inspecting the hold this afternoon. But first I want breakfast. I rose at first light to come here, while the opportunity presented itself, and having fought off a pack of Gantese assassins, I'm fair famished."

The steward seemed relieved by this simple request. "Yes, your grace. At once, your grace." He hesitated. "And then will your—your grace wish to—"

"As soon as I've eaten," Dain said, guessing what he was referring to, "I will be going to the chapel to pay my respects to Lord Odfrey."

"Ah." The sadness returned to Rondel's plump face. "Yes, of course. Very proper, your grace." The steward bowed and hastened out.

Dain flung the rest of his cider on the fire, which smoked in retaliation before regaining its flames with an angry pop of sparks. "Gods!" Dain exclaimed. "I thought he would babble all morning."

"He's capable of it," Thum said grimly. "I have endured his chatter since my arrival yesterday. Morde a day, but were we ever this green and ill-mannered when we first went to Savroix?

Since I've arrived yesterday they've been stumbling about in panic, wondering what to do with you."

"How so?"

"Well, the floor rushes were too dirty for a king to see, too common, but the carpets that were in storage have been ravished by moths. That's why your floors are bare. And your chamber . . . damne, but there aren't linens in the hold fine enough for a king to sleep on. Half the servants refuse to believe you're a king. The other half are scared you'll cut off their heads if they do or say the wrong thing."

Hearing this, Dain didn't know whether to laugh or frown. "What gave them such notions? Do they fear Verence this much?"

"Thod knows," Thum said, throwing up his hands. "The house servants would probably fall in dead swoons if they heard his majesty was coming here. Normally, of course, their chevard would keep them in order, but that's been knocked awry."

"Of course it has." Dain looked helplessly at his friend. "I do not want them to fear me."

"No help for it. At least your chamber is ready. If you want a change of clothing while I brush your surcoat clean of mud, there are Lord Odfrey's tunics. Everything you left behind is probably too small."

"No, I thank you!" Dain said in instant refusal. "I'll wear what I have on."

Thum nodded in understanding. "The wardroom has been left locked and untouched since—since we all set out for Savroix a few months ago."

"Good. I have the key."

"But first, pray tell me what really befell you this morning," Thum said in concern, fingering a tear in Dain's cloak. "Gantese assassins? In truth?"

"Aye. They shot us with arrows before we knew what was afoot, then they came on."

"Six to three is heavy work," Thum said. "I'm sorry I was not there to fight at your side. It is Thod's mercy you were not killed."

"Thod didn't save us. 'Twas their own orders."

"What?"

"You heard aright," Dain said grimly. "They were trying to take me alive, else short work would they have made of us. 'Tis no accident that the only arrow which actually met its mark struck my protector."

Thum's eyes narrowed, and spots of anger burned in his cheeks. "Damne! What villains!"

"I feel certain they were my uncle's agents," Dain said.

"Then you must go no farther," Thum said in alarm. "Your journey ends now, for there's no chance of you sneaking undetected across the border."

Dain eyed him as though he'd lost his wits. "Not if I ride through a checkpoint on a main road, no," he said impatiently. "Which I have no intention of doing."

"But Muncel's onto your plan. He knows where to find you."

"Would you have me turn back at the first trouble?"

"Nay, but a new plan must be—"

"I have more than four thousand men at my disposal if I can get to them," Dain said in excitement. "A courier reached me at the camp last night, bringing pledges from two Netheran generals. Thum, I care not if Muncel knows I've left Savroix. I intend to declare myself at once, so that more men can rally to my cause."

"But, sire—"

"The time for secrecy is over!"

"How will you search for the eldin if—"

"I will do all," Dain said with a swift frown. "If the eldfolk hear of my return, perhaps they will come forth from hiding. General Matkevskiet is bound to know where they may be found."

"Muncel will not stop with one tiny ambush."

"Agreed. I'll need more men to guard me," Dain said.

Thum drew in a sharp breath. "You mean Thirst knights."

Dain said nothing. His gaze was answer enough.

Thum's eyes widened. "Will you take them across the border?"

"Do you think they will follow me there?"

"I—I know not. Do you realize what that would mean?"

Dain nodded. "The original charter of this hold was granted by the kings of Edonia—the old kingdom—"

"It's treason to say that name," Thum said with a nervous glance over his shoulder.

"Thirst pledges fealty to Mandria's kings, but it does not owe its existence to them," Dain said. "I have studied the complex law of the ancient charters for some time. King Verence and I also discussed it."

"Do not expect me to believe he gives you his blessing!"

Dain frowned at Thum. He felt a little surprised by his friend's protests. "Not his blessing, no," he said slowly. "But he will not oppose me."

"Dain—"

"Are you against this?" Dain asked with more sharpness than he intended. "Tell me true. I'll hold it not against you, but I must know if you remain with me."

"Of course I remain with you," Thum said angrily. "Never question my loyalty."

"Then why balk at what I'm saying?"

"Because if you pull Thirst away, the uplands could fall again into divisionism. Civil war could return to Mandria, at a time when she must remain strong." Thum's mouth turned down worriedly. "Gavril would love an excuse to batter the uplands into fresh submission."

"Gavril will not dare."

But Thum still looked unconvinced. Dain frowned at the fire, and realized that in truth, neither of them knew what Gavril might choose to do, only that it would be cruel and merciless.

Dain sighed. "I must have men."

"And if you take Thirst's knights with you, who will guard the hold? Who will guard this area of the northeastern borders? There has been much trouble here."

"Aye," Dain said, knowing Thum's points were valid. He shrugged. "I have no solution to these many problems. Thum, where would the records of the household be kept?"

"You mean the inventories?" Thum asked, looking startled by the sudden change of subject. "In the wardroom, no doubt."

Dain tossed him the key. "Find them. And then you can inform the steward there is to be a new inventory conducted."

"In the Hall?"

"The Hall. The guardhouse. The barns. The entire hold.

Everything. I want it all written down and checked against the previous entries."

Thum looked daunted. "That will take days."

"Perhaps we have them, while Lady Pheresa is unable to travel," Dain said. "This hold has grown slack."

"Aye," Sir Polquin spoke up. "That it has."

"Also," Dain said, "I want Lander the smith brought to me for questioning about that sword he made."

Thum frowned. "He's no longer at the hold."

"What? Gone for good?"

"So I understand. Sir Bosquecel kicked him out."

"And good riddance," Sir Polquin said. "Making magic rubbish like that sword Tanengard. He was naught but a foreign blasphemer."

Dain's brows drew together. "Tanengard, whatever its flaws, saved a few of us from dying on the Charva's banks that day. Remember that before you judge its maker so harshly."

Sir Polquin reddened at the rebuke and dropped his gaze.

"Er, is there anything else, sire?" Thum asked to break up the uncomfortable silence.

At that moment, something unseen, an intangible force or presence, engulfed Dain without warning. Failing to answer Thum, he turned away and walked over to the northeast wall. There he stood, staring into what seemed to be a mist, and could not speak or think. He felt an overwhelming sense of pressure, as though his entire body was being compressed or even crushed. It was an effort to breathe.

Then in the next instant, he found himself seated on a stool and being shaken by a worried-looking Sir Polquin. Thum was holding a fresh cup of cider to his lips.

Scowling, Dain twisted his head away from the liquid. "Get that far from me!" he said sharply.

Sir Polquin released his grip on Dain's shoulders. "Thanks be to Thod! He's come back to his senses."

Dain blinked at the two of them in bewilderment. "What are you saying? I haven't left my senses. I—"

"You did," Thum said hoarsely, looking frightened. "For several minutes—just now—you stared as though you saw something we could not see. You would not answer us. You seemed not to hear us at all, though we did speak to you most urgently and called your name."

Dain rubbed his eyes. "I have no recollection of this."

"Were you seeing a vision?" Thum asked him anxiously.

"Nay. I saw nothing. Are you sure?"

Sir Polquin gripped his arm to keep him from standing. "Your grace had better stay seated for a bit."

"Nay." Dain shook him off and rose to his feet. His knees felt wobbly, and he couldn't understand why. "I'm well. Don't fuss over me."

"Maybe you should have that cut on your hand looked at. Could have Gantese poison in it."

"It's already closing," Dain said impatiently. He felt unsettled and alarmed by what they'd told him. "There's no poison."

"You're not yourself, just the same," Sir Polquin insisted. "Pale as washed linen. Better sit a while and rest."

"Nay, there's too much to do. I've got—"

"All will keep," Sir Polquin told him with gruff kindness. "Bide quietly until you get your breakfast."

There was no satisfying either of them until Dain sat down in a chair by the fire. He frowned at the flames while Sir Polquin and Thum conferred in soft voices they thought too low for his keen ears to overhear. Dain knew there was nothing wrong with him. But something had indeed reached out from a far distance and touched him.

A cold shudder passed through his frame. He felt momentarily as though he'd eaten something rotten that needed spewing up. There were more kinds of pursuit, he realized, than riders on horseback. If Muncel was casting spells his way, even at this great distance, the net was definitely closing in on him. Clearly Muncel would use any means—assassination by eldpoison, kidnapping, even employment of the dark arts—to stop Dain's return to Nether. His uncle was no ordinary enemy, and the struggle for Nether's throne would be no ordinary battle.

He knows where I am, Dain thought with a fresh shudder. *I have been touched by him, and now—wherever I go—he can find me.*

4

IN HIS CASTLE stronghold at Belrad, King Muncel paced back and forth impatiently, glaring frequently at the huddle of three Gantese *magemons* kneeling on the floor in the center of his private council room. Impassive guards stood shoulder to shoulder across the closed doors. Muncel's own lord protector, Prince Anjilihov, and his personal *sorcerel,* Tulvak Sahm, hovered close by, watching alertly for the least sign of trouble. Tulvak Sahm, insulted by the importation of the *magemons,* glittered with resentment. He was capable of thwarting the spell from sheer spite, but if he attempted it, King Muncel vowed to make him regret such folly.

The air smelled of fire and ash and burned hair, scents of magic. A sort of crackling energy rose about the three *magemons,* strong enough to prickle against Muncel's face. He stopped pacing and watched with hope, but at that moment the energy ebbed low again. Closing their eyes, the *magemons* bent lower so that their foreheads were almost touching. They hummed softly, uttering words that seemed to draw a cord tight around Muncel's heart.

He feared their dreadful powers; he was taking a terrible risk in bringing them here so openly, to his own stronghold. But if all went well this day, their dire task would be done and they could leave by eventide, paid and dismissed, never to return.

Restless and impatient, Muncel resumed pacing.

Outside the windows, the day looked bleak and gray. Huge white snowflakes fell rapidly, swirling against the glass in frozen patterns of lace. The snowfall was heavy enough to build large drifts across the keep and extended grounds. Muncel could hear a fierce wind howling and scratching outside.

Over in one corner, a large stove of vivid red and blue tiles radiated heat. Beyar skin rugs covered the stone floor, and on one side of the room stood a massive council table surrounded by leather-covered chairs.

There would be no council meeting today. Muncel had canceled all audiences and appointments to receive only this delegation from Sindeul, Gant's capital city. He would speak to no one in his palace until this spell was completed and the threat from the pretender vanquished for good.

Muncel was a gaunt-faced man with deep lines carved around his mouth and between his brows. His black hair and beard were streaked with gray. He was not as tall as his father, King Runtha II, had been, nor did he have the splendid physique of his half-brother Tobeszijian. Narrow-shouldered and thin, he seldom wore a sword and disliked the heavy weight of armor. Because he suffered from a dyspeptic stomach, his posture was slightly hunched and there was always a slight twist to his mouth that spoke of his discomfort. But his eyes were dark and fierce, and his temper legendary. Muncel possessed the subtle mind that Tobeszijian had lacked. As a result, he had held his throne far longer than had his half-brother simply because he could foresee potential problems and eliminate them. Shrewd and cunning, he never took risks unless he was prepared to deal with the consequences. And he was absolutely, utterly ruthless when he chose to be.

Garbed today in fur-lined velvet, with a jeweled dagger on his belt, many rings glittering on his long, pale fingers, and a narrow circlet of gold on his brow, Muncel glared even more harshly at the triad of *magemons* and barely restrained himself from yelling at their Gantese handlers.

The Believers, clad in fur cloaks and long tunics of heavy wool, themselves looked uneasy. Muncel began to entertain the unwelcome worry that he had exposed himself to censure and condemnation for nothing. And that made him even angrier, for he could not bear the thought of failure, much less ridicule. The churchmen would harass him endlessly about this; he might even be required to do public penance.

Tulvak Sahm, always sensitive to his moods, glided over to him and bowed as though he'd been summoned.

"This is taking too long, *too long*," Muncel muttered. "Clearly the distance is too far."

"Distance slows the power of the spell," Tulvak Sahm murmured back, his deep voice so quiet it was almost a whisper in

Muncel's mind. "But it does not dilute it. Since you have summoned these creatures, majesty, have patience with their antiquated methods. Wait."

Muncel's fists clenched. He *had* waited, damn the man. He'd waited nearly two decades to find this brat of Tobeszijian's, and now he wanted the boy *crushed*.

"Eee-ah!"

That shrill outcry from one of the *magemons* startled even Tulvak Sahm and made Muncel spin around just as the *magemons* lifted their hands in unison. They started chanting hoarse, unintelligible words that made his skin crawl.

The crackling energy intensified in the room. The guards had their hands on their sword hilts now while their eyes shifted uneasily.

Muncel saw rainbow hues of power shimmer in the air above the *magemons'* heads, and even Tulvak Sahm stood rooted in place, staring at them in wonder and dread as the others did.

Although Muncel himself possessed no magical gifts or special powers—for which he thanked Tomias—he drew in an unsteady breath and willed success in the *magemons'* direction.

Find him, he commanded in his mind. *Smother his lungs. Stop his heart. Crush his soul!*

Abruptly the spell ended. The kneeling *magemons* moved away from each other and rose to their feet. The rainbow colors vanished from the air, and the humming sense of energy dissipated. There was only a feeling of emptiness in the room now, along with the stench of burned hair and flesh overlying the putrid stink of the *magemons* themselves.

One of the three turned over his hand, and Muncel saw large blisters rising on the creature's palm as though the energy he'd commanded had scorched it.

Muncel felt no sympathy. Instead, he grew puzzled, then angry. "What's happened?" he demanded. "Why did you stop?"

In unison the three *magemons* turned to face him. As they did so, Prince Anjilihov drew his sword and Tulvak Sahm glided quickly to stand partially in front of Muncel. In his hand glowed a small crystal orb, its yellow light shining through his fingers, and his muscles were tense, as though he was preparing himself to hurl this magical weapon at the *magemons* should it prove necessary.

Over the years, Muncel had learned that weavers of all kinds of magic—*sorcerels* included—could be strange, unpredictable, even dangerous creatures in the moments immediately after a spell was concluded, especially when they had been spellcasting for any intense period of time.

But Muncel had risked too much to permit failure now. His anger—swollen by a sense of desperation—rose in him like a tide.

"You did not finish!" he shouted at the *magemons*. "Why did you stop? Did you even find him? Why have you failed?"

The three creatures might have been one, so similar in appearance were they. In some sense they could be called men, for they stood upright and walked as men walk. Perhaps once they had even been human, before their training changed them into what they were now. On the whole, they were far less fathomable than Tulvak Sahm, who at least looked human, even if he was not.

Moon-faced, with dark slits for eyes and mouths that issued smoke whenever they spoke, the *magemons* possessed skin so white and pale its pallor rivaled the snow outside. They towered above Muncel and his guards as giants, their bulk robed in shapeless garments that covered them from throat to foot. Dried blood and food stains dotted the front of their clothing. Their huge, three-fingered hands were filthy with dirt-rimmed nails as long and untrimmed as talons. They stank of death, filth, rot, and burned magic.

As they stared at him impassively, responding not at all to his questions, Muncel felt bitter disappointment flood his mouth like bile. He wanted to order the guards to hurl them from the windows to their deaths on the frozen ground below. He had imported this trio from Gant at great expense and trouble. He had housed them in a locked tower within the palace walls, supplied them with raw meat, and even permitted them to roam freely at night. He had paid a king's ransom in gold coin for them to be bound to his service by a powerful spell-agreement that guaranteed him two requests. And Muncel's requests were very simple: he wanted them to find Faldain and kill him.

But they were not keeping their end of the bargain. They stared at him now, huge, impassive, and silent, as though they understood nothing he said.

To be cheated was unbearable to Muncel. He refused to let these dirty fiends make a fool of him.

"Answer me!" Muncel demanded of them now. "Why did you stop?"

Still they said nothing. Fuming, Muncel turned on the foremost Gantese handler. "Well?" he demanded. "If they will not speak, do so for them!"

Scowling, the Believer bared his fangs at the *magemons.* "*Chynta!*" he said sharply, snapping his fingers.

"Faldain is found," one of the *magemons* said, his heavily accented words issuing in a wreath of smoke.

Muncel's head lifted. He felt like a pilgrim who sees the shrine ahead. "And is he dead?"

"He is not dead. He is young and strong."

Muncel gritted his teeth. "Sing not his praises to me. I want him killed!"

"Cannot be done in first touch."

"You told me it could!"

"Human, yes. Human can be crushed inside so he die." As he spoke, the *magemon* clenched his large fist, then opened it so that his blisters were revealed, now broken and running with pus. But even as Muncel stared in revulsion, the sores dried up and became ashes. The *magemon* wiggled his three fingers and the ashes drifted to the floor, revealing a hand smooth-skinned and whole once more. "But Faldain not much human."

"All the more reason for him to die."

"He has been touched. Can be touched again more easily now."

"Can you kill him the next time?"

"Must be touched thrice. Then will he die."

Muncel bottled his anger and listened. "Three times. How long will this take? How soon can you touch him again?"

The *magemon* did not answer. His eye slits closed, and he drew his round head down upon his shoulders.

Tulvak Sahm uttered a harsh word and raised his hand swiftly.

A puff of vapor exploded against his hand and dissipated into the air with a sour smell.

Muncel stared, belatedly realizing that the *magemon* had dared attempt to attack him, might have even harmed him had Tulvak Sahm not intervened.

"Unholy monsters!" Anjilihov shouted. The protector swung his sword high and charged.

Shouting in alarm, the Gantese handler stretched out his hands to Muncel. "Majesty! Stop him or we'll all perish!"

"Anjilihov!" Muncel roared.

The protector paid no heed. As he launched himself at the *magemon,* Tulvak Sahm flung himself bodily against Anjilihov and blocked his path.

With an oath of frustration, Anjilihov shoved Tulvak Sahm roughly out of his way. Stumbling, the *sorcerel* whirled and spoke a single word.

Anjilihov froze in mid-step. A look of bewilderment crossed his face before it, too, froze. All he could move was his eyes, and they shifted wildly as though imploring the king to order his release.

At the moment, however, Muncel was too outraged to care how long his protector remained trapped in Tulvak Sahm's spell.

The air in the council room reeked of conflicting kinds of magic. The three *magemons* stood shoulder to shoulder, humming something ominous. The power they gave off crackled along Muncel's skin and lifted his hair. He wanted to flee, but he dared not make any sudden moves.

Instead, he shifted his gaze to the horrified handlers. "Get them out," he ordered. "Get them out!"

The Gantese hurried forward to surround the *magemons,* speaking to the creatures in singsong voices, and slowly began to herd them away.

As soon as they were gone and the door shut with a heavy boom, Muncel closed his eyes and drew in several deep breaths. His stomach was burning with fire, and he felt almost faint. Sinking into a tall-backed chair, he pressed his hand to his belly and fought both his anger and the strong urge to be sick.

With the utterance of a word, Tulvak Sahm released Anjilihov, who went staggering across the room before he caught his balance and turned on the *sorcerel* with a snarl.

"Gods rot your evil heart!" Anjilihov said furiously, swinging his sword. "When you put your damnable spell on me, you imperiled his majesty's life. You—"

"'Twas *you* who imperiled us all," Muncel broke in. "Anjilihov, you fool!"

The protector looked at his king in bewilderment. "But your majesty was attacked by that demon. 'Tis my responsibility to—"

"Tulvak Sahm had already dealt with the matter," Muncel told him, leaning forward. "You made it worse."

"Your majesty, I do protest." Anjilihov shot Tulvak Sahm a jealous glare as he spoke. "I thought only of your safety."

"You thought only of plunging your sword into the guts of a *magemon*!" Muncel shouted. "Gods, man! Those creatures could level this stronghold to a pile of rubble in a matter of minutes if they chose to unleash their full powers. Had you harmed one, we would have been smote dead."

Anjilihov's gaze dropped from his. He sheathed his sword and knelt before Muncel. "Majesty, I ask your forgiveness. I did not realize this danger."

"Obviously," Muncel said, unmoved. Tulvak Sahm circled them both, breathing harshly. Trying to ignore him, Muncel kept his gaze on Anjilihov. "When I commanded you to stop, you disobeyed me."

Anjilihov turned pale. He bowed his head nearly to the floor. "Forgive me, majesty! I thought only of your—"

"You are not to think!" Muncel said angrily. "You are to obey."

"Yes, majesty," Anjilihov whispered.

"One more failure, and I'll see you and your family banished to the World's Rim. Is that clear?"

"Yes, majesty."

Muncel's stomach was burning with pain. A cold chill passed through him, and he suddenly found the lingering stench in the air unbearable. "Open a window. The air in here is foul."

Anjilihov jumped to his feet and obeyed, rather than calling a servant to do it.

Tulvak Sahm continued to circle Muncel's chair. "The *mage-mons* are savages," he murmured. "More dangerous than even I expected. I do not believe the handlers have much control over them. Not as much as your majesty was led to expect."

A blast of icy wind filled the room and stirred the tapestries. Snow blew in and sank into the fur rugs. Muncel inhaled the clean, brisk air with relief and felt his head clear.

"They should not be brought here again," Tulvak Sahm said. "Let them finish their spellcasting in the tower."

"I want to be present," Muncel said stubbornly. "I want to know the instant they kill the pretender."

"Then more *sorcerels* should be summoned here to guard your majesty," Tulvak Sahm said.

Muncel stared up at the man in astonishment. Tulvak Sahm was close to admitting that his powers were less than those of the *magemons*.

"How long would it take to summon your colleagues?"

Tulvak Sahm's face remained inscrutable as he tucked his hands into his sleeves. "I can reach them with the power of my mind immediately. Their coming would take less than five days."

"Too long. I want this matter finished before then."

"Half of your majesty's bargain has been accomplished today," Tulvak Sahm said. "That is great progress. A few more days will scarcely matter."

"Every day matters!" Muncel shouted, only to wince as the pain in his stomach grew worse. "The pretender is nearly to the border now."

Word of Faldain's return was flying across the kingdom as fast as the news could spread, Muncel thought worriedly. There'd already been an outbreak of trouble in Grov itself, traditional seat of Netheran kings, just when half his army had been sent west to put down a Grethori uprising. And the northern settlements were always rebellious; Muncel could only imagine how the troublemakers there would react when news of the pretender's return reached them.

He pounded his fist on the arm of his chair. "I will not have Faldain set foot on Netheran soil, Tulvak Sahm. I dare not!"

"It does not matter where he dies," the *sorcerel* assured him.

"The false one will not prevail against your majesty. This have I foretold."

Horoscope castings no longer reassured Muncel. Where Faldain was concerned, Muncel could not rest easy. In his nightmares, he'd dreamed of lying on the ground, bloody from numerous wounds, while Faldain—looking exactly like Tobeszijian—stood over him victorious. As for his half-brother, who'd disappeared so mysteriously into thin air nearly two decades ago on his demonic mount, who was to say that Tobeszijian himself might not somehow return? There was no proof that he was dead, although Tulvak Sahm repeatedly assured Muncel that his half-brother no longer existed in the first world.

Muncel dared not believe in anything except his own fears and instincts.

Had he waited for destiny all those years ago, he'd still be nothing but Tobeszijian's half-brother, lower in rank than those eldin brats Tobeszijian had sired. Muncel believed not in fate, but in planning ahead. In poisoning an enemy before the battle. In crushing an enemy's insides via magic before he could incite the people to revolt.

Glaring at his *sorcerel,* Muncel said, "If the pretender reaches Nether and proclaims himself king before the *magemons* kill him, the people will make a martyr of him. From his grave, he can still cause me trouble."

Tulvak Sahm shrugged. "Ghosts have never troubled your majesty before. Why should this one?"

Angrily Muncel refused to answer. He had no intention of admitting the panic he felt whenever he heard Faldain's name spoken.

In rational terms, there was little to worry about. The boy was untried and had few resources. He had failed to get the support of the Mandrian army, which had been Muncel's greatest worry. Rumor said that he could not even speak Netheran.

Muncel had a powerful army supplemented by Gantese and Nonkind auxiliaries. Ruthless and capable, Muncel ruled this kingdom with an iron fist and was well-established on the throne. Moreover, Faldain was more eld than human. After all these years, the anti-eld teachings of the Reformed Church had had time to take solid hold in the realm. Many people would reject the pretender for his mixed blood alone.

Yet despite his advantages, in the deepest corners of his heart Muncel still feared the boy's return. No matter how many reassuring horoscopes Tulvak Sahm cast, Muncel remained afraid. No matter how often he counted the size of his army, he felt little confidence. Still, he was determined that Faldain would never sit on Nether's throne. *Never.* This, Muncel had sworn long ago in his darkest days, before he overthrew Tobeszijian. He'd made a secret pilgrimage to Gant and knelt to the evil god Ashnod. He'd drunk a cup of bitterness, wormwood, and gall, said to represent the souls of the condemned. He'd eaten ashes said to be the burned bodies of the dead. He'd even spoken words of submission and worship to Ashnod, a statue of black stone that smoked and roared in a chamber of flame.

All this had he done, privately casting aside his belief in Thod and Tomias and selling his soul to the Believers in order to seize the birthright that should have been his. Paying such a price had been worthwhile, for he'd prevailed against Tobeszijian. But now, to grant even an hour of life to Tobeszijian's son would be to cheapen and reject all he'd sacrificed in order to get his throne.

As for Muncel's own son . . . although the child was sickly now, he would grow out of his afflictions and one day succeed to his father's throne. For his sake also, Muncel mused, must Faldain die; the people of Nether should never have the chance to compare Faldain's sturdy frame and straight limbs to Jonan's frailty.

Lifting his gaze to Tulvak Sahm, Muncel said, "The pretender must die before he sets foot on Netheran soil. I will not wait."

A knock on the door kept Tulvak Sahm from replying. Hearing the sound of several voices outside, Muncel frowned wearily.

"No," he said to Anjilihov. "Send whoever it is away. I am unwell and can give no audiences now."

Unbidden, Tulvak Sahm glided over to the open window and shut it. Bowing to Muncel, he said, "Churchmen are without. I will go."

"Yes, yes, go," Muncel agreed, and leaned his head back

against the chair with a sigh. No doubt word had spread through the court about the *magemons*. That the church was sending a delegation to protest their presence was no more than he'd expected. But he did not want to deal with them now.

Anjilihov closed the door firmly and came to him. "Cardinal Pernal sought an audience with your majesty, but I told him—"

"Are you truly unwell, majesty?" Pernal's voice said clearly. "I have no doubt of it."

Opening his eyes, Muncel saw the cardinal advancing into the room, alone and without the pair of acolytes who usually helped him walk. Despite his advanced age, Pernal's mind was as razor-sharp and cunning as ever. He'd suffered a mysterious illness ever since the day he'd grabbed the Chalice of Eternal Life in an effort to keep Tobeszijian from stealing it. No remedy in all these years had cured him or given him much relief from his sufferings. Yet, like Muncel, Pernal remained ambitious, too ambitious for him to surrender to his affliction. Thus, he refused to retire, and still clung to his role as Muncel's chief spiritual guide and adviser, although Muncel no longer wanted either.

Now, leaning heavily on his cane, Cardinal Pernal limped across the room toward the king. His face, terribly scarred from the old burns, contorted with pain as he came forward, but his eyes were alert and outraged.

"Lord cardinal," Muncel said in cold greeting. "It seems you are determined to force an audience today."

The old man halted, then bowed with difficulty. "Your majesty," he said, sounding out of breath. "Word reached me this morning that Prince Jonan has fallen ill again. I came to pray for the boy, but instead I found your grace closeted with creatures of sin and evil, rather than seeking Tomias's mercy for your son."

Muncel's temper blazed, yet he withheld a reply. Had Pernal been any other man in his court, he would have ordered his death for such bold condemnation. But Pernal had never feared him. They knew too many of each other's secrets; they were locked forever in uneasy alliance, friends once, and now enemies chained by mutual purpose.

In the silence, a look of sadness filled the old man's eyes. "This room is far too cold. No doubt you've had it aired to hide your misdeeds, like a schoolboy concealing evidence of his pranks."

Muncel frowned.

"But of course your majesty is no schoolboy, and the evil that was done in this chamber is no prank. Alas, that such foul creatures are now permitted free run of your majesty's court."

"They are locked away," Muncel said. "They will harm no one."

"And your tame *sorcerel*? Is he also locked away?"

Gritting his teeth, Muncel said nothing. That Pernal dared to stand here and chastise him was almost more than he was willing to take. The cardinal, Muncel vowed, had best take care.

"I grieve to see this," Pernal said relentlessly. "Long ago when you and I plotted the firm establishment of the Reformed Church in this realm, I never dreamed things would come to this."

"I have no time for reminiscences," Muncel said impatiently. "Was there something in particular you wished to ask me, lord cardinal?"

"I come not to ask but to rebuke."

"That, you have done."

"And your heart remains hard and closed." Pernal shook his head sadly. "I wish to pray for your majesty's soul. Come with me to the chapel for a short while. Let us refresh our spirits together."

Despite himself, Muncel stiffened. Rising to his feet, he snapped, "Another time. Not today."

"No," Pernal said softly. "I thought not. You have been giving me that same answer for many years now, majesty. You cannot delay seeking the merciful forgiveness of Tomias forever."

"I need no forgiveness," Muncel said angrily. "Thank you for the offer. I must continue with other matters now."

He started to step around the cardinal, but Pernal was not finished with him. "There is something else I must tell your majesty."

"Then say it quickly!"

"My agents have found Faldain."

Feeling as though he'd been struck, Muncel glared at the cardinal. "What mean you by this? On whose authority do you seek out the pretender?"

"On the authority of the church, your majesty."

"He is *my* enemy," Muncel declared. "I will deal with him in my own fashion."

"You want him dead. No doubt those creatures in your employ have been casting their evil spells, blaspheming here, in order to destroy Tobeszijian's son."

"Yes, I want him dead," Muncel growled. "And I will have him so."

"My men have orders to capture Prince Faldain alive and to bring him to Belrad without delay."

Taken aback by this audacity, Muncel stared at the old man for a full moment before he managed to speak. "Belrad? Why not Grov? Why not put the scepter in his hand? How *dare* you?"

"Nay, majesty! How dare *you* jeopardize the Chalice?"

"What? I don't understand."

Pernal's eyes were blazing. "Of course you don't. You haven't been thinking clearly since the boy was discovered at Savroix."

Muncel's brows knotted. He felt his anger building inside him like an explosive force. Growling in his throat, he began to pace back and forth, making curt, chopping gestures with his hands. "The pretender seeks to have me overthrown. He is too great a danger."

"He is the only link we have to the Chalice's whereabouts. He must not be killed until that knowledge is wrested from him."

Pernal's words rang through the chamber. Some of Muncel's panic and anger diminished, yet he was also aghast at what the old man wanted.

"Yes," Pernal said, nodding his scarred head. His eyes, clear and commanding, bored deep into Muncel. "He knows where it's hidden."

"How can you be sure?"

"Was he not with his father when the Chalice was taken? Think of it, majesty! In all likelihood he has lived with it, grown up with it. Undoubtedly he possesses it now, or has left it concealed where no one but himself can find it. He must be captured and brought here alive."

"He won't tell us what he knows," Muncel said. "Why should he?"

"But if he carries the Chalice with him, we shall have it!" Holy fervor shone in Pernal's eyes. "The sacred vessel will be restored to its rightful place in the cathedral. Its blessed light will once again shine on this afflicted land."

"You think it will heal you."

Pernal bowed his head. "It will heal many. Perhaps it will show mercy to me as well."

Muncel snorted. "Have you forgotten how it maimed you?"

"That was Tobeszijian's doing. The Chalice itself does only good."

Clasping his hands at his back, Muncel resumed pacing. "You should have consulted me first."

"Your majesty is not the head of the Reformed Church. Thod and his prophet Tomias rule our souls."

Muncel scowled, but he knew when to give in. "Very well. If your agents have found the pretender, send them word to seize him where he is. Have him searched. Reclaim the Chalice if you can, but do not have him brought to Belrad. That would be the gravest folly."

"But if he does not travel with the Chalice, we must wrest the knowledge of its location from him. At the cathedral, we can hold him prisoner and open his mind."

"Would you force him?" Muncel asked, curious as to how far Pernal would go.

"If he will not aid us willingly, aye." There was no mercy now in Pernal's voice. It rang out as harshly as Muncel's own. "The true test of his worthiness to rule Nether is if he will sacrifice himself to restore the Chalice to its rightful place. If he resists, then he is unworthy."

"What gibberish is this?" Muncel roared, losing his temper completely. His pulse was throbbing in his temples and his stomach churned as though he'd swallowed fire. "You would give him a test before you hand him *my* throne? You speak treason, old man!"

"Proving his worthiness to rule does not mean he will have your throne," Pernal replied without flinching. "But I will have the Chalice from him before I permit him to fall into your majesty's hands."

"Permit?" Muncel repeated, choking. "*Permit?* How dare you! I—"

"You are not thinking!" Pernal snapped. "You are letting your emotions rule your actions, and that is always fatal, majesty! It was the first lesson in statecraft that I taught you."

Furious, Muncel drew his dagger, but instead of fear contempt blazed in the cardinal's eyes. "No matter that you've abandoned your faith. I must uphold it," he said with conviction. "For Nether's sake, I must! It's my sworn duty to see that the Chalice returns to us."

Muncel stared at the dagger clenched in his hand. A deep shudder shook his frame, and he felt tired to the depths of his soul.

"Do you not realize," he asked quietly, "that if the Chalice returns it will cast me out for all I have done?"

Pernal's eyes widened, and he drew in a sharp breath. "Majesty," he said in a tone of compassion, "allow me to heal your soul before it's too late. Let the Chalice restore the faith you gave away—"

Muncel stepped up to him and plunged his dagger deep into the old man's stomach.

Disbelief filled Pernal's eyes. He stared at Muncel, and although his mouth worked no words came out.

"At last you have gone too far," Muncel said to him, and twisted the knife deeper into Pernal's vitals. "You fool! You should have understood that I do not want the Chalice back. Not now. Not at any price."

Pernal's scarred, hideous face looked frozen. His eyes stared, the vital force inside them dimming slowly. "You have condemned yourself," he whispered, and died.

Muncel pulled out his dagger as the old man crumpled to the floor, and absently the king handed his weapon to Prince Anjilihov. As his protector wiped off the dagger, Muncel stared at the corpse at his feet. He felt empty and foreign to himself.

"I was condemned long ago," he said softly, and nudged the body with his toe. "You were a fool, Pernal, not to see it sooner."

5

AT THIRST HOLD Dain looked in on Sir Terent, who lay bandaged and sleeping, then made his way to the chapel. The interior of this small place of worship was as shadowy as usual. Just inside the threshold, Dain paused to let his eyes adjust. The air was cold, dry, and musty, smelling of incense and candle wax.

The religious murals painted on the walls—crude renderings indeed after the sophisticated art Dain had seen at Savroix—looked dusty and blurred in the shadows. Tiny motes of dust danced in the sunlight pouring down through the oculus overhead. This was a simple place of worship, built for simple folk, yet pride and reverence showed in the immaculate snowiness of the altar cloth and in the brightly polished brass Circle hanging from the ceiling.

There came a pattering of footsteps, and the priest appeared, greeting Dain with restrained courtesy. As soon as he was informed of Dain's errand, he lit a torch and led the way down a flight of shallow stone steps into the crypt below the chapel floor.

"Alas, our poor Lord Odfrey, cut down too early. Far too early," the priest said mournfully. "The people have not yet recovered from the loss. They loved him like children love a parent. They have been lost without him here, guiding and providing for them."

Dain took the torch from the priest's hand and dismissed him. Glancing at Sir Polquin, he said, "Wait for me here."

Nodding, the temporary knight protector positioned himself at the foot of the steps. "I'll see you're not disturbed."

"Thank you."

Dain made his way slowly through the tombs. He found this to be a strange and eerie place of death. Sensitive to the eternal quiet, the musty shadows, and how the slightest of sounds echoed, Dain preferred the dwarf custom of burying the dead beneath dirt or inside wood. He believed that the spirit was long gone to the third world; why not let the body decay as all living things in the forest eventually returned to the soil? But it seemed Mandrians valued stone to guard their bones.

At the far end of the crypt he came at last to Odfrey's tomb. As yet it was only a plain box of stone. No statue lay atop it, and Dain supposed the carving was not yet finished. He would have to inquire, and make sure all was done in accordance with the customs of Odfrey's family.

A small plaque inscribed with Odfrey's full name and the dates of his birth and death was all that adorned the plain surface. In Dain's eyes, it seemed fitting that Odfrey should lie in such simple state. He had lived a plain, utilitarian life, avoiding frills and finery as much as he could. Yet there was one thing his tomb lacked that Dain could supply.

Dain quietly slid his torch into a wall sconce, then drew his sword—Odfrey's sword—from its scabbard. As plain and well-worn as its former master, the weapon had never quite fit Dain's hand, and he knew where this blade belonged.

With reverence, Dain kissed the hilt of the sword and laid it atop Odfrey's tomb before he knelt at its base.

It felt strange to be in a place of death without the proper Elements to conduct a service of respect. Dain had no salt, no stones, no basin of water, no candles, no fresh-peeled rods of ash. He had not brought such things with him because Odfrey had not believed in them. Therefore, he would honor the man who'd befriended him and given him so much by praying as Odfrey had taught him to pray.

Closing his eyes, he offered his short, simple request to Thod the Mighty. He asked that Odfrey's soul abide happily in the third world, reunited there with his son Hilard and his lady wife, who had both died years ago. There had been much grief and loneliness hidden in the chevard's heart. Now Dain hoped his sorrow had vanished forever.

At the end of his prayer, Dain sighed, knowing that according to the teachings of the Reformed Church, he had done his duty.

But he was not finished. Still kneeling, he bowed his head and communed with his memories of the man who'd become like a father to him, even though they had known each other less than a year. He had respected and admired Odfrey so much. He had yearned to please the man, to make the chevard proud of him. Odfrey had been the first man Dain trusted, the first Mandrian to show him kindness. It was thanks to Odfrey that Dain had discovered his own royal heritage, for without the chevard's quest to see him officially adopted, Dain would have never met King Verence, who'd recognized his pendant of bard crystal for what it really was.

So much had happened of late. Dain longed to be walking about the hold at Lord Odfrey's side, seeking his counsel, for there was much ahead of him that he did not know how to handle. He wished that, just one last time, he could see the calm good sense in the chevard's dark eyes, could hear the man talking to him about strategy and planning. In his young life, Dain had lost first his true father, who left him in the Dark Forest and never returned; then Jorb, the dwarf swordmaker who'd served as a guardian while Dain was growing up; and now Odfrey, a decent man of generous heart and open mind who'd seen past Dain's rough edges to show him a future beyond his wildest dreams.

Suddenly, Dain could no longer hold back his feelings. He knew this was against Writ, but he could not stop the ache in his heart. Closing his eyes, he found himself praying fervently to Odfrey himself.

"I go to fight a great war, lord," he cast forth in his mind. "I am barely a knight, barely a lord, barely a king, yet I must fight as all three. How can I be seasoned and wily? What must I know? What must I learn to prepare myself for the trials that lie ahead of me? Oh, lord, if only your spirit could ride with me into battle, then I would not fear what is to come."

He waited a moment, but sensed no response. "It is custom

with your people and mine that a son should inherit his father's sword. I have carried yours, lord, the one that you used daily with honor, the one that you died with. And now I have brought it back to you."

He paused, concentrating so hard that sweat beaded up along his temples. Around him pressed the silence of eternity. He heard nothing but the steady boom of his own heartbeat.

"Lord, if you are aware of me still, hear my request. I need Truthseeker in order to fight the darkness that will be my foe. You taught me that this weapon is not to be used for trivial battles. I ask for its use to regain my throne, and surely that cause is worthy. If my taking it offends you, show me the breath of your displeasure and I swear that I will not carry it away. But if you approve, fill my heart with your strength."

He waited a long while, waited until all he could hear was the muted hissing of the torch as it burned low. He waited until his knees ached on the stone floor, but nothing came to him. No murmur of approval or disapproval. No breath of benediction or protest.

Nothing at all.

Sighing, Dain had never felt more pagan and apart from the ways of Mandria than at that moment, for surely Lord Odfrey's soul had not heard his prayer at all.

It had been futile to believe his troubles could be eased this way. Dain raised himself stiffly, then placed both hands on the stone box which surrounded Lord Odfrey's bones and bade him farewell.

Although he'd gained no answer, at least he'd performed the courtesy of asking. Henceforth, if Odfrey's spirit grew wroth at Dain's use of Truthseeker and chose to haunt him, so be it. He would take what he needed. He would take what he wanted. All that was here belonged to him, by man-law, and he would claim it.

He did not let himself glance back as he strode from the crypt.

Once outside, he paused in the courtyard and looked at Sir Polquin. "What is the custom here, in the swearing of oaths to a new chevard?"

Sir Polquin blinked at the question. "Well now, it's custom to end the mourning with a feast—a great banquet in the Hall."

"Go on."

"And then toasts are drunk, and the men come forward to swear themselves into your service."

"The vaulted swords, the honor they showed me this morning. What was that?"

"Another custom of respect," Sir Polquin replied, squinting against the sunshine. "Respect due to the chevard's heir."

Dain's throat was suddenly full. He struggled to swallow before he could command his voice. "And if I asked them to swear their service this afternoon, in this yard?" He swept his arm in a gesture at the paved courtyard. "Would that break custom too much, if we had the oaths *before* the banquet feast?"

Sir Polquin stared at him hard. "What's turning in that head of yours, sire? What're you up to?"

"We have little time before we must resume our journey," Dain said. "I would see this done before I leave for Nether."

"But surely there's a few days yet. The poor lady's too ill to be moved now. And word has to be sent to the nearby holds, at least the upland ones, so that the other chevards can come and stand as witnesses."

Frustrated, Dain swore softly beneath his breath. "But if they are not present? Does that invalidate the oaths?"

"Nay. It's just an upland custom from the old days. It makes sure that no false claims can be brought against you."

Dain turned to scowl across the courtyard at the opposite wall rising behind Sulein's tower.

"Why?" Sir Polquin asked. "Have you a worry that the men'll balk? I'll cram my sword down their gullets if they don't line up proper."

"Nay, there'll be no oaths at swordpoint, if you please, sir knight!"

"What then? What's the hurry?"

"I can't say. I just have a feeling. . . . " Dain abruptly made up his mind. "Let the order be given. Notify Sir Bosquecel that I want the oaths given this afternoon. A rider will take the announcement to the other holds. We'll feast tonight, and be ready to rejoin Gavril's company on the morrow."

Sir Polquin started to speak, then held his tongue with a frown.

Dain glanced at him. "I don't trust his highness. It troubles me to stay too long from where I can keep my eye on him."

"Seems to me, sire, that Prince Gavril has his eye on *you*."

"Perhaps. But there's also Sulein to think of, now that he's been pressed into serving as a guardian."

"Sulein!" Sir Polquin snorted in disgust. "Good riddance, I say. That smelly hedge-pig of a physician ought to—"

"I need him," Dain broke in.

"Why? According to what I hear from Terent, you've never liked the foreign scoundrel. Haven't from the first day of your being here. Why, your grace even ran off in the forest just to escape having lessons with him."

This last was not true, but Dain had long ago given up trying to set common misconception straight. "I need him," he repeated. "He has something that belongs to me, and until I can get it away from him—"

"Tell me what it is, and I'll have it off his miserable hide in a twinkling," Sir Polquin said fiercely. "Why didn't your grace speak up about it sooner?"

"He's concealed it with a spell, and I can't get it away from him until he releases it."

"Morde!" Sir Polquin stared wide-eyed at Dain. "Even more reason to get rid of him. Why Lord Odfrey put up with his nasty ways, I've never understood. He only brought him here to see if he could cure Master Hilard. Which he didn't."

"Believe me," Dain said, "once I have my property, you may do with him as you will."

"A thief," Sir Polquin muttered, glaring beneath his knotted brows. "Well, now. I'll have to see what I can do."

"Nothing at present," Dain reminded him. "Not as long as he's a guardian."

"Probably put himself there just to keep himself out of our clutches. Fear not: Terent and I will get him."

"You can't as long as he's a guardian."

"Casting spells is against Writ," Sir Polquin said sternly. "Thod may strike him down for it. But what is it he's taken?"

"He wears a ring, very old, carved with runes and set with

a smooth white stone," Dain said, striving to keep his voice casual. He dared not tell even Sir Polquin just how valuable this ring was. "If you ever see it on his hand, that means the spell concealing it has faded. It can be plucked from his finger then, and only then."

"I'll keep that in mind, sire. But I never saw you wearing such a ring when you came to Thirst."

Dain frowned. Sir Polquin's memory remained as sharp as ever, and he was notoriously hard to fool. "It belonged to my father," he said with honesty. "How Sulein came by it, I know not. But it's important."

"Then I'll warn Terent, and we'll keep watch for it. Now for this business of the oath-giving. By your leave, I'll send a page to summon Sir Bosquecel."

Shortly thereafter the captain of the guard arrived. He looked thinner and grayer these days, but he still carried himself straight and erect. Although he blinked at Dain's request, he bowed in immediate, unquestioning obedience as a knight and hold officer was expected to.

"The oath service can take place just after midday, m'lord," he said brusquely. "I'm sorry to hear that you cannot be staying with us long, but I'll have the men ready."

"Thank you," Dain said, grateful for the man's efficiency.

Sir Bosquecel saluted, then strode away to attend to his duties, and Dain turned toward his wardroom.

But he'd barely reached the steps leading indoors when there came a shout from the sentries atop the wall. "Riders on the approach!"

Dain looked around with a grin. "It's Gavril! He's brought her here after all."

Feeling a rush of joy, he threw away his new dignity and ran for the steps leading up to the sentry walk. With Sir Polquin at his heels, Dain hurried along, his shoulder brushing the stone crenellations. At the vantage point overlooking the southwest, he paused and leaned out to watch the group approaching.

The crisp wind ruffled his hair. He saw a small party of ten riders riding beneath the Lunt colors of scarlet and black, and disappointment stabbed him.

At his shoulder, Sir Polquin grunted. "Those aren't the

prince's colors. Why, it's men from Lunt. Odd that they've come here. Probably just a patrol checking in to see that all's well."

Shortly thereafter, the Lunt men were admitted through the gates, and a sentry knight came striding up to where Dain still waited on the ramparts.

"M'lord," he said in a thick uplander accent. "It's Lord Renald come asking for audience wi' ye."

Dain frowned, impatient with the prospect of a visit he had no desire for. His time here was short; he had many things to do.

Sir Polquin breathed down the back of Dain's neck. "Here's your chevard witness for the oath-giving. Come like a gift of providence."

Some of Dain's impatience faded. "Did Chevard Renald say what business brings him hence?" he asked the sentry.

"Nay, m'lord," the knight replied. "Seems a bit rattled. There's been plenty of trouble hereabouts wi' raids and such like. Mayhap he's seeking Thirst men to ride forth wi' Lunt."

Dain thought of Pheresa lying in a tent with only a fence of wattle built around her. She had no salt or sticks of peeled ash to protect her from Nonkind raiders. Only those damned church soldiers, who were too arrogant to learn or listen.

"M'lord—"

"Yes! Of course," Dain said hastily, pulling himself from his worried thoughts. "See that the chevard is bid welcome. I'll receive him at once."

The sentry bowed and hurried away.

Dain looked at Sir Polquin, who said grimly, "Sounds like trouble's afoot."

"Aye. But where do I receive him?" Dain asked. "The wardroom's been locked. Lord Odfrey's things are still—" He choked up and suddenly could not finish his sentence.

Had Sir Terent been with him, the man would have reached out and gripped his shoulder in the way he used to comfort Dain. "Aye, lad," he would have said softly. " 'Tis hard to bear."

But the master-at-arms crossed his muscular arms over his chest. "Wardroom's the proper place for such," he said gruffly. "Best get used to it, now that it's yours."

His words were like a dash of cold water, and Dain nodded. "Very well," he said, and spun on his heel to return the way he'd come.

A few minutes later, he was standing at Lord Odfrey's desk in the lord's small, homey chamber, which had grown stale and musty in its owner's absence. He was conscious of the presence of Truthseeker, lying in the chest behind his chair. He could feel the subtle throb of it, a whisper of its voice, as though the sword was stirring to life because of Dain's proximity. An involuntary thrill raced up Dain's spine. *It knows,* he thought in excitement. *It knows I mean to carry it into battle.* Cobwebs had been spun over the hearth, and their delicate tracery shimmered in the sunlight slanting in through the window. Parchments, maps, and dispatches littered the top of the desk, and that huge beautifully illustrated map of the kingdoms that Dain had once admired was still draped over the tall-backed chair.

Hearing booted footsteps approaching his door, Dain whisked the map off the chair. He was still rolling it up when a knock sounded.

Sir Polquin swung open the door, then stepped back. "Lord Renald, your grace."

The Chevard of Lunt Hold entered with a swagger. His black cloak was thrown back over his shoulders, and his scarlet surcoat was wrinkled and mud-splattered from hard riding. Young and strongly built, with an elegant chin-beard and mustache, Lord Renald looked exactly as Dain remembered him from the night of Dain's trial in the Hall, when Dain had killed the shapeshifter and saved Gavril's life. Renald's intelligent eyes were fairly snapping just now with impatience and disappointment.

"Lord Renald," Dain said with his best court manners, "welcome to Thirst. As always, our hospitality is—"

"Thank you. Most kind," Lord Renald broke in curtly with none of his usual suavity. He seemed to notice his abruptness and checked himself. "Forgive me. I've been up since before dawn, riding like I had hurlhounds on my heels."

"There's trouble, then," Dain said with a sinking heart. He didn't want to get caught up in the problems of this land. His way still led north. "What sort?"

As he spoke, he pointed to the chair, and Lord Renald dropped into it heavily. A servant entered with a tray of cider in cups, and Lord Renald drained his in one swallow.

Grimacing, he slammed the empty cup down. "Damne, that's the sourest vintage I've yet drunk from Thirst orchards."

Dain left his own cup untouched and seated himself behind the desk. It felt strange indeed to have Lord Odfrey's things around him. He kept thinking that Lord Odfrey would come striding in at any moment and take charge, but of course that could not happen.

"I'm sorry there's no stronger drink to offer," Dain said. "The hold cellars need filling with wine and mead."

Lord Renald shrugged, dismissing the matter. His shrewd eyes regarded Dain for a moment, sizing him up. Dain felt his face grow hot beneath that intent gaze, but he returned it with equal steadiness.

"I own myself astonished to see you here, Lord Dain," the man said after a pause. "The word we had of you was that you were lying ill abed at Savroix. Yet you're here, looking hale and hearty."

"My recovery progressed quicker than expected."

Lord Renald's brows shot up. "And is it truth or rumor that you're the lost king of Nether?"

The direct question took Dain aback. "You're well-informed, my lord."

Lord Renald's gaze did not waver. "Truth or rumor?"

"Truth."

The chevard rose to his feet and bowed. "Then your majesty honors me with this audience."

"Please be seated," Dain said. "You've ridden hard. Rest yourself."

Lord Renald hesitated, then resumed his seat. "Morde a day, but you're a casual king."

"I'm not crowned yet," Dain replied.

Lord Renald grinned and suddenly looked not much older than Dain himself. "Aye, that's a valid point. May I bring my business here before your majesty?"

Dain nodded.

"I come looking for Prince Gavril. The word is that he's on his road northward to Nether."

"Aye, he is."

"Well, damne! Isn't he here?"

"No."

"Morde. These raids keep me sore pressed of late. Thod knows I have better things to do than chase in every direction in search of his highness. But I'm bidden to tell him he must turn back."

"Turn back!" Dain echoed in surprise. "But why?"

"That should be obvious."

Dain found himself flushing. "You must explain. It is not obvious to me."

Lord Renald looked at him as though he were a fool. "Has his highness—have you—given no thought to the reports we've been sending to Savroix since early autumn?"

"His highness is on a mission of mercy. He does not intend to turn back."

Lord Renald grunted. "I have received direct orders from King Verence to stop Prince Gavril and turn him homeward. If he'd sought shelter for the night at Lunt, as I expected him to, it would have been an easy matter. As 'tis, now I must hunt him. I tell you, Lord Dain, I have neither the time nor the manpower to spare for such a task."

Understanding now why Gavril had been so intent on avoiding Lunt and other holds, Dain drew in his breath sharply. "He must have received a warning."

"What?"

"He must have been warned of the king's intent," Dain said. "He's insisted we camp on the road every night since we left Tuisons and started overland. Not even here to Thirst will he come."

A line appeared between Lord Renald's brows. "And have you also a missive from the king, telling you to turn his highness back?"

"Nay. Unless it's come without my being told." Dain leaned forward. "I arrived but this morning."

Lord Renald rose to his feet. "Then you've a host of things to do. And I have more riding before me."

"Will you not bide long enough to take a midday meal here?"

Lord Renald seemed pleased by the offer. "Your grace is indeed hospitable. Certainly you've grown more polished than you were when I saw you last."

Flushing at the compliment, Dain also rose to his feet. "At Savroix, it was necessary to learn quickly."

"So I imagine. Well now, thank you for your kindness, but I dare not tarry while this task is on me."

"His highness is camped but a few miles from here. No more than a league, if that far," Dain said.

Lord Renald stared at him in astonishment. "Then why does he not come here? Why risk—"

"I told you. He obviously intends to avoid receiving his father's order."

The chevard frowned, a muscle working in his jaw. "Well, no matter what he intends, his highness is to return to Savroix at once. He can't evade the order now, no matter how he tries."

"But why must he turn back?" Dain asked. "There is Lady Pheresa to consider. If we abandon the journey now, she will surely perish."

Lord Renald shrugged. "I know nothing of that. I have my orders, and his highness is soon to have his."

"But what has alarmed King Verence so?" Dain asked. "Trouble with Nonkind?"

"Aye, all the usual mess and more," the chevard said with feeling. "There have been three trolk attacks on Lunt in the past month. We'll probably eat our Aelintide feast with our hands on our weapons."

"Trolks haven't banded together in years."

"They're at it now. As many as fifty to a pack sometimes. Thod knows how we'll keep them off if they continue to come. But there's some new trouble between King Verence and Nether, or so I hear. That's why his majesty doesn't want the prince to continue northward."

"The treaty," Dain said in dismay. "There must be a disagreement on terms."

"Aye. Now I'd best go."

"Wait, my lord," Dain said quickly. "There is a favor I would ask you."

"Better to ask it after I speak to his highness," Lord Renald said, and turned to go.

"It's about my oath service," Dain said quickly.

Lord Renald halted in his tracks, then swung back. "You have a kingdom north of here. Will you claim a mere hold for yourself as well?"

"Thirst is mine," Dain said harshly. "By Verence's warrant and Lord Odfrey's wish."

"Did Odfrey know your true identity?"

Dain met the chevard's probing eyes and made no reply.

After a moment Lord Renald blinked. "Morde," he said softly. "I always knew there was more to Odfrey than duties and battle. The only reason he accepted Prince Gavril as a foster here was to measure what kind of man—aye, and king—he would grow into. How *you* fell into his hands as well, Thod only knows."

"Will you witness my oath service?" Dain asked again.

"I'll come back for it, if the raids allow."

"My lord, I'm having it this day."

"Your grace seems to be in a great hurry."

"I am."

Lord Renald waited, but when Dain explained nothing more, he raised his brows. "I find it interesting that a pagan such as yourself seeks to follow our conventions."

Dain's shoulders stiffened. "I was named knight and chevard by his majesty, King Verence," he said curtly. "No longer am I considered pagan, but a lord of Mandria—"

"Mandria or Edonia?" Lord Renald asked with equal sharpness. "Rumor says you favor division."

"You hear perhaps too many rumors, my lord. This one is wrong," Dain declared. "I favor keeping Thirst strong enough to withstand what Gant will one day send at it."

"Nether will be coming at it soon enough," Lord Renald said. "This treaty offered to King Verence mocks us, and I pray to Thod he will reject it, even if it means war."

"Nether is not an enemy yet," Dain said.

"Are you promising to keep it allied to Mandria?"

Dain's head lifted at that challenge. "King Verence and my father were friends, and they kept friendship between their realms. I would do the same."

"Easy to say. Harder, perhaps, to do. I have been to Nether

once, four years past. 'Tis a filthy land, full of pestilence and thieves."

Dain's nostrils flared, but he kept his temper. "Once more will I ask you, Lord Renald. Will you, as Chevard of Lunt, witness my oath service as Chevard of Thirst?"

"Do you understand that by so doing I put myself and my hold at risk?"

"How so?"

"Obviously you mean to lead Thirst knights into Nether," Lord Renald said. "There can be no other reason for such haste. I know my king. He will be furious if you do this. I do not care to risk his ire."

"You are more at risk if you fail to convey his message to Prince Gavril."

"How so? You said his highness is close by."

"I did not say he would be easy to find. Is he on the main highway or a lesser road? How much time have you to search for him?"

"Damne! What games do you play with me now?"

Dain crossed his arms over his chest and simply watched Lord Renald. "'Twas you who said you haven't much time."

"'Tis unfriendly to force a man to take risks he shouldn't."

Dain shrugged. "You uplanders are perhaps too cautious."

"We uplanders have reason to be!" Lord Renald retorted. "My grandfather survived the War of Union, when Edonia was brought to heel. He survived, but he struggled thereafter with harsh taxation and was forced to surrender half his lands. The lowlanders have stamped their feet hard on our necks, and only in recent years have the penalties eased. We are trusted now, but we paid a bitter price for it. I'll not be accused of joining the divisionists."

"I do not ask you to do that," Dain replied. He saw that he was not going to budge Lord Renald by any means of persuasion he'd tried thus far. It was time for frank speaking. "I'm no intriguer, my lord. I do not plot political strategies here. When I ride into Nether, possibly I shall never return. But if I do not validate my warrant of inheritance by receiving the oaths of Thirst's men . . . if I do not follow the customs and complete my duties as an adopted son of Odfrey's, then my departure and absence will render Thirst unclaimed. Its ancient charter will be dissolved, and it will pass into King Verence's hands. I have heard that Prince Gavril is counting on this and intends to use the hold for a hunting lodge."

Lord Renald blinked.

Dain nodded. "Perhaps you do not care if the Thirst crest is chiseled off the walls and the royal seal replaces it. But I care. This is perhaps the last thing I can do to preserve Odfrey's ancestral lands as they were meant to be. I seek to honor his wishes as best I can."

Lord Renald looked increasingly thoughtful as he listened. "I see. But if you keep ownership of Thirst, the hold will have no chevard to manage it, or to help protect this part of the border."

"If I survive what lies before me, I shall remedy that," Dain said. "I should like a son of mine to return here."

Lord Renald shot him a wry look. "In that case Thirst would belong to Nether, and it would still be lost to the uplands."

"But it will not belong to Prince Gavril," Dain said through his teeth.

"Is that all this is? A ploy to keep his highness from seizing the hold for his own?"

Dain hesitated, then nodded. "Aye."

Lord Renald laughed. "At least that's honest. Is this how you mean to get back at his highness for having falsely accused you at trial here?"

"It's not about revenge," Dain said stiffly, thinking of that night in Thirst's Hall when he'd saved Gavril's life from the shapeshifter. "It's . . . Much lies between us, my lord. 'Tis complicated to explain."

"Never mind," Lord Renald said with a shrug. "I know enough about feuds. They never stop, and they can consume you if you are not careful."

Dain said nothing, just gazed steadily at the man.

"Very well, King Dain," Lord Renald conceded with a sigh. "I will witness your oath service and see you rightfully placed as chevard. If you fail at being a king, perhaps you can come back and run this hold, eh?"

Dain's smile soured a bit. As an endorsement of support, it

wasn't much, but he supposed he should be grateful that Lord
Renald was agreeing at all.

"I thank you," he said formally. "Come, let us eat together.
Then as soon as the ceremony is finished, I will direct you to
Prince Gavril's camp."

"He will hate us both for this," Lord Renald said with a sigh.

"Aye, he will," Dain agreed. "But I, at least, am used to it."

6

DESPITE THE BRIGHTNESS of the midday sun, the wind blew cold.
The banners of Thirst Hold snapped in the breeze while a trumpet rang out and drumbeats rolled.

In solemn procession, the knights of Thirst marched forth
from the guardhouse before an awestruck crowd of servants,
villagers, and serfs. Each knight wore full armor and carried
arms. Each knight led his charger, with his shield tied to his
saddle. The horses were caprisoned for war with armored saddlecloths and head plates. Their iron shoes scraped and rang on
the paving stones as they filed into the innermost courtyard.
The knights came in order of rank. Sir Bosquecel led the line,
followed by Sir Alard and the other first-rank knights, then the
middle-rank knights, then the sentry-rank knights, and at the
rear, the elderly or battle-maimed knights who no longer rode
to war but served light duties as door guards and strategists.
Behind this procession came the delegation of squires, squirm-
ing and nervous in their dark green tunics and wool cloaks.

Atop the stone steps leading to the Hall, Dain sat in a tall-
backed chair. He still wore his mail hauberk, but had donned
one of Lord Odfrey's dark green surcoats for the occasion. His
thick black hair had been braided up the back of his skull, war-

rior fashion, revealing his pointed ears. A narrow circlet of gold—a gift from Prince Spirin before Dain left Savroix—rested on his brow for the first time. His magnificent ruby ring gleamed on his finger.

Behind his chair stood Sir Terent, looking pale and drawn but proud. Sir Polquin was beside him, with his bullish shoulders drawn back and his head high. It was a king's right to have two protectors if he chose, and Dain had just named Sir Polquin to the second position a few minutes earlier. For once, the master-at-arms had been struck speechless, but his eyes were shining over the honor bestowed on him.

To Dain's left stood Lord Renald with his small band of Lunt knights. To his right were the priest and Thum, who kept grinning despite his attempts to stay solemn.

The procession of knights halted at the foot of the steps, and the drums fell silent.

The herald stepped forward. "By the right of inheritance and the warrant of his majesty, King Verence, this man Faldain is proclaimed Chevard of Thirst. According to law, the oaths of service which bind these assembled men of arms to Odfrey, Lord of Thirst, are hereby dissolved and void."

Some of the knights bowed their heads. Dain's keen ears caught the faintest murmur of whispering among the house servants and pages looking on.

This was the moment, Dain told himself, where everything could go awry. Freed of all allegiance, the knights could now ride forth from Thirst and pledge their service elsewhere. No one could forcibly bind them to Dain, whether he was the lawful chevard or not. He sat there trying to look impassive, but his mouth was dry and his heart was thumping hard inside his chest. If he had not been eld he would not have been much worried, but uplanders were notoriously prejudiced against those of his kind.

"The claims of Faldain begin," the herald announced, his voice ringing forth across the assembly. "He is knight-at-arms, Chevard of Thirst, and uncrowned King of Nether. He asks for your oaths of service, which you may give or withhold by the laws of Mandria."

The drumbeats resumed.

Dain rose to his feet and went down the steps to where the knights stood in a long row before their horses. Behind him, Sir Terent and Sir Polquin followed. It was required that Dain go to each knight in turn, the action a symbol of his humble supplication. Once the oaths were given, his every command would have to be obeyed without question or hesitation, but until then he was to think of how bereft and insignificant he would be without his men. The ceremony and its meanings had all been explained to him, and he felt nervous and stiff in the knees.

As he reached Sir Bosquecel, he stopped and turned to face the man, who stared back from beneath his upraised visor.

"Ask the question," Sir Terent mumbled in Dain's ear.

Thus prompted, Dain said, "I come to you in need, Sir Bosquecel. What am I given?"

The hold commander drew his sword and knelt before Dain to lay his weapon on the ground between them. "I give you my sword in service, loyalty, and honor," he replied, his voice firm and clear. "I swear to obey and fight in the name of Faldain, until my days be ended. *Aelmn*."

"Aelmn," intoned the priest, stepping up to anoint Sir Bosquecel's brow in blessing.

Drawing in an unsteady breath, Dain moved to the next man in line. "Sir Alard," he said. "I come to you once more in need. Although you gave your oath before, what will you give now?"

Sir Alard knelt and laid his sword on the ground between them. He gave the same answer Sir Bosquecel had, with equal assurance and conviction in his voice.

The priest anointed him, while Dain moved to the next man and the next. By the end of the ceremony, Dain felt numb from repeating the same words over and over. Only four knights had withdrawn, refusing to serve. They were new men, strangers, and of the lower ranks. The rest, however, now stood proud and erect as Dain came striding back up the line. When he started to climb steps, they swung their swords aloft and shouted his name.

"Faldain! Faldain of Thirst!"

He turned to face them, pride and gratitude tangled in his throat, and returned the salute. Then he resumed his seat while the squires came, one by one, up the steps to kneel before him and make their pledges. After the squires came the servants, beginning with Julth Rondel and continuing down to the lowest scullions. Many sounded nervous or even frightened as they spoke their pledges. One woman covered her face with her hands lest he gaze into her eyes and enspell her. Two of the maids broke into tears, but the rest kept their composure.

Dain smiled at each servant who dared meet his gaze. He spoke to them with kind gentleness, taking care to do or say nothing to alarm them.

At last it was all done. The villagers gawked from afar at their new master. The serfs had no pledge to make; they were bound from one lord to another with no choice in the matter. A brief benediction was spoken by the priest, and the herald announced Dain's invitation that all help themselves to the cider barrels in celebration.

Feeling as though a heavy weight had come off his shoulders, Dain left his chair and found himself surrounded by his men, all talking at once and grinning like fools.

Lord Renald came over with a cool smile on his lips, but he offered Dain his hand in friendship. "Well done. You have won their loyalty, and I hope Lunt and Thirst will continue to share the accord they have known in times past."

"It's my hope as well," Dain replied. "And now for my end of our agreement. You will find Prince Gavril less than a—"

Suddenly distant trumpets sounded and a shout rose from the lone lookout on the walls. Muttering curses, the sentry knights bolted for the ramparts.

Lord Renald gripped his sword hilt. "It's trolks. Morde a day, but I shouldn't have left—"

A wide-eyed page came running up to Dain. "Lord grace," he said, garbling Dain's titles, "'tis Prince Gavril coming to the gates."

Astonished, Dain stared at the child. He couldn't help but think how close the ceremony had come to being interrupted by Gavril's arrival.

"Tell me swiftly," he said to the page. "Does the whole company come with his highness, or rides he alone?"

"It's everyone!" the page replied. "Such a large number of

wagons, and the church soldiers are carrying demons tied to a pole."

Dain and Lord Renald exchanged startled looks.

"Alive?" Dain asked.

"Nay, my lord grace," the little boy replied with excitement. "Their heads are cut off, and are swinging in a sack beside them. I *saw*—"

The trumpets sounded again, and two men in white surcoats came riding into the courtyard. The crowd parted, and Dain walked down the steps to meet them.

As he drew near, he saw it was Lord Barthomew and Sir Wiltem. The commander was glancing around at the crowd and signs of panoply with narrowed eyes. When he saw Dain, he stiffened in his saddle.

"Lord Faldain," Lord Barthomew said with a sneer, "I am to convey to you compliments of his highness. Prince Gavril and his party seek the hospitality of Thirst Hold."

The formal request was worded with correct courtesy, but the tone that delivered it held contempt and mockery.

Behind Dain, Sir Terent growled in his throat like an old dog, and Sir Polquin turned red over the affront.

Ignoring Lord Barthomew's insulting tone, Dain felt relief that Gavril was finally showing some common sense. "Bid his highness and companions welcome," Dain replied formally. "Report to Sir Bosquecel for instructions in how your knights will be billeted here."

After Lord Barthomew had bowed and ridden off, looking surly, Dain turned and issued orders to the steward.

"Lady Pheresa must not be stared at by the servants," he said sternly. "Above all, we must respect her privacy. Give her an excellent chamber, one that is easily kept warm. Let there be chairs and cushions to soften the furnishings. Damne, I wish we'd known sooner to prepare for her."

A few minutes thereafter, Gavril came riding into the courtyard on his black stallion, his banners flying and his entourage in tow. His pack of dogs barked and milled around the horses in excitement. Today he wore his golden breastplate, polished to a blinding sheen. His dark blue cloak flowed from his shoulders to hang in heavy folds over the hindquarters of his prancing mount. The sunlight glinted on his blond hair, and his vivid blue eyes were glittering with anger as he saw the gathering of knights in their finery.

Dismounting onto a tiny velvet stool that his page hurried to place beneath his stirrup, Gavril ignored the crowd staring at him and started up the steps, Lord Kress at his heels.

Dain met Gavril halfway. With his brows knotted in acute dislike, the prince looked Dain up and down.

"So you would wear a crown now," he said scornfully, referring to the circlet on Dain's brow.

"This is no crown," Dain replied. "By Nether custom, the circlet is worn as a badge of royalty, just as you wear your bracelet."

Gavril's cheeks flushed at the comparison, but he made no further protest. "I thought you intended to keep your identity discreet."

"My intentions have changed."

"Clearly. Well, it seems I have interrupted your ceremony. What a pity. I would urge you to continue, but alas, seeing Lady Pheresa settled will occupy us both."

Dain smiled, keeping his voice as silky as Gavril's. "Your highness is kind, but there is no interruption. My oath service has been completed, and all is well."

Gavril's smile dropped from his face, to be replaced by a thunderous scowl. "Impossible! You are too hasty. The oath service cannot possibly have been conducted this quickly."

"It has."

"But improperly. There are no witnesses. At least four chevards must be present—"

"My pardon for correcting your highness," Lord Renald said quietly, stepping forward, "but according to law a minimum of only one chevard is needed for witnessing."

Gavril's cheeks were ablaze. He glared at Lord Renald, then shifted his gaze back to Dain. "How convenient to find Lunt here as well. You have been busy indeed this day."

Bowing, Dain kept silent. He was eager to get away from the prince and devote his attention to Pheresa.

"Your highness," Lord Renald was saying, "I bear messages

from your father the king, which I am to speak to you without delay."

Gavril took a step back. "Not now."

"But, your highness—"

"Not now!" Gavril turned away from Lord Renald and stared at Dain. "I must speak to you in private."

Dain frowned. "Perhaps after—"

"At once! It cannot be delayed."

"Yes, very well," Dain said.

By this time, Noncire and his attendant priests were riding into the courtyard, followed by a stream of church soldiers. The latter should have remained in the stableyard, but no one appeared to be directing them properly. Sir Bosquecel was busy ordering Thirst knights to disperse into the outermost bailey. The result was milling confusion, added to by the crowd of gawking villagers.

It was almost impossible to hear or speak over the general din. With a glance at the exasperated Lord Renald, Dain led the way inside. He and Gavril were followed by their protectors, and Lord Renald with his man brought up the rear.

Halfway up the stairs, Gavril paused and gave Lord Renald a cold look indeed. "Forgive me, sir, but why do you accompany us?" he inquired.

Lord Renald's face turned pink, but he met Gavril's gaze without flinching. "I must give your highness the king's orders."

"And I told you I would not hear that message now."

"Then I shall wait outside Faldain's wardroom until it pleases your highness to receive me."

Gavril's face grew stony. "When I am ready to receive you, I shall send for you. At present you are dismissed."

Lord Renald's flush darkened to crimson. Although his eyes were blazing, he kept his temper at having been treated like a mere lackey. He bowed, then turned on his heel and went back downstairs without another word.

Gavril sighed. "These provincial lords are so tiresome."

Dain felt angry on Renald's behalf. Although he knew it was probably best to hold his tongue, he could not help but say,

"Your highness should not chastise him for trying to obey his orders."

Gavril, however, was gazing about the corridor they now walked along, and appeared not to be listening. "I see you've adopted the kingly privilege of two protectors for yourself. Is it not best to see yourself crowned first?"

Dain met Gavril's eyes. They were bright and vivid, even here in the shadowy corridor. There was an air of suppressed excitement about him, a fevered impatience, that made Dain uneasy.

"It's just," Gavril went on, "that I feel myself outnumbered."

As Dain unlocked the wardroom door, he reminded himself to post a guard here as long as Gavril's men were running loose about the place. He glanced at Sir Terent, who had held up well during the ceremony, but now looked paler than he should have.

"Go and rest," Dain said.

Sir Terent frowned immediately. "I'm fine, sire. Fit as can be."

"I shall wish you to stand duty with me later," Dain said. "Rest now, and let Sir Polquin serve in your place."

Sir Polquin grinned. With a deeper frown, Sir Terent bowed and left.

Dain pushed open the door to the wardroom, wincing as it creaked rustily. Light and fresh air poured in through the open window.

Gavril looked around at the cluttered space, and sneered. "It appears to be a shrine to Lord Odfrey."

"There hasn't been time to put things in new order," Dain said, then refused to defend himself further. "Please be seated. I'll send a servant to fetch your highness some wine, if—"

"Wine?" Gavril interrupted with a grin. "Not that sour vinegar Thirst is so famous for?"

"Indeed not," Dain said, grinning back. For an instant he and Gavril were in perfect accord. "Rest assured, there will be changes made at Thirst."

"Clearly you are already busy." Gavril glanced at Lord Kress. "Protector, would you step outside?"

Kress bowed at once, but hesitated, then looked at Sir Polquin, who bristled instantly.

"Our conversation must be completely private," Gavril said to Dain in appeal. "You understand."

Dain frowned, suspecting that Gavril had some question about Tanengard he wanted no one to overhear. Dain thought it best to humor him, lest the prince change his mind about staying and drag Pheresa back into the cold wilderness once again.

"If you please, Sir Polquin," Dain said. "Perhaps you and Lord Kress would care to stroll in the corridor."

Sir Polquin looked like he'd eaten sour grapes. He scowled and hesitated, obviously reluctant to leave, but with more meekness than Dain expected he walked out with Kress, slamming the door behind them.

"Now," Gavril said as though in relief, "we can speak plainly."

"What about?"

"This foreign physician of yours," Gavril said.

Dain blinked. The topic of Sulein surely did not merit such privacy. "Is he not able to sustain his place among the guardians?"

"He seems to be doing adequately. My concern lies with his trustworthiness. Will he harm her?"

"No."

Gavril nodded and began to pace back and forth. "In all frankness, I dislike his presence. The guardians sustain her life with a weaving of faith, but Sulein believes not in Writ. He is using power of a different sort. It could taint the entire proceedings. I think Noncire should take his place."

"Noncire!" Dain said in amazement.

Gavril's gaze, as cold and alert as a lyng's, met his. "You object?"

"Nay, I do not object," Dain said, thinking rapidly. "But—but I did not know him capable—"

"He is a cardinal, Dain. Of course he's capable!"

Stung, Dain said, "Very well. But at his age, is he strong enough?"

"I know not," Gavril admitted with a sigh. "Of late his judgment seems to be faltering. He and I disagree more and more."

"Better leave Sulein in place," Dain said, "and save the cardinal in case another guardian falls."

"Aye, your advice is sound," Gavril agreed.

This strange conversation made Dain uneasy and suspicious. "And now, your highness, what is it you really want to discuss with me? Tanengard?"

Gavril stopped pacing and whirled around. "Do not mock me! Thod curse your bones, I would have it still if not for you."

"The king forbade you its use," Dain said coldly. "Not I."

"You—" Gavril stopped and appeared to struggle with himself. "Nay, there is another matter I would discuss with you."

"Then discuss it," Dain said impatiently. "I have much to do."

"This Sulein," Gavril said. "Can he peer into the minds of men?"

"No," Dain replied without thinking. "Why?"

"What is it called, this looking that the pagans do?"

Dain felt astonishment. To his knowledge, Gavril had never before shown any curiosity about the special abilities belonging to some eldin and Netheran priests. "It's called parting the veils of seeing, but—"

"Can you do it?"

"Nay. Women with eld blood and many *sorcerelles* have this gift. For men it often comes harder, if at all. Why—"

"Strange, these different terms for similar things," Gavril mused. "Noncire calls it faith with sight, but it must be the same thing. Don't you agree?"

Dain was starting to think that Gavril's wits were wandering. He could make little sense of this conversation that went first in one direction, then in another. It was unlike Gavril to act this way.

"I wish I could see into the future," Gavril said with a sigh. "In my nightly prayers, I ask Tomias for his benevolence on my plans, but prayers are not always answered. Did you know that I used to believe with all my heart and soul that I would find the Chalice?"

Dain's frown deepened. He eyed the door. "I know that you wanted to find it while you were here as a foster."

"No one searched harder than did I," Gavril said sadly. "No

one prayed for the honor of its discovery more than I. And all the time, you were here with me. You, who have known since infancy where to find it."

Alarm spread through Dain. He moved around the end of the desk, heading for the door, but Gavril crashed into him and hit him hard across his temple with the hilt of his poniard.

Dain's head rang. He saw the world tilt, fade, and tilt again. Blinking, he came to and found himself down on one knee, rigid with the determination not to faint. His head throbbed like a drumbeat.

Gavril stood over him, twisting his fingers into the cloth at Dain's shoulder. "How you must have laughed at me this past year, watching me struggle with my faith and effort, while you knew the secret all the time."

The room spun again, making Dain feel dizzy and sick. He squinted, desperate to make Gavril understand. "No," he struggled to say. His voice croaked like a stranger's. "Don't know."

"You told my father you could find it. You pledged your word of honor to bring its cure to Pheresa."

"Eldin can cure her," Dain said, wincing as Gavril's grip tightened on his shoulder, twisting a fold of the cloth across his windpipe. He coughed for air and reached for his dagger, but it was gone from his belt. "Chalice—"

Gavril rapped his skull again with the hilt of the poniard, and Dain dipped into a place of darkness, only to be shaken out of it by Gavril. Pain throbbed in his head. He smelled blood and could feel it streaking down the side of his face.

In a dim corner of his scattered wits, he felt anger at himself for having been caught off guard like this. He shouldn't have trusted Gavril for an instant.

"Listen to me!" Gavril was saying, shaking him again. "I will give you one chance. Tell me where the Chalice is hidden. Show me where the Chalice is hidden, and I will not deliver you into Muncel's hands."

Dain blinked slowly, feeling his brain turning like thick treacle. "Muncel?" he echoed.

"A message from Nether reached me this morning," Gavril said impatiently. "I have been asked by a man named Pernal to hand you over as an unlawful pretender to Nether's throne. Your secret is out, Dain. They know you are here and not in Savroix."

"Uh—"

"This is a chance for Mandria to create new ties of friendship with Nether, to strengthen an old alliance."

"Don't—"

"Cardinal Pernal offers much for you on King Muncel's behalf! Do you want to hear the terms?"

Dain closed his eyes for a moment, feeling gray and clammy. He knew he must not pass out. His only chance was to stay conscious.

"How naive you are," Gavril said with something close to pity in his voice. "No doubt you thought you could just ride across the border, and the Netherans would receive you with joyous welcome. Hah! This is what comes of a weak mind and small education. You are no king. You have no right to swagger about with a circlet of gold on your head—" He ripped the ornament from Dain's brow and flung it across the room. "You have no right to appoint *two* protectors to guard you. Your folly and conceit are as unfounded as they are pathetic. You're naught but a pretender, Dain! A pretender!"

"What," Dain asked, trying to buy time, "do they offer for me?"

"A potion which will cure Pheresa instantly."

"Doesn't exist—"

"You want me to believe so," Gavril said with a harsh laugh. "But you are as full of lies and trickery as all your kind. Do you not think I know what will happen if you find the eld-folk? You will betray me, enspell me, and hold me hostage for ransom."

Dain frowned, wondering if he was dreaming this. How had Gavril thought up such nonsense? Except . . . except that such an act of foul betrayal was perhaps exactly what Gavril himself would commit in Dain's place.

"Gavril," he said, fighting off another bout of dizziness, "listen to me. I—"

"No, *you* listen! I am offered five times your weight in gold, plus the cure for Pheresa, plus a suit of Nethcran-forged armor, plus a new treaty granting many concessions to Mandria, plus the altar cloth where the Chalice once rested, if I will hand you over intact."

Dain swallowed a groan. He longed to sink to the floor, but Gavril's grip did not loosen.

"Well? What say you to such generosity? Do you think you are worth that much?"

"A fine payment," Dain said with an effort. He was sweating, but he still felt cold. "Worth a prince."

"Yes, indeed."

"If I am really a pretender, would they offer so much?"

Gavril clamped his hand atop Dain's skull, and Dain nearly passed out. "Hold your tongue, trickster! I have something else in mind. Dain! Hear me!" He gave Dain another shake to bring him back. "As appealing as these offers are, I will ignore them. I will set you free if you will take me straight to the Chalice. Right now. This very day."

"You—you would leave Pheresa here?" Dain asked, wincing as the throbbing in his head grew worse. "To die?"

"Nay, fool! You said the Chalice would cure her. And so it will when I bring it back from where your father concealed it. Why should she suffer more, being dragged about in a wagon, when we can bring the cure to her?"

Dain frowned, and Gavril shook him again. "Come! Let us ride forth this very afternoon. I give you this chance to decide; otherwise, we depart tomorrow with you in chains."

Dain summoned all his strength to send Gavril a look of scorn. "You will never give me to the Netherans as long as you think I know where to find the Chalice. Threaten all you like, but you won't do it."

Gavril bared his teeth. His blue eyes shone with triumph. "You're forgetting something. Because I am a fair man, I have given you a chance to spare your life. Help me, and I'll set you free. Oppose me, and I'll let Noncire open your mind for the secrets it contains. I am told it is a procedure rarely done, for it brings terrible pain to the victim. Afterwards, you will be quite mad."

While Dain looked up at him in horror, Gavril flung back his golden head and laughed.

"The Netherans don't care if you're mad or sane," he said,

still chuckling. "I will know where to find the Chalice, and I can still deliver you—poor wretch that you'll be—to collect my reward in Grov."

Dain knelt there, desperately struggling to pull his wits together. "Sir Polquin!" he shouted, although the effort made his head ring. "Sir Polquin, come to me!"

Cursing, Gavril gave him a shove that toppled him over. The door swung open. Expecting Sir Polquin to come charging inside to his rescue, Dain felt his heart lift with relief.

But as the door opened, he saw two figures struggling on the threshold. Dain tried to get to his feet but failed, and at that moment Sir Polquin cried out and sagged in Lord Kress's arms.

Kress, out of breath, his face a grim mask, manhandled Sir Polquin inside the wardroom and shoved him to the floor.

Sir Polquin hit on his side with a thud, his back to Dain, and lay there unmoving and far too still. Dain picked himself up, swaying unsteadily on his hands and knees, and crawled to him. But he knew the truth before he touched Sir Polquin's shoulder.

"No," he whispered in anguish. "No!"

Dain rolled Sir Polquin onto his back, then stared down into his sightless eyes. Lord Kress's dagger still protruded from Sir Polquin's heart. As Dain stared in horror, Kress bent down, bracing his foot on Sir Polquin's ribs, and pulled the dagger out.

"Good work," Gavril said.

"And this one gave your highness no trouble?" Kress asked, cleaning his blade matter-of-factly.

Gavril laughed. "Nay. He was easily tricked. Go outside and keep watch. I'll join you in a moment."

Kress obeyed, closing the door behind him.

Dain knelt there, too frozen with grief to act. Sir Polquin, so stern, so brusque, so gruff-spoken, had taught Dain his very first lessons in swordplay. A relentless taskmaster who demanded perfection, he had run Dain and the other fosters through endless practice drills. Quick to criticize, slow to praise, Sir Polquin had never treated Dain as less than the others because of his mixed blood. Now, grief swelled in Dain's heart. He could not believe he had lost this man. Sir Polquin's unfriendliness was surface only; inside, his heart had been true and loyal. Protector for less than one day, Dain thought, bowing his head as his eyes burned and stung.

"Mandrians slaying Mandrians," Dain said hoarsely. "What vile infamy is this?"

"Get up, if you can," Gavril said impatiently. "Do not keep me waiting for your answer."

"Was this necessary?" Dain asked. "Killing Polquin?"

"You called him to you," Gavril said without mercy. "You sounded the alarm that brought his death. If you want to blame anyone, blame yourself."

Dain felt the guilt twist inside him like the plunge of a knife. But it had been Kress's hand that had done this black deed, not his. He glared at Gavril, hating him, and felt a terrible anger burn through his veins. He reached out, gripped the leg of a chair, and shoved it into Gavril with all his might.

The prince grunted with pain and surprise, and went staggering to one side. Desperate to make an end of him before Lord Kress came back in, Dain tried to tackle him by his ankles, but Gavril dodged him.

With a curse, Dain turned to pull Sir Polquin's dagger from his belt, but his body couldn't obey him fast enough. He gripped the hilt, but he felt as though he were trapped in deep mud. His coordination, his balance, his strength had all gone elsewhere.

Gavril kicked him in the ribs, knocking him flat and sending him skidding across the floor. "I see I have your answer," he said. "Very well! You were always a fool, Dain. I offered you mercy, but now you are finished."

As he spoke, he hit Dain again with his poniard. The weighted hilt felt like a hammer smashing into Dain's browbone. His bones seemed to melt, and he fell. He tried to move, but his limbs would not obey him. Instead, he felt himself sinking into darkness.

Gavril's voice, mocking and merciless, followed him down: "I shall send Noncire to you as soon as we have Thirst subdued and in our power. You fool! You have only yourself to blame for your destruction."

There was no answer Dain could make. The darkness swallowed him then, and would not give him up.

7

THE SOUND OF voices arguing above him brought Dain back to consciousness. He came swimming up through the darkness reluctantly, feeling the headache still pounding in his skull.

He felt himself lifted onto a hard surface. The back of his head thumping against it jolted him to full awareness. He opened his eyes, and was instantly dazzled by golden light that made him squint.

"Hurry," a voice said sharply. "He awakes."

Ropes were tied to Dain's arms and legs, and he was lashed in place before he could make more than a token struggle. As yet he could see nothing more than silhouettes against the bright candlelight. He frowned, trying to figure out where he was and how he'd gotten here. If only his head would stop hurting.

"Sulein?" he said thickly. His mouth was so dry he spoke in a rasp. "Sir Terent?"

"Quick," one of the men said, and a cloth was draped across Dain's face.

The folds were heavy enough to make him feel smothered. He jerked his head but could not shake it off. He heard the rasp of a strikebox and smelled the sharp acrid scent of flame. Moments later, the cloying stench of incense coiled through the air. Trying not to breathe it, Dain grimaced beneath the cloth.

A knock sounded on the door, and when it was opened Dain heard the rustle of thick robes and the whisper of soft leather shoes. He recognized the slow ponderous gait and inhaled a familiar scent of pomade.

"My lord cardinal!" one of the men said nervously. "All is in readiness."

"Good," Noncire replied. "Why is his face covered?"

"Er, to—to keep his gaze from enspelling us, your eminence."

"Foolish superstitions," Noncire said. "Take it off."

The cloth was whisked away from Dain's face. He squinted against the dazzle of light, but this time his eyes adjusted quickly and he saw that he was still in the wardroom. Candles blazed around him. In one corner a small iron brazier burned incense, sending forth thick crimson smoke.

Shimmering in white silk robes, a yellow sash of office encircling his vast middle, the cardinal gazed down at Dain with his small, beady eyes before he held aloft his diamond-studded Circle, which winked and glittered in the candlelight.

Angrily, Dain jerked against his bonds, but the ropes were new and tight. He felt neither slack nor give in them.

"Now, do not be tiresome," the cardinal said to him softly. "Had you been cooperative with his highness, this rather tedious business would not be necessary."

Feeling his heartbeat race, Dain glared at him. "You cannot part the veils of seeing! You have no such powers to look into my mind!"

Noncire's expression never changed. "But of course I do. And if you submit, it will be over quickly, with less damage." He paused a moment, his eyes boring into Dain's. "If you resist, you will suffer terribly."

Dain frowned at him, seeking pity or compassion, and finding none.

"The Chalice of Eternal Life must be found," Noncire said. "It is a terrible sin to keep something so holy hidden away where its tremendous powers and benevolence are wasted."

"Sin?" Dain echoed with a hollow laugh. "And is there no sin in destroying my mind?"

"Tell your secret and you will not be harmed."

Dain heard the lie in Noncire's voice. "Its guardianship is my responsibility," Dain said. "As it was my father's before me, and his father's before him."

"But you've been a poor guardian, Faldain of Nether," Noncire said softly. His plump hand, the pale pudgy fingers adorned with rings of his high rank and estate, stretched out and gripped the front of Dain's surcoat. A cold, smothering force seemed to ripple forth from his touch, sinking through Dain's clothing into his skin and the very marrow of his bones.

Dain could not hold back his gasp of surprise. His eyes widened, and he stared very hard at Noncire, but he could detect nothing in the man, no hint of extraordinary powers at all.

"Your church training was a travesty." Noncire gestured with his free hand, and the assistant priests began to chant something that made Dain flinch. Every word in the chant was like a pinprick, then a nick, then a stab.

"Clearly," Noncire said, looming large over Dain, "you understand almost nothing of Writ, or you would know that our priestly training is based on ancient principles indeed. We are taught those first, before we proceed to the ceremonies of holding mass and giving benedictions."

"But you are against magic," Dain said breathlessly, stiffening in his bonds as Noncire's grasp tightened. "Tomias forbade it."

Noncire chuckled. "How refreshing, to hear a pagan such as yourself call on the Prophet for aid. This is not magic, Faldain. It is something far older."

He pressed his palm across Dain's nose and mouth, and his thick fingers were like iron, digging into Dain's flesh. The clammy sense of smothering engulfed Dain, filling him with panic, for he could not breathe. Only vaguely did he realize that he was jerking against his bindings, jerking so hard the ropes sawed at his wrists. But his struggles began to ebb, for his body seemed to be freezing, growing turgid, inert, and unresponsive. Such a terrible coldness flowed from Noncire's hands. It filled Dain, submerged him, slowed his heartbeat to a mere thread.

Desperate, Dain reached deep inside himself and thought of fire, thought of flames, smoke, and heat. Though it was a strain to even open his mouth, he sang of fire and flicker, of heat and hunger, of crackling, jumping, hissing, blazing fire.

Noncire closed his eyes, and the coldness in Dain increased, hurting now. Dain felt something clawing at his mind, trying to force its way in.

With all his strength, Dain struggled for breath to swell his song. He sang of Jorb's forge, of the roar of flames beneath the bellows, of the sere, crackling heat dancing in the air above the firepit, of the glowing orange metal, half-molten and sparking beneath the skilled tap of Jorb's hammer. And at last he felt the coldness thawing in him and believed, with a spurt of relief, that he was winning.

Then new pain spiked through his head, and Dain's song faltered.

"*The Chalice!*" said a voice inside his head. "*The Chalice! Where is it?*"

Memory came to Dain of the last time he'd seen the sacred vessel. He was high above the ground, perched on a beast that breathed fire and ashes. His father was nearby and they were surrounded by a crowd of people. There was an altar. A man with a cruel face wore a crown. Another man in pale robes held the Chalice aloft. How white it was. How brightly it shone, casting a clear pure light of its own.

When the man holding it aloft shouted words of anger and strife, the Chalice burned him so much he dropped it, dropped the sacred Chalice the way Dain dropped his cup at nursery suppers. And then his father started shouting words of power. Flames shot forth from the end of a mighty sword, and all the bad men fled.

"Fire!" Dain sang now, resisting Noncire. "Fire most holy. Fire of ash and wood. Fire of power. Fire of sky. Fire of earth and mountain. Burn away the impurities. Burn away the dross."

Noncire spoke and his grip tightened, but the cold was still thawing. Dain could breathe again, and the more air that filled his lungs, the louder he sang. Until . . . he felt something stir inside him, something he had never felt before. It was similar to what he felt when he'd wielded Truthseeker or Tanengard, and yet far different.

Tiny little flames sprang up along the ropes binding Dain's arms. In seconds, the ropes were burned through, and Dain yanked his arms free. He knocked Noncire away from him, sending the obese cardinal staggering across the wardroom. His assistants scattered with cries of alarm, forgetting their chant entirely. The spell collapsed.

Sitting up, Dain tugged at the ropes still holding his legs.

"Guards!" one of the assistants shouted.

Dain swore. He yanked the last knot free, then flung himself off the desk just as the door crashed open. A church knight, clad in mail and holding a sword, loomed in the doorway.

Dain kicked the incense brazier over in the guard's path.

Coals spilled out across the man's feet, making him swear and jump back. Crimson smoke gusted up, filling the room.

Noncire's fat face was blotched with anger, and his black eyes narrowed to mere slits. "Put that sword away," he said harshly to the guard. "Seize him and hold him fast."

Dain retreated a step. The wardroom was small, crowded with too many people and the heavy furniture. He backed toward the cold fireplace, remembering the secret passage concealed behind it that Lord Odfrey had once shown him.

But there was no chance to reach it. The church knight charged him, and although Dain dodged, he knew he had no real hope of eluding capture. Not when one of the assistant priests gripped him by the back of his tunic and held him just long enough for the knight to pounce.

Dain sent the assistant reeling back with a little yelp of pain. But then the knight reached him and put his dagger to Dain's throat.

Dain froze, breathing hard.

"Good," Noncire said. "Hold him fast."

The guard seized Dain's right arm and twisted it hard behind his back. He tried to resist, but the dagger point pressed harder, and Dain felt blood trickle down his throat.

Raging inside with frustration, Dain kept still.

Noncire came to him with malevolence glittering in his tiny black eyes. "Your eld magic has availed you little," he said. "Now your defiance will cost you dearly." His gaze flicked to the guard. "Hold him."

Before Dain could react, pain skewered his skull with such violence and force he thought it had been split open. There was no fighting this time, no resisting. The brutal, destructive agony seemed to have no end until at last . . . at long last . . . Noncire stepped back with a tiny smirk of satisfaction.

"Release him," the cardinal said.

The guard obeyed, and Dain swayed on his feet a moment, wide-eyed and shaken, before he fainted into a black aftermath.

The sound of knocking brought him back. He lay in darkness, hardly breathing, his eyes staring at the shadows. After a while, the door creaked open and someone entered.

"Dain?"

Torchlight cast a glow through the room that drove back the shadows. Dain squinted, retreating inside himself as the footsteps came closer.

"What has happened in here?" Thum said in wonder. "It looks like everything has been . . . Dain! Great Thod above, Dain!"

Thum knelt beside him, gripped his shoulders, and rolled him over.

Dain winced and turned his face away from the light. It hurt. Sound hurt. Even darkness and silence hurt.

Thum touched his face, and Dain flinched. "I'm sorry," Thum said, snatching his hand away. "Can you hear me? Can you speak? Morde a day, what's bashed your head? Can you answer me? Dain? Sire? What's happened to you? I've been searching everywhere."

Dain wished he could just lie there forever. He wished he could burrow deep into the earth and never come out. He felt sick and gray and clammy. It was impossible to speak, yet somehow he had to know, had to find the strength to ask questions.

"You . . . well?" His voice was a croak he couldn't recognize as his own.

"Of course I am. How can you think of me when you are in this state? Let me call the servants—"

"No!" The effort of making that protest exhausted Dain. He reached out blindly, groping until Thum gripped his hand. Dain squeezed his fingers weakly. "No one," he whispered.

"But what's happened? I thought you were visiting Lady Pheresa all this time, yet when I went to fetch you for supper you were not with her. Her serving woman said you never came."

Dain closed his eyes on a laugh he lacked the strength to utter. How normal it all sounded. He felt as though he was lying in a place thousands of leagues away.

"Still here," he murmured. "Gavril. Not taken her away."

"Why should his highness go?" Thum asked in surprise. "He just came this afternoon. When you did not come to your chamber to change for the feast, I decided to look for you. I didn't want you to miss the banqueting or the toasts. Already the men are calling for their new chevard. Gavril is downstairs in his finery and has ordered his musicians to play merry tunes for everyone's enjoyment."

"Still here."

"Aye, of course he's here. I'll tell you, he looked sour for a while about the oath service, but tonight his mood has greatly improved."

"Still here," Dain repeated again, unable to believe it.

"I must fetch help for you," Thum said worriedly. "Or has Sir Polquin gone for it?"

Dain laughed, a low, gutless chuckle that he could not stop until Thum gave him a little shake.

"In Thod's name, sire, you're in a bad way. Can you sit up?"

Too late did Dain try to protest. As soon as Thum sat him up, he hunched over and was violently sick. Sinking back, he felt exhausted and wrenched. A cold sweat covered him, and he couldn't seem to collect his thoughts, no matter how much he tried. There was something he needed to do, something he kept forgetting as quickly as he thought of it.

I am alive, he thought in wonder. *I am not insane, and I am alive.*

"I must get you to your chamber," Thum said.

"No," Dain whispered, trying again to think of what he needed to do. "Let me bide here a moment longer."

They sat in silence a little while, then Thum asked, "Where *is* Sir Polquin? Has he gone to get help for you? Why isn't he here? Who attacked you, Dain? What villainy has been done?"

Dain's anger returned, and, though splintered and damaged, it revived him a little. "Kress," he finally managed to say.

"Lord Kress? Did he strike you on Gavril's orders? I hope Sir Polquin has treated him as he deserves!"

Sighing, Dain gave up the attempt to explain. Perhaps later, after he remembered what he had to do, he would be able to tell Thum what had happened. If he tried now, he feared, he would weep.

"Sir Terent," he whispered in dread. "Safe?"

"Of course he's safe. The arrow did not go deep into his shoulder. Do you want me to fetch him to you?"

Dain gripped Thum's sleeve in alarm. "Don't go."

Thum patted his shoulder. "No, of course I won't go. You needn't worry."

"Must rest," Dain said.

"Of course. When you think you can stand, we'll go to your chamber."

"Must remember. Must think."

"Not now," Thum told him. "I am going to lay you down again and call a servant—"

"Call no one!" Dain snapped, then sagged over and retched again. Nothing came up this time but misery.

"Your head must be pounding like a drum," Thum said in sympathy. "I remember hitting mine once when I was little and fell out of a tree. I was sick too, and dizzy. I had to lie abed all day until I felt myself again. Gods! How dare these scoundrels attack you in your own wardroom. Their boldness is an insult that must be repaid in like kind!"

Dain, however, did not answer Thum, for he suddenly heard a low, humming melody that he vaguely recognized. It was a song, yet not a song. Although low and quiet, it seemed very clear.

"Dain—"

"Hush!" he said. "Listen."

"To what? I hear nothing."

But Dain heard it clearly, for the humming was louder now. And in his mind called a familiar, resonant voice: *"Come to Truthseeker!"*

He drew in his breath sharply. That was what he was supposed to remember. Truthseeker was in this room. It knew somehow that he intended to carry it . . . carry it . . . to where?

"Can you stand now?" Thum asked. "Your skin feels very cold. You have lain too long in this unheated room. Come, let me help you up."

Dain shut his eyes, saying nothing. Thum rose to his feet and pulled Dain upright with a grunt, his arm tight and steady around Dain's ribs.

"All right?" he asked. "You aren't feeling sick again, are you?"

The room spun for a moment. Dain felt fresh sweat break

out across his body. With Thum's help he took a single, feeble step, nearly fell, and managed another.

The torchlight glinted on something lying in the corner. It was Dain's circlet of gold, lying where Gavril had flung it. In silence he pointed, and Thum bent to pick it up for him.

"Villains!" Thum said in a furious, strangled voice. He'd gone suddenly pale behind his narrow beard, and his freckles stood out plainly. "They who serve Gavril are cowards and knaves. To attack you like this! It isn't to be borne! I'll give the order and have them thrown out of the hold this very night."

Dain lost interest in Thum's outrage and turned instead toward the large wooden chest standing against the wall. Staggering and dizzy, he struggled toward it.

"Easy now," Thum said. "You're going the wrong way. The door lies in yon direction."

But Dain would not be turned around. He reached the chest and sank to his knees despite Thum's efforts to catch him.

"Please," Thum said worriedly. "Come away. There's nothing here to be done right now. Dain, come with me."

Ignoring him, Dain struggled to lift the lid of the chest, found it too heavy, and nearly mashed his fingers before Thum raised it for him.

"There's nothing in here," Thum said impatiently. "Dain? Sire!"

Reluctantly Dain turned his head to look up at his friend. "Have to," he said, and reached inside the chest.

"What are you looking for? Tell me and I'll get it for you."

Without answering, Dain shifted through the chest's contents, pawing aside a stack of vellum and leather books, a cloak so old the cloth was rotting, a purse of gold dreits, a pair of lady's gloves in finest silk yellowed with age, a worn dog collar, and a musty fur robe. Beneath all this lay a plain leather scabbard sheathing the magnificent sword made of god-steel.

Peering over his shoulder, Thum sucked in an audible breath. "Ah, yes. I'd forgotten about this sword. Shall I lift it out for you?"

"Nay."

Fighting off another bout of dizziness, Dain gripped the weapon with both hands. The ancient metal, wrought in ways mysterious, resonated with power that made Dain's hair stand on end. He shuddered involuntarily, feeling the contact with it even through the leather and wood scabbard.

A surge of energy jolted through him, filling him with new strength until he no longer felt sick and dizzy. Some of the confusion fell from his mind. He remembered what Noncire had done to him, tearing into his mind to find hidden secrets. He remembered that he had conjured in his mind a false location for the Chalice. Only then had the dreadful attack ceased.

He'd saved himself, but even so he'd come far too close to destruction. Gripping Truthseeker now, he drew in several deep breaths and squared his shoulders. He hoped Gavril and Noncire sought the Chalice so far and long in the wrong direction that they both rotted of futility.

Dain shook off Thum's helping hands and rose to his feet. Truthseeker hummed in his hands, its deep song for him alone.

No dwarf swordmaker had crafted this weapon. It was far older, made from metal so hard no ordinary steel could prevail against it. The guard, studded with a row of glittering emeralds, was straight, not circular, in a style predating the long-ago establishment of the Church. The gold wire wrapping the long hilt gleamed richly in the candlelight. The blade itself was carved, Dain remembered, but he did not draw it now to look. Although he'd used the weapon once, to fight and destroy a shapeshifter, he found himself wary and a bit afraid of Truthseeker's tremendous power.

"I know your hand," the sword said to him. *"Fear me not."*

Breathless, Dain gripped the hilt, and felt it twist in his hand as though fitting itself to his grasp. It almost hurt him to hold it, yet he hung on, his heart racing.

"To war," Truthseeker urged him.

"It's beautiful," Thum said, staring at it. "I remember how you used it to kill the shapeshifter. We would all have died that night if not for you." His eyes met Dain's and widened in wonder. "You're well again. Is it—is it the sword's doing?"

"Aye," Dain replied, soaking in the power that Truthseeker shared with him.

"Is it magicked, like Tanengard?"

Dain shook his head, and saw no reason to keep Lord Odfrey's secret now. "It's made of god-steel."

Thum's mouth opened, but nothing came out. His hazel-green eyes were popping. To his credit, he didn't flee, although he'd turned nearly as pale as Dain felt.

"'Tis very old," Dain said when Thum remained silent. "The dwarves search the ancient battlegrounds sometimes in hopes of finding god-steel. They can't work it, though. My old guardian Jorb told me no one has the knowledge of how to make such metal as this."

"What is it doing here?" Thum whispered.

"You mean, how came Lord Odfrey to own such a weapon?" Dain asked wryly. "It has been handed down secretly from father to son for generations in his family. He was afraid to carry it, afraid the priests would condemn it and order it destroyed."

Thum made a strangled, involuntary noise of protest in his throat.

Dain smiled wanly at him. "No," he assured his friend. "Nothing like that will happen to this blade. It has missed war for centuries. It has been locked away, hidden and feared, but it was made for battle and justice. I will take it back to both."

At that moment footsteps sounded in the corridor outside the wardroom door. With them, came the sound of voices.

Frowning, Thum turned in that direction. "Blackguards," he said angrily. "Come to finish the job, no doubt. I'll—"

Dain shushed him quickly. He knew not why church soldiers were returning here, but he didn't want to learn the reason. He and Thum could not be found, and there was only one other way out.

Swiftly he hurried over to the desk and yanked open the drawer where Lord Odfrey had kept a spare dagger. The weapon was still there. Gripping it and Truthseeker, Dain went to the fireplace and pressed the stone as Lord Odfrey had once shown him.

A small, concealed door slid open in the wall, and a dark passageway yawned there, smelling musty and dank.

Picking up his torch, Thum stared with his mouth open.

The door rattled. "I told you to keep this door locked," someone outside said in annoyance. "His eminence gave strict orders about it."

Dain beckoned to Thum, and the squire followed him into the passageway like a rabbit bolting into its hole. Inside, Dain saw an iron lever draped with cobwebs. Swiftly he pulled it down, and the hidden door slid shut just as the wardroom door slammed open with a bang.

Crowded together in the narrow space, with the torch held between them close enough to scorch their eyebrows, Dain and Thum listened in silence.

"Damne, he's gone!" one of the men shouted.

"If you'd locked the door instead of coming to me—"

"No one gave me a key."

Their bickering continued, then faded away as the door slammed again.

Dain realized he was holding his breath, and slowly eased it out. He met Thum's gaze. "I think they're gone."

"Morde a day, but where does this passage go?" Thum asked.

"I don't know. Out of the hold somewhere. Come."

Thum gripped Dain's arm to keep him from starting down the passageway. "You don't mean to explore it, surely!"

Dain frowned. "We're leaving this hold tonight, this very hour. I must get to Nether without delay."

"But, Dain, what about his highness? What about your attackers?"

Dain thought about Sir Polquin, whose death cried out for vengeance. "I will rejoin with Gavril later," he said grimly. "His villainy will not go unchecked forever. This, I do swear."

"But you must denounce him. Do it here, before your own men."

"I will not set Mandrians against Mandrians," Dain said grimly.

"Then—"

"Thum, I must get away, now, before they discover me gone. Gavril means to betray me to King Muncel for a price. I will not fall victim to his plan."

Thum swore viciously. "He is evil through and through. He has hated you from the very beginning and will see no good in you at all. But why attack you here at Thirst? Why not wait until we reached Grov to betray you? It makes no sense."

"Have you ever heard of faith with sight?"

Thum jerked back from him and drew the Circle hastily. "Damne, to talk of that is forbidden by Writ!"

"Cardinal Noncire did it to me," Dain said, even while Thum shook his head. "I have no reason to lie. You saw my state before the sword revived me."

"But why would he do such a thing?"

"He and Gavril think I know where the Chalice is hidden." Dain scowled, hating them more than ever. "Sir Polquin is dead, Thum. Killed by Lord Kress while trying to defend me."

"Great Thod, no!"

Dain stared at the wall, and felt a bitter surge of memory. "My father warned me in a vision that I would be betrayed. I always felt sure it would be Gavril who did so, but I never thought—I didn't expect this—"

He broke off, unable to command his voice.

After a moment of silence, Thum gripped his shoulder. "They are foul to the core," Thum said angrily. "Gavril has always rammed his piety down our throats, but he is the very worst blasphemer I have ever seen. I suppose he thinks that if he but gives the orders for his evil to be carried out, and takes no action himself, Thod will look the other way."

"There isn't much time," Dain said. "They'll be looking for me. Somehow we've got to warn Sir Terent and—"

"They're looking for you, but *I* am not suspect," Thum said. He pointed at the hidden door. "Let me back through."

"Nay!" Dain protested in alarm. "You're safe with—"

"'Tis *your* safety we must worry about. Let me go back and announce that you've taken to your chamber with illness."

"No—"

"Dain, hear me," Thum said with urgency. "We'll need horses, and money. You can't walk to Nether, can you?"

Realizing Thum was right, Dain put aside his protests. "You're thinking more clearly than I am."

"And small wonder. I'll take those coins from that purse we saw in the chest. Aye, and clean out your strongbox as well. There's food too—"

"No food. Don't risk it."

"Very well, but you must have your hauberk, your cloak, and your boots. Besides Sir Terent, who else do you want?"

"Sir Alard," Dain said, thinking it over.

"No one else?"

"We can't smuggle out the entire force without arousing suspicion. As 'tis, how will you get yourself, and horses besides, out of the hold without being stopped?"

Thum looked grim indeed. "Unless Gavril's men have taken the hold by force, the sentries are *your* men, sire. I have only to say we act on your orders, and they'll let us out."

Dain nodded and clapped him on the shoulder. "Go then, and take care."

"'Tis yourself who must take care," Thum said worriedly. "Were there any other way, I would not leave you. What if your illness returns?"

"It won't," Dain assured him, and then stilled his protests.

Dain listened at the door a moment, then pulled up the lever. The panel slid open and, after handing Dain the torch, Thum stepped back into the wardroom.

They stared at each other a moment, and Dain wondered if he would ever see his friend again.

"Go with Thod," Thum said.

"You as well."

As Thum lifted his hand, Dain pushed down the lever. The hidden door slid between them, and Dain was left in the cramped passageway with only the weapons and the torch for company.

He took a moment to thread the dagger and Truthseeker's scabbard onto his belt. Truthseeker was so long its tip nearly dragged on the ground. As Dain picked up the torch again, a wave of dizziness passed through him.

He leaned against the wall until the trembling aftershock passed, then wiped the sweat from his brow with an unsteady hand and regathered his strength with determination. Pushing himself forward, he followed the passageway to wherever it might lead him.

——— PART TWO ———

8

IN THE LONG twilight of evening, when the sky darkened to indigo and falling snowflakes swirled thickly in the gusts of wind, Alexeika Volvn crept from one snowdrift to another until she reached the back of the inn. There, she eased herself into cover behind a stack of empty wooden crates and hunkered low with a sense of relief.

It was bitterly cold tonight, the wind cutting through her cloak and hauberk. Shivering, she flexed her fingers inside her fur-lined gloves in an effort to keep them from stiffening.

Snow season was just beginning in southern Nether. Up north, where she'd lately been, snow lay waist-deep over the ground and drifted high against trees and shepherds' crofts. Travel in such climate was hard indeed, and Alexeika was grateful to have come down here near the border, to better weather and riper pluckings.

On the other side of the wall, she heard muffled sounds as the small party of king's soldiers she'd been tracking all afternoon rode into the stableyard and shouted for the landlord.

Grinning to herself, Alexeika thought of the eight stalwart horses shortly to be stabled in this ramshackle structure at her back. In two or three hours, when the inn's customers had dined and bedded down for the night, she would slip over the wall and take her pick.

Four stolen horses with bridles would be about all she could handle. They would fetch a good price from Costma and add to her growing stash of coin. She had almost enough money to pay for her lodging and food for the duration of the winter. Time was growing short before the deep cold came, but tonight's work would bring her very near her goal.

Born a princess and the daughter of Nether's most famous general, Alexeika now lived a dangerous and solitary life. Since her escape from the savage Grethori tribes up in the far mountains, she'd avoided most folk. The price on her head was high enough to tempt one to betrayal. Twice she'd asked Costma to let her join his bandits, but he refused, saying his men would not tolerate her presence in their company, not even if she wore chain mail and wielded a sword like a man. She would cause trouble, he said.

And so she'd become a horse thief, working alone and taking dangerous risks, selling her prizes to Costma and other bandit chieftains for the coinage that would see her through the winter. She had no home, no family, no one to give her charity. She had no choice but to provide for herself as best she could.

Hunkered in the dark, sheltered by the crates with the stable wall at her back, Alexeika supped on hard cheese and a withered apple and ate snow to quench her thirst. The falling snowflakes filled the folds of her cloak and dampened her hair.

Gradually the village grew quiet as folk shut themselves in for the night. The smell of woodsmoke drifted to her nostrils now and then. In the forest beyond the outskirts of the village, she heard the distant howling of wolves, and shivered involuntarily. The voices and bustle inside the inn, accompanied by the aromas of hot stew and dran tea, eventually faded. When all lay quiet, and even the wind died down to a light breeze that swept snow across a sleeping world, Alexeika rose to her feet and stamped them a while to bring back feeling in her toes.

She shook the snow from her cloak and climbed the wall. After she paused on top to look around, she dropped lightly into a snowdrift in a corner near the fodder pile.

No alarm sounded, and she drew in a deep breath of relief. Dusting snow off her clothing, she glanced around to get the lay of the place. The inn was a crumbling structure built of timber and daub in the shape of an L. The stables were hardly more than a rickety lean-to attached to the longest section of the inn. The walls extended from there, forming the whole into a rectangular-shaped compound. Double gates made of thin wood slats that creaked and rattled in the wind provided the only exit or entrance. Although they'd been shut for the night, they were hardly stout enough to provide any real protection in case of trouble; nor, Alexeika saw at a glance, were they locked. Only a wooden pole dropped across two brackets held them closed.

Light shone across the yard from a large window, throwing an oblong spangle of gold upon the snow. The window gave anyone inside a clear view across the yard, and Alexeika's heart sank as she saw it. For a second she considered abandoning her plan, but she could hear the horses moving about inside the lean-to, tantalizingly close and too tempting to resist.

Although the penalty for stealing army horses was a beheading on the spot, Alexeika never stole any other kind. Most village folk were too poor to own or feed horses; besides, they were not her enemies. Muncel's soldiers were, and she gladly ran the risk to do them whatever harm she could.

Now, firming her resolve, she edged along the inside of the wall, staying well within shadow as she circumnavigated the yard. A dog lying curled up against the door barked sleepily at her. She gave it the rest of her cheese, rubbing its upright ears and making friends with it. When it saw she had no more food, the watchdog yawned and put its head down on its paws.

Grinning to herself, Alexeika slipped up to the large window and peered cautiously inside. The light came from a dying fire on the hearth. It glowed in a mass of collapsed embers and ash. All the torches and lamps had been extinguished; she saw no sign of servants.

The soldiers snored with their heads on the table, their hands still curled around their tankards. By the look of their uncleared trenchers, they'd drunk more than they'd eaten. Over in one corner near the fire, a communal heap of straw provided bedding for a small group of travelers huddled together for warmth under fur robes and blankets. Alexeika hardly spared them a glance. They would not have horses to steal. Hardly anyone could afford a mount these days except soldiers and the aristocrats in favor with the usurper.

Silently Alexeika moved away from the window. If she kept quiet enough, no one indoors would rouse. Now she had to make sure no guard had been posted at the stables themselves. Keeping one hand on her dagger hilt, Alexeika made her way cautiously in that direction.

Close up, the stables looked even more dilapidated than they had at a distance. The structure seemed to have been built of whatever scraps of timber and board the owner could scrounge together. Wattle panels divided the stalls, and Alexeika could hear the wind whistling through the gaps and chinks in the lean-to.

The horses—large shadows she could barely see—shifted about placidly in the dark. The wealth they represented made her shiver with anticipation.

Swiftly she forced herself to concentrate. This was no time to be dreaming of the coins Costma would count into her palm. The hardest part of her task still lay ahead of her.

The wind died down completely, and all the world fell into a hush. It grew even colder. Alexeika's feet and hands were numb, and her cloak might as well have been made of paper for all the warmth it provided tonight. Forcing herself to be patient, she waited and listened for a long while until she felt sure no guard was present, then eased inside the shelter and made soft clicking noises with her tongue to alert the horses to her presence. Stretching out her hand, she touched the hindquarters of one animal, and patted it in reassurance as she moved up alongside it.

"Easy there. Easy," she murmured, and the horse dipped its head and rumbled softly in its nostrils.

In her father's youth, knights of family and proud lineage, and not hired soldiers, formed the bulk of the king's army. Such knights had possessed war horses trained to submit to them alone. Nearly impossible to handle, fierce, and trained to strike down any stranger who put his hand on them, those chargers would have attacked her, whereas these horses were sleepy and docile. The king's agents bought them in herds from the Kladites, and they were assigned to the soldiers at random. These nags were light-boned coursers, underbred and thin-necked beneath shaggy winter coats, but they would fetch her money from the bandits. That was all she cared about.

Not wanting to alarm the horses, Alexeika forced herself to take her time. Fumbling in the dark, she found the bridle of the nearest horse hanging on a peg and slipped it on the animal, then did the same with the horse next to it. The bemused pair turned about and came with her willingly.

Drawing in a deep breath, Alexeika glanced once more at the window of the inn, wishing it did not overlook the yard, and told herself that now was the time for boldness.

She led the horses across the yard in full sight, feeling her heartbeat pound nervously. Her senses were stretched tight. When one of the horses nudged her back, she nearly jumped.

Alexeika slipped the pole out of the gate brackets, eased open a panel, which creaked loudly, and led the horses out into the road.

There, she came face-to-face with four men on horseback, cloaked and hooded, and standing squarely in her path.

Gasping with alarm, Alexeika froze in her tracks and stood there staring. The snow had stopped falling, and overhead the clouds had parted enough to show stars and moonlight. She could see these travelers well enough, but from whence had they come? She'd heard no hoofbeats, no sounds of approach. It was as though they had dropped from the second world, yet they were not Nonkind. In fact, they looked foreign, for their cloaks were thick and neither patched nor mended. Their horses were twice as fat and sleek as her pair.

Her heart was hammering with fright, but almost at once she regained her wits and told herself to act nonchalant.

So she gave them a nod and clucked to her horses, then attempted to lead them past the strangers.

"Hold there, if you will," called out one of the four. His voice was clear, strong, and foreign. He spoke Netheran with a strange accent indeed, but she could understand him.

The problem was, she feared the soldiers asleep in the inn would also hear him.

"Is this an inn?" the stranger asked her.

Alexeika shook her head.

The four travelers exchanged looks and sighs of obvious disappointment. Alexeika hardened her heart to their plight. It was late and cold, but if they were foreign and soft they'd not find this lodging to their satisfaction. Better to spend the night in the forest with beyars and wolves than to share a roof with the king's men.

Holding her head down, she tried again to lead the horses past them, and again the spokesman blocked her path. "We were told we could find lodging in this village. Where is it, if not here?"

Silently, Alexeika pointed down the road the way they'd come.

One of the other men, a large shadow with bulky shoulders, growled within the dark folds of his hood. "Nay, sire," he said in Mandrian, which Alexeika understood, "this lad's playing us for a fool. We've found the place, right enough."

Their leader raised his gloved hand for silence and regarded Alexeika from within the dark folds of his hood. "Guide us to the inn, and I'll pay you for your trouble."

Again Alexeika shook her head. She dared not speak. Although she looked enough like a boy in the moonlight in her masculine garments, her voice was unmistakably feminine and melodious, difficult to disguise.

"Might be a half-wit," growled the large man who'd spoken earlier.

Alexeika did not wait for the leader to respond. She tightened her grip on her horses' bridles and led them forward past his stirrup.

In silence he did nothing to stop her, and she was just feeling the first stir of relief when she overheard him say to his men, "Thum, see if you can rouse the landlord. If nothing else, perhaps we can pay the owner of a private dwelling to let us lodge for the night."

"Aye—"

Alexeika spun around. "Do not call out," she pleaded urgently, keeping her voice as low as she could. "Your kind are not welcome here, and King Muncel's soldiers lodge within."

At that moment the watchdog set up a furious barking, and a shout came from inside the inn. Alexeika swore and jumped onto the bony back of one of her acquisitions. She kicked it forward and yanked on the reins of the other just as some of the soldiers came bursting out into the yard and ran to the gates.

"Thief! Bandits!"

The clash of steel made Alexeika glance back. She saw the four strangers fighting off the soldiers' disorganized attack. Grinning to herself, Alexeika kicked her mount to a gallop, and the horse she led broke into an unwilling run alongside.

Seconds later, she heard the thunder of hoofbeats behind her and saw that the four strangers were following her. She swore in annoyance, for they would lead the soldiers onto her trail.

By now, torchlight was flaring in the stableyard. Men shouted, and already some of the soldiers were mounted in pursuit.

Alexeika leaned low over the neck of her horse, urging it faster. But it was a sorry steed, far inferior to the Mandrian horses. They were gaining on her easily, and she knew she could not elude them, especially while she was hampered with the spare horse.

Reluctantly she dropped its reins, and the animal blundered over into the path of one of her pursuers. As the man cursed in Mandrian, Alexeika yanked on the reins and left the road, ducking low as she plunged into the forest. Here, no moonlight penetrated the interlaced boughs of pine and fir. She rode recklessly through the darkness, pressing her cheek to her horse's rough mane to keep from being whipped by branches.

If Thod favored her, as she prayed he would, the Mandrians would not leave the safety of the road.

But Thod did not favor her.

The Mandrians fell back slightly and Alexeika thought her ploy had worked, but then two riders began to follow her while the others stopped to engage the soldiers. Again she heard the clash of swords, along with a choked cry of pain.

The second skirmish ended nearly as soon as it began. Alexeika glanced back, and now she saw a shadowy figure racing behind her, closing the narrow gap. Worriedly she tried to think of another trick to throw him off, but at that moment her horse plunged into a thicket of briers and reared with a squeal of pain.

With no stirrups or saddle to aid her, Alexeika nearly fell off. Clinging to the horse's neck, she hung on desperately while it lunged out of the thicket. Then it halted with a lurch that sent her flying.

She landed on her hands and knees with a jolt that snapped her teeth together. As her horse whinnied and tried to run backward from her, she staggered upright in an attempt to grab the dangling reins, stumbled in the deep snow, and fell again.

Meanwhile, the Mandrian in pursuit galloped up so fast she feared she would be trampled. She rolled frantically to one side even as his mount plunged to a halt, throwing a spume of snow over her. Snorting white jets of air, the horse tossed its fine head and pawed the ground.

Alexeika's horse flicked its moth-eaten tail and darted into the undergrowth. Seeing a long day's worth of hard work vanish like mist, she knelt in the snow and swore long and loud.

The Mandrian laughed at her. "I understand one word in four," he said, still chuckling, "but for a maid verily you do curse as well as any knight I've known."

Vexed beyond measure, Alexeika fell silent. To be laughed at, after having failed so completely in her objective, made her furious.

The other Mandrians joined their leader, who glanced their way. "Any more to follow?" he asked.

"Nay, sire," said the largest one. "They fought ill indeed. Why they thought us bandits I—"

The leader pointed at Alexeika. "There is the bandit, but she has lost both her horses in the chase."

"*She?*" one of them asked him. "You mean—"

"Aye, a maid," the leader said. Amusement still colored his voice, and Alexeika's cheeks burned like fire.

She rose to her feet and looked carefully to one side to see if she could escape this clearing for the nearby thicket before they had time to stop her. Her hands settled themselves unobtrusively on the hilts of her daggers, ready to throw with deadly accuracy if these men decided to try other sport with her.

"Come, lass," the leader said to Alexeika, stretching out his hand. "Climb behind my saddle and guide us to where we can shelter for the night in this blighted cold."

While Alexeika hesitated, the biggest man cleared his throat. "Nay, sire," he protested, "be not so generous or so trusting."

"She's a proven thief," another one remarked.

"I'm not leaving her here in the cold," the leader said. "Come, maid. We mean you no harm, as long as you try not to steal *our* horses."

Stung by that remark, Alexeika tossed her head. "I'm no thief."

"Were those horses yours?"

Grinding her teeth together, she would not answer.

"A thief," the large man said with a growl. "Leave her be, yer grace, and let's quit this wood as fast as we can."

"Thod knows how far it is to the next settlement," the leader said with a weary sigh. "And we've ridden hard this day. We need rest and warmth for a while." His gaze returned to Alexeika. "Will you guide us?"

"How much coin do you offer?"

"Two silver dreits."

In Mandrian coin? Her mouth opened in shock even as she thought he must be a fool. The offer was too generous, which meant he knew nothing about Nether at all.

"I know more than you think," he said gently, as though he could read her very thoughts. "Would you rather have skannen instead—"

"I'll take the dreits," she said swiftly, and gripped his stirrup.

The large man kicked his horse forward. "Nay, lass, you'll ride with me. And you'll hand over both daggers and the sword first."

She backed up at once. "Never!"

"Sir Terent, you affront her at every turn," the leader chided the man gently. Despite his odd accent, there was something familiar about his voice, something that toyed with her memory. "She's no enemy of ours."

"Don't be so sure," Sir Terent replied sourly. "We've met no friend in this forsaken land yet, and—"

"What is your name?" the leader asked her.

"Alexeika."

He waited a moment as though he expected her to tell him the rest of it, but when she did not he bowed to her from his saddle. "Alexeika is a highborn name, is it not? Very pretty."

She flushed at the compliment, then felt renewed anger at herself for being swayed by his charm and manners.

"You are welcome to come with us, Alexeika, and show us to good shelter. Will you give me your word that you will not use your weapons against me or my companions?"

She hesitated, sensing the suspicion and distrust that surrounded her from everyone except the leader. "You're no enemy of mine," she said begrudgingly. "I'll strike you not, providing none of you strike me."

"Fair enough," the leader announced, and held out his hand to her again. "Climb up behind me."

The thought of those two silver dreits decided her, for they were a fortune. At best, Costma would have given her only a few skannen for the horses. But Mandrian dreits would put an end to the shortage in her purse, meaning she'd have enough to live on for the rest of the winter. It was incredibly good fortune, and she hesitated no longer.

When she grasped the stranger's hand he pulled his foot from his stirrup, and she climbed up behind him with quick agility. Settled at his back, she resisted the impulse to put her arms around him and clutched the back of his fine thick cloak instead. He was a rich man, this stranger, and why he'd chosen to travel into Nether at this time of year was a mystery she did not care to unravel. Soon enough he'd run into more trouble than his three men could handle, and then he'd be shorn of his fine clothes, his boots, and his fancy horse, not to mention his fat purse. For a moment it was tempting to consider guiding him to Costma's camp and turning him over to the bandits.

But then she thought of her father and what he would have said to such a dishonorable scheme. Ashamed of herself for even thinking it, Alexeika tapped the Mandrian lord's shoulder and pointed deeper into the forest. "That way."

• • •

In less than an hour they reached a sheltered spot that was Alex-eika's camp. Nestled beneath the overhanging bank of a small stream that was now a half-frozen rivulet in the snow, it was a good place, protected from the wind and easily defended. Alex-eika showed the men where they could tether their horses in a small, sheltering grove of shtac. She dismounted, then ducked beneath the overhang and pulled aside the stone where she kept her strikebox and tinder dry.

A few moments later she had a fire going. The men moved back and forth, unsaddling and caring for their horses, talking softly among themselves as they decided who would stand watch and in what order. Alexeika fed sticks to her small fire, which blazed stronger, and watched the men without appearing to. She found herself approving of their camaraderie and discipline. Three of them, the lord included, were clearly knights, for the firelight glinted off their mail hauberks and spurs. The fourth individual, young and very thin with freckles and dark red hair, served the lord as squire.

It was he who spied the bark bucket Alexeika left hanging on a tree branch. And he who used it to carry water to the fire.

Giving her a tentative smile, he said, "I am Thum du Maltie, squire to our master. May I heat this water for his comfort?"

She nodded, not yet ready to smile back. "If you don't set my bucket afire."

There was a simple trick to heating bark containers, but it seemed the squire intended to take no chances. He produced a metal pot from his saddlebags and used it to heat the water. Then he set about unwrapping some bundles of waxed linen to produce a feast of cold meat, cheese, flat cakes, and apples.

Although Alexeika had eaten, her supper had been meager fare indeed compared with this. As the men gathered around the fire, crouching low to keep from bumping their heads on the overhang, Alexeika shyly retreated deeper into the shadows.

The largest man was clearly the lowest born. Sir Terent, the lord had called him, and he was rough-edged and plain, sitting there with his ruddy face and gapped teeth. His green eyes re-mained forever watchful for trouble in the dark woods beyond their fire. Now and then he glanced at her, alert to her movements.

By his actions, he was clearly the lord's protector, she realized.

The other knight was fair-haired and soft-spoken, a courtly man whose manner reminded her of her father's. Suddenly she yearned for her old life, when her father had still lived and there had been a few remnants of civility and grace in their camp.

"I am Sir Alard," he said to Alexeika as he carved himself a hearty slice of meat with his dagger. "Will you eat with us?"

She'd had no meat in several days. Game had grown scarce here, and she knew she'd have to move her camp soon. Silently she nodded her acceptance of the man's offer, and grew round-eyed as he handed her the large slice of meat he'd cut for himself.

"Cold rations again," Sir Terent grumbled between bites of flat cake. "Nothing to warm a man's bones in this supper."

"Be glad you've got food at all," Sir Alard told him, and offered Alexeika a flat cake.

She took it politely. The cake was light in texture, baked of fine flour with no coarse grain in it. Ravenous, she devoured it in four bites and gnawed happily at her meat, grateful for the men's casual generosity.

Thum took the heated water and carried it out to the shadows for the lord to wash with.

Warmed by the fire, Alexeika pulled off her tattered cloak and knelt to put another stick on the blaze.

"Thod's mercy!" Sir Terent shouted, reaching for his sword.

That was all the warning Alexeika had before she found herself knocked sprawling. Coughing, she lifted her head and found Sir Terent's sword tip at her throat. Sir Alard's foot pinned her arm.

She lay there, half-winded and paralyzed with alarm. "What—"

"Silence!" Sir Terent roared. "You'll have steel down your gullet if you try your wiles on me."

She could not understand what had turned them so suddenly against her. Sir Terent's hostility, however, could not be doubted, and when she shifted her gaze to Sir Alard, that knight looked no less dangerous.

"I'll hold her," Sir Terent said grimly to his fellow knight. "Run and tell his grace that we've caught ourselves a Nonkind witch."

Sir Alard obeyed, while Alexeika glared up at Sir Terent. She realized now that it was the sight of her red hauberk that had alarmed him. He was a fool to jump to conclusions, but when she opened her mouth to tell him so, he pressed harder with his sword, and she felt the tip break her skin. She froze, hardly daring to breathe, and moved no more.

At that moment, the lord strode up. He had thrown back his cloak hood like the others, but unlike them, he had removed his mail coif and washed the road grime from his face and hands. His black hair fell, neatly combed, to his shoulders. When he stopped next to her, he stood so that the fire was at his back and his face remained cast in shadow.

"What's this about Nonkind?" he asked sharply.

"Look at her, sire," Sir Terent said roughly. "Look at what she's wearing."

"Gantese mail."

"Aye. That makes her one of the murdering savages if not—"

"She's Netheran, not a Believer," the lord said sharply.

"But we know that Nether and Gant are allies now," Sir Alard said. "Strange how neatly we fell into her path. She could have led us into a trap and—"

"There's no trap here," their master said. "Let her up."

"But, sire—"

"Let her up. She intends us no harm, no matter what she wears."

Sir Terent looked as though he wanted to argue, but he obeyed the command. As soon as his sword tip swung away from her throat, Alexeika scrambled up and tackled him by his ankles, knocking him to the ground. He fell with a howling curse of fury, but she was already swarming him and had drawn one of her daggers. She pricked his throat, and had the satisfaction of seeing his green eyes flare wide with alarm, before she sprang off him and whirled to face the others, crouching low, her dagger ready in her hand.

"Get away from me, you Mandrian devils!" she snarled. "I curse this fire I've shared with you! I—"

"Alexeika! Be at peace," the lord said to her, holding up his hand placatingly. The firelight gleamed in the ruby on his finger. "It was a mistake, nothing more."

Sir Terent rose to his feet, dabbing at the trickle of blood on his neck, and scowling. "Damne, I'll show her what a mistake is."

"You'll stand!" the lord commanded in a voice like thunder. "You've caused enough trouble, sir."

Sir Terent turned bright red. "Sire, we've seen the women-folk of Nether. Ain't none of them like this. She's a shapeshifter or Believer or both. What's more, she's likely to cast a—"

"Enough!" the lord snapped, and Sir Terent fell reluctantly silent. "I have already said she's not Nonkind. Even the mail she wears carries no taint."

"I cleaned it well after I killed the Believer it belonged to," Alexeika said fiercely, glaring at Sir Terent.

He glared back. "Ain't likely," he growled. "Horse thief, liar, and idle boaster."

His master gestured in visible annoyance, and Sir Terent uttered no more taunts.

Furious with herself for having brought these men here, Alexeika glared at them all. They had no right to judge her or insult her by calling her a liar. They were foreign dogs, louts of no breeding and less worth. And if Sir Terent insulted her once more, she'd hurl this dagger at his throat and silence him forever.

"Enough of this," the lord said, cutting across the hostile quiet. "Let us all return to the fire and sup together. We've no right to judge Alexeika, no right to force explanations. She—"

"You owe me two silver dreits," Alexeika broke in, interrupting his attempt to restore peace. "I'll have my payment now. Then I'm going. Keep the camp. I care not, but I'll share no fire with you again. Nay, and I want no more of your putrid food, either!"

As she spoke, she vowed to spend the rest of the night walking to Costma's camp. She'd tell him where these rich strangers were and see him pluck them the way they deserved. That ruby ring alone would fetch a good price.

"Very well, Alexeika," the lord said mildly. He ignored his men's protests and turned toward the fire to pick out the coins from his purse.

As he did so, Alexeika caught a clear view of his face for the first time that night. To her total astonishment, she recognized his lean chiseled face, slanted cheekbones, keen pale gray eyes, and mouth both sensitive and determined. Now she knew why his voice had sounded familiar. She had seen this man, seen him in a vision on the fjord long months ago, when she'd tried to conjure forth her dead father's spirit and had brought forth King Faldain's image instead.

Disbelief flooded her, yet she was certain he was one and the same. Dropping her dagger unheeded on the ground, she retreated from him and nearly lost her balance on the sloping bank.

The men stared at her as though she'd lost her wits.

"Alexeika?" The lord's voice was both gentle and commanding.

She felt faint at the sound of it, faint and on fire all at the same time. This was the man she'd cursed; this was the man she'd considered betraying to Costina's bandits. Thod above, but she was unworthy to have found him, unworthy of his kindness and his valor in saving her tonight from the usurper's soldiers.

"What's amiss with you now?" Faldain asked.

"She's lost her wits," Sir Terent said gruffly. "That is, if she ever had any."

Ignoring his insult, Alexeika went on staring at Faldain. Her heart was thudding so hard it hurt. He was no apparition this time, but actual flesh and bone.

"She's staring hard at his grace," Sir Alard said in alarm. "If she means to cast a spell—"

"She doesn't," Faldain said quickly. "Put aside your superstitions, men. She cannot harm you that way."

Thum stepped forward. "Be at ease, Alexeika. This is our lord and master, the Chevard of Thirst—"

"Nay, he is not!" she broke in, refusing the lie.

"He is!" Thum said hotly.

"Liar! I know different."

Faldain gripped Thum's arm to hold him still and walked toward her with a frown.

"Sire, don't go near her!" Sir Terent pleaded, but Faldain ignored him.

As he approached, it was all Alexeika could do to hold her ground. Her knees were shaking so she feared they might buckle.

"Alexeika," Faldain said gently. "What ails you?"

Her ears were roaring. She kept staring at him, telling herself that he was real. She had ridden at his back. She had gripped his hand in hers.

"Alexeika?"

"You," she said, forcing herself to speak at last. In some dim corner of her brain, she realized she was acting like a fool, like the basest, most unlettered peasant, but all her training seemed to have deserted her. In truth, she could scarcely command her wits. "You are King Faldain."

He halted in his tracks.

Alexeika's gaze never left his face. She had dreamed of him often, trying to imagine where he was, what he might be like. In her mind she had made a valiant hero of him, hoping that one day he would return to his kingdom and free his people. But in all her dreams and imaginings, she had not quite conjured him into this tall, broad-shouldered, handsome man. She had not prepared herself for the keen force of his penetrating gaze, for his intelligence and perception. She stared at him now, and wondered if he would admit his true identity to her.

"You are," she insisted, although he'd neither confirmed nor denied what she'd said. "You're King Faldain. You have returned."

Still he did not speak.

His squire frowned at her. "Why do you say this? How do you know?"

"I have seen him before."

"And I say her wits are clean addled," Sir Terent said loudly. "She's no—"

Faldain, however, held up his hand. Recognition suddenly flashed in his eyes. "The lake," he said. "You were the one who brought me there!"

Her knees failed her then. She sank to the ground and bowed low, overwhelmed by the desire to weep and laugh at the same time. "Your majesty," she said through her tears. "Oh, that my father could have lived to see your return."

Faldain bent over her and pulled her upright. "You parted the veils of seeing to find me many months ago," he said to her in wonder. "Who are you?"

And now at last she remembered her training and her lineage. Lifting her head proudly to belie her ragged clothing and dirt-smeared face, she said, "I am the Princess Alexeika Volvn, daughter of Prince Ilymir Volvn, former general of King Tobeszijian's forces. My mother was lady in waiting to Queen Nereisse and later served Queen Neaglis under duress until Neaglis had her executed as a spy."

Faldain said nothing, and Alexeika swiftly dashed her tears away. She drew Severgard, ignoring Sir Terent's swift reach for his own weapon, and held its hilt up before Faldain.

"My father's sword. He has no sons to carry it, and so I bear it in the cause of restoration of your majesty's throne, and the defeat of the usurper."

Faldain reached out and gently touched the hilt for a brief moment. "Your service honors me," he said quietly. "As does the noble blade Severgard."

Awestruck, Alexeika realized she had not said the sword's name aloud. "How did you—you—"

Faldain smiled. "It told me."

She knew that swords made of magicked metal were supposed to speak to their masters, but although Severgard obeyed her hand and had glowed with power when she'd wielded it against the creatures of darkness, never had she actually heard its song. That he could astonished her. In truth he *was* the king.

Faldain gestured. "Come, my lady," he said with courtesy, as though her hair was combed and braided with jewels and she wore a fine gown of silk velvet. "Come and retake your place at the fire. We've much to discuss."

Feeling numb, she obeyed, and hardly noticed when he bent to pick up her dropped dagger and hand it back to her. Absently she sheathed the weapon and sat down across the fire from him.

The ruddy light cast shadows and angles over his face, as sparks and flame danced between them.

When the others crowded around, Alexeika leaned forward. "Your army," she said eagerly. "How far behind you does it come? How many troops have you? Infantry or calvary? Or both?"

Embarrassment colored his face. He shook his head. "Nay, good lady. I come not leading an army. I am here with these men only, traveling in secret to find the eld-folk."

His answer was so unexpected she could but stare at him at first. "I must have misheard your majesty," she said slowly. "You come not with an army?"

He shrugged. "Do you see one encamped here? Nay. As I said, I travel with these men only."

"But what mean you by this?" she cried, forgetting she spoke to a king. "Have you not come to Nether to claim your throne, as is your right?"

"In time, yes, but first—"

"First? What could be more important?"

His gray eyes flashed angrily. "That, good lady, is not your concern. "

"Isn't it? Why come here at all, if you mean to ignore the plight of your people?" she cried, ignoring the anger in his face. Disappointment and outrage choked her. She could not help thinking of her father's slain body lying on that battlefield, a brave and noble man who had fought for this—this craven's cause. Tears burned her eyes. "Do you care nothing for the sacrifices that have been made on your behalf? Do you have no heart, that you can ignore the misery and wretchedness that you've seen?"

Rigid with anger, he jumped to his feet.

She also stood up, glaring at him with a spirit fed by years of hope now crushed past bearing. "Sneaking into Nether like a thief, hiding yourself as though you are ashamed of who you are—"

"That's enough!" he snapped. "I do not answer to you. I need not explain my actions."

"Why?" she taunted him. "Because you are king?"

Nostrils flaring, he said nothing.

"If you will not declare yourself, and act like a king, then you cannot expect me to treat you as one," she told him. "I have seen five hundred valiant knights, brave warriors all, slain to the last man by trickery and evil. They died in your cause, and my father died with them. He believed in you and your father to the last." Her voice nearly broke, but she managed to control it. "I am glad now that he did not live to see this day, did not live to see you as you really are, unworthy of his sacrifice and devotion."

Faldain had turned white. His lips were clamped in a thin line, and his pale eyes blazed at her. "You are quick to judge, my lady," he said at last, his voice hoarse with the effort of controlling it. "You are quick to condemn matters you understand not."

She despised him for keeping his temper, for refusing to defend himself against her accusations. Worse, she despised him because she'd been infatuated with him all this time, and now that she'd seen him she was forced to realize that she'd been thoroughly deluded. He looked strong and handsome, yes. He had civil manners, and intelligent, well-governed men around him, but he was all show and good clothing. She'd seen nothing of worth in him except his innate kindness. But kindness did not make a king. Kindness did not win a stolen throne from the hands of one so evil and unscrupulous she could barely say his name aloud.

"By what right do you judge me?" he asked coldly. "If your father died, I am sorry for it—"

"You are not sorry," she broke in with scorn. "You did not know him. You did not watch him cut down, as I did. Why should you care?"

His pale gray eyes raked her. "I, too, have seen loved ones die. Do you think you are the only one in this world who has suffered loss or deprivation, princess?"

"You have grown up in Mandrian ease," she said scornfully, glancing at the other men, who were looking on in complete silence. "A prince of royal blood, pampered and given every—"

Faldain laughed, the sound cutting across her words and driving her to furious silence. Even worse, some of his men began to smile. They exchanged glances as though they shared some private joke. She despised them for laughing at her.

"Well?" she demanded, refusing to back down. "What does your majesty know of want? When have you ever gone hungry or slept in the wilderness like an animal with only a pile of leaves to serve as a bed?"

A muscle leaped in his jaw, but he answered not.

Instead, his squire spoke up: "Truly, my lady, you do discuss matters of which you are woefully ignorant. It has only been this autumn that his majesty learned his true identity and royal lineage. He grew up in Nold, apprenticed to a swordmaker, and would remain there still had his family not been slaughtered in a dwarf war."

"That's enough, Thum," Faldain said.

But Thum squared his shoulders and continued. "He has known both whippings and near-starvation. People of eld blood fare poorly in Mandria, and had he not come to the favor of King Verence he might be beggared still."

Alexeika's eyes widened. She felt a roaring in her ears, and her face was on fire.

"You call yourself highborn," Thum continued scathingly, "but you have the appearance of a harridan. You are wild, tattered, and dirty, with sticks and leaves in your hair. You are garbed immodestly in men's clothing. When we saw you this evening, you were stealing horses, yet you think you have the right to scream at our master and accuse him of cowardice and worse. You are not fit to speak his name, much less judge his actions."

"Enough, Thum," Faldain said sharply, and this time his squire colored and obeyed.

Alexeika stood there as though frozen while they all stared at her in disapproval. Inside, she raged at what Thum had said, yet his words carried the ring of truth. And she was mortified by how much she deserved his reprimand. Her father would have been ashamed of her for the way she'd acted tonight, and she wished the ground would open now and swallow her.

Living alone these past few weeks had been hard indeed. Since her escape from the Grethori, she had been all internal fire and steely determination. It had driven her and given her purpose so that she could survive on her own. But perhaps she'd become too hard, too fierce. If what Thum said was true, she'd made a dreadful error.

Somehow, although she wanted to die, she managed to bring up her gaze to meet Faldain's. What must he think of her? What had she done?

"Your majesty," she said so softly her words were barely above a whisper. "My behavior has been inexcusable. I forgot my place. I—"

"Let us say no more about it," he interrupted coldly, and turned away. "We'd better get some rest if we're to make an early start come morning."

"Aye," Sir Terent said. "I'm to take first watch. You use my blanket as well as your own, sire."

Then they went on about their business of shaking out bedrolls and banking the fire, all of them ignoring Alexeika as though she'd ceased to exist.

She stood there, appalled and horrified by how quickly their acceptance of her had turned into contempt.

Then Faldain glanced at her and held out the spare blanket. "Come to the fire, Alexeika," he said. "Use this blanket, if you have none of your own."

His kindness was even worse. She turned away and stumbled out into the darkness to the edge of the trees. Her throat ached, and tears spilled down her cheeks, freezing there in the frosty air. She felt as though she'd failed her father and all his expectations of her. And yet, what was she to think of a king who would not seize his throne, would not take the risk of standing forth and making his claim openly?

After a few minutes, she heard footsteps behind her and whirled around, her hand on her dagger.

"Alexeika," Faldain said quietly, "fear not. I mean you no harm."

Her hand dropped from the weapon, and she drew a long, shuddering sigh. "Please," she whispered, wiping furtively at her eyes in the dark, "leave me alone."

"If that's your wish. I came to pay you the coinage I owe you."

Pride surged hot in her throat. She wanted to throw the money in his face, but her common sense and desperation made her stretch out her hand to take the coins. She gripped them hard, and fresh shame branded her all over again.

"You are no common lass. Forgive me, but I meant 'no common lady,' " he said, breaking the silence. "Your way of life has taken you cross-country many times?"

"Yes."

"Good. I could hunt the eld-folk on my own, but winter is coming soon, and I must find what I seek without delay. Will you guide me to my mother's people, Alexeika? I will pay you well for your trouble."

She sniffed, and wiped her eyes again. "I don't understand. The eldin will not fight. They will give you no army."

He snorted impatiently. "Do not worry about my army. I have one already in place."

She stared at him in astonishment, wishing she could see his face through the darkness. "But—but your majesty said you had none."

"I said I have come to Nether with only the men who are with me tonight. That does not mean I have no warriors to fight in my name."

Her sense of astonishment grew, and rapidly she reviewed in her mind the remaining bands of rebels that she knew about. So many had given up and dispersed.

"Will you guide me to the eld-folk?" he asked again.

She frowned. "They cannot be found, not now. Perhaps in the spring, when thaw begins, but—"

"But do you know where they are? Where to look for them?"

She hesitated, then shook her head. "No, majesty."

Without warning, he pounced on her, pushing her back against a tree and pinning her there. She tried to fight him off, but he gripped her wrist with crushing strength.

"Never lie to me again," he said harshly.

Her mouth went dry. She could feel her heart thudding against her ribs, even after he released her and turned away. He was incredibly quick. She realized she had underestimated him, misjudged him, perhaps completely.

Confused and embarrassed, she swallowed with difficulty and tried to amend her mistake. "Forgive me," she whispered.

"You have judged me, insulted me, and now lied to me," he said, his voice like iron. "Why should I forgive you anything? I will find another guide."

He started to walk away, but she ran after him. "Your majesty, wait! I didn't mean to lie. It's just that searching for the eldin is a waste of time. They—"

"It is *my* time to waste," he said harshly. "Mine, and that of the one I love. How dare you decide such things for me?"

"I'm sorry," she whispered, feeling as though she'd been struck. "I—I have been used to giving orders. I don't take them very well."

"It would seem you do not take them at all. If your father was a general, my lady, I wonder you are not better trained."

He could not have said anything that hurt her more. She shut her eyes a moment, and forced her pride to bend.

"Please," she said, letting herself plead. "I would be honored to guide your majesty anywhere. I just thought I—"

"You must give me your word never to lie to me again, Alexeika. I will not tolerate it, not in anyone who serves me."

He spoke to her the way he might have spoken to a servant. Irritation flared inside her, but she stamped it out. If he was really the king, he could speak to her any way he chose, and she would have to accept it.

She bowed her head. "I swear my honesty, your majesty."

"Then on the morrow you will guide me to the eld-folk?"

She hesitated. "I will take you where I think they might be found. I cannot promise success. They no longer trust men."

"Then I shall find much in common with them," he said dryly.

She frowned. "If your majesty would but strike first at Grov, and proclaim yourself there, the people would rally to you. And the eldin would come forth from hiding. It would not be necessary to seek them."

"I have asked you to be my guide, not my adviser," he said firmly. "If I want your counsel I will ask you for it; otherwise, my actions and decisions are not yours to question."

She could not rein in her pride. "You misjudge me if you think I am some meek maiden fit only for pointing you down a road," she told him plainly. "I know this land, yes, especially the mountain and fjord country. But I know much more that could be of use to your majesty, if you would but allow it."

"You—"

"I have been trained in battle strategy."

He laughed. "Am I to be taught by a girl? Nay, my lady, you won't—"

"Hear me!" she said furiously. "Of course I do not intend to teach your majesty simple battle skills, but do you know the Netheran style of fighting? Do you know how to face Nonkind and *sorcerels*? Do you even know what they are?"

"Aye," he said brusquely. "I do."

She realized she was offending him again, but she had to prove her point. "I am not helpless. See these?" She drew her daggers and held them out for him to see. "I have slain the men who carried them. One was a Grethori chieftain; the other was a Believer. I have used my father's sword in battle. I have fought in your majesty's name, struggled to keep your cause alive. There is a price on my head, as there was on my father's. I tell you all this not to boast, but to show you the value of my advice. Heed me, majesty, and let me guide you in more than following a trail."

"You have been accustomed perhaps to giving orders in your father's camp," he replied, "but you will not give them here. There can be but one leader among us. If you are a true supporter in my cause, you will accept this. Well?"

Alexeika felt as though she'd been flattened again, and a mixture of resentment and exasperation stirred her. After all, her father had trained her to use her intelligence and abilities. She wasn't trying to compete with Faldain; she only wanted to help him. But it seemed that wasn't what he wanted.

She had often imagined what it would be like if she were to ever meet him. She believed he would instantly acknowledge her to be no ordinary woman, and he would be grateful for her help. Instead, she had found herself reprimanded harshly and put firmly in her place. It seemed her expectations had been far too idealistic. He had a mule's stubbornness, and a poor grasp of his kingdom's political situation. Such a combination could be deadly. She should perhaps abandon him now, she reflected, before she was forced to witness disaster.

And yet, she could not go. She had spent her life wondering what he would be like. After she'd seen the vision of him on the fjord, she had been infatuated with him. Now that she'd met him in person and felt the force of his charm and magnetism, she could not imagine herself anywhere except at his side. Yet that confused her too.

"Well?" he asked again, impatiently this time. "We must get this settled, for I do not want to repeat this argument with you."

She bowed in the darkness. "I accept your majesty's terms."

"Good." He did not seem to notice how hard it had been for her to say that. "I am in great haste to find the eld-folk. I seek a cure, one that they alone can give—"

"Are you ill, majesty?" she asked in alarm.

"Nay, it is for someone . . . very dear to me," he said.

She tried to draw breath, but her lungs did not seem to be working very well. Her dreams were bursting in rapid succession tonight. How could she have ever hoped he would see her and instantly lose his heart? She was rough and unfeminine, her maidenly wiles forgotten. Naturally he would have a lady he loved. He might even be married, although he wore no marriage ring. Feeling foolish, Alexeika told herself her dream of winning him was girlish nonsense that must come to an end. But it hurt just the same.

As Faldain walked back toward the fire, with Alexeika following, he said, "When we have found the eld-folk, then I hope you will guide me to General Matkevskiet."

Surprised yet again, she stopped in her tracks to stare at him.

He did not pause, but continued walking so that she was forced to hurry to catch up.

"If you are indeed the daughter of a rebel leader, then you must know this man."

"Of course." She frowned. "I mean, I know who he is. I saw him once when I was a child. He—he refused to join the Agya forces with my father's men. If he had, they could have crippled Muncel's army before he gained troops from Gant. It might have made all the difference, or so my father used to say. There was no communication between them after that."

"And Count Romsalkin?"

Again he surprised her. "These men support you?"

"Aye."

"And you tell me this?" she said, marveling. "You do not suspect that I might betray you at the first village we come to? The usurper's spies and paid informants are everywhere. I could betray you, and Matkevskiet and Romsalkin as well, for a few pieces of—"

"But you won't," Faldain broke in calmly.

Their gazes locked for a long time. "No," she said, lifting her head proudly. "I won't. But I do not think you should trust me—or anyone—as quickly as this."

He grinned, and in that moment she lost her heart to him forever. There was such charm in his face, such a winning look, that she could not resist him. "You need not worry," he told her. "You seem to think me something of a fool, Alexeika, but fear not. I was raised by dwarves, and I know more than you suppose."

Her face flamed anew. It seemed she had made every mistake possible tonight. "Majesty, I—"

"It grows late, and we must ride at first light," he said in dismissal, and climbed into the bedroll his squire had prepared for him.

Disgruntled, Alexeika hesitantly took up the blanket they had generously left for her use, and wrapped herself in its folds. She settled herself a little apart from the men, with her back propped against the bank for security.

Sir Alard was the last to settle himself by the fire's glowing embers. Rolling over so that he could look at her, he smiled and said softly for her ears alone, "We have all tried to dissuade him from this quest, and cannot. You will not succeed either."

She frowned. "Not even if we are trapped up by the World's Rim when the deep cold comes? It is folly to seek the eldin this time of year." It was folly to seek them at any time of year, for they refused to be found, but she did not say that aloud.

Sir Alard shrugged and burrowed deeper into his blankets, saying nothing else. Soon the men were snoring.

Alexeika lay there, wide-awake and unable to calm herself. She listened to the sentry stamp his feet out in the darkness to keep them warm. She listened to her own heartbeat thrumming with excitement that Faldain was so near. He was stubborn, impossible to manage, ruthless beneath his courtesy, and completely fascinating. She had done everything wrong tonight, and yet he had still offered her a place in his service.

Tomorrow, she thought, *I ride with the king.*

If only they were riding in the right direction, instead of on this mysterious quest of his. She thought briefly of misleading him and guiding his path straight to the Agya hideouts, but at once she dismissed the temptation. He had too much eld blood in him to be so easily fooled. Besides, there was more to this matter than he'd yet revealed. She warned herself to bite her tongue and take care.

And for the first time in her life, she could not sleep.

9

WITH HIS HORSE plodding in Lord Barthomew's wake, Prince Gavril squinted into the driving snow, and huddled deeper inside his fur-lined cloak. He was exhausted and half-frozen. His joints ached from long hours in the saddle, but he had too much pride to rest himself in one of the wagons. Cardinal Noncire had retired from riding horseback many days ago, and now rode in state beneath an arched canopy that protected him from the worst of the wind and cold, with a little portable brazier burning with coals, soft cushions to recline on, and his scrolls and books to read. Each day he invited Gavril to share his comforts, and each day Gavril gave him a curt refusal.

He had yet to forgive Noncire for his failure to learn the true whereabouts of the Chalice from Dain. After all, Gavril had warned Noncire that Dain required special handling, but the cardinal had been too arrogant, too self-confident, to listen.

As a result, Dain had deceived them all, his vile trickery sending Gavril on a futile chase to an abandoned shepherd's hut in the meadows far west of Thirst Hold. That escapade cost them three days of time they could ill afford to spare. Dain seemed incapable of understanding how holy and precious the Chalice was, or how vitally important it was to recover the sacred vessel.

Now, riding along the road while the wind blew right through his cloak and furs and the snow stung his face, Gavril fumed and clenched his cold fingers harder on the reins. He vowed that if ever again his path crossed with Dain's, he would make that pagan dog pay dearly for misleading them.

In the first place, Dain should have been forthcoming about the Chalice's whereabouts. When Noncire questioned him, Dain should have submitted himself willingly, even eagerly, to the cardinal's interrogation. After all, he'd sworn to help save Pheresa's life. The liar had claimed he would do anything for her.

To Gavril had fallen the unpleasant task of explaining Dain's defection to Pheresa. She had lain there, wan of face, with her reddish-gold hair brushed and shining, and listened to him gravely. Tears had welled up in her brown eyes as he told her how Dain had betrayed her, and Gavril had pledged anew that he would never desert her, that he would do everything humanly possible to find her cure.

Yet hardly had they set out from Thirst to resume their journey when another guardian had collapsed. Despite Noncire's previous avowal that he could replace a guardian if necessary, he immediately claimed that he was too fatigued from the effort to open Dain's mind to be able to serve the lady. Gavril, disgusted by the cardinal's cowardice, made no effort to coerce him. He knew the spell could not work under duress.

Thus far, Pheresa still lived, even with the spell out of balance, but at night her moans and weeping could be heard across the sleeping camp. She looked so ill and hollow-eyed that Gavril could hardly bear to visit her these days. He no longer knew how to alleviate her fears.

"We'll be in Nether soon," he told her day after day while the belief in her eyes gradually dimmed.

At first she'd tried to ask him questions about the remedy the Netherans promised. What was it? How would it work? But in the last week, she'd grown too weak to bother. She only stared at him with grave, pain-filled eyes, clearly no longer trusting him to save her. And what if he did fail? For the first time in his life, Gavril was not entirely sure he would triumph. He found such a possibility disquieting, and it was difficult not to resent the lady for having brought him to such a state. If Pheresa died soon, in a way it would almost be a relief.

Such thoughts shamed him, making him pray long into the nights in atonement. But sweet mercy of Tomias, he was tired of responsibility, tired of this long trek, tired of the endless small difficulties of traveling with an invalid, tired of the boring exhaustion of it all.

Nevertheless, here he was, pressing on at the head of their company. Nether was a country as bleak and forbidding as anything he'd ever seen. The snow was driving harder in their faces today, and Gavril had never been colder in his life. There was no way to get warm, not even when they set up camp for the night. No fire, tent, or blankets could ward off the numbing cold, which seemed to freeze the very marrow of his bones. Aching, tired, and miserable, he slept poorly, if at all, yet he kept forcing himself and his men onward.

Since they'd crossed the Netheran border, it had snowed every day. They could not find adequate forage for their horses. The kine bawled hungrily at night. Their own food supplies grew short, and there seemed to be almost nothing they could purchase or scavenge. This was a land marred by hovels of starving peasants, blighted crops withering unharvested in paltry fields, meager villages lacking the most basic amenities, and this bleak climate of unremitting cold.

Worse, time was running out. He'd intended to reach Grov and return home to Savroix by Selwinmas, but that holy day was drawing nigh. After it would come winter. He had to get out of this Thodforsaken realm before the weather became too harsh for travel. The thought of being trapped here all winter filled him with dread.

As for Dain, ever since his escape from Thirst Hold in the dead of night, along with one of his protectors, du Maltie, and one other Thirst knight, there had been no sight of him, no trail to follow, no whisper along the border that he'd been sighted. It was as though the forest had swallowed him. And no matter how much Gavril craved vengeance, there was no time to spare in hunting him down.

Noncire swore that Dain would forever go in want of his wits, but Gavril did not believe him. Gavril no longer believed much of anything the cardinal said. Dain hadn't been too insane to escape Thirst or elude them since. Gavril believed that Dain must carry blasphemous protections of magic and evil that gave him more lives than a cat.

Blessed Thod, Gavril prayed now, *have mercy on me and let me find this creature, that I may destroy him once and for all.*

"Your highness."

The voice of Lord Barthomew intruded on Gavril's thoughts. Seeing the church knight commander blocking the road, Gavril reined up with a scowl. Around him, his squires and Lord Kress drew rein as well.

"Yes?" Gavril snapped.

"The Netherans, your highness. They've passed along a message that we approach Grov."

Gavril's ill temper fell away, and excitement made him straighten in his saddle. "Where?"

Lord Barthomew pointed, and Gavril saw Commander Ognyoska of their Netheran escort a short distance ahead, beckoning to him. Since they'd crossed the border, this large, armed force of Netheran soldiers had traveled with them, claiming to be escorts. Ognyoska said that he and his men rode along for Gavril's protection, but Gavril considered their presence an insult, most especially since there were exactly the same number of Netheran knights to match his church soldiers.

But right now, Gavril forgot his resentment and felt overwhelming relief at having finally reached their destination. Spurring his horse forward, he joined Ognyoska.

A burly, taciturn man with a thick mustache and a tall hat of black beyar hide, Ognyoska wore a cloak of shaggy fur. His chain mail was rusted in places, his horse was a spindly, rough-coated nag, and his marriage ring was tarnished. When he grinned at Gavril, he showed a mouthful of rotten teeth.

Pointing ahead into the swirling snow, the commander spoke with more animation than he'd showed in days. His translator, a scrawny man going bald and suffering from a perpetual head cold, sniffed and said, "Compliments to your royal highness. The city lies ahead. Permit Commander Ognyoska to show you the vista."

Glancing at Lord Kress and Lord Barthomew to make sure they stayed close by, Gavril spurred his black stallion ahead of the pennon-bearers to follow Ognyoska to the top of a small rise.

As Gavril drew rein there, the wind died down for a moment and the snow stopped swirling in his face.

Ognyoska gestured proudly. "Grov!" he stated.

A valley bathed in misty white lay before them. Bordered on one side by the half-frozen Velga River, the city sprawled across the valley floor with clusters of wooden houses painted in garish colors, gilded church spires, and defense towers of stone. Although it was barely mid-afternoon, dusk was drawing near and many windows already shone with light. The falling snow blurred the scene, softening the outlines of the buildings. Plenty of people could be seen thronging the streets of frozen mud, and barges bobbed on the river amidst small ice floes. Across the city, rising high atop a bluff that overlooked the river, stood the palace of Nether's kings, a fortress of massive stone walls and tall towers wreathed in mist and snow flurries.

Gavril had not expected the city to be this big. It fully rivaled Savroix-en-Charva in size. But large or not, it was no doubt populated with barbarians, if the Netherans he'd met thus far were anything to judge by. Still, his relief grew as he stared at the city. Suddenly the hard journey and its difficulties seemed worthwhile, and his spirits lifted.

But a new problem loomed before him. Part of the cost of Pheresa's cure was to deliver Dain alive into the hands of Cardinal Pernal. How, Gavril wondered bleakly, was he to explain to the Netheran cardinal that he would not be delivering Dain as promised? He'd received no communications from Pernal in days, and he had not wanted to send news to the Netheran that Dain had escaped through the incompetency of his men.

Well, he couldn't repine over it now. There must be something else the Netherans would accept in Dain's place, he told himself. Perhaps the wagons of costly gifts would be enough.

Swinging his gaze away from the city, Gavril looked at Ognyoska. "Where are we to go? To the palace?"

The translator chattered between them. "No, no," he said earnestly. "Not enough space for all in King Muncel's court. Your highness will lodge in fine house. All has been made ready for comfort."

"House?" Gavril stiffened in affront. "Whose house? How dare you suggest that I take up residence in some ordinary dwelling? I—"

Ognyoska spoke again in Netheran, his words coming rapid-fire. The translator blew his red nose and sniffed miserably.

"Your highness mistakes my words," he said with a mendicant smile and a little bow from atop his donkey. "This is house of very fine personage. Very fine. Will be satisfactory much. It belongs to family of Count Mradvior and is grand indeed. You will see."

Scowling, Gavril did not see why he should not stay in the palace or even reside with King Muncel in his stronghold at Belrad. However, when Ognyoska shouted orders they moved forward, following the road down into the city as twilight closed about them.

With wolves howling in the woods and nightfall making the cold bite even deeper, all Gavril could think about was getting indoors and finding fire and food.

Grov itself was an ominous place, however. As he drew near, Gavril felt the strangeness of the city reach out to him. Unease prickled along his spine and he rode with one hand clutching the hilt of his sword.

Since they'd entered Nether, he'd resumed carrying Tanengard, despite Noncire's protests. Gavril felt as though a missing piece of him had been restored, making him whole again, for the sword was no longer silent. It muttered constantly in the back of his mind, a closer companion than even his protector.

Just now, the blade was glowing white inside its scabbard, which meant Nonkind lurked nearby. Dry-mouthed, he stared hard into every deep shadow and sat tense and alert in his saddle, certain that death was going to attack.

In silence, the townspeople pushed back to let them pass.

No cheers of greeting were raised, and yet the crowd—ominously quiet—grew ever larger as they passed. Hordes of beggars followed at their heels. With the grim-faced Netheran knights trotting at front and rear, and the church soldiers angry still at having these foreign nursemaids, as they called them, it was a solemn procession indeed that wended its way through the fetid streets.

Garbage and filth lay where it had been tossed. Starving mongrels scavenged what they could, snarling as they ran from the horsemen. Most of the buildings Gavril saw stood in disrepair. Some had been grand in the past but were now deserted. Weeds grew up through broken steps and snow drifted in through open windows.

They crossed a fine square, paved in stone and surrounded by beautiful villas, but whatever statues had once stood on a trio of bases in the center had been pulled down and smashed to bits.

Gavril glanced back over his shoulder at Pheresa's wagon and was glad the cloth canopy remained in place, not so much to shield her from the eyes of the curious as to keep her from seeing what a dreadful place he'd brought her to.

What have I done? he asked himself.

In the very heart of this dreadful city, he found himself riding at last through tall gates of intricately worked iron and entered a compound of ornate gardens, pools, and fountains blanketed with snow and ice.

The house itself was an immense structure that towered at least four stories overhead. Broad steps of pale stone jutted forth from its red-painted entrance, and mythical creatures carved from finest agate guarded either side.

Servants clad in livery came out to greet them with welcoming smiles and steaming flagons of hot drink. Distracted by the spiced and rather appealing brew, which warmed him from the first sip, Gavril saw Ognyoska's knights close the iron gates just as the crowd surged forward. Now the peculiar silence was broken, and many people howled like wolves, reaching through the gates with imploring hands and crying out words Gavril did not understand.

Shouting, the guards drove the horde of people back with

pikes, for it seemed they might break open the gates if left unchecked. Some even attempted to climb over, only to be knocked off by the guards.

It made no sense to Gavril, who turned his back on the sight and went inside, leaving the church soldiers to be directed to barracks in another wing of the compound. Stout men came forth to gently carry Lady Pheresa's glass encasement up the steps, which had been swept clean of snow.

Warmth was Gavril's first impression as he strode through the tall doors. The air was so comfortable he immediately felt overdressed in his gloves and heavy cloak. A long vestibule painted in garish colors of scarlet, black, and blue stretched before him, but he saw no hearth or burning fire. Puzzled at first and fearing the use of some magic, he soon realized the warmth was radiating from a tall construction of glazed tiles standing in one corner.

Unctuous servants ushered him forward into a spacious chamber of regal proportions. The ceiling, carved and gilded in a riot of creatures and floral motifs, soared high overhead.

Noncire, puffing in his fur-lined cloak, his long black traveling robes snow-soaked at the hem, waddled up beside Gavril and smiled in approval as he glanced around. "Very fine."

Indeed, Gavril could find no fault with the soft carpets underfoot, the exotic woods which paneled the walls, or the marquetry and carving of the furniture. More servants appeared like magic to anticipate his every wish. And so efficient were they that he felt instantly at home. His initial misgivings faded.

Lady Pheresa had been set down in the center of the room. Her serving woman hovered nearby, and Gavril strode over to check on his lady. Pulling back a corner of the blanket covering her encasement, he found her either asleep or unconscious; her skin was pasty white, with a light sheen of perspiration. He wanted to wake her and tell her the good news of their arrival, but just then the guardians filed in silently to surround her, and Gavril retreated from them.

Throwing off his cloak and gloves, he accepted another flagon of the spiced drink and stood near the tile stove to bask in its wonderful warmth. What a luxury to feel the frozen marrow in his bones thawing. For the first time since he'd left Savroix, he felt warm enough.

A gray-haired Netheran, clad in a velvet tunic trimmed with islean fur and a heavy gold chain studded with jewels, appeared and bowed deeply to Gavril.

"I am Lord Mradvior," he announced in heavily accented Mandrian while Gavril's brows rose in both astonishment and affront. "All is to your comfort, yes? All is to your liking?"

Gavril set down his flagon and turned his back on the man, leaving Noncire to quietly explain Mandrian protocol to him.

"Ah, yes," Mradvior said. He smiled, but there was a flash of anger in his dark eyes. "I understand. But your highness is a guest in my house, by orders of our esteemed majesty the king. I will, I think, introduce myself as I please."

There was something slightly hostile in the man's tone. Still annoyed by his presumption, Gavril turned around with the intention of ordering his men to usher Mradvior out.

Only, none of the guards in the room wore white surcoats. Aside from himself, Kress, Noncire, and the guardians, every one else present was a stranger. Alarmed, Gavril wondered what had become of his companions—his squires and minstrels, the royal physicians, the assistant priests, and most important, Lord Barthomew.

"Where are the church knights?" he asked sharply. "Kress! Where is Lord Barthomew?"

"Your knights have been shown to their quarters," Mradvior said before Kress could reply. "There they will stay. Your highness has no need of armed men to protect him while he is the guest of our most excellent majesty."

Gavril felt uneasy. He realized he was deep inside a foreign kingdom, inside a strange and foreign city, now isolated from his own men and at the dubious mercy of his hosts. For the first time he understood his father's fears and why Verence had been so reluctant to let him come here.

However, Gavril refused to let himself be rattled. Facing Count Mradvior with all the icy disdain he could summon, he said, "Your hospitality is most gracious. When will I see King Muncel?"

"Ah, very soon. Very soon. An audience has been arranged.

His majesty is always pressed by the many demands of his high
estate, but he, too, is anxious to meet. In the meantime, I am
to see to your every comfort. If you wish anything—"

"Lady Pheresa," Gavril cut in. "Her comfort is paramount.
She has need, at this moment, of her physicians."

"Of course. Her affliction is surely most curious." As he
spoke, Mradvior walked over to Pheresa and swept the blanket
to the floor. He stared at her, his eyes gleaming. "Well, well, a
beauty."

"Stand away from her!" Gavril commanded furiously. "How
dare you invade her privacy in such a way."

Mradvior ignored his protest and walked around the circle
of guardians, now and then tapping one of them on the shoulder. Gavril saw one of these men, Dain's peculiar physician
Sulein, twitch violently and sway where he knelt.

Alarm filled Gavril's throat. He stepped forward with his
hand outstretched. "You must not distract the guardians, Count
Mradvior. Her life depends on their complete concentration."

"Really?" Mradvior's thick brows shot up, and he smiled.
"This is most fascinating. I will tell the king of these details.
They will amuse him, I am sure."

Gavril's hands curled into fists. He could not believe this
creature's insolence. But without his men to put Mradvior out,
Gavril could do little to silence him.

"The lady's affliction," Gavril said through his teeth, "is
surely too tragic to afford amusement to anyone of civility and
kindness."

Mradvior tossed back his head in a bellow of laughter so
loud several of the guardians swayed. Gavril watched them in
alarm, wondering how to get this idiot away from them.

"Ah, your highness," Mradvior said at last, wiping his eyes.
He laughed again. "You will find that his majesty is neither
civil nor kind."

"If you have any regard for the lady's malady, please grant
her some privacy and quiet," Gavril said, resenting having to
plead on her behalf. He'd never begged for anything in his life.
"She needs her physicians at once. The journey has taken its
toll on her."

"Do you want her moved again?" Mradvior asked, looking

surprised. "This chamber is surely good enough. It is warm and dry."

"She requires a solitary chamber where no one will disturb her and the guardians," Gavril said impatiently. "Please."

Mradvior shrugged and issued a series of rapid orders in Netheran. Servants came to lift Pheresa's encasement and carry her away, with the silent guardians filing out in her wake. Megala followed fearfully.

Noncire leaned over Gavril's shoulder. "I am not sure this separation is wise, your highness," he murmured into Gavril's ear. "Perhaps it would have been better to keep her close by."

Gavril glared at him. "Your advice comes too late."

Noncire's answer was cut off by Mradvior, who said, "There! She will be placed in my wife's apartments. Perhaps she will amuse the ladies of my household, for they will be curious to see her style of hair and gown."

Dismay sank through Gavril. "I pray they will not disturb her. She needs her physicians, for she—"

"My physician attends her now," Mradvior said with a shrug. "It is enough."

Gavril shut his mouth on more protests. "Then I wish to bathe and dine. Afterwards I will write letters. Have you messengers that will carry them for me? Or may I dispatch my own men?"

"All will be seen to, your highness."

The evasive answer set Gavril's teeth on edge. If he was a prisoner, he wished Mradvior would come out and say so openly.

"Please notify Cardinal Pernal of my arrival. As soon as possible, he must come to me."

Mradvior's smile faded. He pressed his palms together and sighed. "Regrettably, his eminence is away."

"Where?"

"Far from here. He has gone on a long journey."

"And when will he return?"

For some reason this question seemed to amuse Mradvior very much. "Not for a very long time."

"But I have been exchanging letters with him," Gavril protested. "We were engaged in negotiations for—"

"Ah, yes, negotiations for the return of the pretender," Mradvior broke in with a bow. "But I am informed by Commander Ognyoska that the pretender is not with you."

"Unfortunately, no." Gavril shot a look of blame at Noncire. "He escaped us."

"Pity." Mradvior's smile disappeared, and his dark eyes bored into Gavril with implacable force. "Ognyoska had orders to give the pretender a proper greeting at the border. His majesty will be . . . disappointed."

An involuntary shiver ran up Gavril's spine. "It could not be helped."

"Oh, you need not make your excuses to me, your highness. It is King Muncel you will be held accountable to."

Anger flashed through Gavril. He tossed his head. "I am accountable to no one, Count Mradvior. As Heir to the Realm of Mandria, I—"

"Oh, your highness is of very great importance," Mradvior agreed. "Very great. Yes, yes, this is understood."

"Your highness," Kress whispered hoarsely at Gavril's shoulder. "This feels like a trap."

Gavril was amazed it had taken Kress this long to grasp the obvious. Glaring at his protector, all he said was "Netheran manners are poor, but they do understand the rules of safe conduct and hospitality."

"Yes, yes! We do understand," Mradvior said with a smile. "You will be treated very well during your stay here. Of course, how long you stay depends on many factors."

"The health of the lady," Gavril said sharply. "If she can be cured quickly, I hope to depart before—"

Mradvior shook his head as though she were of no importance. "Not the lady, no. You will stay as long as it takes King Verence to become generous."

Stiffening with alarm, Gavril gripped his sword hilt. "What do you mean?"

Mradvior gave him a sly grin. "Yes, yes, I think he will be anxious to see his son and only heir come home again. We Netherans are not fools, your highness. When you give us such a ripe opportunity, how can we resist grabbing it?"

"Speak plainly, sir. Say what you mean!"

But Mradvior only laughed.

"We had an agreement," Gavril said angrily. "We came here under stated truce and a flag of pilgrimage to save the lady's life."

"Well, she'll be a curiosity for the court, I am sure," Mradvior said with a shrug. "Everyone is agog to see her. We have heard the rumors of her beauty. This spell which keeps her alive is strange magic indeed, which the king wants to study."

"Take me to King Muncel at once!" Gavril commanded.

"When it is time for your appointed audience, of course."

"No! I demand to see him now."

"When it is time for your appointed audience."

Gavril muttered under his breath and strode for the door. The guards who stood in front of it, however, refused to budge. Gavril glared at them, trying hard to keep his dignity even as his heart started pounding.

"Let me pass!" he commanded.

"They do not obey your highness's orders," Mradvior said from behind him. "Your highness may have full run of my house, but your highness may not leave."

Gavril stiffened and turned back to face him. "Am I a prisoner here?"

Mradvior spread wide his hands with a shrug. "I prefer the word guest."

"You cannot hold me. To do so is tantamount to a declaration of war."

"Yes, yes, of course," Mradvior replied. "But since King Verence has refused agreement to the terms of the new treaty, Nether and Mandria are no longer friends."

Gavril listened to this news and felt sick. Was this why his father wanted him to turn back? Why had his message not said so in plain explanation? But even worse, what had possessed Verence to be so stubborn at this delicate time?

"Still," Mradvior was saying merrily, "what do the terms matter? You will bring a very fine ransom that will swell King Muncel's treasury. Of course if your father does not act quickly, you cannot be released before the deep cold, and then I'm afraid it will be thaw-time before you can journey homeward. Do you think the lady will live that long?"

"Kress!" Gavril shouted, and sprang forward as he drew

Tanengard. Behind him, he heard Kress draw steel. His protector took on some of the guards, who shouted in Netheran as they engaged in combat.

Gavril charged Mradvior, who carried no weapon other than a small dagger. Although he wanted to run the villain through, Gavril intended to hold him at swordpoint and force a way to freedom.

Noncire called out a warning that Gavril ignored.

Just as he reached the count, however, an invisible force slammed into him. Tanengard grew too heavy to hold, and as he went staggering back, he dropped the sword.

Across the room, Kress screamed in agony. Gavril looked over his shoulder in time to see one of the guards yanking his sword from the protector's chest. Blood spurted, and Kress crumpled to the floor.

Looking around wildly, Gavril found himself entirely on his own. He lunged toward Tanengard, but the invisible force struck him again, and knocked him away from the sword.

Fearful of this magic, he retreated a step and desperately tried to remember his Sebein training in how to properly channel Tanengard's special powers. If he could just close his eyes and concentrate a moment, he would remember how to—

"In the name of Tomias, begone!" Noncire shouted sternly, and the memory shattered in Gavril's mind.

Enraged, he turned on the cardinal. "This is no time for piety! How dare you interfere!"

"And how dare you risk your soul when your very life is in mortal danger?" the cardinal retorted. "Do not reach for that weapon in anger, your highness. I warn you most urgently. It will consume you as it did before."

Gavril opened his mouth to argue, but by then Mradvior had picked up Tanengard and was examining it with interest.

"A magicked blade," he said, pursing his lips. "I thought Mandrians never carried them."

"You thought wrong," Gavril said proudly.

Noncire clutched his sleeve. "Have a care, highness."

Furious with him, Gavril shook off his grasp. He sprang at Mradvior again, intending to wrest Tanengard from his hand.

This time the invisible force walloped him so hard the world grew dim. Only his quick grab at a table kept him from falling.

Noncire gripped his shoulders to steady him. "Desist, I beg you! He is using magic and you will only do yourself harm."

"I will not be made a fool by this blackguard!" As he straightened, Gavril tried to reach for his Circle, but it was inside his hauberk where he could not get at it.

Chuckling, Mradvior came forward and handed Tanengard to him hilt-first. "My master-at-arms would be interested to know where this weapon was forged. It has an unusual vibrancy in the blade. Does it not affect you? Some men go mad when they carry something flawed like this."

As Gavril's hand closed on the hilt, he felt Tanengard's rage ignite from his own, and he was filled with an overwhelming urge to strike. With one blow, he could send Mradvior's head rolling across the soft carpet.

"Gavril!" Noncire said urgently. "In the name of Tomias, take care! He *wants* you to act rashly."

The prince bared his teeth, but he saw the taunting challenge in Mradvior's dark eyes, and knew that Noncire's warning was true.

Struggling to master his emotions, Gavril slid Tanengard into its scabbard. He could not fight spellcasting, no matter how much he might want to try. He must bide his time for the right moment, and then, by Thod, he would run Mradvior through.

Looking disappointed at his restraint, Mradvior beckoned to a wide-eyed servant. "His highness looks fatigued. Conduct him and his eminence to their apartments. Oh, and clean up this mess."

Feeling hollow, Gavril walked past Kress's body to follow the servant through a door and up a long flight of stairs to an elegant suite of rooms. Gavril hardly spared a look for his new surroundings. He seemed unable to concentrate. He had been tricked. He'd been made into a fool. First by Dain, and now . . .

"Highness," the servant said, handing him what looked like a clear stone. "Speak aloud where you wish to go, and the stone will guide you."

"Great Tomias!" Gavril said in startlement. He dropped the

stone, which bounced on the thick rug and rolled partway under a chair.

Clucking in distress, the servant retrieved it, seemed about to repeat his instructions, then bowed and carefully set the stone on a small table of inlaid wood. Bowing again, he backed out past Noncire, and vanished.

Gavril's fear rushed up and over him like a gigantic wave. He shut his eyes, fighting the desire to scream aloud. "What in Thod's name have we come to?" he whispered.

"We have come to betrayal and villainy," Noncire said softly. Shrugging off his cloak, he looked at the ornate furnishings and heavy hangings. "Well, Gavril, your pride has brought you here. Since you refused to listen to anyone's counsel except your own, you—"

"Oh, end your recriminations," Gavril said sharply, recovering from his momentary weakness. He began to pace back and forth. "I take no blame for this. I came here in good faith. Is it my fault that I have been betrayed?"

"Yes."

Gavril glared at him. "How dare you say so!"

"Why should I not tell the truth? I am equally a prisoner here, but no one will ransom *me,* I think."

Gavril resumed pacing. Another wave of indignation swept over him. "We had Muncel's assurance, his word!"

"This situation cannot be entirely unexpected," Noncire said scornfully. "The risk has always been a factor. King Verence feared something like this—"

"My father is the very reason we are now prisoners!" Gavril said furiously. "I blame him entirely for this."

Noncire's small black eyes turned stony with disappointment. "Of course you do."

"Why don't you make yourself useful? Instead of casting blame, you can better serve me by finding a way to reach Cardinal Pernal and—what? Why do you shake your head at me?"

"Did your highness not understand Mradvior's hints? Cardinal Pernal is surely dead."

"You imagine things!" Gavril said with a sharp laugh of disbelief. "Why should he be dead?"

"Because in this realm, enemies of the king vanish, never to be seen again."

"Fie! We know Pernal to be Muncel's chief spiritual adviser. He has been so for years. You can hardly label him one of Muncel's enemies."

"If you wish to delude yourself, do so," Noncire said with uncharacteristic asperity. "I think he is dead."

"Then find someone else to aid us."

Noncire's fat face never changed expression. "I think it must be your highness who finds a way out of this predicament."

"How so?"

"When you meet with King Muncel—"

"*If* I meet with him," Gavril said glumly.

"I believe you shall. He will want to gloat over his catch, if nothing else."

Gavril ground his teeth together and abandoned this useless conversation. The fact of having been tricked made him boil. That Muncel dared betray him seemed inconceivable. Never in his life had Gavril met with more disrespect or insult than today. And yet, had his father not bungled the treaty with Nether, none of this would have happened. Gavril's eyes narrowed. It seemed Verence wasn't as concerned for his son's welfare as he pretended. Well, let him pay a hefty ransom for their return. Perhaps that would teach him to be less careless with his treaties in the future.

"It is said that King Muncel has an uncertain temper," Noncire was saying. "When you talk to him, take care that you do not arouse it."

Gavril turned on him impatiently. "I do not require your counsel on this."

"I think you do!" Noncire said sharply. "All our lives are at risk here."

"He will not dare kill me," Gavril said haughtily.

Noncire's fat face turned red. It was one of the few times he had ever displayed his temper. "You might consider the safety of those you have brought here with you," he said very quietly indeed.

Gavril shrugged. "Do not lose your nerve simply because

Mradvior has wielded a bit of magic. Muncel and Mradvior
know that if *I* am harmed, my father will send no ransom."

"And your men are therefore expendable?" Noncire said in
rebuke. "Like Lord Kress?"

"I cannot help the man now," Gavril said in irritation. "What
is the point of dwelling on his loss?"

"And Lady Pheresa?"

"Ah, yes. I must see that she gets the care she needs. You
will work to negotiate our freedom."

"With whom?"

Gavril shrugged. "You must have allies in the church here.
Contact them."

"And if I cannot?"

"Stop arguing with me, and do as you are told!" Gavril
shouted. "I wish to Thod I'd never brought you along."

"I wish to Thod I had not come."

Hot, angry silence fell between them. Gavril looked at his
former tutor with contempt. Although the man had once seemed
to be so intelligent and clever, he'd proven himself both spineless and weak.

"You're here at your own insistence," he reminded the cardinal icily.

"Someone must protect your soul." Noncire pointed at Tanengard. "Your blasphemy in carrying that vile weapon puts you
in mortal danger."

"Without it to protect us, we—"

"Did you not hear Mradvior say it will eventually drive you
mad?"

Worry touched Gavril for only a moment before he dismissed
it. "Why should I believe what that villain says? Tanengard will
protect us from the evil here."

"Tanengard will only draw you into the darkness. Have
care—"

"Be silent!" Gavril roared, losing his temper entirely. "I will
hear no more on the matter, lord cardinal! Must I use this weapon
to silence you forever?"

Noncire stood very still, his face as immobile as stone. For
a long moment he stared at Gavril. "I have lost you," he said
sorrowfully. "All the training and instruction in the faith that I

gave you since your infancy is now as nothing. You are lost, Gavril, and I cannot get you back."

"You old fool!" Gavril pointed at the door. "Get out! *Get out!*"

In cold, disapproving silence, Noncire drew the sign of the Circle between them and went.

10

DAIN AND HIS companions were five days into the forest of central Nether and looking for a place to camp for the night when the attack came.

It had been overcast all day. No snow was falling, but the air smelled damp and frosty. It was bitterly cold, and as dusk drew nigh, shadows began to pool beneath the trees. Keebacks flew overhead, calling their plaintive *kee . . . kee . . . kee.* A young danselk, his antlers spreading to only two points, foraged noisily in a stand of colorful harlberries until he heard their approach; panic-stricken, the danselk flung himself from the thicket and raced away.

"Damne!" Sir Terent said. "An easy shot, that, if I had a bow."

"Do you want to course him?" Thum asked.

"And do what? Stab him with my sword?" Sir Terent snorted. "Nay. He's gone already."

Meeting Thum's smiling eyes, Dain gave his squire a small nod of approval. That was the most Sir Terent had said in days. Ever since Sir Polquin's death, Sir Terent had gone about in a black mood indeed. Gone were his sunny, gap-toothed smiles. Instead, his brow was often furrowed, and grim lines bracketed his mouth. Dain left him alone to his grieving for his friend.

There was no comfort to offer; nothing would bring Sir Polquin back.

At present, Alexeika and Sir Alard had ridden ahead, scouting for a campsite. Dain, Sir Terent, and Thum allowed their horses to plod along at a walk. It was getting more and more difficult to find forage for the animals, and their own food supplies had dwindled to whatever they could manage to hunt on the way. Early this morning, Sir Terent's traps had caught two hares. Tied to his saddle, they dangled and bobbed with the promise of tasty eating tonight.

Dain's head was aching a little, in the way it did occasionally since Cardinal Noncire had tried to force open his mind. As a result, he wasn't alert. All he could think of was stopping for the night, eating something hot, and not moving until his headache eased.

Had he felt well, they might have had some warning before gray shadows came flying at them from the trees.

Larger than bats and much faster, two of the creatures zoomed over Dain's head. He ducked instinctively and heard Thum shout in alarm. Drawing rein, they all bunched together, ducking and swatting the things in bewilderment. Sir Terent drew his sword with an oath, but he could not swing it fast enough to strike whatever these things were that darted and circled.

His headache forgotten, Dain tried to contact them with his mind, but was brushed aside. One came right at him, and Dain ducked just in time.

"Morde a day!" Sir Terent swore, swinging his sword in vain. "What are they?"

"Nothing of this world," Dain said as one struck his shoulder. From the corner of his eye, he caught a confused impression of gray fur and beady malevolent eyes. Its claws were like needles, and with an oath, he knocked it off. Before it hit the ground, however, it turned over in midair and suddenly zoomed away.

Thum screamed, arching his back, and Dain saw that one of the small gray shapes had fastened itself to his shoulder. "Get it off me!" Thum shouted. "Damne! It's—" He halted in midsentence and screamed again.

Unsure what to do, Dain drew Truthseeker and plunged its

tip into the creature. Flames burst the thing apart, and the others flew off with tiny screeches just as Sir Alard came galloping out of the trees, with Alexeika clinging behind him.

Sir Alard had his sword drawn. His eyes were on fire and he was ready for battle. "What is it? What happened?" he demanded.

Dain had no time to answer him. Leaning over from his saddle, he pounded out the flames burning through Thum's cloak, using his gloved hands to smother the fire. Thum was huddled over his horse's neck, moaning softly. Dain stopped slapping flames long enough to give him a light shake.

"Are you much hurt? Did it bite you? Thum, are you hurt?"

Thum didn't answer. At that moment, the fire in his cloak shot back to life, nearly scorching Dain's hand.

Sir Terent gripped Thum by his collar and shoved him out of the saddle. Even as Thum hit the ground with a startled yelp, Sir Terent was dismounting. He ran to roll Thum over and over in the snow until the fire was truly extinguished from his clothing. Even then, Sir Terent took no chances. He yanked off Thum's ruined cloak, flung it on the ground, and kicked snow over it.

"These damned swords," he grumbled. "'Tis against Writ to put magic in a blade, aye, and I can see why."

By then they were all off their horses, except Alexeika, who remained on Sir Alard's steed. Holding her daggers in her hands, she kept a sharp watch on the sky and trees around them.

"We must leave this place," she announced. "Now."

Dain glanced up at her. She was an odd maiden, to be sure, with her brusque manners and masculine clothing. Her tongue was sharp, and she was quick to criticize, quick to voice her opinion, whether asked for or not. But since that first night, when they'd argued so fiercely, she'd taken care not to contradict Dain's orders. On his part, he tried to talk to her only when it was absolutely necessary.

He noticed now that she was looking tense, even a little frightened. That increased his sense of unease.

"It is not good to be here," she said. "They are a warning."

"What are they?"

"*Krenjin.* Imps. They're dangerous."

Dain had never heard of the creatures. But although they were not Nonkind, they were certainly hostile. "What kind of warning?"

She glanced overhead again with such apprehension that Dain looked skyward too, half-expecting to see another formation of the creatures in renewed attack.

"Alexeika, what kind of warning? Against what?"

"I don't know." She gestured impatiently. "We must go!"

By now Sir Terent and Sir Alard were helping Thum to his feet. The squire's face was bone white beneath his freckles. His hazel-green eyes were round and wide with shock.

"All right?" Dain asked him worriedly. "Can you ride?"

He gave Dain an unsteady nod. "Aye."

"We'll tend him later!" Alexeika called out. "Only let us get away from here!"

Dain had many questions about these mysterious *krenjin*, but he would ask them later. While Thum was helped back astride his horse, Dain swung into Soleil's saddle.

"They came at us from the direction we were heading," he said to Alexeika.

She frowned. "Then let's turn aside. We'll circle east a ways before we head north again."

Mindful of Thum, who looked none too steady in the saddle, Dain kicked his horse to a trot and ducked beneath the bare branches of a tree entwined with woody vines. The others followed him, and for a moment there was only the sound of their horses crashing through the snow-crusted undergrowth.

Then Dain sensed something ahead, something he did not know or recognize. Fearing another attack of *krenjin*, he turned Soleil aside, but an enormous gray beyar came loping across his path.

Soleil reared in fright, and suddenly they were surrounded by more of the huge, shaggy animals.

By the time Dain had his panicked horse back under control, it was too late to run. Only then did he notice that some of the beyars had riders. Slim, cloaked figures, they were but half-seen in the gloomy shadows among the trees.

"Merciful Thod," Sir Terent whispered hoarsely, "what lies before us now?"

But Dain started grinning in relief. "Eld-folk!" he said with a laugh. "We have found them."

Sir Terent's eyes shifted and darted warily. "Looks more like they've found *us*. Aye, and caught us fast."

"There's nothing to fear," Dain proclaimed. For the first time since he'd sneaked out of Thirst Hold via its secret passageway and waited long, bleak hours in the darkness until Sir Terent, Thum, and Sir Alard rode through the gates at dawn's light, concealed among Lord Renald's small squadron of knights, Dain felt optimism. No matter how much the others had doubted the course he'd set them on, he'd always believed that he could find the elusive eldin. And now that he had, he felt that many of his troubles were over. After all, these were his mother's people. As soon as they knew who he was, they would help him.

Raising his hand in peace, he called out a greeting.

"Take care, sire," Alexeika warned softly.

Ignoring her, Dain kicked his trembling horse forward.

A slim, short arrow hurtled through the air, missing him by inches. He halted, his heart pounding fast.

"In Thod's name, sire!" Sir Terent called out in alarm. "Come back!"

"Be still," Dain told his protector, and stared at the silent, hostile eldin around him. He wished he could see their faces more clearly in the darkening shadows. Again he raised his hand. "I am Faldain," he said loudly. "Son of King Tobeszijian and Queen Nereisse. I come seeking my mother's people."

When no one responded, Dain frowned. "I bring no harm to you," he said. "I seek my mother's people, and come with friendship and good intentions."

Finally the beyars parted, and a single rider approached Dain. His mount was a stout, black-furred beast with a band of white at its throat. When the beyar halted in front of Dain, its rider pushed back his hood with a frown.

Dain found himself looking into a pair of amber eyes flecked with glints of silver. The eld's hair—blond as tasseled grain—fell nearly to his slim shoulders, and the pale locks twisted and writhed constantly as though a wind blew through them.

A pang of familiarity shot through Dain's heart. Thia's hair had been that same pale color. It, too, had moved and curled incessantly as though possessing life of its own. He wished fiercely that she were here at his side for this reunion with their mother's people.

The eld's face was triangular, with pronounced cheekbones and a narrow chin. A single gold earring dangled from one of his pointed ears. Beneath his cloak, he was clad in a fur-lined jerkin and leggings of soft, fawn-colored leather.

"You call yourself Faldain, son of Tobeszijian," he replied at last when he had finished his scrutiny of Dain. "How will you prove it?"

Dain frowned. "How will you test me?"

The eld glanced at the darkening sky and shrugged. In silence he started to turn his beyar around.

"Wait!" Dain called out desperately. "Please. I've come seeking your help."

"You wear man-stink and think man-thoughts," the eld said to him harshly. "We no longer walk among men."

"I would change that, if I could," Dain said. "I know many injustices have harmed the eld-folk, and hope to put an end to such wrongs."

"Then end them," the eld said indifferently. "It is nothing to us."

"Wait!" Dain called again. "Please take me to your king. Let me plead my cause to him."

"Your cause has no meaning to us."

"How do you know?" Dain asked.

The eld glared at him. "Leave this land. You have intruded on sacred ground, and your presence offends us. Take your men and go!"

"I ask your pardon for our intrusion," Dain said quickly. "I didn't know—"

"The markings are plain."

Embarrassed by his ignorance, Dain sighed. "I know only dwarf runes, not eldin ones."

The eld gestured with contempt. "We do not scratch runes into trees like barbarians. You were warned away by the *krenjin,* but you heeded them not. You have intruded, and I will give you but one more chance to go with your lives intact."

"Sire," Sir Terent said softly behind him. "You better back away now, nice and quiet."

But Dain couldn't face defeat now, not when he was so close to achieving this part of his objective. He drew a deep breath. "In the name of Solder, I—"

Roaring, several of the beyars reared up on their hindquarters. Their eldin riders exchanged glances and called out sharply in a language Dain did not understand.

Their leader narrowed his amber eyes at Dain. "What do you know of the old favors?" he demanded angrily. "What do you call for in the name of the First?"

Dain realized his mouth was hanging open. He shut it hastily as he tried to hide his delight in what Solder's name had invoked. He'd only intended to urge them to listen to him; he knew nothing about any "old favors." But now it seemed he had some leverage, and he intended to use it.

"Take me to your king," he said. "I must talk to him."

The eld scowled at him through the gathering shadows, then said something rapidly that Dain did not understand. He pointed behind Dain, and several eld riders closed in on Dain's companions.

"No *man* may come past this point," the eld said to Dain. "Your companions will stay here, guarded close."

"But—"

"There will be no trickery." The eld issued another order.

One of his riders gripped Alexeika's arm and pulled her off Sir Alard's horse.

She twisted, kicking in midair, and landed on her feet with a stumble. Snarling something, she reached for her daggers.

"Alexeika, no!" Dain commanded.

She froze. Curly tendrils of her dark hair framed her face, and a long strand that had escaped her braid hung crookedly over one ear. "I'll not be taken prisoner," she said gruffly. "Never again will I be held against my will."

The eld leader swung his attention back to Dain. "You are both mixed-bloods. Is she your sister, Thiatereika?"

Again, a pang of regret stabbed through Dain. He was relieved that they knew him, even recognized him, but deeply saddened that Thia would never meet her mother's people.

"Thiatereika is not with us," Dain said formally. His throat felt like it had something wedged in it; he could not seem to make himself phrase his answer differently.

"Who is this maiden?" the eld leader asked suspiciously.

With a proud toss of her head, Alexeika walked up to stand at Dain's stirrup. "I am Alexeika, daughter of Prince Ilymir Volvn. My mother was half-eldin and from—"

"Both of you will come," the eld leader said. As he lifted his hand, tiny flames ignited from the tips of his fingers and cast a faint, pearly glow of light. "Your mixed blood will enable you to go across."

"Sire!" Sir Terent called in alarm. "Don't go off with them! They mean you no good—"

"Sir Terent, hold your tongue!" Dain ordered furiously. "I will not hear you insult their hospitality."

"Ain't hospitality to part you from your protector and haul you off at spearpoint," Sir Terent said stubbornly.

"I am in no danger," Dain retorted. "They will treat me well. Bide here quietly until my return. I won't be long."

"I must go with you," Sir Terent said stubbornly, coming forward.

The eld leader spoke a sharp command, and one of the riders bounded across Sir Terent's path. Confronted by a huge, snarling beyar and a rider holding a javelin in readiness to throw, Sir Terent backed down.

"In Thod's name, sire, take not this risk!" he pleaded one last time.

The eld leader was glaring at Dain; clearly the scant patience he'd possessed was gone. "They cannot enter our sacred groves," he said in outrage. "They profane the very ground."

"I give you my word they will not stir from this place," Dain said, making sure he spoke loudly enough for Sir Terent and the others to hear him. "They will cause no trouble. You have my bond on this."

The eld leader looked at Dain with open distrust, but after a moment his scrutiny swung away. He nodded, then wheeled his beyar around. "Very well. Come."

Alexeika stepped forward, her blue-gray eyes large and luminous.

Dain reached down to give her a hand so she could climb on Soleil behind him. She hesitated, but he gave her a quick smile, and something softened in her eyes. She climbed up behind his saddle with quick agility, and in that momentary clasp of their hands, he sensed the excitement that pulsed inside her.

Dain felt the same way, for he was certain he was going to meet a part of his heritage and find out more about who he was. He would meet his family. There would be celebrations and long talks. And best of all, he would learn how to cure Pheresa.

The beyars padded silently over the crusted snow. Night fell over the forest, but the fairlight flickering from the eld riders' fingers provided enough illumination to guide Dain through trees and brush nearly as choked and thick as that to be found in the Dark Forest. Gradually Dain grew conscious of something very strange. The trees around them were alive, for he could sense their low, dormant life force. But there seemed to be nothing else alive in this forest: no little animals hibernating in their burrows, no birds, no predators—nothing.

In all directions he sensed only a silent stillness that made the hair prickle beneath his mail coif. He stayed alert in the saddle, riding with one hand resting on his sword hilt. Beneath him, Soleil pranced along like a coiled spring, ready to bolt at the least provocation.

At last, they came to a stream, narrow and incredibly swift. The water rushed past a scrim of ice trying with little success to form along the edge of the bank. The riders around Dain parted to allow him to ride alongside their leader.

A narrow bridge spanned the stream. Access to it was guarded by a pair of life-sized, carved wooden beyars standing on their hind legs.

The leader dismounted with a gesture for Dain to do likewise. An eld rider hurried forward to take Soleil's reins.

Dain watched him with a frown, but the eld's hands were gentle with the nervous horse. He murmured softly to Soleil as the eld led the steed away.

"Come," the leader said, then walked across the bridge, the sound of his footsteps masked by the rushing water.

Dain walked between the carved beyars, and was startled to

feel himself brushed by some essence of the animal, as though beyar spirit resided in these statues. Warily, he quickened his stride across the bridge planks, with Alexeika hurrying at his heels, and joined the leader on the other side of the stream.

The moment his foot stepped off the bridge onto solid ground, the entire world changed with a suddenness that took him aback.

Where before there had been nightfall, bone-numbing cold, and crunchy snow underfoot, now there was light as though a hundred lanterns had been lit at once. The warm breeze was fragrant with the scents of flowers and foliage. The trees towering around them were fully leafed in green, their canopies whispering and rustling softly.

The ground itself was carpeted with moss that released a pungent, almost spicy aroma when stepped on. A path edged with glowstones wended its way toward a collection of dwellings close by, and Dain could hear the sound of voices and laughter.

He glanced back across the bridge at the other side, but all lay shrouded in darkness, and he could see nothing now of the other riders or his horse.

Alexeika was gazing around in wonder. Meeting his eyes, she smiled with the delight of a child.

He felt himself relaxing in these gentle surroundings. This was all he could have imagined and more; once again he thought of his sister, and how wherever she'd been present, plants grew lush and flowers bloomed with an intensely sweet fragrance.

Their guide, however, looked as stern and unfriendly as ever. He gestured impatiently, and they followed him up the path to the village.

Tidy dwellings enclosed within blooming hedges circled a grassy clearing. In its center stood a tree growing straight and true. Although it was fully leafed, it cast no shade. The same gentle clear light seemed to shine everywhere. Eldin children were at play, running and chasing a ball made of leather, but at the sight of Dain and Alexeika they stopped their game and scattered for home.

That's when Dain noticed an individual sitting on a wooden chair beneath the tree. The chair had sprouted leaves along its surface, as though the wood it was carved from remained alive and rooted. Robed in clothing of soft green, wearing shoes of supple leather, and holding a leafy staff in his hand, this individual had the distinctive eldin features. His face was unlined, but as Dain met his rain-colored eyes he knew instinctively that the eld was very old. His pointed ears were pierced by multiple gold rings, and in his white, constantly stirring hair he wore a gold diadem.

A few eldin, both male and female, stood near him. One of them held a small harp, although Dain had heard no singing. The pleasant expressions on their faces dropped away and hardened as they caught sight of Dain and Alexeika.

Their hostility was like a blow. Dain frowned, wondering what had happened to the famed gentleness and hospitality of the eld-folk. What had made them so tense and wary of strangers?

The guide gestured for Dain to stop, then walked forward alone to kneel before the old eld.

"Grandfather," he said reverently, and kissed the hem of his garment.

The old eld leaned forward to place his hand benevolently on the younger one's head. He asked a question in the eldin dialect that Dain did not understand.

Still kneeling, the young eld replied in kind.

Something familiar about the words flickered and shifted in Dain's mind. He frowned, feeling he should be able to understand if only he concentrated a little harder.

Alexeika edged closer to him. "Do you know what he is saying?" she whispered.

"No."

She frowned. "Did your lady mother teach you nothing when you were a child?"

He glared at her. "Did not yours?"

Her face puckered angrily as though she'd bitten into a sour grape, but before she could retort, the old eld was beckoning to Dain.

"Come forth," he said in Netheran.

Not sure whether to be elated or nervous, Dain swallowed and walked up to him. He bowed in the Mandrian way, then dropped to his knees, willing to humble himself if it would help.

"This is King Kaxiniz," the younger eld announced. "Leader of the eight Tribes . . . and father of she who was Nereisse."

Dain looked up in startlement, realizing he was staring into the pale gray eyes of his own grandfather. At last, against all odds, he had found his true family. Tangled emotions surged into Dain's throat. For a moment he was too choked up to speak.

Kaxiniz stared at him and through him, offering no greeting. Dain met his regard steadily for a moment, then shifted his gaze to the younger eld, who had taken a place beside Kaxiniz's chair as though he had the right to do so.

"You called his majesty 'grandfather,'" Dain said in puzzlement. "Is he in truth your relation, or do you call him so as a title of respect?"

The young eld's amber eyes flashed proudly. "I am Potanderzin," he stated. "Grandson and heir to King Kaxiniz."

Dain smiled in genuine pleasure. "Then we are cousins. I am glad to find family."

Potanderzin stiffened. "We are not your family, mixed-blood!"

Kaxiniz held up his hand, and Potanderzin subsided with a glare.

The king of the eldin turned his pale gaze back on Dain and said, "You have invoked the old favors owed to Solder the First. What would you ask of us?"

Dain blinked at the direct question. He was still trying to adjust to the fact that he possessed both a grandfather and a cousin, and possibly numerous other relatives as well. He wanted to meet them all, to be welcomed. However, plainly he was not going to be accepted here. It saddened him to discover that the eldin were in their own way as bigoted as humans.

"Ask your favor!" Kaxiniz said impatiently. "Let us settle all debts and be done with them."

Dain frowned, certain he faced a trap of some kind. Solder had been the first king of Nether; for a debt to have lasted over the course of several centuries, Dain realized, it must be great indeed. He had no intention of squandering it through ignorance.

"Perhaps I will not ask my favor now," Dain said, and saw the old king's eyes narrow.

"What, then, do you want?"

"I am Nereisse's son," Dain said in appeal.

Kaxiniz's eyes were like river pebbles. "So it has been said. What proof have you?"

Dain slid a finger inside the neck of his hauberk and pulled out his bard crystal pendant. As he held it up, the multifaceted glass caught the special light of this place and flashed to life in a rainbow of colors and hues that it had never reflected before. The breeze stirred it, and the crystal began to sing with a purity that took Dain's breath away. Before he realized it, he was singing with it, his voice blending in perfect harmony.

Potanderzin caught his breath audibly, and Kaxiniz closed his eyes. No one else present moved or spoke until the song ended.

Trembling a little with emotions he could not name, Dain closed his hand around the crystal. It felt strangely warm and alive against his palm, more so than ever before. He drew in several deep breaths to steady himself.

"I am Faldain," he whispered.

When Kaxiniz opened his eyes, tears shimmered in them. "I heard Nereisse's voice in your song."

Dain bowed his head, missing the mother he had never known.

"And the voice of someone else. Who?"

"Thiatereika," Dain said hoarsely, and cleared his throat. "My sister."

Kaxiniz's gaze shifted to Alexeika, who stood behind Dain. "Not this maiden?"

"No," Dain answered. "Thiatereika is dead."

Murmurs came from the onlookers, and Kaxiniz's hands clenched hard in his lap.

His expression, however, did not change. "Killed by *men*?" he asked harshly.

"No, by dwarves. My—Tobeszijian left Thia and me in the guardianship of Jorb the Swordmaker. We grew up in Nold, and might be there still except for a war that broke out among the clans. Jorb died in one of the attacks, and so did Thia."

"How were you spared?" Potanderzin asked.

Hearing criticism and an unspoken accusation of cowardice in his voice, Dain frowned and rose to his feet to face his cousin. He was a full head taller than Potanderzin, with twice the muscles and breadth of shoulder. He was getting tired of being judged and found lacking by someone he could break in half.

"I was away, buying ore for the forge," he replied, his voice quiet but brittle. "Be assured I took vengeance on those who slew her. They live no more."

"Ah, the man-taint covers you well," Kaxiniz said. "Why come you here to boast of killing and death?"

"I come here to ask for your help in saving someone's life."

"Whose?"

"Lady Pheresa du Lindier," Dain replied. "She is of Mandria."

The eldin all stared at him, and no one spoke. Dain struggled on with his explanation.

"By accident she drank eld-poison which was intended for me. She lies near death, and has been kept alive only through a spell. It cannot hold her much longer. I came here for the cure."

Kaxiniz's brows drew together. "You come invoking the old favors for *this*?"

Dain did not understand his anger. "I need your help. I don't know where else to turn."

"Nereisse died because of eld-poison meant for you," the old one said. "Why do you come before me with this tale told anew? To wound my heart? To stir up old grief? She was my only daughter. With the greatest misgivings did I bestow her hand in marriage to a man-king. I did it only because Tobeszijian had eldin blood in his veins. And see what became of her! See!"

He flung out his hand as he spoke, and a small vapor formed in the air. For a moment it roiled upon itself, then it cleared to show Dain an image of a woman lying in bed, writhing in fevered delirium. He stared at her, realizing this slender, beautiful woman who looked so much like Thia was the mother he'd never known.

Unable to stop himself, he took at step toward the image, and it vanished with a small pop.

"She died because of you!" Kaxiniz said. "Died to save her child from poison."

"I—"

"And now you claim another woman will die by the same cause, and for the same reasons."

"I didn't come to bring you pain!" Dain said vehemently. "I came in an effort to save a life."

"She cannot be saved."

"But she's human. There's no eld blood in her. Surely something can be done to rid her of the poison," Dain said desperately. "Please, sir. I beg for your mercy."

"There is no cure," Kaxiniz said gruffly. "It is a poison like no other, conjured forth from the foul breath of Ashnod of Gant to destroy us. It is destruction. Its source is the very antithesis of life. There is no cure."

"But—"

"Accept this. Your quest is a false one, born of pride and a sense of false responsibility."

"I *am* responsible!" Dain retorted, reeling from what Kaxiniz had said. "I love her. I—"

"And that is another lie." As Kaxiniz leaned forward, his pale gray eyes were relentless. "You claim love for the bride of another man. No eld would dare do this. You are immoral and tainted by man-ways."

Dain stiffened. "I fell in love with her before she belonged to another. I—"

"No, Faldain. No. I read the truth in your heart, truth which you will not accept. You sought this maiden because she was forbidden. You sought her because you are the enemy of the man she belongs to. This is evil. Great evil!"

"But I—"

"You have grown up to be unworthy of your mother's sacrifice," Kaxiniz said with contempt. "Nereisse never lacked courage. She never told lies, not even to herself. She never evaded her duty."

"Are you saying I do?"

Kaxiniz said nothing, but the expression in his eyes was damning.

Feeling whipped by the old king's scorn, Dain stood there with his face on fire and his temper in shreds. He hadn't come here to be called an immoral coward. Kaxiniz was a stranger, with no right to judge him.

Except . . . Kaxiniz was his grandfather, and he *did* have the right to judge.

Feeling ashamed and confused, Dain bowed his head. "I do intend to claim my throne," he said stiffly, wanting the old eld to understand. "But I have felt it necessary to save Pheresa if I could. I don't expect her gratitude. I—I know that if she lives she will marry Prince Gavril of Mandria. But why should I let her die, if I could do anything to prevent it?" He looked up, frowning earnestly. "I thought the eldin revered life. Why are you so eager to condemn this young woman? You don't even know her."

"I do not judge her. I do not condemn her," Kaxiniz said. "Her fate lies not in my hands."

"The eldin are healers," Dain said, pleading with him. "Can no one try to help her? If not for my sake, then for hers? She is innocent. No enemy of any man. Why should she suffer? Why should she die because an assassin sought *my* death?"

Kaxiniz stared at him stonily. "You could journey to the pits of hell and beg Ashnod for his dire mercy on her behalf, and it would avail you nothing. There is no cure."

"But I thought an eldin healer could draw the—"

"No eld can draw the poison from her without dying in the attempt. As your mother died, drawing the poison from her child."

Dain flinched, for again he heard the accusation and bitterness in Kaxiniz's voice. He had no memory of having been poisoned as a young child, no memory of having been seriously ill. Thia would have told him about it if it had really happened. Yet he heard no lie in Kaxiniz's words.

Dain sighed, then said, "Can the Chalice of Eternal Life not create a cure?"

Behind him, Alexeika gasped aloud. Potanderzin blinked in shock. Kaxiniz drew back deeper within the embrace of his leafy chair. Dain did not know what had shocked them this time, but he was getting tired of how these people took offense at everything he said or asked.

"Do you know where the Chalice is hidden?" he persisted.

"I do not."

Dain's last hope crashed. He couldn't believe he had come all this way, risked his life and the lives of his friends, only to meet now with failure. He'd been so sure the eldin would help Pheresa. Had Thiatereika still been alive, she would have stretched out her hand instantly to help a stranger. He realized he'd expected all the eldin to be like her, but clearly they weren't.

And yet, there was another mystery lying concealed beneath Kaxiniz's hostility, a secret of some kind, a . . . a sort of wariness tinged with fear. Dain glanced around at the handful of eldin looking on, then turned his frown on the nearby dwellings. There weren't many of them. There seemed to be almost no folk in this enchanted village. And why had the little ones fled at the sight of him? Were they so wary of strangers? Why? Who could harm them, much less find them here?

"Why do you hide yourselves?" he asked. "What do you all fear?"

Kaxiniz's and Potanderzin's faces were like stone. Dain sensed a flash of panic between grandfather and grandson, felt it as sharply as though it had been shared with him.

"Something is wrong," Dain said. "You fear me? Why?"

The two of them exchanged glances that only confirmed Dain's suspicions.

"Why?" he repeated. "All my life I have heard of the eldin ways, of eldin gentleness, of eldin hospitality, of eldin grace and love of beauty. I saw it in my sister, who never spoke from unkindness, who cherished all living creatures."

"Your sister is dead," Potanderzin said harshly. "You said she died by violence. So has it been for most of our folk. We have been *too* gentle, *too* trusting. Well, no more!"

Kaxiniz reached out and touched his wrist, but Potanderzin scowled and jerked away from the old eld's touch.

"You ask why we fear you?" Potanderzin said angrily to Dain. "You stand here, in our last place of refuge, and feel hurt because we abhor you!"

Kaxiniz sighed. "Potanderzin, do not—"

"Yes, Grandfather! I must tell him. Why shouldn't he know?"

"Tell me what?" Dain demanded.

Potanderzin's amber and silver eyes blazed at him. "You mean our destruction."

"What?"

"It has been foretold! The son of Tobeszijian will find us, even in refuge where no man may enter. No matter where we hide, he will ride straight to us with eyes that see past the veils of concealment. And when he goes forth from us, he will betray us to our worst enemies. Then will we be driven forever from this place of safety, nevermore to dwell here beyond the reach of men."

Stunned, Dain could only stand there, staring at his cousin in astonishment. "But such a prophecy is impossible," he said at last. "I would never bring harm to you. I—"

"Save your lies," Potanderzin said roughly. "I tell you it has been foretold. The veils of seeing have been parted several times, and always we see ourselves in flight, moving eastward, toward the lands of our enemies."

"Visions can be misinterpreted," Dain said desperately. "I would not act against you. This, I swear!"

"Knowledge of our hiding place now lies in your mind," Kaxiniz said with quiet weariness. "Among the Nonkind, knowledge can be plucked from anyone's thoughts, whether he wishes it to happen or not."

Potanderzin nodded. "You are our downfall, Faldain. Our last destruction. This is why we wish you ill."

"But—"

"It is time for you to go," Kaxiniz said. He met Dain's eyes as he spoke, and there was no relenting in his gaze. "If you invoke the old favors, we will dishonor ourselves and refuse. For we cannot help you. Now go, and bring about our destiny."

11

"No," DAIN SAID. "No! Please, I swear to you that—"

"We do not want your oaths," Potanderzin said with a sneer. "The king has bade you go. In the name of courtesy, do as he asks. Or must you be forced out?"

From the corner of his eye, Dain saw Alexeika stiffen and reach for her daggers.

Not wanting violence, Dain held up his hand. "Wait!" he called out, as much to her as to Potanderzin. "I will go, but I ask one last question."

Potanderzin looked as though he would refuse, but Kaxiniz gestured to Dain. "Speak."

"Could *I* draw the poison from Pheresa?" Dain asked. Alexeika gave an involuntary start, but he ignored her and kept his gaze firmly on Kaxiniz. "If I were shown the gifts of healing, could I save her?"

Emotions shimmered in Kaxiniz's eyes, but he gave Dain no answer.

Alexeika gripped his sleeve. "You'll die," she said fiercely. "If you attempt such a thing, you will kill yourself. What good to us is that?"

"It would clear a debt," Dain said stubbornly. "One life for another. Isn't that right, Grandfather?"

Kaxiniz's face had lost all color. Even his curls stopped moving. "No," he said hoarsely. "No!"

"Teach me this skill," Dain said. "I was too young to remember where my father hid the Chalice, so I cannot bring it forth from hiding to heal many who suffer. I can think of no other way to save Pheresa's life. Even if you think I am wrong, she is my friend. I have to save her, no matter what the cost!"

"And do you understand the cost?" Potanderzin asked him fiercely. "Do you?"

"Yes," Dain said. "My life for hers."

"No," Alexeika moaned, but Dain ignored her.

"With you will die the true line of Netheran kings," Kaxiniz said. "The chain of descendants from Solder will lie broken forever."

Dain flinched slightly at that, but he did not yield. "I am sorry," he said. "I was not raised to preserve kingdoms, but instead to keep my word. And I gave it to—"

"Foolish boy, consider more than your own boastful arrogance!" Kaxiniz broke in. "Long, long ago in the time of the ancients, Solder did dare to intervene in the Battles of the Gods. Partly because of his courage and valor, Ashnod and the lesser dark gods were defeated. The mortals who worshipped them became the first Nonkind, and all were driven far across the Charva into a desolate place that we now know as Gant.

"In reward, Thod made Solder first king over Nether and entrusted him with the Chalice of Eternal Life and many secrets of power and magic to enable him to rule long and well. This, Faldain, is your heritage. This is your beginning."

Dain frowned. He dared not interrupt the old eld, but so far nothing Kaxiniz said had changed his mind.

"Since that dawning of time, Ashnod has focused on one primary objective."

"Revenge?" Dain said impatiently.

Kaxiniz frowned at him in severe disapproval. "It is Ashnod's will that Solder's line be broken forever, crushed from existence. The Chalice of Eternal Life is to be either destroyed or else lost for all eternity. Nether is to sink into the darkness and be consumed by evil. Why do you think Muncel was befriended years ago by agents of the Believers? Who do you think dripped the poison of jealousy into his ear, day after day, until he actually struck against your parents?"

Dain dropped his gaze, ashamed of his earlier flippancy.

"Hear me," Kaxiniz said. "When Tobeszijian was forced from his throne and vanished, never to return, evil took great strides against us. Your father condemned his realm to death when he removed the Chalice—"

"He had to," Dain said in automatic defense of his father. "He couldn't let it fall into their hands."

Kaxiniz's face twisted with bitterness. "Your father was a brave warrior in battle. The rest of the time he was a fool who did not think ahead. He reacted. He never planned. Time after time, I warned Nereisse of the dangers, yet Tobeszijian would not heed them."

"Anyone can make mistakes," Dain said. "Why can you not forgive his?"

"Because he carelessly allowed himself and his entire family to fall into the enemy's hands."

Dain's head lifted in contradiction. "Nay, he kept my sister and me from harm. We were well-hidden until this year."

"Too well-hidden," Kaxiniz said bitterly. "He could have brought you to my keeping, but he did not. Despite his eld blood, he did not trust me with your welfare. Now you stand here, looking brave and manly, yet how ignorant of the true situation you are. By hiding you from your own heritage, Tobeszijian played once more into the enemy's plans. To some Netherans you are a myth, a savior whose eventual return has been foretold. To others, you are nothing at all, for they do not believe in you. To us, you are disaster."

"I—"

"Hear me! Your coming is likely too late, but if you do nothing except go questing to save a foreign girl whose destiny has no place in Nether, then you finish Ashnod's work for him."

"I gave her my word," Dain said stubbornly.

Kaxiniz's stony gray eyes bored into him. "When?" he asked sharply. "Before or after you learned your true identity?"

Dain frowned. He had the feeling that Kaxiniz already knew the answer to his question, yet Dain knew he was expected to reply. "After."

"Aye, after," Kaxiniz said with a nod. "After you knew you were required to be elsewhere."

"Nether has grown dark indeed," Dain told him coldly. "For I see that the eldin have come to despise kindness."

Kaxiniz stared at him a long moment before he shook his head. "Alas, kindness is not despised, but the good of many must come before the good of one. Has no one taught you this?"

Dain refused to answer.

Kaxiniz sighed. "It would seem you are exactly like your father."

"Am I?" Dain retorted with heat, wondering what the old eld

would say if he knew how strongly Tobeszijian's vision had urged him to return and rectify his mistakes by fighting for the throne. "Then I am proud to be like him. He kept the Chalice from danger."

"But at the cost of his kingdom's well-being!" Potanderzin burst out, as though he couldn't keep quiet any longer. His eyes were blazing. "The land has grown tainted and foul. We eldin can no longer heal it, for Muncel's evil has destroyed the Tree of Life that we worship. If you throw yourself away on a cause that does not belong to you, who will restore the tree? Who will restore the Chalice? Who will restore the kingdom?"

Dain's face was burning. He glared back. "You revile me in one breath and beg me to save you in the next. Is this not the way of men, and far beneath the honor of the eld-folk?"

Potanderzin reached for his dagger, but quickly Kaxiniz rose to his feet and stepped between them.

"You hide here, fearing foretellings that may or may not come true," Dain said in disgust. "Yet what do you for the cause? Will you come forth and fight the evil? Or am I supposed to do it all alone?"

Kaxiniz faced him with stony dignity. The expression in his gray eyes was terrible to behold. "When you have proven yourself a king, you may criticize us. Not before." He pointed a trembling finger at Dain. "Go from us. Go!"

Dain bowed to the old king, his anger like something alive in his chest. Tight-lipped, he took no farewell and gave no other courtesy, but simply turned on his heel and strode away.

Potanderzin hurried to catch up with him. "I will lead you back to the bridge."

"No need," Dain said angrily. "I can follow the path."

"You are blind and foolish," Potanderzin said. "Just like your father. You are unworthy of Solder's heritage."

"Thank you," Dain said through his teeth, "for repeating the old king's words. I would not want to forget them."

"Perhaps repetition will break through the stone of your stubbornness."

Fuming, Dain followed Potanderzin back along the village path to the bridge. There, he hesitated, seeking one last way to appeal to his cousin's sense of mercy.

But Potanderzin gave him no chance. He pointed at the bridge. "Go from here, and do not return."

"My blood is pale," Dain said resentfully. "Just like yours. We're kin, whether you like it or not."

"Until you are worthy, you are no kin of mine."

"Worthy?" Dain shot at him. "Worthy of what? My throne? How dare you judge me like this. You have closed your minds, without giving me a chance."

"We have seen what is to come," Potanderzin intoned.

"Aye, so you keep saying, but what do you intend to do about it?"

"Do?" Potanderzin said blankly. "What can be done?"

"When you can answer that question, perhaps at last *you* will be worthy to sit on our grandfather's throne."

Potanderzin's eyes narrowed. "Do not mock me. This war against Ashnod has nothing to do with the folk of eld."

Dain snorted. "Of course not. Yet you hide."

"You were born under great auspices to sit on Nether's throne. It is *your* responsibility to guard the Chalice, to keep back the powers of darkness. We are not required to help you."

"Clearly," Dain retorted. "You hide here in your enchanted wood, safe from Muncel's army, safe from Gantese assassins. You criticize me yet take no risks yourself. I wonder you do not slaughter me to prevent this betrayal I'm supposed to commit."

"Great Thod, no!" Alexeika said in alarm.

Dain went on glaring at Potanderzin. "Or do you intend to strike me down after I cross this bridge?"

"You speak evil insult," Potanderzin said through his teeth. His hands were clenched at his sides. "We eldin are not assassins."

"No, indeed. Your destiny has been foretold; therefore, you will fold your hands like old women and make it come true. Why not help fight the darkness? Why not seek to restore this Tree of Life you count so high?"

Potanderzin's amber eyes narrowed to slits. He glared at Dain in silence.

"Yes, I thought so," Dain said with contempt. "You will do nothing. I may be wrong, as my grandfather has said, but at least I am no coward."

"Go from here," Potanderzin said furiously, and the flowers blooming next to the path withered and died as he spoke. "You understand nothing. *Nothing!* Go and do not come back!"

Dain shot him a final steely look. "I am ashamed," he said, "to know you are my kin."

Potanderzin stiffened, but Dain turned away from him and stepped onto the bridge.

Instantly the light and warmth vanished, and all was dark and bitterly cold once more. Dain strode across, his boots echoing on the rough planks, and stepped off between the carved beyars.

He found the other eldin riders gone. Only a lingering scent of rank beyar musk remained on the frosty air. Soleil, nickering a welcome, stood tied to a tree.

Dain untied the reins and waited in the darkness, fuming, as Alexeika crossed the bridge and hurried to join him.

"Your majesty," she said quietly, her voice holding a mixture of sympathy and pity, "I'm sorry—"

"Yes, thank you," he said, cutting her off. He wanted no comforting. He was too angry, too resentful. His eldin relatives had condemned Pheresa to death, and he would never forgive them for it. "Let's find the others and go from here."

But Alexeika blocked his path. "I'm sorry I had to hear of your shame," she said. "I swear I will never speak of it."

"Shame? What say you?"

She was only a shadow in the darkness, lean and straight and stalwart. Her hair and skin smelled of frost. "This awful thing that you will do—"

"I will *not* betray them!" Dain said angrily. "Gods! Is this your belief as well, that fate comes to us as an assignment we cannot escape?"

"No, but—"

"They are sore afraid," he said, cutting across her words. "There are few of them left—no doubt from persecution. Clearly it has softened their thinking and made them weak."

"Fear is always the greatest enemy," Alexeika said. "Or so my father always told me."

"Your father," Dain said grimly, "was wise."

"Sire, you won't—I mean, you really don't intend to draw this lady's poison into yourself, do you?"

He looked away, staring into the blackness of the forest with his heart still on fire. Never, since Thia's death, could he remember feeling so bleak inside.

"No," he said curtly.

Alexeika sighed in obvious relief. "Thank the—"

"If she were nearby, I would try something . . . anything," he said raggedly, clenching and unclenching his fists. "But surely she's in Grov by now."

"Grov!"

"Aye. Unless she died on the journey." Dain tipped back his head and blinked fiercely in an effort to control himself. He wanted to yell, to draw his sword and cleave something in twain. He wanted to trample, to destroy, to run with the wind until he could feel nothing at all.

"Your majesty cannot go to Grov!" Alexeika said in alarm.

"I know. My uncle's men would cut me down. No, Alexeika, I'm turning west to find the Agyas. It's time for war."

She made a soft little cry in the back of her throat and suddenly dropped to her knees in the snow before him, clutching the hem of his hauberk, "At last," she murmured, her voice raw with emotions he did not want to witness. "At last! Oh—"

He gripped her shoulders, and gave her a rough shake. "On your feet. There's nothing to rejoice about."

"But there is!"

"No, Alexeika." He sighed harshly in the darkness. "Come, let us get back to the others."

Just as he slid his foot into the stirrup to mount his horse, a peculiar feeling swept him, rendering him dizzy and suddenly weak. Letting his foot drop back to the ground, he closed his eyes and leaned against Soleil's reassuring bulk. A terrible coldness suffused him, starting at the top of his head and descending through his body. He felt as though his very life was sinking into the ground with it. He could feel his heart slowing, his energy draining away until there was nothing . . . nothing . . .

"Dain!"

A rattling thump jolted his bones and brought him back from the icy darkness of nowhere.

Opening his eyes with a wince, Dain found himself lying on

the ground, which was very cold and hard beneath him. He blinked, momentarily dazzled by the orange flames of a campfire. Thum knelt over him, gripping the front of his surcoat with both fists.

"Dain!" he shouted again with more urgency than before.

"Easy, lad," Sir Terent's voice said. "He's coming around."

Dain tried to lift his hand to his head. He felt dizzy and strange. Nothing looked right to him. He could not figure out what had happened.

"Here, Terent, lift him while I put this blanket under him."

"Aye, Alard. Here, Thum, move out of the way. You're of no help lifting."

Thum vanished, and Dain felt himself lifted and set down again. The ground still felt cold beneath him.

Frowning, he gazed up into Sir Terent's worried face. His head dawdled like an infant's, and he had to concentrate to hold it steady. "What happened to me?"

Sir Terent pressed a callused hand to his cheek and smiled. "Ah, now, that's what we'd like to know. That lass came riding into camp here like a wild woman, with you draped unconscious over the saddle. She said you were hale and hearty and talking to her one minute, and the next you fainted flat on the ground."

"Oh." Dain's frown deepened. He tried to remember and couldn't. "Is that what—"

"As for me," Sir Terent said grimly, "I'm wondering what those queer eldin did to you. What kind of spell did they cast on you, eh?"

"Move back!" another voice said before Dain could answer.

Alexeika rushed up to elbow Sir Terent aside. She lifted Dain's head and pressed a bark cup of water to his lips. "Drink this."

Realizing he was thirsty, Dain gulped down the icy cold liquid with gratitude. His weakness was wearing off now. He pushed her hands aside and sat up, thrusting against Sir Terent's attempt to press him back down.

"I'm well, sir," he said sharply, and glanced around.

The camp lay in a tiny clearing banked with snowdrifts beneath the laden branches of pine and fir. A fire was crackling briskly, casting out enough warmth to hold back the night's raw cold. Hare carcasses, long since roasted and stripped to the bones, lay atop a flat stone by the flames. Dain could smell the lingering aroma of roasted meat, and his mouth watered.

"Is aught left for me to eat?"

Sir Terent chuckled and clapped him hard on the shoulder. "Aye, that there is. Now I know you're well again. Here, Alard! Hand over that morsel of hare we saved back."

Sir Terent's idea of a morsel was the entire haunch. But clearly they'd all eaten while he was unconscious, so Dain took it and ate it hungrily.

While he did so, they gathered round and stared at him with blatant concern.

"I like this not," Sir Terent said finally when Dain was snapping the bones and sucking marrow from them. "You faltered at Thirst and did act most strange. Now you've swooned. Perhaps it's some illness and—"

"No," Dain said with a frown, tossing the bones into the fire and wiping his greasy fingers. "I have been thinking about this, for it's passing strange."

"But if you're ill "

"I can't be," Dain said. "My eldin blood would protect me from common malady."

Sir Terent's face turned red, and he slapped a hand around his sword hilt. "Then these eldin have enspelled you—"

"Easy, sir," Dain said to restrain him. "Someone is trying to do it, but it's not the eld-folk."

Alexeika's intelligent gaze was intent as she leaned forward. "No, it can't be," she agreed. "I sense none of their type of magic near you."

"Hush, lass!" Sir Terent said gruffly to her. "This discussion has no need of your opinion."

For an instant she looked hurt; then anger flashed in her eyes and she jumped to her feet. "Wisely spoken, sir lout!" she said contemptuously. "Since you are foreign-born and too stupid to know magic when it's burning your ears, I'll leave you to it."

"Alexeika!" Dain called after her, but she turned so fast her long braid of hair swung behind her. Away she strode into the night.

Thum and Sir Alard kept silent, but Sir Terent showed no remorse.

"Good riddance," he said in satisfaction, rubbing his hands. "Bold as brass and a tongue of vinegar. Now, sire, about these eldin—"

"She was absolutely right, Sir Terent," Dain cut him off coldly. "This could not be their magic turned against me."

"Don't see why not," Sir Terent replied stubbornly. "No friendliness in them, and the lass told us they refused to help you."

"That doesn't mean they're trying to kill me," Dain said.

"Kill you!" Thum exclaimed in horror. "You think someone intends your death?"

"Aye." Frowning, Dain rubbed his chest. "It's like lying in a snowdrift for hours, unable to move, and growing colder all the while. But it's worse than that. It's feeling everything sinking away, fading . . . " He sat in silence a long moment, trying to shake off the confused memories. "It comes from afar."

"From who?" Thum asked. "Who attacks you like this?"

Dain shook his head. "Choose from my enemies, since they're so plentiful. But this is strange magic. I don't know it, and yet I . . . " He frowned, but the thought that had almost come to him vanished and would not return. Frustrated, he sighed. "All I know is that it's getting stronger."

His men exchanged uneasy glances. Sir Alard had pulled out his Circle and was turning the brass piece over and over in his fingers.

Thum's hazel-green eyes held horror. "But what can you do to stop it? You must know something!"

"I don't. I never know when it's going to overtake me." Dain's frown deepened, and he shivered despite his nearness to the fire. "With the Nonkind, I often have some inkling, but this is nothing of their ilk."

"Can you not sense when it will strike again?" Thum asked.

Dain met his eyes with a sense of foreboding. "Nay. I only know that it will."

That night he dreamed of riding through driving sleet, the air so cold it burned his nostrils and fingers. He dreamed of hurlhounds— red-eyed, acid-slavering beasts that surrounded him so that there was no way out. He dreamed of fire and smoke, hearing Thia's screams, feeling her life force ebb away as he gripped her in grief and denial. He dreamed of a place harsh and terrible, where the wind blew sand that abraded his face and choked his breath. And he dreamed of his father, ghostly pale astride his darsteed, blood streaming from terrible wounds, his sword, Mirengard, glowing white in his hands.

"Father!" Dain called out desperately, racing after Tobeszijian. There was so much he wanted to ask, so much he needed to know. "Father! Wait for me!"

But Tobeszijian seemed not to hear him. Moaning in pain, the great king reeled in his saddle as though he would fall from it. On his ungloved hand, the Ring of Solder glowed brightly against the gloom. Dain saw his father hesitate, nearly swoon again with a shuddering grimace, and mouth words that Dain could not overhear.

A blinding explosion of sparks enveloped him, and in an instant he vanished into thin air. Only a few golden sparks lingered in the air, raining down slowly where he had been a moment before.

Dain felt an overwhelming sense of loss and dread. "Father!" he called. "Come back! Please!"

But Tobeszijian did not return.

The next morning, they arose and broke camp in dawn's bleak light. Dain felt tired and heavy-eyed from poor rest. He caught the others glancing at him in concern, but with a frown he brushed aside their inquiries and climbed into the saddle.

As had become their custom, Alexeika walked over to climb up behind Sir Alard, but Dain stopped her.

"Ride with me today," he said. "We will turn westward and set a hard pace. Soleil is better able to carry two than is Sir Alard's steed."

Alexeika's cheeks took on a pale tinge of pink. In silence, her red chain mail looking vivid and outlandish against the frosty gray backdrop of the woods, she climbed behind his saddle.

"I'm sorry for Sir Terent's words to you last night," Dain said quietly for her ears alone.

The color in her cheeks intensified. Her blue-gray eyes were fierce with resentment as she nodded stiffly to him. "The apology is not yours to make, sire," she said.

"Perhaps not," Dain said. "But he is my man and I am responsible for him. He never means to be as rough as he sounds."

"Your majesty is wrong!" she said sharply. "He means exactly what he says. But I need no protecting from the bigotry of your men. I can take care of myself."

She was so prickly that Dain was tempted to drop the matter, but he could hear genuine hurt beneath her bravado, and he remained troubled by the look that had crossed her face last night. It was the first sign of vulnerability he'd seen in her, the first sign that she was neither as tough nor as hard as she tried to appear.

"I faced their bigotry myself not so long past," he told her mildly. "Few Mandrians will accept anyone of eld blood in their company. Gaining their loyalty did not come quickly . . . or easily."

"I suppose your majesty is telling me that in the fullness of time they will befriend me too?"

"Aye."

She snorted. "Why think you I want their friendship?"

"Everyone needs friends, Alexeika. Even you."

She fell silent at his back, and Dain added, "Besides, we're comrades. It's best to be on good terms before battle."

She ducked in unison with him as they rode beneath a low-hanging branch. "Battle won't come before the thaw of spring. We—"

She broke off with a gasp of alarm. At that moment, the stench of fetid decay filled Dain's nostrils.

He nearly stood in the stirrups as he drew Truthseeker. "Terent, Thum, Alard!" he shouted. "Nonkind!"

12

Just as Dain shouted his warning, a pair of hurlhounds burst from the undergrowth and came bounding straight for him. Black as eternity they were, their hides scaled and oily, and their eyes glowed with red fire. Venom dripped from their slavering jaws, and they stank of the grave.

At his back, Alexeika shouted a war cry and drew her sword, which was glowing white in the presence of evil. Dain spurred Soleil forward, intending to meet the onrush of the two hurlhounds with steel, but his beautiful steed had been bred in the gentle stables of Savroix, far to the south where monsters such as these were unknown. Soleil was only a courser, trained to the hunt, and no horse of war.

Just as Dain leaned over and swung, intending to use his horse's momentum to drive his sword with additional power through the spine of the nearest hurlhound, Soleil squealed in terror and sprang away from the snarling, snapping monster. Truthseeker whistled harmlessly through the air without striking its target, and Dain nearly tumbled from the saddle. Righting himself with an oath of frustration, Dain pulled hard on the reins, and tried to turn his panicked horse back toward the fray.

Then Sir Terent came galloping up on his heavy charger. With a shout, he beheaded one of the hurlhounds before it could leap at Dain. Coming up on the other side, Sir Alard attacked the second monster. Their ordinary swords could not prevail, however. Refusing to fall over, the headless hound went staggering back and forth until at last Dain was able to stab it with Truthseeker. Flames shot forth from the blade, and the hurlhound burst into ashes with a thin, wailing scream.

Sir Alard was still hacking at the other monster, mercilessly cutting it to pieces until his charger finally reared and brought both forefeet down on the hurlhound's skull with a mighty crack of bone. Only then did the monster fall.

A terrible quiet fell over the wood, broken only by everyone's harsh breathing. Jets of white wreathed from their mouths, and there was no need to say aloud what they were all thinking: where two hurlhounds were to be found, a whole pack would surely follow.

Alexeika gripped the back of Dain's cloak. "This horse of yours is a fool!" she said in fury.

Dain didn't bother to reply; he was too busy using his mind to soothe Soleil's fear and bring the trembling horse back under his control.

"I hear more coming," Sir Terent said.

For once his hearing proved more keen than Dain's. Lifting his head, Dain shook off his preoccupation with Soleil to listen, and now he heard the baying of more hurlhounds, coming fast. Worse, he heard the thunder of hoofbeats, and he sensed the minds of many riders. Some were filled with evil intent; others were simply empty. His mouth went dry.

"Believers and Nonkind," he said hoarsely.

Sir Terent stood up in his stirrups, listening with all his might. "How many, think you?"

Dain's mind was working rapidly. Not for the first time did he feel exasperation at being in a strange land. He knew not the lay of this country, knew not the streams, nor the ravines and hiding places.

"Sire?" Sir Terent said. "How many—"

"Too many for us to fight," Dain replied quickly. "Damne, but we should have ridden hard all night, gotten ourselves far from here. We—"

"After your swoon last night, you were in no condition to ride," Sir Terent reminded him gruffly.

"That's my point," Dain said impatiently, reining Soleil around. "Clearly my uncle's agents have been hunting me since I left Savroix. Last night, somehow, they—or some *sorcerel* working in concert with them—managed to mark me."

"Mercy of Riva," Alexeika whispered in dismay.

Ignoring her, he kept his gaze on his protector. "That must be why I fainted."

A deep crease furrowed between Sir Terent's brows. While Sir Alard drew a Circle on his breast, Sir Terent stared hard at Dain. "You're saying some kind of spell's been cast o'er your mind?"

"Not to control me," Dain assured him. "But these hurlhounds made straight for *me* alone. We've been found, here in the midst of nowhere. How else, unless they have marked me in some way?"

Alexeika gripped his shoulder. "If that's so, then by camping here near where you collapsed, we've given these riders all night to catch up with us. Thod above, I never thought of that!"

Comprehension and worry flashed across all their faces, but there was no time to discuss it further. The sounds of pursuit were coming closer, a crashing thunder through the forest that made birds fly up from the treetops into the sky and set Soleil's ears pricking nervously. A terrible howl rose in the air, and Dain felt his heart lurch in his chest, for he was the quarry.

"We've got to run for it," Sir Terent said grimly, and Sir Alard was nodding with nervous glances over his shoulder.

"If you're marked," Alexeika said quietly to Dain, "then they'll follow you no matter where you run."

"I've thought of that," Dain said. He forced himself to speak crisply, with no evidence of fear, in order to steady the rest of them. "I think I can make myself elusive and counteract whatever they've put on me. Quick, Alexeika, is there a place of refuge nearby? An old shrine, perhaps? A place to hide?"

She was frowning. "I think so. About half a league that way." She pointed. "There's a little river, the Tan. On the other side are small hills riddled with caves. I've heard there are old shrines there."

"Morde a day!" Sir Terent said in frustration. "What good is some pagan cave—"

"A river!" Dain said in relief, paying his protector no heed. "That's even better. Come—"

"Wait, sire!" Thum said urgently, moving his horse to block Dain's path. "Why take the chance of running that far when the eldin sanctuary is close by? If you hide yourself there, surely the Nonkind cannot follow you to that enchanted place."

Sir Alard's head whipped around, and hope flashed across his face. "Yes, that's it! Go there now, while we hold them—"

"Nay!" Dain said angrily, as Soleil bunched and pranced beneath him. He thought of the prophecy that said he would lead destruction to the eldin, and shook his head. "Not there. None of us are welcome, and I will not lead Nonkind to—"

"Never mind us," Sir Terent said gruffly. "Get yourself to safety at once, Dain lad. We'll take a stand here to give you what time we can."

Dain met Sir Terent's green eyes and saw in them all the man's stalwart love and loyalty, offered with the gift of his life. "Nay! I'll leave none behind. Quick! We ride toward the river."

"Go to your folks," Sir Terent said. "They'll hide you. I'll lay odds they know how to hide from the Nonkind better than anyone."

The kind intentions of his friends filled Dain with frustration. There was no time to explain how he'd been treated by the eldin, and clearly Alexeika had not spoken of it to anyone.

Another howl filled the air, followed by fearsome baying, and Soleil reared in fright. Fighting with the horse, Dain shouted breathlessly, "I'm riding to the river, and all of you will follow. You can't defend this ground. Come!"

Not allowing them to waste more time by arguing, Dain wheeled Soleil around and let him run. Spurred by panic, the fleet-footed courser would have ordinarily left the heavier horses behind, but Soleil was carrying the weight of two, and that helped Dain slow him to a pace the others could match.

They'd very nearly argued too long. A pack of hurlhounds came into sight, gaining rapidly on their heels, then splitting into two smaller packs that ran through the undergrowth on either side of Dain and his companions. Making no attempt to attack, they merely paced them, their black scaly hides flashing through gaps in the undergrowth as they ran alongside.

"Sire!" Alexeika shouted in his ear, but Dain was watching the hurlhounds closely and made no reply.

He leaned forward over Soleil's whipping mane, steadying the frightened horse all he could. The hurlhounds kept pace easily, never drawing closer, and Dain wondered why they did not attack.

A horn wailed in the distance behind them, and Dain's heart nearly jumped from his throat. He remembered the day when Gavril had coursed him through the Dark Forest with hounds and men, all because he'd tried to steal a horse and a bit of food. And now he was the quarry again.

Battling down fear, he forced himself to think. They couldn't ride at this blistering pace all the way to the river. Therefore, it was time for trickery.

With determination, he reached deep inside his mind, seeking the mark that had been placed on him. Because he was no *sorcerel,* he could not work complex magic. He knew only the simple, instinctive spells of life and nature, but thus far simplicity had always served him well. He drew in a breath, then began to sing softly of salt.

"What are you doing?" Alexeika asked, but with a shake of his head Dain kept singing.

He sang of salt mines, places where the ground turned barren and salt lay white atop the soil. He sang of salt on food, salt on altars, salt on the tongue. He sang of salt in the sea, salt in wounds, salt to cure meat, salt for cleaning. He sang of the coarse grittiness of it, of its radiant sparkle in sunlight, of its white purity when finely ground. He sang of its flavor. He sang of its sting.

He sang until he felt the mark wither slightly, then he yanked the reins and veered Soleil toward the hurlhounds paralleling him on the right. Neighing in fright, the horse fought him, but Dain pressed at its mind with his own.

Soleil leaped a fallen log, burst through a thicket, and nearly crashed broadside into one of the monsters.

Drawing Truthseeker, Dain struck fast and hard before the horse could scramble away from the hurlhound. Flames and ash flew in all directions, and the hurlhound was no more.

Behind him, Alexeika was wielding her own sword, chanting, "Severgard! Severgard!" as she sliced through another creature.

Wild baying broke out. The hurlhounds that had been running on their left came to the fray, just as Sir Alard, Sir Terent, and Thum caught up and desperately joined Dain in the fight he'd started. For a moment there was only wild shouting and the frenzied snarling of the monsters.

Truthseeker sang in Dain's hands as he caught another hurlhound in mid-leap and sent it crashing to the ground. He could hear Severgard singing as well, in a kind of peculiar harmony, as though the two blades—despite being forged so differently—were aware of each other.

A few seconds later, the battle ended, and all lay momentarily quiet in the forest. Weak sunlight filtered through the bare branches of the trees and glittered atop the trampled snow. Breathing hard, Dain felt Truthseeker still humming in his grasp. The sword glowed and rippled from hilt to tip, cleaning itself of gore and blood, which dripped off to hiss and steam on the ground.

Dain sheathed the sword and glanced around swiftly to take stock. Alexeika slid off Soleil's rump without a word and darted over to Sir Alard. Meanwhile, Thum was doubled over his saddle, wincing and gasping. Dain saw him clutching his leg, saw the claw marks and blood, now dripping onto the snow.

Swearing in alarm, Dain reached into the purse of salt that he'd brought with him from Mandria and rode over to his friend. Swiftly he brushed Thum's hand away from his injury and salted the wound.

Stiffening, Thum jerked back his head with a shout of agony that he bit off. Dain gripped his arm hard until the spasm eased and Thum began gasping and swearing.

Dain grinned at him, but Thum grimaced back. "I like not your tending," he said.

"You'd like dying of poison less," Dain said bluntly, and glanced at Sir Terent. "Are you well?" he asked.

"Aye." The protector's gaze was shifting in all directions. "We can't tarry here."

"Bind his leg for him. And quickly." Dain handed over the purse of salt. "Paste those cuts well with more salt first."

"Morde! Nay," Thum said shakily.

Dain looked at Sir Terent sternly. "Be sure it's done. It means his life."

"Aye, your grace," Sir Terent said.

Dain nodded, then rode over to see about Sir Alard just as Alexeika was pressing the flat side of her sword against a bite wound in his arm. His mail sleeve hung in tatters, and he gritted his teeth in obvious pain, the cords in his neck standing out until at last she released him. Sir Alard's aristocratic face turned as pale as the snow. He drew in several shuddering breaths before at last he recovered enough to lift his head.

"Does that work better than salt?" Dain asked Alexeika.

She grinned. "The same, but while I can run out of salt, Severgard is always with me."

Dain gave Sir Alard's shoulder a little shake. "Well again?"

The knight's brows rose. "If you call being branded alive a cure."

"If you can joke, you can ride." Dain swung his gaze back to Alexeika. "Come, my lady. Back up behind me."

She frowned, hesitating between the two of them. "Perhaps I should ride with Sir Alard and steady him."

"I'm well," Sir Alard said, straightening in the saddle.

"Come," Dain said to her, listening to the wail of the horn coming closer. His heartbeat quickened. "His horse carried you yesterday. Today 'tis Soleil's turn."

Alexeika climbed on behind him, and they rode onward at a brisk trot. "Soleil," Alexeika said in Dain's ear, "is likely to buck both of us off before this day is over."

Dain grinned, although it wasn't much of a joke. Then three riders appeared ahead of them. Clad in dark mail and heavily armed, they made no noise, raised no shout. They ranged themselves across the trail, blocking it, and simply waited.

Alexeika moaned. "Thod's mercy."

"We can take them, sire," Sir Terent said softly, looking grim indeed as he gripped his sword hilt.

Dain frowned and drew rein. "Nay," he said in alarm. "There's a trap here. Turn back!"

But as he whirled Soleil around, it was only to see another group of five riders block them from behind. This latter group was close enough for Dain to see that their mail was made from something that looked like black obsidian, yet that was flexible enough to allow them movement. He was reminded of scales on a serpent, or some Nonkind creature. Swiftly he drew his sword.

Alexeika gripped his shoulder hard. "Fire-knights!" she whispered.

He frowned. "Believers?"

"Aye, the worst kind."

The fire-knights slowly trotted forward from both sides, closing in on them. Dain's men were brave fighters, but were outnumbered and tired. Even as Sir Terent and Sir Alard drew their swords, Dain turned Soleil southward and headed into the forest. "Come!" he shouted, and kicked his horse to a gallop.

The others tried to follow, but one of the Believers shouted something in his bizarre, clacking language. Strange symbols drawn in flames appeared suddenly in midair before Dain.

Startled, he jerked involuntarily on the reins, and Soleil reared in panic. The flaming symbols cast off sparks and ashes that elongated as they fell to the ground. But instead of snuffing out in the snow, they blazed on the ground, cutting him off from the forest.

"Thod and Riva, have mercy on our souls," Alexeika was praying at Dain's back.

He brought Soleil under control and wheeled the horse in another direction, but again the Believer shouted, and again fire symbols blazed in the air, cutting Dain off.

Sir Terent swore a string of violent oaths. "Here's where we fight these devils, sire."

"Aye," Dain agreed grimly, and brandished Truthseeker.

It was not humming with power, and neither was Severgard aglow. Whatever these fire-knights might be, they were not Nonkind. Thod only knew what they were.

"Thum," Dain said rapidly to his friend. "Get you away into the trees."

"Nay, sire."

"Do not engage!" Dain said angrily. "You've no armor. You're not required to fight."

Holding his sword, Thum looked grim indeed as he positioned his horse beside Dain. They were arranged now in a tight circle, facing all four directions as the Believers closed in. "I doubt these creatures understand Mandrian rules of combat, sire," he said in a tight, strained voice.

"Squires do not fight," Dain said harshly. "I'll not put you at risk. As soon as we engage, slip away and—"

"Nay!"

"Hush, the pair of you," Sir Terent muttered, just as he used to when they were fosters in training. He drew the sign of a Circle on his breast, as did Sir Alard.

With shouts, the Believers charged at a gallop.

Dain lifted Truthseeker. "For Nether!" he shouted.

"For Faldain!" his men roared in response.

Then they were surrounded, and the crash of swords rang through the trees. Sir Terent's war charger reared up and struck with deadly forefeet, driving one Believer back just as the protector swung his sword at one of the foes closing in on Dain.

Then another opponent rushed at Dain, and he had no more chance to see what was happening to his companions. Looking massive in the black stone armor, this Believer kept his helmet visor closed, and Dain could see only darkness where his eyes should have been.

Fear stabbed through Dain, but he pushed it away as he met the Believer's attack. God-steel collided with iron, and the Believer's sword shattered in the first blow. The Believer stared at the broken weapon in his fist, then shouted something and hurled it at Dain like a knife.

Dain batted it away, but by then the Believer had drawn a curved dagger that flashed in the final slanting rays of sunlight. As he charged again, Dain swung his ancient sword with both hands and struck the man at the base of his shoulder.

Obsidian plates cracked into tiny slivers of stone that went flying as Truthseeker cleaved the Believer in twain to his waist. As the Believer fell, blood gushing from the fearsome wound, Dain sought another opponent.

Sir Terent was hacking lustily away, and Sir Alard was holding his own, but Thum was outnumbered by two Believers, who were ignoring his squire status entirely. While one kept Thum's sword engaged, the other hit him from behind.

Knocked from his saddle, Thum went crashing to the ground and lay there unmoving.

"No!" In a fury, Dain attacked the Believer who'd struck his friend down, thrusting Truthseeker through his back. Screaming, the Believer toppled over. Dain twisted Truthseeker desperately to keep it from being wrenched from his hand, but before he could withdraw his weapon, the fire-knight who'd been fighting Thum hurriedly pulled the dead man from Dain's reach. Truthseeker, still lodged in the dead man, was wrested from Dain's grasp.

With a laugh, the Believer galloped off, dragging the corpse and Truthseeker alike.

Armed now with nothing more than his dagger, Dain gulped. For a moment he was too horrified to think.

"Two down to our one," Alexeika shouted over the clang of weapons. "Six now against our four."

Dain looked at Thum, who was still lying on the ground. Dead or stunned, Dain knew not, but he feared the worst. Grief swelled through him, and with it came fresh anger.

"I'll take his sword," Dain said, and started to dismount.

Alexeika, however, gripped him in warning. "Look!"

He turned his head and saw another Believer approaching him at a gallop, sword brandished aloft. Straight at Dain came this new opponent, looking huge in his stone armor, his black cloak billowing from his shoulders as his horse jumped Thum's body. The Believer's horse was snorting jets of white breath, and tendrils of smoke curled through slits in the Believer's visor.

Desperate to get Thum's sword, Dain again started to dismount, but Alexeika reached around him to press Severgard into his hand. "Take mine!" she shouted, and jumped off before Dain could stop her.

Severgard protested by nearly twisting itself from Dain's hand. It was all he could do not to drop it. By then Alexeika had darted behind the fire-knight to seize Thum's sword. Holding it aloft, she went running to rejoin the fray, and there was no chance to swap weapons with her. Desperately Dain managed to force his fingers around Severgard's silver and gold wire hilt just as his opponent struck.

Despite mustering a desperate parry just in the nick of time, Dain knew himself to be in trouble.

Severgard was not forged for him, was never destined for his use. Its weight and balance were off; having held Truthseeker only moments before, Dain was painfully aware of this fact. He struggled with the sword, fighting it as much as he fought his opponent, who kept him hard pressed.

Severgard was a magicked blade, but it had none of the advantages of god-steel. It did not shatter the Believer's weapon. It could not cut through his obsidian armor. With every blow, Dain felt the Believer's strength jolt through his blade, his wrists, and his arms. He was tiring, sweating heavily inside his hauberk, and all the while in the back of his mind he was cursing himself for having foolishly thrust Truthseeker into that last man.

How many times in sword drills had Sir Polquin taught him and the other fosters never to run a mounted man through? Always cut, but never stab. Not while in the saddle.

He'd made a terrible error, a green boy's error, and now he was paying for it. It was only by Thod's grace and Alexeika's generosity that he was still armed and able to fight at all.

Determined to prevail, Dain stopped defending himself and instead swung aggressively, feinting, then striking low, just above the fire-knight's hipbone. The blade bounced off the stone armor, unable to cut through it. Had the man been wearing normal chain mail, it would have been a mortal blow. Ignoring his disappointment, swiftly Dain reversed his swing and brought Severgard up to meet the Believer's response.

The sword was no longer fighting him, but it remained something lifeless in his hands. Dain sent his mind to it in appeal.

Nothing in Severgard responded to him.

The Believer got in past Dain's guard and struck his upper arm. It was a glancing blow that did no damage, but the jolt of it was a warning. Gritting his teeth, Dain swung back in a fury, striking again and again with all his skill and might.

The Believer faltered a little. His guard slipped more than once, only to recover before Dain could take advantage of it. Clearly the Believer was tiring too, although not as much as Dain. With leaden arms, Dain forced himself to keep fighting. When he saw smoke curl through the slits of the fire-knight's visor, he felt a weary stab of alarm. What was this creature if not a man? And if he was Nonkind, why didn't Severgard's magical power come alive?

Nearby, the others fought equally hard. Heartened by the shouts and ringing steel, knowing his comrades refused defeat, Dain kept on, but he was grunting now with every blow he delivered and feeling a burn in his arms that warned him he had little strength left.

Knowing that he would soon falter from exhaustion, Dain sang Severgard's song raggedly, although such notes were hard for his throat to imitate. He sang them anyway, panting between notes as he sweated and fought against his indefatigable foe.

Severgard shuddered in his hands. He felt its power come reluctantly to life, flashing from hilt to sword tip in an instant, and making the blade glow white.

The Believer shouted something in Gantese and tilted his head away, as though it hurt him to gaze on that glowing light. Seizing his momentary advantage, Dain swung Severgard with all his strength.

The blow overpowered the Believer's defense. He went reeling back, toppling from his saddle to roll over in the snow. The advantage was now Dain's. Kicking Soleil faster, he swung Severgard high and charged. The fire-knight regained his feet, but he did not parry, did not even look up at Dain. Instead, he shifted his stance as Soleil came at him, and with one powerful blow sliced through the horse's throat a split second before Dain's sword hit him.

A spray of blood splattered the snow and blew back across Dain's thighs. In mid-stride, Soleil went down, crashing to his side and kicking his legs convulsively as his powerful heart pumped his life away.

Knocked flying from the saddle in the fall, Dain hit hard and tumbled over twice from the impetus of impact.

Although his mind urged him up, he lay there a moment, half-stunned. Blearily he saw Soleil lying on blood-soaked snow, the horse's strength, beauty, and speed gone forever. It was impossible to believe, too terrible to believe. Dain wanted to close his eyes and just lie there, but he knew better.

Somehow he forced himself to his hands and knees, shaking his head in an effort to get his wits moving. He saw a shadow rushing at him, and desperately lifted Severgard.

He was too slow, too dazed from his fall.

The Believer he'd been fighting knocked Severgard from his hands, then kicked him hard in the ribs. Wheezing from having all the wind driven out of his lungs, Dain toppled onto his side and knew he was finished.

"Dain!" Sir Terent bellowed in the distance. *"Dain, no!"*

Looming over him, the fire-knight lowered his sword, and Dain expected him to drive it through his heart in a final thrust. Instead, he nudged Dain's leg with his toe.

"Up," he said.

At first Dain could not believe his ears; then he realized he was to be made a prisoner.

A sickening sense of defeat flowed over him as he floundered unsteadily to his feet.

A short distance away, Alexeika was screaming defiance. Dain saw her crouched with Thum's sword in her hands, turning while a Believer circled her. They sprang at each other and engaged in a swift flurry of blows, but a moment later she cried out in pain and her sword went spinning from her hand. She drew a dagger and hurled it, but the Believer batted it aside and grabbed her. Shrieking, she tried to stab him with her remaining weapon, but could not pierce his armor. Then she was knocked to the ground and pinned there by her opponent's foot.

Only then did Dain see Sir Alard lying on the ground and Sir Terent kneeling in defeat with two opponents holding their weapons on him. Blood streamed down his face, and his head was bowed.

Dain dragged in a breath of relief. At least the man was still alive. It was a mercy any of them had survived.

The Believer who had defeated Dain held his sword aimed warily at Dain's throat, as though he expected Dain to give him more trouble. "I am Quar," he said. His voice was rough and guttural. "You are my prisoner, Faldain of Nether."

Dain gritted his teeth and forced himself to speak calmly. "Raise your visor, Quar. Let me see who has captured me."

He intended to hurl his dagger into the man's eye if he could get him to raise his visor, but Quar only laughed. It was a low, horrid sound, like stone grating on stone. Smoke curled forth from beneath the man's helmet, and Dain caught a whiff of something charred.

"My face is not for you to see, Faldain," the Believer said. "I have walked through the fire of Ashnod. I live in fire, for his glory. And for his glory will your blood be served to him."

Dain swallowed hard. "You're taking us to Gant?"

"You, I take to Gant. You will be served to Ashnod."

"Then let my friends go," Dain said quickly. "You have no need of them. Spare their lives and release them."

Turning partially away from Dain, Quar gestured at the men standing over Sir Terent. *"Ch't kvm'styk mut!"*

One of the Believers reached down and yanked off Sir Terent's mail coif. The other swung his sword in one swift, flashing blow.

Sir Terent's head went rolling across the ground beneath the feet of a horse. While the animal neighed and pranced in fright, Sir Terent's body toppled over.

Dain stared openmouthed, unable to believe it. So swiftly, so cruelly had it happened, he could not absorb the horror of it. Sir Terent had been their prisoner, disarmed. He had surrendered and was at their mercy. The casual brutality of Quar's order stunned Dain.

He slowly wrenched his gaze away from the gruesome sight of the man who had befriended him, trained him, protected him, and served him with the most loyal heart of all. Quar met Dain's gaze steadily but said nothing.

That's when the rage came, a fury that burned away everything inside Dain and left only a white-hot force. He felt the anger flash through him, then he shouted, and his rage came forth like flames of power, knocking Quar reeling.

Ducking recklessly under Quar's sword, Dain drove his shoulder into the man's gut, pushing him backward with all his might as he drew his dagger.

Still shouting words that cracked and trembled in the air, Dain struck at Quar again and again, but his dagger point skidded harmlessly off the stone armor. Quar's fist, sheathed by an obsidian-encrusted glove, smashed into Dain's face.

The world blackened and shrank in an instant. Dain staggered backward, feeling as though he'd been sucked into a vortex. It pulled him down before he could even struggle, and he was smothered in dark nothing.

PART THREE

13

FOR DAYS, GAVRIL waited in vain for an audience with King Muncel as though he were nothing more than an emissary. It was a terrible insult, and with every passing day Gavril's temper grew more frayed. Truly he had come to a land of barbarians.

He was given the run of one wing of Count Mradvior's palatial house, but he quickly discovered that aside from a handful of graciously furnished chambers, the rest of the building stood empty.

Denied the most basic amusements, Gavril prowled restlessly through the desolate, unheated rooms, preoccupied with finding a way to escape his trap. A trap he still blamed on Verence.

"Father, you fool!" Gavril muttered aloud as he paced up and down. "Why do you delay? Why do you not hurry?"

He'd written several letters to Verence, until he'd figured out that Mradvior was burning them.

Caged and thwarted at every turn, Gavril had thought up several plans to escape the house and round up his church knights. But every exit was guarded and when he'd drawn his sword on some of the guards, he found that they were protected by the same mysterious spell that safeguarded

Mradvior. Tanengard could not harm them. In sheer frustration, he'd even tried throwing a chair through a window, but the glass would not break.

Megala came searching for him. "Your highness—"

"What are you doing away from your post?" he asked in annoyance. "Get back to Lady Pheresa at once."

The serving woman curtsied deeply. "I ask pardon of your highness," she said nervously, twisting her hands together. "The lady has sent me to fetch you."

Gavril was startled. "She's awake?"

"Aye, your highness. Weak and doing poorly, but—"

He strode out of the room, with Megala trotting at his heels. When they'd first arrived in this terrible place, Mradvior's wife had stolen Pheresa's ball gown, for apparently it was dyed a shade of blue impossible to obtain in Nether. Thereafter, they'd ignored her, for she gave them little amusement.

Presently Pheresa was installed in a tiny chamber hardly large enough to hold her encasement and the guardians. Sometimes her room was heated; sometimes it was not. More guardians had collapsed, until now she had only six to hold the spell together. Gavril could not believe Pheresa remained alive. Her survival had seemed tenuous enough when there'd been thirteen guardians, let alone less than half that number.

Now, as he hurried into her tiny, poorly lit chamber, he hoped that she was finally dying. She'd suffered long enough, and the Netherans weren't going to help her. Why should she not at last have the relief of death?

At first, Gavril had considered it both noble and tragic to have his betrothed stricken this way. The spells, the encasement, and the trappings necessary to preserve her life had lent the situation a certain dignity, as had the dangerous quest to save her. She remained beautiful, and her helpless vulnerability rendered her appealing to him. During their journey, Gavril had felt proud of himself for taking such good care of her. In return, she'd shown him gratitude, and he'd felt sure that once she was cured, she would become a dutiful, compliant wife.

But the quest had ended in failure, and Pheresa wasn't going to be saved. Instead, she was dying slowly and terribly. He gazed at her now where she lay within a dim circle of candlelight. She wore a dingy white gown of cheap cloth, plain of embellishment and so poorly constructed that one of the sleeves was noticeably shorter than the other. Her thick reddish-gold hair lay matted to her skull like dull straw, and her eyes were deeply sunk into their sockets.

A dark cloud settled over his spirits, and he bowed his head, feeling a tangle of resentment, self-pity, and deep unhappiness. It was one thing to undertake a difficult endeavor with shining confidence and every hope of success; it was quite another to stand among the ruins of failure and despair.

The shining glass encasement had grown dusty and scratched. There was something tawdry about it all—the plainness of the dying girl, her cheap gown, the stink of a sickroom, the desperate exhaustion so obvious in the few remaining guardians kneeling around her.

Feeling repulsed, Gavril lifted his head and took a step back from her. For this, he had risked his life. For this, he now was kept prisoner in this vile place. He turned to leave, but at that moment Pheresa opened dull, unfocused eyes.

Gavril could barely stand to look at her pale face and wasting form. In that moment he despised her for what she'd become as much as for what she'd brought him to.

"Gavril." Her voice was the merest whisper, and she struggled to smile. "Sweet prince, you are still with me."

Still chained to you, he thought, and averted his face without reply.

"Don't weep for me," she said. "My dearest prince, how good you are. I didn't think you loved me at first. Now I know that you care deeply. You've done so much for me. Thank you, my love."

Overwhelmed with revulsion and embarrassment, Gavril felt as though he'd been swept by fire. Her words made her even more pathetic, and he was filled with the urge to turn on her viciously, to say how he hated her, how she'd put him in the gravest danger, how he wished he'd never known her. He felt like shattering the encasement and stabbing her through the heart. Even then, he decided contemptuously, she would probably think him a hero for releasing her from this misery.

Somehow, he restrained his wild urges and even forced himself to meet her gaze. "Pheresa," he said unsteadily, and stopped. He could think of nothing to say.

"Don't blame yourself," she whispered. Her brown eyes gazed up at him with tenderness. "You tried your very best. I love you for that. My last prayers will be for you."

As her voice drifted off, her eyes fell closed. Choking, Gavril retreated from her while Megala hurried forward to tend her mistress.

"Is she . . . dead?" he asked hoarsely, gripping his sword hilt while Tanengard chanted *Death, death, death, death* in his mind.

"Nay, your highness," Megala replied. "The sweet lady sleeps again. But her fever burns strong today. The physicians have not come to her recently. Where are they? Can nothing be done to ease her suffering?"

Gavril envisioned endless months imprisoned here, trapped by the guards, trapped by the terrible cold and snow outside, trapped by this maiden who would not die. His brain felt as though ants were crawling inside it. He wanted to scream, and then to laugh. Above all, he wanted to draw Tanengard and behead each of the remaining guardians. Then Pheresa would die. And then . . . he would still be a prisoner.

"Your highness?"

Gavril shot Megala a wild look, then whirled around and fled the room. He collared the first servant he encountered. "Your master. I want him at once!"

The servant looked bewildered. "Count wants you," he replied in his thick Netheran accent. "I come to bring you."

A little surprised, for he hadn't spoken to the count in days, Gavril followed the servant to the sumptuous chamber where he'd first met Mradvior. It seemed to be the count's favorite room. When Gavril arrived, the count was sitting near the warm tiled stove, sipping spiced wine from a jewel-encrusted cup and munching on toasted nuts.

He grinned at Gavril and raised his cup in greeting. "Your highness!" he said merrily. "I have a surprise for you. Tonight begins the festival of lights. It is a great favorite here in Grov. I shall take you in a sleigh down to the river if you give your word not to—"

"I want to see the king," Gavril said angrily.

"Yes, yes, it takes time. But the festival is really—"

"A plague on your festival! I want to see the king! I *demand* to see him."

Tossing more nuts in his mouth, Mradvior shrugged. "Why? Your royal father will pay your ransom. Be patient, and enjoy yourself. Enjoy Netheran hospitality."

"No, thank you," Gavril snapped. "I have asked repeatedly for audience with King Muncel. What is necessary to achieve it? Bribes? Promises of—"

"No, no, no." Mradvior grew serious. "You are fine prince, fine young man. I like you. And so I will give you advice. Is good the king has not sent for you." He pointed at Gavril. "You do not ever tell him I say this to you, eh?"

Gavril shrugged. "I want to see him. *Now,* with no more delay."

"Why?"

Gavril's anger swelled inside him. "That is no concern of yours."

"If you have question, or request, ask me. I will find out answer."

"No," Gavril said through his teeth. "I want to speak to the king myself."

"Is not good for you to do this," Mradvior insisted.

"Morde a day!" Gavril screamed, losing his temper completely. He drew Tanengard and used it to smash a small table to pieces.

Mradvior jumped to his feet, dropping his fancy cup and scattering the toasted nuts over the floor. His protector came running, but Gavril turned aside from the count and started pacing back and forth. "I want to see the king!" he shouted, still brandishing his sword. "Make it so, Lord Mradvior, and do it *now!*"

"As you command," Mradvior said warily. "So will I inquire."

"Insist, damn you! Don't inquire!"

Bowing repeatedly, Mradvior backed away from him and beckoned to two of his guards. "Watch his highness," he said in a low voice. "Do not let him destroy more furniture."

Overhearing, Gavril snorted to himself with bleak amusement and kept pacing back and forth. It pleased him to hold Tanengard in his hands, pleased him to swing it about and attack imaginary foes.

After a long while, one of Mradvior's minions came for him, followed by a servant carrying Gavril's cloak and gloves. Smiling, Gavril put them on and followed the man outside.

Snow was falling, and the air felt damp and bitterly cold. Shivering beneath his heavy cloak, Gavril climbed into the horse-drawn sleigh next to Mradvior and allowed servants to spread a heavy robe of beyar fur across his lap. Mounted guards, snow collecting in the folds of their fur hats, surrounded the sleigh.

An order was given, and the sleigh went racing toward the tall gates, which swung open at their approach. The gliding smoothness of the sleigh amazed Gavril. It was far more comfortable than a wagon.

The mounted guards stayed close, pressing on all sides, so that it was impossible to see anything of the streets or the city.

Mradvior's dark mustache turned white with snow. He sat tensely, looking neither right nor left. A large basin of salt was balanced on his lap, and in his hand he clutched a long dagger. He seemed unwilling to talk to Gavril.

The prince wondered what Mradvior was afraid of, yet the count seemed unwilling to talk. At last they passed through a set of tall gates and wound through a wood up a short hill to a castle fortress. An entire army seemed to be camped on the grounds. Gantese marched by, and in the distance Gavril heard an animal bugle loudly.

He jumped, his heart thudding in his chest. "A shapeshifter?" he gasped out.

"Darsteed," Mradvior told him without expression. "Foul creatures."

In its scabbard, Tanengard glowed white. Gripping the hilt for courage, Gavril saw a black, scaly monster that looked like a dog—but that was much larger, and horrible—go padding around the corner of a tent. His mouth went dry, and his grip tightened.

"That—that beast," he said breathlessly.

"Hmm? I didn't see it."

" 'Twas vile," Gavril said. "Like a—" He stopped, unable to go on.

Mradvior stared at him. "Haven't you seen Nonkind before?"

"Of course I have! I—" Gavril thought of the shapeshifter, a horrifying, shrieking, winged creature that had clawed him with its talons. He still bore deep scars on his legs, still remembered his terror, still recalled how his gold Circle had not deflected the monster's attack.

Suddenly the bowl of salt that Mradvior held made perfect sense. Staring at it, Gavril swallowed hard.

"Have you any salt in your pockets?" Mradvior asked him, proffering the bowl. "Take some."

Gavril frowned, affronted as always by the man's familiarity, and turned his head away. "No, thank you."

"Take some. Is best to be prepared."

"Nothing would *dare* attack me," Gavril said, and heard the hollow bravado in his voice. "Certainly not in the presence of your king."

"If you want to think so. But is never good, to be in presence of king."

Gavril ignored him.

The sleigh crossed a moat and drawbridge into what seemed more like a cave than a fortress. They passed through a long, rough-hewn tunnel, the runners scraping noisily over paving stones, before they eventually emerged in a cramped courtyard surrounded by towering walls.

Here, the sleigh stopped. Gavril and Mradvior climbed out. The guards dismounted and flanked them on either side as they walked up a set of massive stone steps to enter the fortress through a set of tall, thick doors studded with nails.

Contrary to Gavril's expectations, there was no heat inside. Nor was there much light. He found himself squinting against a pervasive gloom, for only now and then could there be found a burning torch in a wall sconce. The walls were black with grime and smoke, the floors filthy with matted rushes, worn and rat-chewed carpets, bits of bone, and trash. Servants and officials lurked in corners and behind stone pillars, breaking off conversations as Gavril and Mradvior passed.

They climbed a flight of steps into a gallery of long chambers, where one opened directly into another. Again, there were no windows, only a few arrow slits cut high up into the walls. Snow drifted through these openings, and icy drafts whipped through the rooms.

Fur- and velvet-clad courtiers huddled in small clusters. Some were dicing or playing assorted games next to charcoal braziers. Others plinked mournful tunes on lutes and zithrens. And a few talked and drank, passing dishes of little morsels from one to another.

They stared at Gavril openly, making no attempt to mask their curiosity. He walked with his chin held high, annoyed by having to come here under close guard, without his entourage, his heralds, his banners, or the usual fanfare. He was mortified by such treatment, yet with his gloves held elegantly in one hand and the other resting on his sword hilt, he swaggered along like the prince he was, staring back at the curious with all the hauteur he possessed.

He wore a fur-lined doublet of pale blue velvet today, tied with lacings of silver. His snowy, immaculate linen showed at the throat. His leggings and boots were made of supple leather, and his sword belt was chased with silver. His bracelet of royalty glinted gold on his wrist, and his dark blue eyes glowed with defiance and contempt for this ragged, ill-mannered court.

They came at last to a closed door, guarded by knights who held pikes across it. An official shivering in a woolen cloak lurked there.

Mradvior spoke very softly to him, and the official shot Gavril a wide-eyed look before slipping past the guards into the chamber.

"The king waits in yon room?" Gavril asked.

Mradvior bowed and nodded. He seemed nervous.

Gavril turned around and began to pace back and forth. "I will not be kept waiting like this. Let whomever his majesty is receiving be sent out, that I may enter."

As though someone had overheard him, the guards stepped aside and the door swung open. Young pages—pallid, scrawny boys with frightened eyes—hurried out, crying, "Make way! Make way!"

Mradvior drew a sharp breath and jumped aside. As he did so he gripped Gavril's sleeve to pull him out of the way.

"Unhand me!" Gavril said. "How dare you!"

The count shot him a look of warning. "Be quiet, be quiet," he whispered, glancing past Gavril and bowing low. "Call no attention to yourself."

Puzzled, Gavril swung back just as a litter of carved and gilded wood was carried out by eight sweating bearers. Cushioned with scarlet, purple, and gold silk and adorned with long tassels that swung and bobbed, the litter contained a creature such as Gavril could not even have imagined. It might have been a man . . . once. But its skin was charred to a black, leathery texture from the top of its knobby, hairless skull all the way to the elongated, bare feet protruding from the hem of its silk robes. Its hands were strangely shaped, very narrow with fingers of unusual length. Each digit ended in a long, black talon that looked needle-sharp. A stink of sulfur and brimstone hung about this apparition. Draped on its neck was a collar studded with enormous rubies that glowed blood red.

Gavril's jaw dropped and, ignoring Mradvior's surreptitious tug at the hem of his doublet, he stared openly. The creature lifted its gaze to his and stared back. It had a man's eyes, distinctly human no matter what the rest of him looked like.

No word was spoken between them. Gavril barely drew breath. He could make no sound. Inside, his heart was hammering as though he'd run a long distance.

Certain he was gazing on the god of darkness itself, Gavril fumbled inside his doublet for his gold Circle and clutched it hard.

The creature went on its way, and Gavril saw three other vile things emerge from the chamber in its wake. Huge and moon-faced, they stank of carrion. As they shambled past him, Gavril felt a nameless unease coil about his entrails.

As soon as they were gone, he struggled to draw a deep breath. He felt light-headed and strange. He wished he'd never come to this Thodforsaken place.

"What—what—"

He could not seem to force the words past his lips.

"Those were *magemons*," Mradvior said. "Taken away, it looks to be. The king will be angry."

"What are *magemons*?"

"Gantese magicians. Very powerful. Yes, yes, makers of very powerful magic. Very dangerous. *Sorcerels* work alone, but *magemons* cast their spells in teams. Very strong." Mradvior frowned. "Is against Writ to have them here. The king dares much."

Feeling as though he'd been struck, Gavril stared at the count and found nothing to say.

Mradvior scuttled away, beckoning to the official, who had now reappeared. The two put their heads together and consulted in whispers.

Gavril turned and stared down the gallery at the departing *magemons* and the burned creature. Forbidden, blasphemous purveyors of magic . . . everything that was wrong and unholy. To even see such as they was to be defiled. And Muncel openly consorted with such unspeakable evil. It was amazing, Gavril thought in shock, that Thod had not struck the king down for the evil he did.

"Best to go," Mradvior said, returning. "Best to come another day."

"Certainly not," Gavril said with a huff. "I will not be brushed off like a mere courtier. How dare you suggest it."

"Is better to be gone when king is angry, your highness," Mradvior said.

Disdaining the man's cowardice, Gavril stepped past the count. "Announce me," he said to the official hovering at the doorway.

The man only stared at him with bulging eyes.

From inside the king's chamber came a howl of temper, followed by a shattering crash.

Blanching, the official retreated.

"Come away, your highness," Mradvior called softly. "Is not a good time."

Ignoring him, Gavril walked unannounced into the king's chamber, where he saw a cluster of wary-eyed courtiers on one side of a large, sparsely furnished room. Pacing back and forth before a heavily carved throne was a black-haired man garbed in a long velvet tunic trimmed with ermine at cuffs and hem. A half-grown lyng, wearing a studded collar and tethered by a chain, lay near the throne, idly switching its tail and watching the proceedings through slitted, feral eyes. Servants were crouched on their knees, foreheads touching the floor. An over-turned table lay in the midst of broken glass. Wine spread in a large puddle from the mess.

Those who noticed Gavril's entrance ignored him. The king—busy pacing and gesticulating—paid Gavril no heed either.

"This meddling goes too far, Tulvak Sahm," he said furi-ously to a tall, foreign-looking man clad in long robes and a peaked hat. "I will not submit to it!"

"Your majesty has no choice . . . at present," the man replied in a quiet, singsong voice.

Although they were speaking in Netheran, Gavril understood what they were saying. Since childhood, he'd been thoroughly versed in the languages of all Mandria's allies. That did not mean, however, that he would deign to speak anything but his own language.

Short of shouting to bring attention to himself, there was nothing to do but wait. Gavril glanced around. As an audience chamber, this room was half the size of Savroix's. Paneled with wood painted in gaudy colors and lit with torches, it held no fine art at all. A tiled stove checkered in colors of bright blue and red radiated the first heat Gavril had felt since entering this appalling fortress. An enormous mobile of king's glass, cut into rectangular prisms, quivered and danced in the air, singing softly as it refracted light.

"A plague on Gant!" the king shouted. "A plague on the Chief Believer and the minion he has sent to interfere with me! I will not stand for such interference."

"Majesty has no—"

"Bah! I had the pretender in my grasp," the king said, clench-ing his fist. "All I had to do was squeeze the life from him, Tulvak Sahm. But now he is to be saved."

"Not saved, majesty. Delivered unto the Chief Believer and sacrificed to Ashnod. Surely that is a fate dire enough for any—"

"The rabble will make a martyr of him," Muncel said. "It will cause more unrest."

"But the pretender will still be dead," Tulvak Sahm murmured.

Gavril's wandering attention suddenly focused on what they were saying. The "pretender" they referred to could only be Dain, pagan fiend that he was.

"So your majesty's men have captured the upstart," Gavril said loudly, daring to interrupt the king's conversation despite Mradvior's hiss of warning. He walked forward, clapping his hands together. "Well done."

A knight clad in a mail hauberk and fur-trimmed surcoat stepped into Gavril's path. "Halt!"

Gavril struck a disdainful pose, but obeyed. Angered to be treated like some oaf, he told himself these Netherans clearly had no understanding of the proper deference due a prince of royal blood.

"Again, your majesty, I say well done," he called out in Mandrian. "'Twas my intention to bring Faldain to you in chains as a gift, but, alas, he escaped my men through vile trickery."

Muncel stared at Gavril in astonishment. Far from a handsome man, at this close range the king looked even less well-favored. Lines of dissipation were grooved around his eyes and mouth, and his mouth was pinched together. His deep-set brown eyes held chronic dissatisfaction. Gray streaked his black hair and beard, making him look older than he probably was. Stooped and perhaps shortsighted, he lacked the aura of noble majesty which rested so impressively on Verence's broad shoulders.

"Who is this?" he asked.

Belatedly the official at the door announced, "Your majesty, the Prince of Mandria!"

Gavril stood proudly with his head held high, pleased to be the center of attention at last. "I am Prince Gavril of Mandria," he said, giving the correct form of his title. "Heir to the Realm."

Pointing at him, Muncel laughed. "So, Mradvior! You have brought the little cock to me, eh? How he does crow and strut."

Some of the courtiers present joined in the king's derisive laughter.

Heat flooded Gavril's face and burned the tips of his ears,

but calling on all his willpower, he managed to keep his temper. "I thank your majesty for granting me this audience."

Muncel's laughter died. He swung around to the tall, odd-looking man standing beside him. "Eh?" he said sharply. "What does he say?"

The man translated.

"I have been a guest in your majesty's fair city for many days now," Gavril continued, pausing occasionally to allow translation. "It is time your majesty and I had a discussion. I want—"

"Has the ransom come?" Muncel broke in.

"Nay, your majesty," replied a courtier with a deep bow. "King Verence has sent no reply to your majesty's demands."

Muncel leaned forward, peering at the man who spoke. "Nothing?"

"Not a single word."

Muncel's face turned purple. He swung around and glared at Gavril. "That southern dog! I hold his son and heir, and *still* he defies me. Gant meddles. Mandria ignores me. What is next? War?"

"If your majesty will hear me," Gavril said impatiently. "I—"

Muncel gestured angrily. "Get rid of him."

When the protector shoved Gavril back, the prince's temper snapped and he drew Tanengard. "How dare you touch me!" he shouted.

Even as the courtiers called out in alarm, the protector drew his weapon and attacked. Gavril parried, expecting his magicked sword to easily vanquish this opponent. But everything seemed to go wrong at once. The protector had the strength of three men. He overpowered Gavril and knocked Tanengard from his hands in the first exchange of blows.

Before he knew what was happening, Gavril found himself flat on the floor with the protector's sword at his throat.

Dazed by how fast it had happened, Gavril dared not move. His heart was pounding, and to his shame he was afraid that he would die here and now.

"Desist!" Tulvak Sahm called out. "Majesty, he should not be harmed . . . at least not until his ransom is paid."

"It will be paid!" Gavril said through his teeth. "And to the last dreit. That, I swear!"

"What?" Muncel asked Tulvak Sahm. "He says it will be paid?"

"Yes, majesty. He swears it."

Stooping, Muncel peered down at Gavril. His eyes were like stone. They held no humanity, compassion, or mercy. Gavril reflected that the burned creature who'd ridden out of here on that fancy litter had eyes more human than Muncel's. *Here,* he thought with a shudder, *is true evil.*

Tulvak Sahm picked up Tanengard and examined the weapon with interest. "A magicked blade, majesty," he said, sounding amused. "Poorly made. Shall I let your majesty hear its song?"

"No," Gavril whispered, agonized with jealousy. No one was supposed to hear Tanengard except himself. It was his and his alone.

"There are spells and lures woven through the metal," Tulvak Sahm said, letting his fingertips brush the blade lightly. "Look at him, majesty. He's caught fast like a moth in a spider's web. See how much he hates it that I hold his sword?"

Muncel barely glanced at Tanengard. "The workmanship is terrible. Break it."

"No!" Gavril cried out before he could stop himself. With his last remnants of pride, he barely kept himself from pleading.

"And do I release him from its spell first?" Tulvak Sahm asked, tilting his head to one side. His strange, slanted eyes regarded Gavril coldly. "He will go mad if he is not released before it is destroyed."

Muncel walked over to his throne and sat down. He looked petulant and bored. "I care not."

"It is best, majesty, to keep him in good health until he is ransomed. Verence may demand verification of his well-being before he pays."

"Verence is a lying dog!" Muncel said harshly. "And full of trickery. Clearly he cares nothing for this boy. He must have other sons."

"He does not!" Gavril declared hotly.

The Netherans exchanged speculative glances, and Gavril realized it would have been wiser to keep quiet. Swallowing hard, he burned with humiliation.

"Is this how you treat your equals?" he asked, feeling he had nothing left to lose. "This discourtesy, these constant insults . . . they ill-become a monarch. But then, you are only a king by theft and treachery."

Muncel jumped to his feet. "Get him out! Get him out!"

The protector grabbed Gavril by the front of his doublet and shoved him from the chamber with such force that he fell sprawling on the floor. Gavril heard the door slam shut behind him, cutting off the babble and noise inside.

Seething, he picked himself up slowly, glad he'd delivered some insults of his own. Really, Muncel was nothing but an arrogant monster, a ruffian, a usurper, nothing more.

Mradvior hurried to help Gavril up. "Come, come," he said in haste. "We go. We must hurry."

"You are not to touch me!" Gavril roared at him.

But Mradvior gripped his sleeve anyway. "We go now. You have made the king more angry than before. Is not good to stay here."

Planting his feet, Gavril wrenched his arm free. "I'll go nowhere without my sword!" he shouted. "They are not to break it. Not to dishonor me like this. They have no right to—"

"You fool! Forget the sword. We must go before the king orders you killed on the spot, and me with you."

Still protesting, Gavril was whisked from the moldering fortress and packed into the sleigh. Climbing in beside him, Mradvior shouted orders at the driver, and back they went through the city. Dusk was falling now.

Howling for alms, beggars ran beside them in the streets. Mradvior ignored them and the guards kept the beggars away from the sleigh. Gavril huddled under the furs and paid no attention. All he could think about was Tanengard and how Muncel's minion had stolen it from him. He wanted it back most desperately.

In the distance, from down some dark alley came a howling cry that belonged to nothing of this world. Mradvior grimly clutched his dagger and bowl of salt.

"I should not have brought you here," he said over and over.

"I should not. I was fool to bring you to the king. But you are bigger fool to insult him. Thod! The king's temper is terrible thing. And now . . . now perhaps I am ruined."

"Why do you snivel so?" Gavril asked indifferently. His hands stroked Tanengard's empty scabbard. "Why are you not quiet?"

Mradvior drew in a sharp breath. "Do you realize nothing? In morning I could face orders for execution. My house, my family all could be destroyed. Like that." He snapped his fingers. "All because you insult the king."

"Your fate has nothing to do with me," Gavril said with a shrug.

Visibly fuming, Mradvior sat rigidly on the seat beside Gavril, silent all the way back to the gates of his house.

The guards pushed away the rabble that crowded up next to the sleigh as it slipped through the gates. When pikesmen attacked the crowd, the guards galloped inside, urging the sleigh before them. The gates shut with a clang, while the people shouted pleas for food, for money, for mercy . . . unheeded completely by both Gavril and Mradvior.

Gavril found the heat inside the house a blessing. Until then, he had not realized how thoroughly chilled he was. Pulling off his cloak, he glanced around, but Mradvior was already hurrying away into another part of the house, leaving him behind with the servants.

Gavril shrugged. King Muncel was an ill-tempered lout, and Mradvior was a whining fool. It had been a wasted afternoon, and now he'd lost Tanengard.

As Gavril was ordering his supper, a loud series of knocks sounded on the front portal. A few minutes later, Mradvior hurried past to meet the messenger.

Shortly thereafter the count approached Gavril, with a small squadron of guards following at his heels. Pointing at the stairs, Mradvior issued orders in rapid-fire Netheran. The guards trotted off in that direction as the count turned to Gavril.

"Now it begins," he said heavily. "Orders have come from his majesty. You leave my house tonight. You and the lady."

"We are released?" Gavril asked in delight. "Aha! I knew if I could but see his majesty that—"

"Do not mock this, your highness. Of course you are not released."

Gavril's sense of relief crashed to his feet. In its place came alarm, which he tried to mask with a sneer. "I see. Holding us prisoner is unconscionable. We should be set free."

"You are to be moved to old Palace of Runtha and kept there until you are ransomed."

Gavril frowned, thinking of the fortress he'd visited today. "The king's own— "

"Nay, Palace of Runtha. The old place of kings. From before . . . before everything changed. It is a ruin, but not all of it has been torn down. You will live there, with your guards. The lady too."

"She's too ill to be moved," Gavril protested.

"Your highness should have thought of her before you insulted the king."

"He insulted me first!" Gavril said defensively, then stopped himself, for clearly he wasn't going to prevail.

From outside the room he heard the marching cadence of bootsteps. Someone rapped loudly on the panels, and the door swung open to reveal the contingent of guards, cloaked and heavily armed, returning from upstairs.

They shepherded Noncire and four of the guardians inside. One of the latter swooned as soon as he crossed the threshold. A burly knight bent and gave him a vigorous shake, only to straighten and look at Mradvior with a shrug.

"*Vant othyaska,*" he said.

"Another one dead?" Mradvior said with a lift of his heavy brows. "Throw him over wall. The poor will be glad of some meat."

Unprepared for this sudden evidence of brutality in the count, Gavril blinked in shock.

While one of the guards bent to pick up the dead man, Noncire hurried across the room to Gavril's side. The cardinal looked pale and strained.

"Gavril. Your highness," he said in quiet urgency. "Please intervene on our behalf."

Mradvior's laugh rang out loudly. "Look at his eminence

quiver!" he called. "What's amiss, lord cardinal? Does your faith not sustain you now?"

"Your highness must intercede," Noncire said. His small dark eyes were as round as possible within their folds of fat. Perspiration soaked the collar of his robes. "For the love of Thod, your highness, have mercy and do not let them take us to Gant."

Gavril stared at him impatiently. "I think your wits have gone. No one is going to Gant. Who told you such a thing?"

"Please, they—"

Gavril shifted his gaze away from Noncire's gibbering and pointed imperiously at the guardians. "Why are they brought here, Lord Mradvior? It's critical that they be left alone."

"Is excessive to have this many guardians," Mradvior said. "As the lady dies, is less and less need for her to be sustained by so many."

"That is not for you to decide. Send them back to their place," Gavril commanded.

Mradvior's dark gaze did not waver; nor did he obey the order.

"I said—"

"Your highness spoke clearly," Mradvior broke in. "These men, the foreigner especially," he said, pointing at Sulein, who looked at Gavril in silent appeal, "are superfluous. So says the king's orders."

"I don't believe you. There are no such orders."

Quiet fell over the room. Mradvior scowled. "Take care, young prince, that you do not insult me again. You are not among friends."

Gavril narrowed his eyes. A fire was burning in his temples, stabbing sharp little jabs into his brain.

"Your dogs are destined for the cook pots," Mradvior announced. "Your knights and servants can be sold into bondage at good prices."

"You do not dare!" Gavril said furiously. "By the laws of—"

"Laws?" Mradvior broke in with a laugh. "They are for the weak and feeble-minded."

"You're a thief, Mradvior!" Gavril said. "A thief and a barbarian!"

Pursing his lips, the count turned away.

Noncire's gaze flicked desperately to Gavril. "Placate him," he murmured. "Use honey, not a wasp sting. Win back his friendship."

"Be silent," Gavril snapped, but despite his annoyance he tried to take Noncire's advice. "Lord Mradvior, reconsider. I have money. I shall pay you well to keep the guardians in place."

"And me, your highness," Noncire murmured beneath his breath. "Will you pay him to keep me here as well?"

But Mradvior was laughing with both contempt and mockery. "Your highness forgets something important."

"What is that?" Gavril asked haughtily.

"Your money and fine possessions have already been confiscated. Besides, even *you* did not bring enough gold to pay bribes for all your knights and servants."

"I—" Gavril left his sentence unspoken. He could not believe Mradvior intended to send the church knights to Gant as well. Once they were taken away, would he have anyone left with him except a dying girl? Fear washed over him, rendering him mute.

At Mradvior's gesture, two guards gripped Noncire by his fat arms. He struggled against them.

"No!" he shouted. "No! Lord Mradvior, I have a private fortune. It can be yours if you will spare me."

"Gladly would I take your gold," Mradvior replied, "but I do not disobey the king."

"But an arrangement can be made," Noncire said, making a grotesque attempt to smile. "Surely we can reach—"

With Noncire struggling all the way, the guards forced him to the door. "Please!" he called out, throwing aside all dignity to beg. "Prince Gavril, have pity and help me. Don't let them send me to Gant to die."

"Surely your faith will sustain you," Gavril replied.

The cardinal stared at him in disbelief. "What have you become?" he asked.

The guards pushed him from the room. The door slammed, and he was gone.

"My lord count," Gavril said with a sigh, "let us come to fresh terms. I feel we should discuss—"

"Discussion is over." Mradvior paused next to a table to caress a small box of exquisite wood sitting on top of it. "Your belongings should be packed by now."

"I refuse to go," Gavril said, tossing his head. "I refuse to live in a ruin. Your house—"

"Is no longer at your disposal," Mradvior said coldly. "You go quietly or you go by force. The lady has already been loaded on a wagon. Will you ride with her?"

Before he could stop himself, Gavril began laughing. Mradvior looked at him strangely, but Gavril could not stop the laughter as he put on his cloak and gloves.

"And my sword?" he asked when he'd finally regained his breath. "Let it be returned to me."

Mradvior eyed him with something close to pity. "You plead for it, but not for the life of your cardinal or your men. Truly you are caught in its spell."

"I—I need it." Gavril swallowed the last dregs of his pride. "Please, lord count. I can bear to lose anything but Tanengard."

"I think you mean what you say," Mradvior said in wonder.

"Of course I mean it! I must have it with me! Please!"

Mradvior sighed. "I will ask. If Nonkind break into the old palace, you will need defense against them."

"Nonkind!" Gavril said uneasily. "You mean—"

"Is not a good place," Mradvior told him. "Is nothing good left in palace of our former kings. Nothing good at all."

The guards escorted Gavril outside into the snowy darkness, where a cold wind bit deep into his bones and made him shiver. He climbed into the wagon beside Pheresa's encasement. Out near the wall, he could see shadowy figures lined up, and as the wagon lurched past he realized they were his church soldiers, shackled together and about to be marched away to their terrible fate.

"What is to become of us," Megala moaned, weeping into her hands as she crouched in the wagon.

Gavril saw the tall gates swing open, and he felt as though the dark city beyond waited to engulf him. Forcing himself to sit up straight, he smiled and proudly saluted farewell to his men as he was carted away. For surely it was better for a knight and prince to laugh aloud at his enemies than to cower in fear.

Yet his men did not cheer him as he left them. They did not cheer him at all.

14

NIGHT FELL OVER the forest; the wind gusted, bringing sleet and misery; and still the Believers and their prisoners rode at a steady trot. Alexeika was so cold she would have wept, had she any tears left inside her. The dead men—Faldain's companions and the slain fire-knights alike—had been abandoned by Quar to lie where they'd fallen, unshriven and unburied.

Now it was late and the sleet was stinging her face. With her hands bound behind her, she couldn't pull up her hood for protection. Aching with exhaustion, she worried about Faldain, who was still draped unconscious across the back of his horse. His squire Thum swayed in the saddle and made small, involuntary grunts of pain whenever his horse jolted him too much. Alexeika worried that if he could not continue to ride, the fire-knights would probably kill him.

Fear kept gripping her entrails. She did not want to be taken to Gant and sacrificed to Ashnod. All her life she'd heard stories of Gant, of how dreadful it was, of how the taint of evil poisoned the land.

She glanced at Faldain in the darkness, willing him to wake up. There had to be a way to escape these fire-knights. If they ever stopped and camped, she vowed, she'd find a way.

They did not stop. Instead, they rode all night and into the early light of dawn. By then Alexeika was reeling in the saddle. Her eyes were gritty and so heavy she could barely hold them open. When they finally stopped, and she was pulled off her horse, she lay on the cold ground where they tossed her and slept until she was kicked awake.

The sun was shining midday-bright. She sat up awkwardly, her arms aching from being bound so long. Faldain, she was relieved to see, had also awakened. He sat blinking in the sunshine, with a bleak expression of loss and desolation on his face.

Alexeika wanted to offer him comfort, but what could she say? He'd lost his protector, and she knew how deep such a loss could wound. During her childhood, her father's protector had been like a faithful shadow at his heels, watchful and vigilant, until he'd fallen in battle and left Prince Volvn bereft. Another man had of course taken Sir Blenin's place, but Alexeika understood that for her father it had never been the same.

One of their captors walked over and kicked their feet. "Get up," he growled. "We ride."

Realizing they weren't going to be fed, Alexeika fell over and rolled facedown, scooping as much snow into her mouth as she could before she was yanked upright and shoved toward a horse.

The snow tasted old and bitter. It was so cold it numbed her tongue, but she swallowed it in an effort to ease her parched thirst, and longed for more. Her stomach growled loudly, but she knew she could last better without food than she could water.

"Quar!" Faldain said, twisting in his captors' hold when they tried to lift him onto his horse. "Quar!"

The leader turned his head and stared at Faldain through his visor. Alexeika had observed that Quar seemed to respect the young king a little, possibly as a fellow warrior, but they could not count on this for much. She hoped Faldain understood that.

"You must feed us," Faldain said. "We are not like you. We need food and water if we're to keep going."

Quar looked away. "You will last."

"Then at least bind our hands in front. That way, we can—"

"Escape?" Quar broke in harshly. "No."

He signaled, and the other Believers hoisted Faldain into the saddle, then came and tossed Alexeika into hers. As they put

Thum astride his horse, Alexeika noticed that his leg was bleeding again.

"Sire," she said quietly. "Your squire's wound needs tending."

Faldain frowned at Thum. "How bad is it? Have you fever?"

The red-haired squire shook his head valiantly. "Nay, I'll do."

"He's bleeding," Alexeika said.

"Not much," Thum protested.

The Believers kicked their horses into that jolting trot that made Alexeika's spine feel as though it might snap. Gritting her teeth as her sore muscles protested, she jounced along at the mercy of the Believer leading her horse, and ducked a low branch barely in time.

"You must tell me if you feel strange," Faldain said to Thum. "If the hurlhound venom wasn't salted away thoroughly, fever will grip you. Tell me at once if that happens."

Thum's smile was crooked and strained. "And then? Do I become like them?" As he spoke he nodded at their captors' backs.

"Not like them," Faldain said, and stopped with a worried frown to cast a glance of appeal at Alexeika.

"You will not become Nonkind," she said in reassurance, wishing she'd cauterized his wound with Severgard the way she had to Sir Alard's arm. Salt was good, but sometimes it did not work as well as it should. She did not say that, however; Thum looked scared enough already. "But if you keep bleeding, you will weaken."

He nodded, and the two young men began to converse, excluding her. Alexeika's eyes stung, and she told herself not to be so sensitive. After all, she'd been with them only a few days. They barely trusted her. As Faldain had said, they were now comrades, but clearly they were not yet friends.

She tried to content herself by stealing glances at him. She wanted to help him, to make him smile, to see his gray eyes soften toward her. But his heart belonged to another. She wondered what this Lady Pheresa looked like. Was she dark or fair? Did she sing and display the acceptable maidenly accomplishments? Alexeika imagined her wearing a lovely gown, her long tresses combed into soft waves that shone in the candlelight, a piece of exquisite needlework in her white, slender hands. Sighing, Alexeika asked herself why Faldain should look twice at a girl with rough, tanned skin, her hair springing wild from a sloppy braid, who wore masculine clothing and swore like a hire-lance?

Alexeika reminded herself that she had maidenly accomplishments too. She knew how to dance, how to curtsy. She knew court etiquette and ritual. Her needlework was terrible, to be sure, but did that matter? If she could attire herself in a gown and sit posed and quiet for him to see, would he not perhaps look twice at her? If she combed the snarls and tangles from her hair and dressed it in a fashionable way, would he notice?

She used to dream of the day when Faldain would regain his throne, thus restoring peace and prosperity to the kingdom. She would take her place in his court as a princess of high rank. She would wear a gown of silk studded with tiny pearls, and her every movement would shimmer. One glance at her would entrance his gaze, and thus would she capture his heart.

Angrily she now brushed such fantasies aside, telling herself to face reality. Although she'd vowed never to be taken prisoner again by barbarians after her escape from a Grethori tribe, here she was—bound and cold and hungry—riding to Gant to die. Although she'd pledged herself to the cause of helping Nether's rightful king retake his throne, there would be no restoration. Her parents' deaths had been for nothing. Soon Alexeika would die too, ending the line of Volvn forever.

Faldain had been this kingdom's last hope, but it was over.

Dain's head was aching. He rode along, weary from too many hours in the saddle, and tried to think of ways to escape. As long as they were tied up this way, he could think of no solution. Soon, if they were not given food and water, they would become too weak to try anything.

Alexeika, at least, was clever enough to take care of herself. Dain had seen her eating snow just before they set out again. He wished he'd thought of it, for his thirst made him suffer. And Thum was in the worst shape of all. Worried that if Thum weakened more Quar would kill him, Dain chattered in an effort to encourage his friend.

There'd been enough killing. Again and again, the image of Sir Terent's beheading haunted Dain's mind. He wished the memory could be less vivid and terrible, yet his grief kept it sharp and all too clear no matter how many times he forced it away.

Sir Terent would not die unavenged; that, he swore with all the determination in his soul. He kept his eye on the long bundle that held Truthseeker and Severgard. Wrapped in a cloak, the two swords were tied to the back of Quar's saddle. Dain longed to get his hands on his weapon, for the next time he fought Quar, he vowed to himself he would not lose.

When Thum tired of talking and fell into a semi-doze, Dain glanced at Alexeika, who was crying. Her face remained stoic, but tears kept slipping down her dirty cheeks. The remark Dain had intended died in his throat, and he stared at her in consternation. He had not realized she was so afraid. Or perhaps the Believers had hurt her in the battle. Frowning in sudden compassion, Dain started to reassure her, but something about her averted face and the rigid set of her shoulders warned him to leave her be.

Still, it unnerved him to see her so vulnerable. Until now, he'd taken her toughness for granted. She was prickly and fierce, always trying to usurp leadership, voicing her opinions whether anyone wanted them or not. She'd offended Sir Terent by wearing red chain mail and carrying weapons like a knight, when she had not that rank and deserved no such privileges. Even Thum was not allowed to wear mail, and wasn't supposed to fight in battles. Alexeika had ignored all the rules, flaunting her knowledge of strategy and combat when she should have stayed quiet.

Dain frowned, wishing she would not cry. He preferred her to remain tough and boylike. He knew how to deal with her in that guise. But if she became maidenly and soft, then he would feel protective and worry about her safety. He wished he knew what to say to her.

"Alexeika," he said softly.

She glanced up, sniffing and blinking rapidly. He knew that

had her hands been free she would have slapped her tears away. Her face reddened, but she looked at him squarely.

"Yes, sire?"

He kept his voice very low, for he knew not how keen the Believers' ears might be. "Have you marked where your sword is?"

"Aye," she said, just as softly. The look in her eyes grew keen and eager. Dain was glad he'd hit on the very thing to cheer her. "Quar has them."

He nodded. "I need a way to free my hands."

"It won't do. They're alert for trouble. Even if *you* got free, they'd turn on Thum and me."

He'd thought of that. "I want to try something that will free us both, but I don't want to frighten you."

A partial smile quirked her lips. She looked fearless. "Do it."

"I think I can burn off my ropes. If I can burn yours too—"

"Try it now," she said eagerly.

Dain opened his mouth, then sang the first notes of fire.

In the lead, Quar whirled around in his saddle and pointed at Dain. He uttered a single, guttural word, and Dain's throat froze. He could not sing or speak. Try as he might, no sound came forth.

"Sire?" Thum said worriedly, rousing from his doze. "Dain?"

"Hush," Alexeika said angrily. "His majesty has been silenced."

Seething with frustration, Dain glared at Quar, but the fire-knight ignored him.

Within a few minutes, they drew rein short of a stream running swiftly across the road. An ancient, crumbling shrine with unfamiliar symbols stood on its bank. With thirst burning his throat, Dain kicked his feet free of the stirrups, intending to dismount and drink his fill.

"Stay on horse," Quar ordered. He gestured at his men, and they pulled the prisoners' horses closer to their own.

"Please," Alexeika said, her word almost a moan. "Let us drink."

Quar wheeled his mount around to face them. "We go to Gant now. You keep quiet. Say nothing. Do nothing."

Dain and Thum exchanged puzzled looks, but Alexeika turned white. She began to pray rapidly beneath her breath.

Quar pulled a short baton from his belt and held it aloft. As he rode toward the shrine, he uttered words that burned in Dain's mind. The baton suddenly began to glow as though lit from within by fire. There came a rushing sound, like a strong wind, and Dain's horse leaped high. He found himself in midair, then the world around him vanished and he plunged through dense gray mist.

It obscured everything, even the ground and sky. His companions vanished from sight. All he could see was his horse.

The fog flowed damp and cold against his face. He felt as though he were being smothered in it. He breathed it in, choking with the old lifelong, irrational panic. He hated fog, had always feared it.

And now . . .

With a jolt that snapped his teeth together, Dain felt his horse land on solid ground. He blinked and squinted against brilliant light.

The sun blazed down on them from a brassy sky. While the air had been bitterly cold only minutes before, now it felt hot and dry. Dain found himself roasting in his fur-lined surcoat and heavy cloak. Dazed and disbelieving, he stared at a barren landscape where nothing grew—not one tree, not one blade of grass, not even any scrub. Everywhere he looked, he saw an unchanging vista of reddish sand, rock outcroppings, and stony ridges. And here, nearby, stood a stone shrine nearly identical to the one Dain had just seen by the stream in Nether.

Undoubtedly by some magical means, they had passed through the second world, leaving Nether to arrive here. Dain wondered if such shrines were to be found in upper Mandria and Nold as well. Perhaps they were gateways that allowed the Gantese to come and go as they pleased. It would explain how they were able to bypass the Charva, which was supposed to keep them in Gant.

Their captors, having ridden for hours without any evidence of tiring, suddenly seemed exhausted. The man holding Dain's and Alexeika's reins dropped them and nearly fell from his saddle. Puzzled, but determined to seize any advantage he could, Dain kicked his horse hard, but the animal stood with its head down, breathing hard, and did not respond.

Had there been anywhere to run to, Dain would have jumped from the saddle, but this parched, barren land daunted him. He could smell the heavy, putrid stench of Nonkind nearby, but although he stared hard in every direction, he saw nothing except black shapes flying lazily in the sky. Quar, sagging in his saddle, glanced up warily. That alone made Dain decide not to run away, weaponless and bound, an easy target for whatever kept circling overhead.

He watched Quar carefully fit the baton back in his belt, then open a saddle pouch and toss small packets of waxed linen to his men. All three Believers devoured the contents, which looked hard, crumbly, and unappetizing. Still, Dain's stomach rumbled. His mouth was so dry and parched it hurt to swallow. When he glanced at Thum and Alexeika, he saw that both of them were transfixed, unable to do anything except stare at the food.

After the Believers gulped down the morsels, which seemed to restore their strength immediately, one man dismounted and fed bits of the substance to each of the horses. Their heads snapped up and their ears pricked forward as they, too, regained their energy.

"Please," Thum said hoarsely. "May we not eat?"

The dismounted fire-knight glanced at Quar, then held out a piece to Thum, who bent over awkwardly in the saddle to take it. Just as he opened his mouth, however, his face wrinkled in revulsion. Before he could draw back, the Believer laughed and crammed it in his mouth. Making a terrible face, Thum choked and spat it out.

Cursing him in Gantese, the Believer dragged him off his horse and shoved him sprawling to the ground. While the other fire-knights laughed, the Believer kicked and swore at Thum, who tried unsuccessfully to crawl away from him.

"Stop it!" Dain shouted, suddenly regaining his voice. "Leave him alone!"

Ignoring him, the Believer went on kicking Thum until he

lay gasping and shuddering on his side with his knees drawn up.

"Get on horse," the Believer said harshly.

Thum moaned and lay there.

"Thum!" Dain said urgently, afraid they would leave him behind. "Get up! Do as you're told. Thum!"

"Leave him," Quar said.

"No!" Horrified, Dain tried to dismount in order to intervene, but Quar spoke and Dain found his feet glued to the stirrups. Try as he might, he could not kick them free. "We can't leave him here. Thum! You must get up. *Thum!*"

His friend struggled, sat up, fell over, sat up again, and finally knelt, swaying. His face was pasty white.

"Get up, please," Dain said. "I need my squire with me. I need you, Thum."

Once more his friend struggled to gain his feet. Quar growled something impatiently and the other Believers walked over to grip Thum's arms and hoist him to his feet. Roughly they put him back on his horse.

Thum sagged in the saddle, barely staying on.

"Steady," Dain said, trying to think of what Sir Polquin would have said. "Remember you're a Thirst man. Show these Gantese dogs what you're made of."

"Aye," Thum said faintly, and slowly pulled himself more erect.

The Believers mounted their horses, then began to trot across the barren landscape. As they started up a long, stony slope, Dain settled himself deeper in the saddle and tried to ignore his growing list of discomforts even while the sweat poured down his face and the red dust clouded over them.

His mind was awash with a flood of sudden memories, for he remembered that he'd made other journeys through the gray mist. Journeys huddled next to Thia, while she had held something white and large in her small hands.

"Do not drop it, Thiatereika," their father had said.

"I won't, my papa," she'd replied.

"The Chalice," Dain now whispered aloud.

Alexeika glanced at him. "What? It's not to be found here. That much is certain."

He paid her no heed, as amazement filled him. "The Chalice," he said again, thinking of the clear white light which had glowed next to him, his sister, and his father, holding back a cold and rainy darkness. His father's sword had glowed with light also, as had a ring which Tobeszijian wore.

Dain drew a sharp breath. "The Ring!" he said.

"Aye, Quar stole your ruby while you were unconscious."

He felt as though he'd awakened from a very long dream. Turning his head, he stared at Alexeika as though he'd never seen her before. "I know where it is," he said.

"I just said that Quar has it."

He didn't hear her, for he was remembering it all. That long, tiring journey on his father's darsteed. The cold darkness, the leaps through mist, his father's fear and worry mingled with courage. Dain remembered trying to sleep in a cave, and how hungry he'd been. He'd wanted his bed and his nurse singing to him by the firelight, but there'd been neither. His father's cloak had smelled of woodsmoke and leather. There had been prayers said over a circle of stones. And the Chalice had shone its white, peaceful light within the cave, warming him so that at last he could sleep.

A shiver passed through him. "I know where it is," he said in wonder. "I've remembered."

"The Chalice of Eternal Life?" Alexeika asked in a voice so low he could barely hear her. Her eyes were huge as she stared at him.

Thum was staring at him too, in awe mixed with open-mouthed astonishment.

Glancing at them both, Dain nodded, then realized this was not the time or the place to talk about the sacred vessel. To his relief, Thum and Alexeika seemed to come to the same unspoken realization, for with uneasy glances at their captors neither of them asked any questions.

Dain found it astonishing that memory should return to him now in this desolate place. Tobeszijian had hidden the Chalice in a cave in Nold. He had hidden it with honor, making a sacred place for it, and perhaps it was there still. Dain understood that the Ring of Solder was a device similar to Quar's baton; somehow its power enabled its wearer to pass through the second world and return. His father had done so in order to escape his enemies and keep the Chalice from harm.

But how to get there now? Dain wondered. He envisioned the Ring of Solder as he'd last seen it, with its distinctive carved runes on the band and its large, milky-white stone. If only he'd been able to get it from Sulein, it might be encircling his finger at this very moment. Then he could have escaped these fire-knights. But, nay. He would not have abandoned his friends just to save himself.

"Look!" Thum cried.

At the crest of a hill, they paused. Before them stretched a desolate plain leading to a jagged mountain range on the far horizon. A city nestled at the base of the mountains, its domes and spires shimmering slightly in the heat. The buildings were the color of dirt and sand.

A road wound its way toward the city, which sprawled, stark and unadorned, across the desert.

"City is Sindeul," Quar told them.

Dain had heard of Sindeul from peddlers at dwarf clan fairs. It was reputed to be a place of the greatest blasphemy and evil, a place where unmentionable things were practiced. No one traveled willingly to Sindeul, the city of death.

"Look yon," Quar said, pointing. "Behold sacred mountain that is mouth of Ashnod."

Dain stared at the tallest peak, which smoked as though it had fire inside. Dread and foreboding settled over him. He sensed that he might be taken there, and he did not want to go.

After a moment, during which none of the prisoners spoke, Quar led them forward across the hot and dusty plain.

The city was farther away than it looked. They rode, baking in the merciless heat, until Dain thought he would perish of thirst and weariness. In the afternoon they came at last to the gates. Shapeshifters flew overhead like huge vultures, and as they drew near to the walls of towering black stone, Dain saw corpses dangling from the crenellations. Decaying heads stuck on pikes were fought over by ugly, raucous birds with scales instead of feathers. A terrible stink hung over the place.

Quar shouted in his harsh, guttural voice. After a moment the city gates creaked open to allow them entrance. Alexeika cried out in fear. Thum's face turned pale. "Tomias, save us," he said again and again.

Dain gazed up into a hideous face carved in the stone wall, and felt his own courage quail. Surely they were doomed.

His keen ears overheard murmurs of curiosity and eagerness beyond the gates. Although he could not understand Gantese, he heard one familiar word over and over: "Faldain . . . Faldain . . ."

He was surprised they knew of him. And with that surprise came a revival of his spirit. Realizing these cruel people would not respect anything but courage and strength, he proudly straightened in the saddle and squared his shoulders. He was the son of a king, a sworn enemy of this land and its people. He would show them no fear.

"Princess Alexeika!" he said sharply as they passed through the gates. "Remember who you are."

Her eyes, huge and dark with fear, stared at him. Pink tinted her cheeks, and as her chin lifted, he saw the old spirit flash in her eyes.

"Thum du Maltie!" he said, glancing to his right. "Show them a Mandrian uplander. Your ancestors have fought off their raids for centuries. They are dogs and worse. They are carrion-eaters."

"Aye," Thum said in a shaky voice. He frowned and straightened with a wince. "Aye, that's so."

By the time they reached the checkpoint inside the gates, all three prisoners were sitting tall and looking bold.

Glancing about at the curious guards leaning on their spears as they stared, Dain closed his mind to their savage thoughts. He pretended he did not see the shapeshifters flying back and forth overhead. He tried hard to ignore the growling hurlhounds slinking here and there among the crowd, baring venomous fangs. A soultaker—gray, fat, and sated—was lying in a cage hanging overhead, and Dain was obliged to ride directly beneath it.

Aware of its interest in him, he shuddered. His heart thudded hard against his ribs, and sweat poured off him, but with determination he kept his face stony and his eyes calm and steady.

Beyond the guardhouse, they rode along a broad avenue paved with red sandstone. A drum began to pound, and guards in breastplates and metal-studded loincloths fell in behind them. Wearing helmets and carrying spears, they seemed to be primitive warriors indeed, very old-fashioned compared with the fire-knights.

Along the route, they were joined by mounted knights wearing red hauberks similar to Alexeika's. Some of them called out to her, but she merely lifted her chin higher and ignored them all.

Only Dain was close enough to see her mouth quiver now and then, but she had pride and hatred to sustain her, and she did not falter.

Another contingent of armed men joined them, this time with prisoners in tow. Dain saw them shuffling along in shackles, their boots worn nearly through, their mail tarnished and torn, their surcoats in filthy tatters. After a moment he recognized the black circle on their breasts and realized they were church soldiers, Mandrians all.

Dain stared at them in shock, recognizing some of the faces now despite their grime and matted beards.

Thum stared at them too, and gasped. "Sire!"

"Aye," Dain said grimly. "Gavril's church soldiers."

"Great Thod," Thum said, his eyes widening as horror sank in. "That means—"

"Betrayal. Disaster." Dain wondered what had become of Pheresa, and his heart felt like lead in his chest. "When they reached Nether, Muncel must have turned on them."

"Merciful Tomias," Thum whispered in anguish. "Think you that all were captured?"

Dain bowed his head in silence. What was there to reply? After a moment, he roused himself and looked for Gavril among their number, but did not see the prince. Instead, he spied one knight, taller than most of the others, limping along, and recognized him.

"Sir Wiltem," he said.

As though the man had overheard him, Sir Wiltem lifted his head, and his gaze met Dain's. In silence, they stared at each other. Sir Wiltem's eyes held only stoic suffering. Dain had no idea what his own conveyed in return. A whip cracked across Sir Wiltem's shoulders, and Dain's captor tugged his horse into a trot, leading him past. The church soldiers were left behind to join the rear of the procession.

Curious folk emerged from houses of red or tan mud. Most were leather-skinned, burned dark from the relentless sun, with narrow skulls and hostile eyes. Children ran alongside the procession, shrieking insults and pelting the prisoners with dried dung. The city seemed to be a maze of narrow, winding streets, buildings made of stone or mud, and endless dust and filth. Ashy smoke from the volcano polluted the air, making Dain's eyes sting. He sensed a restless energy in the streets, an innate streak of cruelty in the citizens, a feeling of something terrible about to happen.

But even as the end of the avenue came into sight and he saw a domed palace rising before him, Dain continued to ride like a king, ignoring both the jeers and stones that were flung at him. In his mind he made himself as large and regal as possible. He imagined himself to be Tobeszijian and tried to act as his father would have.

Walls of red stone surrounded the palace, which was white, creating strong contrast. The spires towered high, and the hot sun glinted off the hammered gold leaf decorating the domes. At their approach, the ornate gates swung open to admit them.

Impressed in spite of himself, Dain looked around in open curiosity. The palace was enormous, rising white atop a checkerboard foundation of red and white stone. The unpaved courtyard was huge, more than ample to hold all the knights, spearmen, and prisoners, plus the armed men who advanced to surround them all.

Orders rang out, and red-hauberked guards with drawn swords ascended and lined up along the sandstone steps.

At the top of the steps, along a wide veranda that lay deep in shadow, a cluster of individuals stood watching. Glancing in their direction, Dain felt a chill sink through him.

He thought of the mysterious power that had reached him and caused him to swoon twice. He remembered the peculiar coldness that had permeated through his body, taking his consciousness and something of his life force with it. And although nothing attacked him now, he felt that same evil power, that same icy coldness, slither across his being with the lightest possible touch.

A shudder passed through his frame.

Quar dismounted, came over to him, and cut through Dain's ropes. As his arms swung forward, Dain barely managed to bite off a yelp of pain. His arms felt leaden and useless, yet painful prickles rippled through them, bringing a new kind of agony. Gritting his teeth, he made himself flex and work his fingers. They were puffy and dark, with bruised creases cut deeply into his wrists.

Quar cut Alexeika free, then Thum, before he returned to Dain.

"Down," he said.

Dain dismounted, as did the others. Thum staggered slightly and had to grip his stirrup to keep himself on his feet. His thigh wound was seeping blood again.

Quar pointed at Alexeika and Thum, issuing orders.

At once they were shoved over to the line of church soldiers. But when Dain tried to join them, his path was intercepted.

Quar gave him a light shove. "Up the steps. Go."

"What about my friends?"

"Go."

"But—"

"Your majesty!" a singsong voice called out in Mandrian.

Dain whirled, his gaze searching the many faces. "Sulein?"

"Your majesty, have pity!" Sulein came shoving his way through the line, breaking away from any guards who tried to stop him. Hobbled by his shackles, his long robes tattered and torn, his black hair frizzing wildly, the physician stretched out his hands to Dain.

"Do not let them make a slave of me," he begged. "Have mercy, majesty, for I belong to your service. Keep me with you. I was not destined to be broken hauling stone."

"Sulein," Dain said with pity, "I cannot help you. I am a prisoner too."

"No, that cannot be so," Sulein said, shaking his head. Guards caught up with him and grabbed his shoulders. "You are King

Faldain. All in Gant know your name. Your horoscope shows you emblazoned across the heavens."

The guards pushed a struggling Sulein back toward the line of prisoners. "Majesty! Keep me with you! You swore you would."

Dain took a step toward him, but Quar's arm blocked his way.

"Keep your promise!" Sulein called out.

But there was nothing Dain could do for him. When he helplessly shook his head, the physician's face contorted with rage.

"You cannot cheat me!" he cried as he was shoved into line next to Alexeika. She stared at him in amazement, but he never noticed her. His dark eyes blazed at Dain. "If you break your royal promise to me, you'll regret it!"

"Sulein, I can do nothing—"

The physician raised his fist, and Dain saw the Ring of Solder glowing on his finger.

Aghast, he pushed against Quar's restraining arm. "No! Sulein, do not use it! In Thod's name, *don't*!"

But Sulein spoke a word that made the ground rumble. Dain's ears hurt from the sound of it, and with a loud pop the physician disappeared.

Consternation broke out among the Gantese. Even Quar seemed taken aback. His arm dropped, and Dain ran forward a couple of steps, only to stop in dismay.

He couldn't believe Sulein had panicked like that. Sulein, who had never before been seen to lose his nerve. Had the physician kept his head, Dain thought ruefully, perhaps they could have worked out an escape plan for everyone.

At that moment, the air shimmered and seemed to break open. Screaming, Sulein appeared in midair, then plummeted to the ground. He thudded hard and lay there unmoving, almost at Alexeika's feet.

Jabbering in Gantese, the guards surrounded him, shoving Alexeika aside with such force she stumbled and fell. She scrambled out of the way, then quickly regained her feet.

As some of the guards dragged Sulein's body past Dain, he ran to the physician, who was dead. His dark beard and hair had both turned snowy white, and his skin was as cold as ice.

Dain stared at him, unable to believe he'd died in those few seconds. Where had he gone? What had he seen in the second world? What had killed him?

Swiftly Dain gripped Sulein's hands, feeling for the Ring. It was gone.

"Get back!" Quar ordered, pulling Dain away.

Dain offered no resistance, and Sulein was removed, his head lolling, his arms dragging in the dust. Despair settled through Dain. He could not believe Sulein had been so foolish, so utterly stupid. He had thrown the Ring away, lost it forever in the second world. What evil lunacy had possessed him?

Quar gave Dain a push, jolting him from his thoughts. "Up the steps," he ordered. "Now."

Dain had no choice but to obey. Numb, feeling dazed, he stumbled forward. Although he sensed Thum's worry and Alexeika's fear behind him, he didn't glance back. He no longer had any assurances to share. They were all doomed.

15

THE PALACE WAS an edifice of torment. It had been built out of mortar mixed with blood and ground-up bones. Grotesque faces carved from stone leered over the doorways. Disembodied souls, gibbering and moaning, flew about like smoky wraiths and puddled together in shadowy corners. Sticking out from the walls of the dimly lit corridors at regularly spaced intervals were hands, turned palm upward. Fairlight flickered from the fingertips, and Dain dared not look closely enough to see if they were real eldin hands or just carved ones. Ushered along by Quar and additional guards, Dain was startled at first to see doors swing open at his approach without anyone having pushed them. As he walked past, eyes, and sometimes an entire face, would appear in the murky panels of the doors. He sensed the muted screams of whatever was trapped inside, and couldn't keep himself from quickening his pace.

Despite the shadows, the interior of the palace was almost as hot as it was outdoors. As he strode along Dain pulled off his cloak and loosened the throat of his hauberk. He was so hungry and thirsty and his senses felt assaulted on all sides by the torment and misery that seemed to permeate every corner.

At the end of the corridor stood a tall pedestal beneath a window through which sunlight streamed in. Dire curses carved in ancient runes marked each side of the pedestal, and a plain metal bowl stood on top of it. As he drew near, Dain realized the bowl was made of god-steel. He could sense it, as though the metal were alive and calling out to him.

And from behind him, he heard Truthseeker's song, muffled by its heavy wrappings. Faltering, Dain glanced over his shoulder at the Believer who carried Truthseeker and Severgard so gingerly. The swords were temptingly close, yet he knew Quar would never let him reach one.

The fire-knight prodded his shoulder. "Go," he said. "Cannot linger here."

He seemed uneasy, and he avoided looking in the bowl's direction.

Dain's apathy fell away. Narrowing his eyes, he stared at Quar. "Why do you keep god-steel indoors if you fear it?" he asked.

Smoke curled from beneath Quar's helmet. "Go," he said finally, refusing to answer Dain's question. "Do not stop here."

As Dain passed the bowl, he ran his fingertips across it.

Snarling, Quar struck him so hard he staggered against the wall, but Dain did not care. That brief touch was enough to send tingling energy through him. Much of his fatigue dropped away. Even his thirst lessened, and full feeling returned to his puffy hands. Although he did not yet know how he could possibly escape this place, or even ride across the desert of Gant, he vowed that somehow he would try. He would not give up as long as he drew breath.

Ahead, a door swung open, moaning on its hinges. An embossed face appeared in the panels, and opened its mouth in a soundless scream.

Quar struck the wood with a bad-tempered fist, and the face disappeared. "Inside!" he ordered.

But as Dain stepped over the threshold, he stopped in his tracks with a gasp.

The heat was overwhelming. An immense blaze roared inside a brick firepit in the room's center. Brown lizards with iridescent throats lay basking atop the broad edge of the firepit wall. Now and then one of them blinked bulbous yellow eyes. Believers, both men and women, moaned and chanted in worship. Clad only in loincloths, their oiled bodies tattooed with intricate designs, they crawled to the firepit on hands and knees, threw offerings into the flames, and retreated to allow others to crawl forward. Thus did the group move in a continuous flux. Suddenly one of them leaped to his feet and flung himself into the flames. As he screamed and flailed in the fire—the stench of burning flesh and hair filling the air—the other worshipers lifted their arms and shouted in mindless ecstasy.

Appalled, Dain wondered if this was what the Gantese meant by "eating fire." He cast Quar a sharp look, but dared ask no questions.

Quar gestured, and with reluctance Dain edged his way past the worshipers. When a snake slithered across the floor toward him, he stopped warily, but Quar shoved him forward. At the same time, Quar spoke a sharp command and the serpent turned aside as though it understood him. Enormous tarantulas scuttled out of Dain's way as he left the worshipers behind and crossed the remaining half of the room. Quar pointed at a dais at the opposite end, and Dain headed toward it.

A long bench gilded in gold leaf and padded with scarlet cushions stood centered on the dais. Reclining there was a figure clad in robes of purple silk, a figure who was no more than leathery, deeply scarred skin stretched over a skeleton. He looked as though in the past he'd been burned alive. His lips and nostrils and ears had all been scorched away, leaving slits and orifices. Only his eyes remained human, eyes as intelligent and searching as any Dain had ever seen.

He found his own gaze captured and held by those remarkable eyes, and before he realized it he was nearly kneeling to this creature. At the last second he stiffened his knees and refused to bend to the will exerted against his.

The pressure eased and fell away. Drawing a deep breath, Dain stared hard at this creature and wondered if the fire-knights looked like this beneath their obsidian armor and helmets.

Quar clamped his gloved hand possessively on Dain's shoulder. "Lord Zinxt, I bring Faldain of Nether to thee, as the Chief Believer has ordered."

"Thou has done well, Quar," Lord Zinxt replied. His voice was as ashy, ruined, and hoarse as Quar's. "The Chief Believer will be pleased."

Although they spoke in Gantese, Dain found himself suddenly able to understand them. He glanced at Zinxt in suspicion, suspecting he had made this possible. The Gantese lord dismissed Quar with a gesture, and Quar glanced at Dain before striding out. Four more fire-knights remained at Dain's back; he dared do nothing.

"Indeed, yes, I have made it possible for Faldain to understand our words," Zinxt said, reclaiming Dain's attention. "Faldain's eldin blood makes him quick to learn, quick to see what is before him."

Frowning as he adjusted mentally to Zinxt's strange way of speaking, Dain said nothing. He was too wary to accept the Gantese lord's compliments. Behind Dain, another worshiper flung herself into the fire while her companions shrieked and wailed joyously.

Refusing to look, Dain steeled himself to be as ruthless as possible in order to escape this place.

"Faldain has eluded us a long while," Zinxt continued. "But the Chief Believer's patience is long. When it comes to obeying Ashnod's will, the Chief Believer never stops until he succeeds. Now Faldain is here, and the final steps of the plan can be put in place."

"What plan?" Dain asked sharply. "I've been told I'm to be sacrificed to Ashnod. I promise you I'll make him a poor dinner."

"Do not mock the god!" Zinxt said angrily.

"Or what?" Dain retorted. "I'm doomed to die already. What can you threaten me with?"

For a moment there was silence, then Zinxt's lipless mouth stretched in what was perhaps a smile. "Faldain fears the same things as any other nonbeliever. But when Faldain's soul is eaten and he belongs wholly to us, then, little king, *then* Faldain will be useful indeed."

Dain's defiance dropped away. Trying hard to mask his horror, he stared at Zinxt, and felt suddenly numb. "My soul," he repeated. "Eaten."

"Of course. Faldain will become Nonkind and blessed among us."

"Cursed, you mean," Dain whispered.

"It is not the terrible thing Faldain thinks," Zinxt said with a shrug. "Faldain will have the honor of serving Ashnod. Faldain will be the last piece in a plan that has taken centuries to complete."

Thinking of what the old eldin king had told him, Dain swallowed with difficulty. "What is Ashnod's plan?"

"When Faldain belongs to Ashnod, we will return him to Nether to take his throne. With our help, Faldain will overthrow Muncel's army. The rebel forces will come out of hiding to pay Faldain fealty, and we will destroy them."

Dain frowned, but Zinxt went on:

"According to our agents, Faldain is on excellent terms with Verence of Mandria. He will be eager to sign a new treaty with Faldain. Because of this, Faldain will find it easy to lure him to Grov, where he will be crushed."

"Never!" Dain said. "I won't do any of it."

Zinxt tilted his head. "Does Faldain believe he has a choice? It is Ashnod's will that Gant rule the world. Since the day when we were imprisoned here in this place of desolation and forced to eat sand and bitterness, we have vowed to destroy the order of things. We shall rule over all kingdoms. All people will bend their knees and hearts to the will of Ashnod. No other god will be worshiped. And Faldain will finish this plan when he brings the end of the world. He will provide Gant with its new beginning. So it was with Solder the First. So it is now with Faldain the Last."

Dain set his jaw. "You're wrong, Zinxt," he said defiantly. "Gant will never spread its darkness across the world. Your plan will fail. You will remain here in this desert, where your kind belong."

"Such defiance is as the wind," Zinxt replied. "Once Faldain's soul is eaten, he will not resist. He will be ours."

"Soultakers cannot eat the souls of eldin," Dain said rapidly. He glanced left and right, but the guards still stood between him and the door.

Zinxt emitted a dreadful laugh. "False! Eldin souls are no different from others. It will not hurt unless Faldain fights, but the *magemons* will hold Faldain so that he does no harm to himself, and the soultaker will, I promise, be swift."

Afraid, Dain steeled himself. "Bring on your foul creatures," he said with all the defiance he could muster. "See how well they prevail."

"It was not foretold that Faldain would be a fool," Zinxt said. "Have patience, little king. The *magemons* are still with the Chief Believer. He wants to see Faldain for himself before Faldain is . . . altered."

Fresh perspiration beaded across Dain's brow. He drew in a deep breath, taking little comfort from the delay. *Father, give me courage to meet my death,* he prayed, and let his hand stray casually to his dagger hilt.

Zinxt beckoned to the guard who held the swords. "Show me what thou has brought."

The guard unrolled the swords at the foot of the dais. Severgard's black, rune-carved blade was glowing white in the presence of evil; its huge sapphire gleamed in the firelight. Beside it lay Truthseeker, ancient and deadly, its hilt emeralds glittering with fire of their own. Its song was loud in Dain's mind.

Aching to leap for the weapon and fight his way out of here, he clenched his fists at his sides. He sensed that Zinxt was waiting for him to try something rash, waiting with a trap ready to spring closed around him. Although it cost him all the willpower he possessed, Dain waited.

"These swords are made from the foul metals," Zinxt said, gazing down at them in patent displeasure. His gaze shifted to Dain. "One of them is Faldain's. The other, whose?"

"Alexeika's. The maiden who was brought to Sindeul with me."

"Alexeika." Zinxt repeated her name as though savoring it on his tongue, then reached to the floor and picked up a snake. He allowed it to slither up his arm and curl itself around his neck. "Faldain and Alexeika . . . these names have been spelled out by the bone dice. Faldain and Alexeika are young indeed to carry swords of such antiquity."

"We inherited them from our fathers."

"False!" Zinxt said, pointing a long talon at Dain. "False. The kings of Nether do not carry god-steel."

Dain stiffened. "What do you know about the kings of Nether? What we do and what we carry into battle is no concern of yours."

Lord Zinxt's eyes narrowed. He tipped back his head, then hissed a long stream of smoke from his mouth and threw the snake straight at Dain. As it flew through the air, the snake suddenly shimmered into another shape, something flaccid and gray and amorphous.

It was a soultaker, uncaged, and incredibly dangerous.

Chilled to the marrow despite the hot room, Dain froze for a second. He had no idea these things could transform themselves like shapeshifters. As its putrid smell choked his nostrils, he realized it was going to land right on him if he didn't force himself to move.

Dodging barely in time, so that the soultaker landed with a plop on the floor and came writhing toward him, Dain lunged for Truthseeker and closed his fingers around the hilt just as one of the guards grabbed him from behind. Yanked off balance, Dain swore and managed to keep his footing. As he righted himself, he swung Truthseeker up and around. Chanting ancient words to the weapon's inner song, Dain slashed through obsidian armor and nearly cut the fire-knight in half. As the Believer staggered back, crumpling in a gush of blood, the others charged Dain.

Sidestepping the soultaker once more, he kicked it away from him with all his might and met the guards' swords with Truthseeker, which sang loud and strong. Back and forth their blades flashed. In seconds, two guards were down. The others hesitated uncertainly, and did not charge him.

As the soultaker came his way again, Dain turned and plunged Truthseeker through it.

Screaming, the thing burst into flames.

At the firepit, the chanting and wailing fell abruptly silent. Lord Zinxt shouted something that made the air stink of ashes and smoke. Although Dain felt the power of the spell that was hurled his way, it did not ensnare him. Instead, all he felt was Truthseeker's power throbbing in his hands. Dain ran for the door.

He feared that the worshipers might attack him in a mob, but they knelt where they were and stared at him with dazed eyes.

Before he reached the door, however, it swung open and Quar marched in, weapon in hand, with additional fire-knights at his back.

Retreating, Dain searched for another way out.

"Quar!" Lord Zinxt called. "Leave thy men at the door and come to me."

The fire-knight swung away from Dain as Zinxt began incanting another spell. This one, however, was not directed at Dain but instead at Severgard, which still lay in front of the dais.

The magicked sword lifted into the air and hung there, wobbling and turning slowly.

"Quar, take it," Zinxt commanded.

The fire-knight hesitated only fractionally before he sheathed his weapon and reached out to grip the sword of Alexeika's ancestors. As soon as his gloved hands closed on the long hilt, he flinched with a bellow of pain.

Understanding what Zinxt was trying to do, Dain ran straight at the fire-knight. He swung Truthseeker high, and aimed for Quar's neck, determined to behead him as brutally and mercilessly as Sir Terent had been beheaded.

But at the last second, Quar managed to lift Severgard enough to parry Dain's blow. Quar's movements were jerky and awkward, almost as though another will was directing his. Smoke boiled from beneath the edges of his helmet, and Dain could

hear his ragged breathing, but despite his obvious pain, he
fought.

Magicked steel against god-steel. The two noble blades
clanged loudly as Dain and Quar fought back and forth. Severgard slashed across Dain's forearm, snapping the finely
wrought links of chain mail and drawing blood.

Hissing, the brown lizards around the firepit came to life
and jumped down from their ledge. They crawled through the
crowd of worshipers, and headed straight for Dain as though
drawn by his blood scent.

Keeping a wary eye on the approaching creatures, Dain balanced his weight on his back leg a moment to catch his breath;
then, as Quar lunged at him, Dain crouched low beneath Severgard's thrust and hacked at Quar's knees.

He cut tendons, and although Quar leaped aside, he staggered as he landed, then sank down. Dain charged with all the
strength he had left, raising Truthseeker high.

Gasping, Quar lifted Severgard as though intending to im-
pale Dain, but when Dain spoke in the language of swords,
Severgard twisted in Quar's hands, its point swinging aside.

Down swept Truthseeker, and Quar's head went tumbling
across the floor among the brown lizards and tarantulas. As
Quar's body toppled, Dain scooped up Severgard in his left
hand.

The weapon was throbbing and the hilt felt white-hot. Swiftly
Dain slid the sword through his belt and swung around to face
the charge of the remaining fire-knights.

By now, Zinxt was shouting words that made the air trem-
ble. Flames and sparks burst in midair, yet Dain realized he
was protected as long as he held Truthseeker. Chanting again
the songs of battle and blade, Dain felt tireless as he killed another fire-knight, then charged the next.

This Believer, however, turned and fled from him. Zinxt
shouted a spell that knocked the coward down. Leaping over
the fire-knight, Dain ran for the door.

The lizards scuttled after him, following the pale blood that
still dripped from his arm. As Dain passed the firepit, flames
seemed to explode in all directions.

The worshipers went sprawling, and many of them were set

on fire as the flames caught their hair and spread across their oiled bodies. Knocked off his feet by the explosion, Dain was too dazed at first to know what had happened. His ears rang, and his eyes were dazzled. Squinting, he shook his head and tried to regain his senses.

Something crawled over his leg, and Dain slapped it away with Truthseeker.

His vision cleared, although his hearing still rang. He beat down the sparks smoldering in his clothing, scrambled to his feet, then staggered out the door.

More fire-knights were running up the corridor toward him. Dismay sank through Dain. His rush of energy had spent itself, and exhaustion now trembled in his arms and legs. He was panting from exertion and drenched with sweat. The cut in his arm was no longer bleeding, but it hurt.

Instinct told him that if he tried to fight his way out, he might never reach the last knight ordered against him. He decided to try a different tactic.

Impulsively, he ran to the pedestal and seized the bowl of god-steel. Cradling it against him, he retreated into Lord Zinxt's chamber, kicking lizards and serpents aside and jumping over the burned and injured worshipers.

Zinxt was standing atop his bench, his purple robes falling open to his waist and billowing around his thin form. Tiny flames burned in midair in a circle around him, and with his eyes shut and his talons raised he was weaving a spell that made Dain's hair stand on end. The very air was crackling and popping.

Without hesitation, Dain rushed up to Zinxt and stepped inside the circle of flames. An invisible force tried to push him back, and his mind was assaulted by numerous voices murmuring vile and terrible things in a maddening babble. But Dain slammed the bowl against Zinxt's bare chest.

The Gantese lord reeled back, screaming. The voices babbling filth fell abruptly silent, and the circle of flames vanished. Smoke rose from where the god-steel was blistering Zinxt's scarred flesh. He writhed and screamed again, then jerked himself back with such force that he fell off the dais.

Dain straddled him, pinning him on his back with Truth-

seeker at his throat. Holding the bowl in the crook of his left
arm, Dain felt its strength pour through his body, driving away
his exhaustion and weakness and restoring his strength. He
glared down at Zinxt, who was wide-eyed in fear.

"Give the order," Dain said. "Tell your guards to let me go."

Zinxt defiantly hissed smoke at him. "I cannot defy the Chief
Believer's commands."

Dain pressed Truthseeker against his throat, intending to tor-
ture him until he complied, but suddenly all the air seemed to
leave the room.

Dain tried to breathe, and couldn't. The bowl fell to the floor,
spinning there with an awful clang. As his lungs jerked in panic,
he turned around and saw a tall nightmarish figure standing behind him. Clad in a sleeveless tunic of thin stone disks, a necklace of skulls hanging around its neck, the newcomer had the
shape of a man, yet his entire body was aflame. In one blazing hand this creature held a stone scepter topped by a ball of
crystal in which floated tiny, distorted faces grimacing in perpetual torment. Two snarling slyths—each beast no wider than
Dain's hand— flanked it like sentinels.

The creature stopped blazing orange, its flames dying down
to mere flickers. Air returned to the room, with a gust that blew
Dain's hair back from his face. He could breathe again, but now
the air stank of sulfur and ashes. Inhaling only shallow breaths,
Dain realized belatedly that he was being mesmerized by the
creature's fiery gaze. Somehow he managed to wrench his eyes
away.

"Let Zinxt go," the monster commanded.

"Are you the Chief Believer?" Dain asked.

"Thou are mine, Faldain," the monster replied. Its voice was
like nothing he'd ever heard before. There was no song, no life
in it. Every word it spoke seemed to weaken him, despite the
god-steel in his hands. "Thy soul is mine. Once it is collected,
I shall keep it here." It tapped the crystal of its scepter. "Thy
blood belongs to the Nonkind who serve Zinxt. Thy body will
do the bidding of Ashnod, and lure the mortal kings of this
world to their deaths."

"No," Dain said. "I am sworn to be forever your enemy,
yours and your god's. Faldain of Nether does not serve you."

"Not even if I save the one thou loves?"

Dain jerked involuntarily, and Truthseeker nearly slipped from his hand. The Chief Believer extended the scepter in his direction, and the distorted faces inside the crystal were replaced by a likeness of Pheresa. Her reddish-gold hair framed her oval face; her eyes were shut as though she slept . . . or lay dead.

Dain frowned, believing the latter possibility, but at that moment her brown eyes opened and looked straight at him.

"Dain." Her lips formed his name in silence, but he seemed to hear her melodious voice in his mind.

"I can save her," the Chief Believer said. Its voice was stony and lifeless. "Serve as we bid thee, and she will be whole again."

Dain's heart swelled with hope, but he cut off the temptation as fast as he could. The Chief Believer's offer was a trick, nothing more.

"She's dead already," he said. "I saw the guardians among the prisoners today. She could not live without them. She's dead!"

"Fool!" the Chief Believer said, flames blazing higher. The heat it emitted made Dain back up a step. "She lives, and she can be at thy side."

"Nay!" Dain shouted. "Get back from me, you evil liar!"

"Defy us, and she *will* die," the Chief Believer said. "Defy us, and we will take you into the fire."

On the floor at Dain's feet, Zinxt reached out and gripped his ankle. His talons pierced Dain's boot, holding him with unnatural strength when Dain tried to kick free. Hissing smoke, Zinxt stretched open his mouth very wide and belched forth a small soultaker. Gray and slick, its flesh pulsing in eager quivers, the disgusting thing landed on Dain's foot and began inching up his leg.

Shouting, Dain jerked in Zinxt's hold, but when he could not get free, he plunged Truthseeker through Zinxt's heart. Flames burst from his wound as Dain withdrew the sword. More flames blazed in Zinxt's open mouth and nostrils. His eyes melted in the heat, and his body seemed to collapse in on itself like paper thrown onto a fire.

Retreating, and unable to shake off the soultaker, which was still climbing his leg, Dain reached into his purse and pulled out a handful of salt. He threw it on the soultaker, which shuddered all over, then went rigid and fell off.

Dain stabbed it, and fire exploded it into bits. He whirled and swung Truthseeker at the Chief Believer, not sure how he could fight an entity made of flames. The creature parried with its scepter and deflected Truthseeker's blow. Shocked to find the scepter capable of withstanding god-steel, Dain was caught off guard when the slyths sprang at him, attacking him from two sides. He managed to cut one in half, but the other knocked him down. It bit his shoulder, but its poisonous fangs closed only on Dain's fur-lined surcoat and the mail hauberk beneath it. He rolled over and plunged Truthseeker through its chest. With a scream the slyth crashed to the ground.

Dain jumped to his feet and grabbed the bowl he'd dropped earlier. The Chief Believer shouted words that appeared in midair, flaming and shooting sparks. But once again, the god-steel protected Dain from Gantese spells, and the fire-curses did not entrap him. Without looking back, he fled.

16

A WHIP CRACKED across the shoulders of the man in front of Alexeika, making her flinch reflexively.

"Go!" the guards commanded.

Slowly the line of prisoners shuffled across the baked compound. Alexeika walked with her head down, trying to bring no attention to herself. Thum limped grimly beside her, his hazel eyes filled with both anger and despair.

Alexeika knew he was fretting for his friend and master. She felt sick at heart herself, for the thought of Faldain being sacrificed to Ashnod was impossible to bear. Yet how could they escape? Now that they were separated, what hope had they?

Tears stung her eyes, and angrily she wiped them away. She would not give up as long as she drew breath. Whatever she could do to thwart or harm the evil ones here, she would do. As her father had faced overwhelming forces with courage, defying the darkness to the last, so would she do her best until the very end.

Lifting her head and sniffing, Alexeika stopped her tears, then pulled off her cloak and tied it around her waist.

"Why keep that?" Thum whispered. "Throw it away. I have never known such heat."

She shook her head with a frown. Although she loosened the lacings of her red hauberk, she did not cast it off. She was roasting in her heavy winter clothing, but if she somehow found a way to escape, she would need its protection later.

To the west of the palace sprawled a complex of barracks and stables. Here, the prisoners were separated into groups and led away to various tasks. Alexeika and Thum were among those assigned to the stables. The shadowy interior was cool after the intense heat outdoors. Mixed with the usual rustic smells of straw, fodder, animals, and droppings was a terrible stench, rank and hot, of something not of this world.

With flaring nostrils, Alexeika glanced around with interest. "Darsteeds," she said.

Groaning, Thum limped over to the water trough. He fell to his knees, plunged his face into the greenish water, and drank deeply.

Shouting and cursing in Gantese, a guard yanked him away.

Consumed with thirst, Alexeika headed for the trough, but the guard shoved Thum into her path. As she grabbed the squire to keep him from falling, Thum bent double and retched up the water, spewing it over his boots and leggings.

Concerned, she held his shoulders until he was finished, then helped him straighten. Using a corner of his cloak, she wiped the clammy sweat from his face. He was bone-white and gasping. His hazel eyes looked at her in horror.

"Don't drink it," he whispered, swallowing with a grimace. "It tastes like blood."

She stared at the trough in disbelief.

"That food the fire-knight tried to give me earlier," Thum went on painfully. "It tasted foul and rotted. Horrible. We can't eat or drink anything here."

"But we have to," Alexeika said in alarm. "We can't survive much longer without water."

"Everything is tainted," Thum said despairingly.

Grooms in livery, their narrow faces cruel and hostile, interrupted them then, barking orders in Gantese and putting shovels in their hands. Alexeika and Thum were sent to muck out stalls and spread clean bedding.

She welcomed the work. It was easy, requiring no thought. She worked quickly and methodically, moving from one stall to the next. Now and then she paused to rest and lick the perspiration from her lips for the tiny amount of moisture it brought her. She was soaked to the skin beneath her hauberk, but she forced herself to ignore the discomfort. She'd survived worse.

In the meantime, a plan of sorts was forming in her mind. She observed the layout of the stables, watched the grooms and other workers, made note of the slaves such as herself and what they were permitted to do. Gradually, as she reached the end of her assigned row of stalls late in the day, she found herself near the section of heavy brick pens where the darsteeds were kept.

Bugling challenges, kicking and lunging at each other in an effort to fight, the darsteeds were perpetually restless. Some of them stood looking over the top of their brick pens, red-eyed and snorting flames.

Alexeika kept staring at the animals. They were larger than horses, and capable of covering long distances speedily without tiring. If she found a way to escape and stole a darsteed, she might have a chance.

The idea was so daring and far-fetched it seemed impossible. Yet it would not leave her. She wished she had Quar's magical baton and could just leap home through space and time, but she did not. Therefore, she had to ride across the desolate plains and deserts of Gant until she reached the Charva River.

But how could she steal a darsteed? How could she saddle it, or ride it? The creatures were wild and savage, only mini-

mally trained to saddle and bridle. She knew they were controlled by their riders' minds. Could she somehow control them?

In her mind she heard old Uzfan's scolding voice: *"Nay,
child, you have not the ability. Do not attempt it. Spellcasting
is not your gift."*

Uzfan had always said she was untrainable, and her abilities were indeed erratic. Since her escape from the Grethori,
when she'd called forth *krenjin* and attracted hurlhounds to her
by accident, she'd not dared to try again. Yet despite things going
awry, she *had* escaped the Grethori. She *had* escaped the hurlhounds. She'd even killed their master. It was his hauberk that
she now wore, his dagger she carried. What would it hurt to
try to tame a darsteed with her mind?

One of the darsteeds was staring at her, its eyes red and intent, like a hunter focused on its prey. Alexeika stared back at
it, then closed her eyes and centered her thoughts. *You are mine,*
she thought, sending her will toward the creature. *Serve me.
You are mine.*

For a moment there was nothing at all. Ignoring her frustration, she concentrated harder. *You are mine.*

The darsteed's mind suddenly opened to her, and she was
assaulted by primitive fury and killing lust. *Food/food/food/food!*

Rocked on her feet, Alexeika opened her eyes and broke free
of that savage contact. Her mind felt on fire, and she was panting for breath. Glancing around to make sure she was unob-
served, she put aside her shovel and hurried over to a metal
box by the darsteed's pen. From it she took a chunk of raw
meat that stank and felt sticky with decay. Maggots were crawling in it, and in revulsion she flung it over the top of the wall.
The darsteed's head vanished, and she heard its jaws snap on
the meat. Immediately the darsteed's head appeared again. Its
eyes fastened on her more avidly than before.

She stared back at it. *You are mine. I feed you, and you are
mine.* She reached into the box for another hunk of meat, but
someone grabbed her from behind and spun her around.

A groom glared at her, gesturing and shouting incompre-
hensibly. He slammed the box shut, and shoved Alexeika away
so hard she nearly fell.

Slapping and shoving her, he continued to berate her all the

way over to a stack of filthy straw. Pointing and shouting, he
indicated that she was to shift the entire stack outside, then
handed her a wooden pail and shovel.

Disposing of the refuse stack one bucketful at a time was
total drudgery, but Alexeika hardly minded. She was too busy
planning. The darsteed's response had been encouraging, and
she felt confident now that she could gain influence over it. All
she needed was time and opportunity.

Dain squeezed himself into a shadowy niche behind a contorted
statue of some demonic figure and crouched there, barely daring to breathe as another squadron of guards hurried by. They
were sweeping the palace in search of him, but thus far he'd
been able to elude his pursuers. After all, he was skilled in the
art of hiding.

He knew, of course, that had he not kept his hand constantly
on god-steel the Believers or their *magemons* could have found
him instantly. He'd found other pieces of god-steel displayed
here and there on pedestals throughout the palace, but all of
them were damaged or merely a scrap or two of some item that
he could not identify. He wondered why the Gantese kept such
artifacts, when obviously they abhorred the metal and could not
tolerate touching anything made from it.

Still, it was not a mystery worth solving. All he cared about
was that the god-steel helped him, and he was grateful for it.
At one point he'd come to a water source, a large basin filled
to the brim with stale, brackish water scummed over with algae.
Its smell alone had been foul enough to counteract Dain's terrible thirst. But on instinct he'd dipped the bowl into it. The
water was purified instantly, enabling him to drink it without
harm.

He wished he could find food, but he dared not risk searching for any. His intent was to get out of the palace and somehow find Alexeika and Thum.

As he crouched in this latest hiding place behind the statue,
with the bowl safely tucked away inside his surcoat and Truthseeker lying across his knees, he sensed a stirring of something
inside the stone figure, something malevolent and watchful.

Warily, Dain eased out from behind it as soon as the way

was clear again. As he stood up cautiously in the passageway, the statue's eyes came to life, shifting until they stared down at him.

Swiftly, not even giving himself time to wonder what might be going on, Dain pressed the tip of Truthseeker to its surface.

The statue's demonic eyes flickered, then went dead and stony once more.

Glancing right and left, he hurried silently along the passageway, seeking a way out. This palace would be impossible for any ordinary person to escape, for the trapped and tormented entities within the very floor and walls would surely betray him. But Truthseeker kept them silent.

He came to a door and hesitated there. As he listened, questing cautiously with his senses, he leaned against the door and slowly pushed it open.

Courtiers, knights in red mail, and other Believers milled inside a long gallery. Dain retreated with a grimace of impatience, then looked around until he found a door concealed in the wall panels for servants to use. He opened it cautiously and slipped into a plain, narrow passageway, praying he would not encounter anyone.

He did, of course. Rounding a corner, he came abruptly face-to-face with a female in a sleeveless gown and soiled work apron. She was carrying ashes in a bucket, and her gaunt face creased in dismay equal to Dain's own.

Swiftly he lifted his finger to his lips, pleading silently for her not to betray him. Her eyes stared at him, darting from his face to his drawn sword to his face again. She trembled visibly, and although Dain held up his hand in reassurance, she didn't seem to understand his gestures. He wished he knew some word of Gantese that would soothe her.

She seemed frozen. Finally Dain walked toward her as slowly and gently as he could. He had no doubt that in her eyes he looked foreign and terrifying, garbed in fur and chain mail, his pale eyes wild with strain, a bare sword gripped in his hands. As he brushed past her in the narrow passageway, she uttered a muffled shriek and dropped the bucket of ashes.

But as Dain went on without doing her harm, the terror

abated in her eyes. She frowned, blinking at him, and slowly lifted her dirty hands to her mouth.

He dared give her a tiny smile before he turned and hurried on. She sounded no alarm, and Dain's stride lightened. If even one Gantese could comprehend kindness and mercy, then there was hope for this tainted and blighted land.

Eventually he made his way outdoors. The sun had gone down, leaving the world shrouded in a murky twilight. The air stank of Nonkind and ashes. In the distance beyond the palace walls he could hear the noise of carts and pedestrians. Somewhere a bell rang out in queer, off-key notes that made him wince. Worshipers, chanting and carrying torches, filed through the palace gates and crossed the spacious compound.

Dain crouched behind a stone pillar in the shadows and watched the worshipers impatiently. He had to find his friends in this enormous compound, and the quicker the better. Unwilling to waste time searching in the wrong places, Dain dared allow his senses to quest for them.

At once he picked up Thum's emotions, close by. Pain and fever caused by his wound, mingled with despair and grief, poured into Dain before he closed the contact. Realizing Thum was in a bad way, Dain frowned. It was unlike his friend to lose heart like this.

Moving from shadow to shadow, taking his time and staying careful despite his impatience, Dain made his way to the stables. Row after row of horses were munching contentedly on their bags of fodder. An occasional groom walked up and down the rows, inspecting the animals. On the far side of the large building stood a number of circular darsteed pens.

The sound of voices alerted him that someone was approaching. He flitted deeper into the shadows and hid behind a pile of fodder that smelled sour and moldy. The search party did not enter the stables, but instead marched on into the darkness.

When the grooms ended the inspection of their charges and the torches were extinguished, Dain crept outside and around the end of the stables, seeking the slaves' housing. In a space between the stables and the knight barracks, he found a filthy pesthole crammed with prisoners and slaves. They had nothing to sleep on save the ground, no means by which to keep their areas clean. He smelled the food that had been served to them, but it stank as though half-spoiled.

Most of the wretches were lying down now as the starlight glittered overhead. Dain noticed that a fat white moon was rising above the horizon. Moving cautiously forward, he picked his way about, trying not to step on anyone. Some of the slaves were free; others wore chains and shackles that rattled with their every movement.

He searched slowly, now and then bending over a recumbent form to press his hand to a ragged shoulder. He dared say nothing, dared not utter names. Instead, he relied on touch and his keen sense of smell.

At last he caught Thum's scent. Relieved, he knelt beside his friend and gripped his shoulder to be sure. Thum moaned at his touch and stirred. Dain pressed him down.

"Hush," he whispered, afraid of who or what might overhear. "Say nothing. 'Tis I."

Thum rolled over, then struggled to sit upright. "Thod be praised! You're—"

Exasperated by such foolishness, Dain clamped his hand across Thum's mouth. Thum grew still and touched Dain's wrist. Only then did Dain take his hand away. In silence Thum gripped his fingers hard, awash with emotions. Quietly, Dain slung his arm around Thum's shoulders and held him.

Nearby, another shadow slowly sat up and stared at him. Recognizing Alexeika, Dain mentally applauded her good sense in keeping quiet. She reached across Thum and gripped Dain's sleeve, and only the hard pressure of her fingers betrayed her emotions. When she pointed at the stables, Dain nodded.

"One at a time," he whispered softly. He got to his feet, then retreated slowly and carefully back the way he'd come.

Not until Dain had left the slave area and circled around the end of the stables did Thum follow. Limping heavily, he came stumbling around the corner and nearly blundered into Dain, who gripped him in support.

"Easy!" Dain whispered.

Thum was shuddering from that simple exertion. He sank to the ground despite Dain's attempts to support him, and sat there breathing raggedly. Dain was concerned, but Alexeika arrived before he had a chance to discover what ailed his loyal squire.

She knelt at once next to Dain. "The sentries have counted us once, but I think they will come back in a few hours to check again," she whispered. "I have a plan—"

"Good," Dain said, interrupting. "The compound gates opened tonight to let worshipers inside. If they leave, we should try to get out with them."

"I think I can steal a darsteed," she said. "We can't cross the desert to the Charva on foot. Even a horse or two won't be able to outrun pursuit for long."

Dain frowned in the darkness, for the idea of trying to control one of the monstrous beasts unnerved him. Still, although her suggestion was daring and risky, it was bold enough to have a chance of success.

If he could manage to control one of the beasts.

"All right," he said finally. "I shall try—"

"Nay, sire. *I'll* do the stealing. I'm experienced at this, re-member?"

"Experienced at stealing horses, not darsteeds. They'll eat anyone they can reach."

"I *know* that," she said impatiently. "One has already learned my scent. I've been working to gain its trust."

"Trust?" he echoed more sharply than he intended. "Darsteeds have no trust to give. This is not some skittish horse, but a monster."

"Which I can control," she retorted. "You aren't the only one who—"

"Perhaps," he said, worried that a longer argument would bring discovery. "But you could get eaten while bridling it."

She hesitated. "That part worries me," she admitted at last. "It might take two of us to do that."

It usually took a neck-pole and several stalwart lads man-handling a darsteed to get it saddled and bridled, but Dain did not point out such details. He gave her hand a quick squeeze to indicate agreement and together they rose to their feet.

Thum, however, stayed on the ground where he was. Worried about him, Dain bent down again.

"Can you stand?" he asked softly. "Come, my friend."

Thum struggled upright, gasping with every breath. Dain gripped his arm to support him and felt the heat of Thum's fever through his clothing.

They limped along a few steps before Thum stopped and slumped against the wall. "It's no good," he moaned. "I'm only in the way. Get away if you can. Leave me here."

"Don't be stupid," Dain whispered angrily. "I'm not leaving you behind."

"I can't do it," Thum said, and rubbed his forehead fretfully. "If I only had some water."

Dain looked around at once. "Where's the horse trough?"

Alexeika blocked his path. "No," she whispered. "He tried to drink it earlier. He said the water tastes like blood."

Gently Dain pushed her aside. "Wait and see."

Slipping inside the stables, he dipped the god-steel bowl into the water, carried it outside, and held the brimming vessel to Thum's lips. "Drink."

Thum turned away. "It's no good. It burns like fire and—"

"Drink," Dain urged him. "This is pure."

He supported Thum's head, tightening his grip on the bowl when Thum began to gulp greedily at the water. When he'd drunk it all, Dain slipped back to the trough to fill the bowl for Alexeika.

She took it warily, then nearly dropped it. "What is this?" she asked suspiciously.

Dain held the bowl for her. "Just drink," he said.

She lowered her head to the water and sniffed it. Cautiously she took a sip, then began to drink faster until she was gulping it as greedily as Thum had been. When it was empty she stepped back and wiped her mouth with the back of her hand.

"Praise to Thod," she whispered with a new lilt to her voice. "Nothing has ever tasted sweeter."

Dain tucked the bowl away inside his surcoat, then took Severgard from his belt and handed it to her.

She gasped audibly and gripped the sword with both hands. At once its blade began to glow in warning, and she sheathed it hurriedly.

"Where did you . . . how did you get it?" she asked.

"I'll tell you later," Dain said, casting a look over his shoulder. He heard nothing to alert him, but just the same he felt uneasy. "We'd better hurry."

Leaving Thum outside to keep watch, they hurried into the stables together and slipped over to the darsteed area.

At once, several of the creatures bugled a warning. Stamping and snorting, they peered over the tall walls of their pens, red eyes glowing demonically.

Dain stared at them in annoyance, wanting them to be quiet.

"That one," Alexeika said, pointing.

Without giving Dain a chance to respond, she darted over to its pen and opened the meat box. The darsteed reared up eagerly, its hooves striking sparks off the top bricks.

Dain gripped her arm to stop her. "Don't feed it!"

"Why not?"

"Look!" He gestured at the other darsteeds, now alert and snorting eagerly. "They all want feeding."

"Oh." Alexeika shut the box. "Give me a moment to prepare."

"We don't have a moment," Dain said. He heard a muffled voice of inquiry from the loft where the grooms slept. Swiftly he hurried to the gear hooks and pulled down an odd-shaped saddle and bridle designed for darsteeds. He pushed the saddle into Alexeika's hands. "I'll go in first and bridle it. While I hold it you get the saddle on. Agreed?"

"Aye," she said breathlessly. "But how—"

He reached for the gate, paused a moment to let the hot fury that was the darsteed's mind flood his, then opened the gate, stepped inside, and clamped down hard on the beast with all his willpower.

Stand/stand/stand/stand.

The darsteed snorted and retreated from him, lashing its barbed tail from side to side. Dain kept aiming the mental command at it. Never before had he felt anything fight him so hard. Never before had he had to be so harsh with a wild beast to make it do his bidding.

Sweating in the darkness, he advanced on the creature, aware that if his control slipped the darsteed would attack him instantly.

Stand/stand/stand/stand.

It stopped retreating and lowered its head. Flames rumbled in its nostrils. Dain's heart was thudding hard, but he knew he dared not hesitate now. Swiftly he strode forward and slipped the bridle onto that narrow skull. He fastened the throat latch with a hard tug, then turned around.

"Come."

Alexeika entered the pen, lugging the heavy saddle. The darsteed reared and struck out with a deadly forefoot, missing Dain by inches.

He struck back with his mind, and the darsteed squealed in pain.

"Someone's coming," Alexeika said. "I heard them."

Dain refused to listen. He could feel the animal's savage desire to attack pushing against him. With all his might he struggled to hold it while she fumbled with the saddle and tugged at the girths. Dain helped her, fear giving him the strength to yank them tighter than the darsteed liked.

It pawed and shifted, and its tail nearly struck Alexeika. Her mind reached out, blundering and clumsy, entangling with Dain's as she tried to help him control the darsteed.

Distracted, Dain lost control of it.

The darsteed opened its venomous jaws and charged. Shouting something, Alexeika tried to stop it, but its mind was a maelstrom of fury and attack. It bounded right at Dain, who retreated until his shoulders struck the brick wall behind him. Swiftly he drew Truthseeker, and as the darsteed reared above him, Dain slapped the creature's chest with the flat of his blade.

Truthseeker burned the darsteed. Squalling in pain, it dropped to all four feet and retreated. The stench of burned hide filled the air.

In the distance, shouts rang out, and Dain heard the sound of running feet. Pushing past Alexeika, he sprang into the saddle and beat the darsteed with his mind to regain control of it.

"Quick!" he said to Alexeika.

She climbed on behind him, and the darsteed exploded into a gallop, bursting through the half-open gate. They thundered through the stables, frightening the horses, which neighed and jerked at their ties. The other darsteeds bugled and kicked while grooms came running with torches and shouts of alarm.

The darsteed sprang outside, bounding faster than Dain was prepared for. By the time he stopped it and wrenched it around, precious minutes were lost. It fought him every step as he forced it back to the stables to get Thum.

His friend was standing there openmouthed in the brightening moonlight. He retreated as the darsteed sidled up to him.

"I cannot," he said.

"Quick, Thum!" Dain shouted. "There's no time for your scruples now."

"Leave me. 'Tis blasphemous to ride it."

There was no time to argue with him. Dain urged the darsteed closer, and when Thum turned to run Dain reached down, gripped him by the back of his tunic, and hauled him up across the darsteed's withers. Thum howled in fear and struggled, but Dain held him in place ruthlessly. Dain wheeled the darsteed around so sharply it reared, then let it run.

On the other side of the compound, more worshipers were entering. Now there was no question of trying to slip out unnoticed, but the gates were open, and if he could reach the streets beyond the palace, he vowed, he'd lead his pursuers on a merry chase.

"No! No!" Thum was still protesting.

"Sit up!" Dain shouted at him. "Damne, man, you're alive and we've a chance to get out of here. Sit up and ride like the du Maltie you are, or by Thod I *will* leave you behind."

His words were harsh, his temper ablaze, but Thum stopped whining and struggled erect astride the darsteed's neck. It bounded along with a longer stride than a horse's, awkward and hard to get used to. But Thod's bones, Dain thought in sudden exhilaration as his hair blew back from his face, it was indeed fast.

Scattering worshipers on every side, he came galloping up to the gates. They were wrought of some kind of ornate metalwork, far from the solid and immensely thick portals he was used to in Mandria. Shouting and cursing, the guards were shoving the gates closed, but although Alexeika screamed something in Dain's ear, he did not hesitate.

"For Nether!" he shouted, drawing Truthseeker.

He swung the sword with lethal force, and the guards reaching for him went sprawling. As Dain sent the darsteed leaping straight at the gates, he leaned forward to strike the metal with his sword.

Truthseeker shattered the ornamentation, sending bits of metal flying in all directions. He struck again and again, chopping his way through while the darsteed danced and wheeled.

An arrow flew through the air, missing them by inches. Crying out, Alexeika drew Severgard, which was glowing white, and fought off those who tried to attack them from the rear.

The darsteed kicked with lethal force, knocking a man flying as Dain finished destroying the gates. He gathered the reins and started to turn his mount just as more arrows flew by his ear.

None struck him, however, and by then Dain was sending the darsteed bounding through and out onto the broad avenue that stretched across the entire length of the city.

"Hang on!" he shouted, and let the darsteed gallop.

"Fire-knights pursue us!" Alexeika shouted in his ear.

Nodding, Dain settled deeper into the saddle and let the darsteed run as fast as it wanted. Thum was leaning back against him, hindering his control of their mount. After a moment, Dain gave him a slight push, then had to grab him quickly to keep him from toppling off.

Only then did the moonlight glimmer off the arrow protruding from Thum's chest. Horrified, Dain held him close.

"Thum!" he shouted over the thunder of the darsteed's hooves. "Thum, can you hear me?"

His friend made no answer. Dain realized that had he not forced Thum to sit up, he himself would have been hit by the arrow. Aghast, he wanted to plead forgiveness, but knew it would do no good.

"Damne!"

"What's wrong?" Alexeika asked.

"Thum's hurt. Arrow! I can't hold him up."

"Break it off and let him lie across the darsteed's neck," she suggested. "Hang on. I'll try to reach the arrow if I can."

Her arm snaked past Dain's side. He wanted to protest, for he feared she might kill Thum by yanking the arrow in the wrong direction. But there was nothing else they could do.

She grunted, pressing her cheek hard against Dain's shoulder as she struggled to pull the arrow out from this difficult angle. Finally she gave a shout of triumph and held it up. Blood dripped across her hand, and she flung the arrow away.

"Lower him!" she said. "He'll live or die, but there's naught else we can do right now."

Glancing back, Dain saw a shadowy group of riders in the distance behind them, closing too fast.

Something invisible touched him, and Dain shuddered. Quickly he tightened his grip on Truthseeker. "Alexeika!" he said. "Reach inside my surcoat and put your hand on the bowl. Whatever happens, don't let go of it."

To her credit, she didn't question his odd order but did as he said. The *magemon*'s touch on his mind fell away. Dain gasped in relief.

He felt suddenly tired and weakened from a day too long and too full of exertion. In his heart he was grieving for Thum, yet now was not the time to give way. Mustering his determination, Dain thrust off his fatigue and veered the darsteed abruptly off the wide avenue into one of the dark, twisting streets of the city.

Alexeika's arms tightened around him, but she made no protest. Praying he would not become lost, Dain wound along the narrow streets. Here and there the darsteed's hooves slipped on the filth, but he came to no dead ends, and gradually the sounds of pursuit diminished.

But they had another problem ahead of them, one that Dain had not yet solved.

As though she were thinking the same thing, Alexeika said, "The city gates. How do we get through them?"

"I don't know."

"You can't batter them down. They're too strong, and too heavily guarded."

But Dain was thinking hard. He said, "Can you speak Gantese?"

"Almost none," she said.

"Enough to get past the guards?"

"How—"

"Can you say you have business beyond the city walls?"

"I—I think so," she said doubtfully. "But what—"

"Quick, then," he said, halting the reluctant darsteed. It rumbled and shook its head, snapping the air and lashing its tail, but he held it firmly. "You're wearing red mail, Believer mail."

"Aye, but—oh."

She stared at him as he twisted around to look at her.

"Aye," he said swiftly, and pulled the bowl from his surcoat. "Take off your surcoat and give me your cloak."

She untied the cloak, which was twisted about her waist, and handed it to him. He shook out its folds and flung it over Thum. By then she'd removed her surcoat. Dain wadded it up inside his own before he upended the bowl on her head.

At once she gripped it in protest. "What are you doing?"

"Making you a helmet," he said. "Hush. I can make you look bigger. I can make this bowl look like a helmet. Wait." He paused, surprised to see her still armed with her daggers. "How come you to have those?"

"My daggers?" she asked, and shrugged. "I know not. They never took them from me. Perhaps they're of no use against spell locks and protections."

Dain grunted. "We're trading places. Get off."

"What?"

He elbowed her in the stomach, shoving her off the darsteed's bony hindquarters. She landed on her feet and had to jump quickly to avoid the lash of the creature's tail.

Dain pushed himself back behind the saddle. "Get on, quickly!"

She climbed, avoiding a vicious bite by striking the darsteed's muzzle with her fist, and put the bowl back on her head. "I feel like a fool. This *can't* work."

"Eldin magic is mostly about illusion. You let folks see what they expect to see," Dain said in explanation. He leaned close against her. "I shall make an illusion that we are one rider, masculine and large."

"What about Thum?"

"They won't see him."

"What about my face?"

"I shall make the bowl look like a helmet so they never see your face."

"But it won't *really* be covered."

"In their eyes it will appear so. Remember to speak Gantese. Be gruff. Be curt and impatient. Do nothing else. Make no sudden moves, because the illusion will fail if you do. The spell will be very thin."

"But—"

He gripped her shoulders. "Trust me. And do what I ask."

She nodded, although she still looked doubtful. "But what kind of magic is this? I've never heard of eldin doing such—"

"It's *my* magic," Dain said hurriedly. "Something I taught myself to do."

As she fell silent, the darsteed jumped without warning and nearly unseated both of them.

"Alexeika!" Dain said in exasperation. "You must control it. I can't concentrate on both things at once."

"All right," she muttered beneath her breath. "Just get on with it."

"You won't feel anything. Don't trust your eyes," he warned her. "Trust me, and stay within the illusion."

She nodded, and he closed his eyes. After a moment he was able to clear the darsteed from his mind. He felt it shy again, fighting Alexeika and the reins. Somehow she held it, and Dain concentrated on the spell he was weaving. As once he'd made men look like trees in the Nold forest to save their lives, so now did he weave this illusion, turning Alexeika and himself into one Believer in red mail.

At last he opened his eyes, feeling fresh sweat pop out on his forehead as he struggled to hold the spell in balance. "Now," he whispered.

She eased the darsteed forward, threading it down a dark, narrow street between silent mud houses. In a few minutes they emerged into the open. The city walls rose up before them, and torchlight flared brightly at the gates. Their pursuers milled around there, shouting orders at the sentries, who replied with equal vehemence.

Alexeika checked the darsteed suddenly. "Oh, no!"

Dain felt the spell slip; he nearly lost it entirely. "Join them. Stay at the rear."

She drew in a sharp breath, but then steadied herself. She

rode up to the rear of the party, her darsteed snapping in ill temper at another. She was the only knight in red mail astride a darsteed. All the others of her rank were on horseback, but no one seemed to notice the discrepancy.

The commander of the pursuit party went on arguing with the sentries, then at last issued a series of orders. From their gestures, Dain inferred that they somehow believed he and his friends had already escaped the city. A few minutes later, the gates swung open.

Alexeika rode out behind them, and as the Believers fanned out into the darkness, Dain gradually dropped the illusion, then resumed control of the darsteed. He sent it a firm command—*Quiet/quiet/quiet/quiet*—and the animal for once obeyed him perfectly.

Without even a rumble, it dropped back from the others and picked its way quietly down into the ditch bordering the road.

Cloaked in darkness, keeping well to shadow, they kept going cautiously until the ditch petered out in a dry canyon and the darsteed began to flounder in deep sand.

Giving it a kick, Alexeika sent the beast climbing out of the shallow canyon, then they went galloping into the moonlit desert. Not until they reached the low hill where they'd first seen Sindeul did Alexeika draw rein. Dain looked back at the city, which lay like a long dark smudge at the base of the black mountains. The tallest peak, sacred to Ashnod, was spewing fire at its top, and the smoke it emitted spread into the night sky, obscuring the stars and veiling the bright, round moon.

Dain allowed himself to draw a long, deep breath. It was hard to believe they'd actually escaped, yet at the same time he felt scant relief. He knew the hardest part still lay ahead of them.

As he took the bowl off Alexeika's head and slipped it back inside his surcoat, she laughed aloud. "We did it!" she crowed. "We're free! Free of Gant and all its evil."

"Hush!" he whispered, swiftly gripping her shoulder in warning. "Sound carries far in the desert. Besides, they won't let us go this easily."

"I see no one in pursuit," she said. "We've lost them."

"Have we?" he asked sharply. "Where are the ones we followed out? Why do they not come after us?"

"What does it matter, as long as we're free?"

"While we remain in Gant, we are not free," he said grimly. "I think they may be waiting ahead of us, near the gateway to the second world."

"In ambush?"

"Aye."

As he spoke, the ground rumbled and quaked, causing the darsteed to shy. Dain saw the mountain erupting with fire. Molten lava spilled down its sides. The air, even at this distance, was suddenly filled with ash and smoke.

Alexeika kicked the darsteed forward. "Then we must avoid that trail and choose another. The desert is vast. Surely we can elude them."

Before them stretched a vast sea of sand and bare rock, perhaps empty of life except for themselves. Dain had no idea of how far it was to the Charva, which bordered this land, how many leagues they needed to ride, how many days they had to travel. Was there any water to be found in such a vast wilderness? Was there anything to hunt for food? And if so, would it be edible?

All these questions swam in his mind, but he touched Alexeika's shoulder and said, "Let the darsteed run."

She obeyed, and as the darsteed raced into the desert nightscape, Ashnod shook the ground and rimmed the edges of Sindeul with living fire. Whatever lay ahead did not matter, Dain told himself, because for them there was no going back.

17

THE FOLLOWING MORNING, as the sun came up and grew bright
and hot, they took shelter of sorts beneath a rocky outcropping
that cast scant shade. Keeping a sort of mental leash on the
darsteed, Dain stripped off its bridle and let it roam to hunt.

He and Alexeika had nothing to eat except the pocketful of
grain she'd stolen from mangers in the stables. Dain put the
few precious kernels in the god-steel bowl in hopes of cleaning them of whatever taint they held, then he and Alexeika
chewed them raw. Despite his efforts, the taste was foul, and
the grain proved to be almost too hard to chew. Afterwards, his
stomach hurt, ungrateful for what he'd put into it.

Thum lay where they placed him, gray-faced and hot with
fever. His arrow wound had stopped bleeding on its own, although it looked deep and ugly. The hurlhound bite on his leg
was swollen with infection. Dain salted the wound carefully,
then Alexeika cauterized it with Severgard. Thum screamed in
pain, sitting up for a wild moment while Dain tried to hold him
still, then he fainted again and could not be roused. They bound
up his wounds and let him be.

Throughout the day the heat grew more intense, until they
were panting from it. Dain could think of nothing except water.
He stripped bare to the waist, leaving himself clad only in leggings and boots, and used his clothing for a bed. Sweating and
miserable, he fell into an exhausted sleep while Alexeika kept
watch.

When the sun began to drop low in the sky, Dain awoke,
wiped his perspiring face and licked the sweat off his palms
for moisture, then recalled the darsteed. To his relief, the creature came back, but it was bad-tempered and hungry. With difficulty they loaded Thum across its withers. Dain and Alexeika
got on, and they turned their faces toward the huge, blazing orb
sinking beyond the horizon. Dain rode all night, with Alexeika
dozing against his back.

The next dawn the darsteed found a small oasis with a muddy, brackish puddle beneath a sickly, yellow-green tree. Its dying, thorny foliage lay scattered on the ground and floated on top of the water. Tracks of wild creatures, all small, could be seen in the dried mud.

Dismounting, Dain let the darsteed drink first while he sniffed and prowled hopefully, but he sensed no game nearby. For a moment his head felt light and his knees wobbled under him. He clung, half-swooning from hunger, to the darsteed's side, then pulled himself together and filled the bowl with water.

When it cleared, he gave it first to Alexeika, then drank deeply himself. He refilled the bowl and managed to dribble some water past Thum's dry, crusted lips. Moaning, Thum stirred and seemed about to awaken, but he did not.

Worried about his friend, Dain supposed it was just as well that Thum stayed unconscious. His misery was lessened that way.

In the end, Dain and Alexeika broke off twigs from the odd tree. He peeled back the tough bark with his thumbnail and gnawed the twigs like something demented.

"Sire!"

He looked up, alerted by the strange tone in Alexeika's voice. She'd climbed partway into the tree and was frozen there, staring at something she'd found among the branches.

"What?" he asked, squinting.

At their backs, the sun was coming up, streaking the sky with coral and gold. With it came the heat that was their enemy. Dain frowned at Alexeika, who was making odd little noises in her throat.

"What?" he asked again.

"Eggs," she said reverently. "A nest of eggs."

Nearly overwhelmed by this stroke of good luck, he closed his eyes. "Merciful Thod," he whispered. "Can you reach them?"

"Aye. Here."

With infinite care, she handed the fist-sized eggs down to him one at a time. He fought off the darsteed, which lunged at their bounty, and managed to keep the beast from stealing any. Grumbling, the darsteed lurched off, then stopped, glaring back at them with red, resentful eyes.

Ignoring it, Dain and Alexeika busied themselves making camp a short distance away from the water hole. Alexeika built a fire, while Dain held up the eggs one by one. They were hard-shelled and an ugly greenish-black color. Four of them felt heavy; two did not.

He and Alexeika baked the four heavy eggs in the ashes of the small fire, their mouths watering at the aroma. The darsteed stayed nearby, bugling its desire for food. Finally Dain tossed it the lightweight eggs he'd rejected.

Two snaps of the darsteed's jaws, and the eggs were gone.

Go, Dain commanded, and finally the darsteed ambled off to hunt.

When the eggs were cooked, Alexeika rolled them out of the ashes with a stick. They cracked one carefully on a stone, not sure what they would find inside. But there was a yolk, bright orange and steaming, in the midst of flaky white.

Sniffing it cautiously, Dain smelled nothing foul. At his nod, Alexeika divided the egg between them, and they could barely wait for it to cool. Dain found the flavor too strong to have been appealing under different circumstances, but he ate all of his share and counted himself blessed. Half of an egg, though, was hardly enough. He stared at the rest of the eggs, tempted sorely to eat them all, before his gaze lifted to meet Alexeika's blue-gray eyes. He saw his own desperate hunger reflected in them. He realized that if his willpower weakened, hers would too. Thus far, she'd proven to be resilient, brave, and stalwart. It was a relief to have a companion equal to the task at hand. She was no helpless lady, to be pampered and worried over. She could take care of herself.

With a frown, he pulled his attention back to the situation at hand. "Better save the rest of the eggs, just in case," he said regretfully.

She licked her mouth and dropped her eyes to hide their disappointment. After a moment, she nodded, and he was grateful she did not whine or protest.

"I'm going to make some lures," she said, "and see if I can trap whatever comes to the water today."

"A good idea," Dain told her with a smile. "I'll help you."

Companionably they set to work, cutting supple branches

from the tree and matching them by length. Alexeika unraveled threads from the edge of her cloak and braided them together to make a thin but strong cord. With it, she bent the lures into position while Dain carefully brushed out their tracks. Glancing over at her, he realized they had not argued since their escape. It was pleasant working together on a specific task, such as making these lures.

"Let's shift our camp upwind of the water," he suggested. "And out of earshot. Nothing will come close if it smells or hears us today."

Alexeika's assessing look held a new measure of respect. "It would seem your majesty is a skilled hunter as well as a warrior."

He grinned at her, for he'd learned her compliments were rare. Kicking away a brown, furry spider as large as his hand, Dain settled himself in the scant shade created by spreading his cloak across two branches to form a crude lean-to.

She hesitated a moment, standing there with her gaze on the horizon and her hands resting casually on the hilts of her daggers. "Sire?"

"Hmm?"

"May I ask you about the man who died?"

Dain glanced up. "What man?"

"The one who was a guardian. The one who disappeared in thin air, then died." She was frowning, looking troubled. Her eyes, so clear and intelligent beneath dark brows, met Dain's hesitantly. "Was he your servant?"

Thinking of Sulein's crazed final moments only reminded Dain of the Ring and all that had been lost with it. He scowled and drew up his knees beneath his chin. "He was the physician of Thirst Hold."

"And . . . I think . . . also a *sorcerel*?"

"Nay!" Dain said sharply. "He wanted to be one, wanted others to think him one, but he lacked those powers. His spells were minor ones."

"But he could enter the second world at will," she said. "As Quar took us. Surely that was possession of great ability."

Dain frowned, still angry at the physician for having been such a greedy fool. Jabbing the red dirt with his thumb, Dain gouged a hole as he said, "That was no special power of his. Sulein possessed the Ring of Solder."

Alexeika turned pale. Staring at him, she opened her mouth but no sound came out. She dropped cross-legged on the ground before him. "The Ring!" she finally whispered in awe. "I have heard its legend. But how came he by it?"

Dain shrugged. "He said he bought it from a peddler. How this could be, I know not. When I learned what it was and that it was part of my birthright, I tried to claim it, but Sulein would not release it into my keeping." He paused, his mouth twisting with bitter regrets. "We could be traveling to Nether at this moment, in the blink of an eye." He snapped his fingers, and Alexeika flinched.

"But if he served you and believed you to be king—"

"Oh, aye, he believed that long before I did myself," Dain said. "But he was an ambitious and greedy man. He wanted riches and great rewards, and he thought if he kept the Ring from me I would grant him anything he asked."

Frustration welled up inside Dain and he clenched his fists, wishing he could run and run and run, the way he used to through the Dark Forest when his inner burdens grew too heavy to bear. But he was no longer a child, with a child's solution to problems.

"Why he panicked in Sindeul, I know not."

"Perhaps he was simply afraid," she said softly.

"Aye. It's a terrible place."

"More than terrible."

Dain met her eyes, which held a haunted look. He knew his own must be reflecting back a similar expression.

"An unholy place," she whispered.

He nodded. "But now he is dead. He used the Ring improperly, and lost it forever."

"If you had it," she asked slowly, "would you dare use it to take us from here?"

"Aye." Then he remembered Tobeszijian's warning and abruptly shook his head. "Nay, I suppose not. Its use is for the benefit of the Chalice only. 'Tis what happened to my father, after all. He used the Ring without harm to conceal the Chalice, but then he tried to save himself and is now trapped forever in the second world."

She gasped. "I didn't know this! Merciful Thod, I thought him dead."

Dain sighed. "'Tis worse than being dead. He wanders, trapped between the first world and the third like a ghost."

"Before your path parted from this man Sulein's, why didn't you use the Ring to find the Chalice?"

"Because I didn't know where the Chalice was," Dain told her. "You can't just leap into the second world without a clear destination in mind. You could end up lost like Tobeszijian. Or dead, like Sulcin."

She frowned thoughtfully. "Can anyone use the Ring, if they know how?"

"That, I know not," Dain said. "It is meant to be worn by the king. Sulein dared to use it, and you saw what happened to him."

"Aye," she said softly. "I did."

In the shade of the lean-to, Thum moaned.

Hoping his friend was finally coming round, Dain dusted off his hands. "'Tis no good talking about the Ring now," he said bitterly. "Sulein saw to it that it's gone forever."

He checked on Thum, who was tossing feverishly. The squire's dark red hair looked matted and dull, his eyes were sunk deep in their sockets, and his skin was hot to the touch. Dain gave him more water and tried to keep his face cool.

Out in the sun, Alexeika sat cross-legged on the ground with her back turned slightly toward him as though to give herself privacy. She rolled up the sleeves of her linsey tunic and used a damp rag to clean her face and arms, which were growing bronzed beneath the merciless sun. Then she loosened her hair from its braid and began to work out its many knots and tangles with her fingers.

Dain found himself watching her perform these simple, yet incredibly intimate acts. He felt uncomfortable, as though he'd somehow invaded her privacy, yet there was nowhere else to go unless he were to risk sunstroke by wandering about in the desert. So, tired and stiff from riding all night, he reclined on one elbow under the lean-to and sleepily watched her finger-comb her hair.

He'd had no idea there was such a wealth of it, or that it was so long and thick. Curly from having been braided, it flowed down her back to the ground. He remembered his sister's long hair, so fair and silky, and how Thia used to comb it every night, counting the strokes under her breath, before she went to bed.

The sunlight beamed down upon Alexeika as she loosened snarls and picked out little bits of leaf and twig. At last she finished working through the long tresses, and spread her hair in a luxuriant fan across her shoulders. It was a dark chestnut brown, with highlights of red and gold glinting in the sunshine. Alexeika sighed, tilted back her head, and gave it a shake so that her hair flowed and rippled magnificently.

Then she straightened and looked over her shoulder straight at him. Her blue-gray eyes held his a long, long while, entangled with emotions he could not read.

He sensed nothing from her mind, nothing at all, yet there seemed to be something she expected. He'd noticed that Alexeika watched him often with a brooding frown, as though she wanted to say something to him, or to ask a question, or even perhaps to confide a secret. Yet she seldom spoke except as necessary. Today's questions were unusual for her. He found himself suddenly curious about her past.

"Alexeika," he said.

She blinked, her gaze changing. "Sire?"

"Tell me about Nether. Tell me about its history, about your father and what you know of mine. Tell me about yourself and how you've grown up, what you've done since your father died."

Something eager sparked to life in her remarkable eyes. She nearly smiled, then frowned. "There is much to say in all that. I would bore your majesty."

"Don't be coy," he said sharply. "Were I not interested, I would not ask. Talk to me a while, for tired as I am, I cannot sleep."

"Where do I start?"

"Anywhere you like."

And so she began to talk, keeping her voice low and quiet.

He found her an excellent speaker. Her recountings were clear and concise and well-ordered. After a while she seemed to relax and forget his rank, for she began to sprinkle in pithy comments and observations that made him smile. He saw how keen and logical her mind was. The details she gave him were useful. He learned all she knew about his parents and the betrayal which had led to their doom. But when Alexeika began to talk of her own father, her tone softened and changed, filling with pride, love, and longing all jumbled together. Dain saw how profoundly she had adored and respected Ilymir Volvn, and he envied her for having grown up knowing her parent. Through the spinning of her tales, he could envision that tall, fearless general with his jutting nose and fierce gray eyebrows. When she described Volvn's final battle, how he and his five hundred men took on a force of two thousand, only to be slaughtered by the unexpected arrival of Nonkind against all rules of combat, Dain heard the war cries and saw the terrible massacre as the rebels fell one by one. These had been men loyal to his father, King Tobeszijian. Men loyal to himself, although they'd never seen him.

Bowing his head, Dain knew he owed such men—owed *all* the Netherans who had fought and died in the cause of right— a tremendous debt. It did not matter how much he still felt unworthy and unready for his kingly responsibilities. They had to be carried out. And he vowed anew that he would do what was required.

Unless he failed to escape Gant.

Tears welled up in Alexeika's eyes as she told him how she'd released her father's soul just before the looters returned to the battlefield.

"I'm sorry I asked you to conjure up such painful memories," Dain said softly.

She sniffed, and wiped her eyes as though ashamed to be caught weeping. "I was so certain he would win. Until that day I never doubted that my father could do anything. The possibility of defeat never entered my mind, despite all his cautions." She frowned. "I was such a child."

" 'Tis nothing wrong with being so. With having an innocent hope and belief in good," he said.

Her eyes flashed fiercely. "Nay! 'Tis better to know that life can be cruel indeed. Nothing is ever safe. Nothing ever remains unchanged."

"Would you want things to always be the same, Alexeika?"

"Aye! I would wipe this year away, if I could."

Dain said nothing. Despite all that had happened to him in recent months, he would change little of it. Only the deaths, he thought, would he change. There had been too many of those, too many loved ones, friends, and comrades taken.

Alexeika took out Severgard and rubbed its black blade with sand, polishing it as though her hands knew not how to lie idle. She spoke again, and now her voice was hushed and angry as she told him about the Grethori raid and her days as a captive. She provided few details, but Dain could tell from the suppressed emotion in her voice and the fire in her eyes that it must have been a horrifying time. Yet she'd escaped.

"Only to be pulled back into danger by me," Dain said. "And because of me you were brought here to be a Gantese slave."

"The Grethori were worse," she said, tossing her head. "All my life I have feared Gant, but nothing I've seen here has been worse than the *sheda* and her spells."

She didn't meet Lord Zinxt, Dain thought bleakly. She didn't walk through that palace of the lost and the damned. She didn't face the Chief Believer.

He crawled out from under the lean-to, picked up the bowl, and rose to his feet. Exposed to the full blast of the sun, he felt himself instantly drenched with perspiration. The heat seemed to be baking his brain inside his skull. When he squinted across the horizon, the air shimmered from the heat, and for a wild moment he thought he saw riders coming their way.

But it was only a mirage, and after a moment his racing heart slowed down.

"Get in the shade and rest," he told her. "I'll go fetch more water and check the traps."

"Those should be my jobs," she said at once.

Dain frowned. "Alexeika," he said with more sharpness than he intended. "You are neither my squire nor my servant. Nor do I want you to be. Avail yourself of the shade."

A tide of red rose from her throat into her face, but Dain

swung away from her and strode off toward the watering hole. His senses told him no animals had come to it; thus, he made no effort to be quiet. It was odd how, whenever he found himself starting to like the girl, she did something to irritate him. She had no business groveling around him like some lackey. Indeed, as a maiden—and maiden she was, no matter how good a warrior she might also be—it was unseemly for her to serve him; why didn't she understand that?

He filled the bowl halfway with muddy water and watched it gradually clear. As he carried it carefully back, he checked their empty traps and let his vision sweep the horizon in all directions. The wind blew hot and dry against his face. Every breath he inhaled seemed to desiccate his body from the inside.

When he returned to the lean-to, he found Alexeika sitting in the shade. Her loose tunic sleeves were rolled down to the wrists, concealing her lean, well-toned arms. Her beautiful hair had been pulled back in a severe braid. Looking stern and unhappy, she watched as he crawled next to Thum and began to bathe his friend's feverish face.

"I do not understand how the bowl sweetens the water," she said at last.

Dain finished dribbling a bit of the liquid between Thum's parched lips and sighed. "Be grateful for this gift of the gods."

"Is—is this perhaps the Chalice?" she asked in a hushed voice.

Dain looked at her in surprise. "Nay."

"I thought it must be. It seems to have such amazing powers. It has saved our lives and—"

"The Chalice is in Nold," he said firmly, and handed her the bowl to drink from. "That is where we go next."

She lowered the bowl from her lips and frowned. "Not to Nether?"

"I'll not argue with you on this matter," he said in warning.

Her frown deepened. "I do not argue with you, sire. I merely asked for clarification."

"We go first to Nold, if we can reach it," he said, hardly willing to let himself hope that they might actually get as far as the border. But finding the water and food today had restored his faith in their survival, giving him new energy and optimism.

"With the Chalice in my possession I will rally the scattered rebel forces into an army."

"But would it not be better to rally those forces now, in the last days of autumn?" she countered. "You will have all winter to train them into a strong fighting force. Then you can renew your quest for the Chalice's recovery."

With a snap of his temper, Dain turned away from her. "I told you I would not argue about this."

"It is not argument to discuss—"

"Alexeika," he said sharply, "if you want me to be your king, then let me lead. Let me make the decisions."

She jumped to her feet. "Are you ever willing to be counseled in anything?"

"Are you ever willing to accept it when I do not want such counsel?"

"Why do you reject advice that is wise and sound?"

"Learn to be rejected," he replied harshly. "Learn to be quiet."

Her cheeks grew red. Standing there with her long legs braced apart and her hands resting on her hips, she fumed visibly. "I am only telling you what my father would tell you. I suppose that were he alive, you would pay heed to *him*."

"I thought we had this settled," he said in annoyance.

"I have seen you fight as no other man can fight," she said furiously. "Why, then, do you turn coward whenever joining your army is mentioned? What's amiss with you?"

Had she been a man, he would have struck her for that. As it was, he glared at her with such heat he thought the top of his head might explode. Somehow he held on to his temper and drew in several deep breaths until he thought he could control his voice.

No doubt she thought he wasn't going to answer, for she continued: "Or is it Lady Pheresa's plight that keeps your wits bound in a knot? Can't you think of anything else? What about your kingdom? What about the people's suffering? You think the Chalice will heal your lady love, but what about—"

"Enough!" he broke in. "You seem to have certain expectations of me, of what I will do, of how I will act. And when I do not conform, you shriek at me like a fishwife."

Her mouth opened, but he held up his hand to silence her.

"Hear me! There can be but one king, one leader. The rest must be followers!"

"Sire—"

"Perhaps your father hoped to make himself king of Nether. Perhaps you think *you* should rule."

She turned bright red and knelt at his feet. "No, sire. I—"

"You want me to be something I am not. You refuse to accept me for what I am."

"Please—"

But he was tired of her criticism. "I am not Netheran-raised, Alexeika. Never will I react as you would probably wish me to. My actions are governed by many factors, some of which you know nothing about."

"I know about them," she said resentfully. "I know you put Lady Pheresa ahead of your own throne."

That again, he thought. As though Alexeika were somehow jealous of Pheresa, whom she'd never met. The absurdity of it only fanned his anger more.

"I see," he said in a clipped voice. "You think that because King Kaxiniz spoke unkindly about the lady you may do the same. No doubt if you were fed adequately and had sufficient sleep, you would show more charity to a maiden who has done you no ill whatsoever."

"I—"

His angry gesture cut her off. "Let us put the lady's misfortunes aside. She is dead by now and beyond my ability to save her."

"Dead!" Alexeika looked shocked. "How know you this?"

"Her guardians were among the prisoners in Sindeul, or have you forgotten? She and Prince Gavril were betrayed. The outcome is only too obvious."

Alexeika's dark brows knotted, and her anger seemed to fade away. "I had not made the connection. I'm sorry."

"Sorry?" he snapped. "Aye, perhaps. Until the next time you see fit to judge my actions. These jealous outbursts become you ill. Did your father teach you to behave so toward your liege and king?"

Her face turned pale. "No, sire," she whispered.

"As for the Chalice, its welfare *is* more important than my throne. It is my duty to return it to Nether first, as I swore to my father I would."

She stared at him, white-faced and silent.

Annoyed that he had revealed his private promise to his father, Dain glared at her. "Yes, Princess Volvn," he said with icy formality, "an oath sworn to Tobeszijian. A promise given. Do you understand that? Do you acknowledge the obligations a son must fulfill?"

Tears shimmered in her eyes. "Yes," she whispered.

He left her then, wishing he could stride out into the desert and work off his fury. Instead, he circled around behind the lean-to and settled himself there with an angry grunt. She'd provoked the stupid argument; he wondered how she liked the outcome.

But he could take neither pride nor satisfaction in having crushed her. Instead, he felt faintly ashamed of himself for having been so harsh, although that only annoyed him more. She needed to be taught a lesson, and that was an end to it.

In the empty silence beneath the wind, he heard her crying, the sound muffled and private.

Feeling more guilty than ever, he scowled. That was the way of females, he thought with resentment. They provoked an argument, then cried when they lost. Well, damne, perhaps she'd learn to bide her tongue. She had no business jumping to conclusions the way she did.

Just before sunset, he awakened from uneasy slumber and sat up stiffly. His skin felt burned and raw. The inside of his mouth was so dry he could not spit. The prospect of riding through another night filled him with dread and an exhaustion so pervasive he did not think he could even stand up.

But he forced himself to his feet. Alexeika was awake, and very subdued. She went to check the traps and came back with a shake of her head.

In silence they shared another egg. Such a meager amount of food was so inadequate against his ravenous hunger he almost didn't want to eat at all. But afterwards he felt strong enough to break camp.

Alexeika tucked their other two eggs away in her pockets while Dain gave more water to Thum. Both Dain and Alexeika drank as much as they could hold. Wishing he had some better means to transport water, Dain filled the bowl one last time and handed it to Alexeika to carry. Recalling the darsteed, which had tried to rub off its saddle during the day, Dain tightened the girths and lifted Thum onto its withers.

Alexeika stood nearby, stiff and almost at attention. Her right hand was white-knuckled on Severgard's hilt. "Sire," she said formally, "I wish to beg your forgiveness. I spoke wrongly to you today and deserved your ire. Please grant me your pardon."

Wrath, resentment, shame, and deep unhappiness were all entangled in her voice. Dain realized she must have battled long and hard with her pride to make this apology.

He also realized that her fiery spirit was far from broken, and that in the future she would likely give him more trouble.

But did he really want to crush her spirit?

Though he felt regret for some of the things he'd said to her, he did not apologize in turn. Instead, he gave her a kingly nod. "It's not the first time we've fought over this same matter," he said sternly.

She bowed her head. "No. I took your majesty's reprimand before, yet I did not learn my lesson."

"You have not learned it now."

Her head snapped up, but he did not let her reply. "You apologize because you think you should, not because your heart has changed. There will be more arguments in the future."

"Sire, I—"

"Don't promise something you can't keep," he said.

"But I—"

"Perhaps it is right that you *do* question me," he said. His anger was gone; he was too weary to find it again. "I think every king should have a friend fearless enough to speak her mind. Even if she's sometimes wrong."

Alexeika stared at him in astonishment. He returned the stare a moment, then smiled. She smiled back, and when he held out his hand to her, she clasped it readily.

He found her grip strong, her long fingers so different from Pheresa's slender, delicate ones. But thinking of Pheresa only stirred up emotions of grief and rage at her fate. Frowning,

Dain swept Pheresa from his mind and climbed into the saddle.

As soon as Alexeika got on behind him, he turned the darsteed westward and set it bounding along at a ground-eating pace. His bones ached. The saddle galled him, and he wondered if there would ever be an end to this desert wasteland.

Even more worrisome was the lack of pursuit, for he knew the Chief Believer would not let him go this easily. He was the linchpin of the Gantese plan of domination. Somewhere, sometime, he knew, there must be a confrontation, or a trap. He told himself to stay alert, but weariness and aches kept dulling his senses.

Yet despite his pessimism, there had been no more attempted contact by *magemons*. They encountered no traps. No riders appeared on the horizon behind them. No shapeshifters flew overhead to mark their location. They faced nothing but the terrible landscape and the deprivations of inadequate food and water.

The following daybreak, the air stayed cooler than it had before. Different scents came to Dain's nostrils, faintly intriguing but elusive, gone before he could identify them. He stiffened in the saddle and leaned forward as the starlight overhead faded and the day steadily brightened. They had left the desert behind. The darsteed's cloven hooves clinked now and then on dislodged pebbles. The terrain had changed, grown hilly and broken.

A breeze picked up, stirred by the rising sun. It came from the west, blowing into Dain's face. He turned his head and prodded Alexeika awake.

"What?" she asked at once, reaching for her daggers.

"I smell water," he said. His heart leaped in hope, and for the first time he allowed himself to believe they were going to make it. "Alexeika, I smell water!"

"Another oasis?" she asked, rubbing her face with her hands. She yawned and stretched while the darsteed plodded steadily onward.

"Nay." Dain lifted his face to the breeze, his nostrils sorting through various scents, which were stronger now. "Trees. A lot of water." He grinned in excitement. "I think it must be the Charva!"

At that moment the darsteed topped a rise, and there before them flowed the river of legend, rippling and rushing along between its rocky banks. On their side the hills dropped abruptly to a narrow beach of pebbles. The river ran glistening and shallow at the edge, so clear Dain could see the bottom pebbles. Here and there it foamed white over boulders in its course. Toward the center, the waters deepened to a swift channel.

On the other side, boulders lay strewn about as though a giant's hand had thrown them in a dicing game. The bank itself was flatter, wider, stretching gradually back toward a forest of pines, where the ground gleamed white beneath them.

Dain inhaled deeply of the pines' clean, pungent scent, and shivered in the cool dawn air. He untied his hauberk from the saddle, slipped it on, and rebelted Truthseeker and his dagger around his waist.

The darsteed stood there atop the rise, surveying the landscape before it with uneasy snorts.

Alexeika chuckled. "It doesn't like the water. Do we release it here?"

Dain shook his head. "Not if I can force it across. I know not exactly where we are, or in what realm we'll land on the other side."

"Pray to Thod it's not Klad," she said. "I know little of that land, and nothing I've heard is promising to our cause."

He smiled, his keen eyes surveying the forest. "Perhaps it's Nold. I'll know as soon as we're across and I find clan markings."

"Whatever it is, let us go there as fast as we can!"

He laughed with her, his weariness forgotten, and kicked the darsteed forward. The sun was climbing ever higher behind him. It did not feel as hot on his back as on previous days, and he rejoiced in that. Despite terrible odds, they had survived the Gantese desert. Perhaps there had been no pursuit because the population of Sindeul had perished in the erupting volcano. Dain knew not what had befallen the Believers, and he did not care. He and Alexeika were going home.

The darsteed flung up its narrow head and bugled. Thinking that it feared the water, Dain kept urging it forward. The darsteed fought him every step, slinging itself from side to side, then rearing.

Dain's temper began to fray, and he lost patience with the animal. They were so close, yet the darsteed refused to enter the water.

"We'll have to leave it behind," Alexeika said breathlessly, clinging to Dain's waist.

But Dain was determined to ride into Nether on a darsteed, determined to create a legend for himself no less than his father's had been.

"Come!" Alexeika urged him. "Let's dismount and be done."

"Nay! I'll try one more time."

He wrenched the darsteed around, but at that moment a terrible, putrid stench filled the air. It was so heavy and rotten it burned his nostrils and filled his mouth. Sick dismay sank his heart.

"Nonkind!" he shouted.

Alexeika was already drawing Severgard, which glowed as though on fire. "Great Olas, protect us now," she prayed aloud.

They came pouring into sight from farther upriver, horses and darsteeds galloping across the rocky beach. As they came, sunlight glinted off the riders' chain mail. The hurlhounds ran in front. Their baying chilled Dain to his very bones. Here, at last, was the ambush he'd feared all along.

18

As the Believers came galloping at them, Dain drew Truthseeker and kicked the darsteed again toward the water. Although reaching the Charva was now their only hope, the darsteed fought every step, costing them more precious minutes. Dain couldn't help but think, with a deep stab of frustration, that had the darsteed gone into the river the first time, they'd be halfway across by now and out of reach.

"Morde a day!" he shouted aloud to the beast. "You *will* go!"

"Get off!" Alexeika shouted. "Let's leave the brute!"

"And what of Thum?" he asked, unwilling to give up. "Am I to fight with him on my back?"

"We'll swim!" Alexeika said. "Never mind fighting."

Baying came from Dain's left, and he saw more Believers and hurlhounds stampeding their way from the opposite end of the rocky beach. They were cut off now on two sides, with the desert behind them. There was no choice but to enter the river.

Dain touched Truthseeker to his darsteed, and the beast squalled in pain. Furiously it galloped forward, splashing into knee-deep water. When it stopped again, rearing and striking the air with its forefeet, it was something crazed, and Dain no longer could control it.

Although the fire-knights on their darsteeds reined up at the water's edge, the red-mailed Believers on horseback charged into the shallows without hesitation. Dain gripped Thum's unconscious form and shoved him off into the water. It was the only place of safety for his helpless friend—unless Thum drowned, and even that would be better than recapture.

Dain twisted in the saddle as the hurlhounds reached them and shoved Alexeika off the darsteed too.

Yelling furiously, she hit the shallow water and floundered there, then jumped to her feet and brandished Severgard. "Are you mad?" she shouted. "What—"

"Get Thum to safety!" he shouted back. "Swim for your life!"

There wasn't time to say more, for the hurlhounds came splashing into the water, only to yelp and leap back.

The Believers on horseback galloped up and surrounded Dain. He could have jumped off and tried to swim away too, but he thought if he held these men for a few minutes it would give Thum and Alexeika a better chance to escape.

Shouting defiance, he swung Truthseeker in ferocious combat. But no matter how mighty his sword, he could not fight all his foes at once. Even as he stood up in his stirrups to strike off one man's head, he was hit in the back with a blow that seemed to break his spine. All the air was driven from his lungs, and he reeled in the saddle.

Somehow, he managed to parry another blow which came at his unprotected head. He figured he should have been dead already, but then realized they were hitting him with the flat sides of their swords, seeking to stun him and take him prisoner rather than kill him.

The Chief Believer must still want him taken alive, Dain realized, and that helped him pull himself together. He fought harder than ever, determined never to be mastered or used for their evil purposes.

His darsteed fought too. It reared up and struck with its forefeet, slashing a horse's shoulder to the bone. The animal fell, taking its rider into the water. More red-mailed Believers rode up to take the place of those who fell. Meanwhile, the obsidian-armored fire-knights and hurlhounds remained on the bank, watching, along with something dreadful. Dain sensed the evil presence of a soultaker nearby, waiting to consume him.

Savagely he fought. He did not know how many came against him, or how many he sent tumbling into the blood-churned water under the darsteed's feet. Then his mount bolted, nearly unseating him, and Dain realized it was heading back to the bank, all but maddened by its partial immersion in running water.

If it left the river, he knew, he would be doomed. With all his strength he wrenched the creature around, the darsteed rearing and fighting him all the way. A blow smote his shoulder, rendering his whole arm numb. He did not know how he managed to retain his grip on Truthseeker, for he could not feel his fingers, much less command them. Unable to lift his sword and gritting his teeth against the pain, he pressed Truthseeker to the darsteed's rump and commanded it with his mind at the same time.

Crazed with agony, the animal bounded past the circle of attackers and jumped into the deeper water, where the swift-moving current made it stagger.

One of the Believers forced his horse to follow and swung

at Dain from behind. Glimpsing him from the corner of his eye, Dain twisted in a weak effort to parry the blow. But as he did so, the floundering darsteed lost its footing in the current.

The water swept it over, and Dain went plunging with it beneath the surface, hopelessly tangled in the stirrups.

The darsteed flailed, legs churning, while Dain struggled to get free. He hardly knew which way was up. His lungs were bursting with the clawing, desperate need for air. Yet no matter how he kicked and jerked in an effort to free his feet and get away from the darsteed, he could not seem to make it.

A force caught him, and he tumbled upward. Breaking the surface briefly, he gulped in air before he was dragged down and away. He realized vaguely that it was the current, sweeping him and the darsteed together into deeper and deeper waters.

Alexeika meant to consign Thum to the mercy of the gods and make a stand with Faldain, but as she jumped to the side to avoid one of the riders rushing at her king, she stepped into a hole and fell. The current grabbed her, and suddenly she was struggling to stay afloat. Her chain mail dragged her under the surface before she was able to kick her way back up. Gulping air and water, she managed to slide Severgard into its scabbard, thus freeing both hands to swim, but her mail and the heavy sword weighed her down so much she could barely keep her head above water.

Behind her, she heard the shouting and clanging swords of battle. Her heart was screaming, for she knew Faldain could not prevail against so many. With all her strength she tried to swim back to him, but the current was too strong for her.

Although she was an excellent swimmer, the deep still waters of the northern fjords were nothing like this river, which swept and tumbled her relentlessly along. She realized that if she were to survive, she had to keep swimming, keep angling against the current in an effort to reach the opposite shore.

As she struggled along, she was swept into a pile of logs caught against some boulders. The impact shook her bones, but she was able to clutch one of the water-slick logs and hang on for a few minutes, long enough to catch her breath and cough some of the water from her lungs.

Shoving her dripping hair out of her face, she stared upriver, but she'd been carried too far away around a bend. She could not see Faldain, and no longer heard the battle sounds, for the rushing water was too loud.

She clung there, her hands slipping periodically, and her face twisted with wrenching grief for all their shattered hopes. Angrily she struck the water with one hand, struck it again and again and again before she stopped and began to sob.

At that moment a body came bobbing past her, and her heart lurched before she saw the red mail and realized that it was a Believer.

"Go to perdition!" she shouted, then lost her handhold and slid back into the water.

The rest, however brief, had revived her strength a bit. Although the strong current still swept her along, she renewed her struggles to keep swimming despite being seriously hampered by boots and clothing. No matter how much Severgard pulled her down, she refused to throw it away. She would drown with it rather than lose it now.

She collided with another body, this one feebly trying to swim and keep its head above water. Furiously she gripped the man with one hand while she drew her dagger.

But just before she struck, she recognized the dark red hair and realized this man wore no mail. Her fury faded in an instant.

"Thum!" she cried out, aghast at what she'd nearly done.

She pulled him close, got her arm around him, then kicked with all her might as she struck out for the bank.

Eventually, when she thought her arms would fall off at the shoulder from sheer exhaustion, she reached shallow water. Her feet touched bottom, slipping as the pebbles and mollusk shells rolled treacherously beneath her. Staggering, she emerged from the river, pulling Thum along with the last dregs of her strength.

A slim, brown-furred weasyn, startled by her appearance, retreated from the water's edge with a fish in its mouth, and dashed into the forest.

She stumbled and fell to her hands and knees in the water,

crying with grief and fatigue, but after a moment she forced herself up and pulled Thum completely out of the water and laid him down gently on the pebble-strewn bank. It was a miracle that he still lived, she mused, then decided that Mandrians must be tougher than they looked. As she knelt over him and pumped the water from his lungs, his hazel-green eyes flickered open momentarily.

"Dain?" he whispered.

Grief overcame Alexeika. She stopped working on him and sat down with her knees drawn up tight within the circle of her arms. She was dripping wet; her clothing was plastered to her body, making her shiver in the crisp early morning air. In sudden fury, she hurled a stone, then another and another until she started sobbing.

The sunlight grew brighter. Birds were singing in the forest behind her. She'd not heard birds the entire time they were in Gant. Yet now that she was back in a normal place, it somehow didn't matter. Nothing did, for Faldain was lost forever.

Tears spilled down her cheeks. She remembered how he'd shoved her into the water, then turned to face the enemy closing in around him. She'd seen no fear on his handsome face, only courage and determination as he put her safety ahead of his own. He was a natural-born champion, a king to his very fingertips.

Yet, what good were his courage and valor now? He'd saved her and Thum but lost himself—and Nether—forever.

"You brave, stubborn fool!" she whispered.

During their days together in the desert, riding at his back with a proximity that made her entrails melt, she'd grown sensitive to his every mood, his every change of expression. When he'd stripped to the waist, revealing powerful muscles and thews, she'd had to busy herself to hide her trembling. During the hot days, she'd often lain awake just so she could watch him sleep, imprinting every detail of his face on her memory.

But no matter how handsome he was, his inner qualities were even finer, for he was kindhearted, gentle, and compassionate. Of course, he had many faults as well. He could be prickly and defensive, seeing criticism too often in remarks that were meant kindly. There could not be a more stubborn man alive. He kept too much to himself, which caused misunderstandings. Yet there was such generosity in him, such a concern for and awareness of the plight of others. Not once had he lost patience with his injured friend Thum or contemplated abandoning him in the wasteland. Even when he'd lost his temper with Alexeika, he'd seen that she drank her fill of water and taken care to share their meager food equally. He'd even given eggs to that hideous darsteed, as though taking pity on it.

Alexeika knew she was wrong to feel jealous of the maiden he'd loved. She'd tried every means she could think of to gain his attention, from demonstrating her skills at swordplay to un-braiding her hair to picking arguments with him. She believed that had she ever managed to win his heart, he would have been as faithful and loyal to her as he'd been to poor Lady Pheresa. How Alexeika craved such devotion and wished that for a single day she could have known it.

What a king he would have made, this handsome, stalwart, brave, loyal, generous Faldain.

And because she'd been jealous and petty, she'd ensured his doom.

Slowly Alexeika reached for the cord that hung about her neck beneath her hauberk. She pulled out the Ring of Solder, which she'd picked up the day it fell from dead Sulein's hand. Now, holding it aloft so that the large milky stone shone in the sunlight, she faced her guilt and shame.

Had she given this to Faldain immediately, he could have recovered the Chalice, perhaps even saved the maiden he loved. He would be free today, maybe already united with his army. He would not be a prisoner of the Gantese, would not at this moment be enduring the horror of losing his soul. Even as she sat here, mourning him, he was being turned into Nonkind, doomed to serve Ashnod's bidding forever.

It was all her fault. She, who had been raised from birth to serve Faldain's cause, had instead destroyed him.

She lowered her head to her knees, and wept with all her heart.

•   •   •

A faint noise startled her from her misery. Fighting back her tears, Alexeika felt a wild stab of hope that Faldain had somehow escaped the Believers and survived unharmed.

She looked up swiftly, but it was not her young king who stood nearby, but instead a band of perhaps twenty dwarves. Shaggy of beard and dressed in coarsely woven clothing as drab as the forest colors of stone, moss, and bark, they stared at her in hostile silence with bows and war clubs in their hands.

Dismayed, Alexeika realized her troubles were far from over. Perhaps justice intended her to meet her end at the hands of these strangers, but she dismissed the thought quickly. She tucked the Ring of Solder out of sight, knowing it was her duty to return to Nether with it. She needed to determine how it could be used to withstand Gant's attack against her homeland. She might even have to use it against Faldain's soulless shell.

Fresh tears spilled down her cheeks, but she put aside her grief and tried to think of how to handle this newest kind of trouble.

Some of the dwarf clans were civilized and peaceful; they traded with men of other lands and worked hard for the gold they hoarded in their burrows. Others were wild—almost feral— and warlike. They raided loot to live on and dealt peaceably with no one except members of their own clan.

She did not know much about dwarves, but she very much feared she was facing the latter kind.

Slowly, trying to make no sudden moves that the dwarves might misconstrue, Alexeika rose to her feet and forced herself to hold out her hands empty of weapons.

Even that peaceful move alarmed them. Several drew their bows and aimed arrows at her. The rest stiffened, glaring at her with more menace than ever.

She knew almost nothing of the dwarf tongue; there were too many confusing dialects. "Peace," she said awkwardly. "Peace to you."

The dwarves stared at her as though they did not understand.

No other words came to her, and in frustration she spoke in Netheran. "I mean you no harm."

One of them shot an arrow at her. It struck the ground just short of her foot, and Alexeika flinched. Her heart thudded against her rib cage, and suddenly she found it hard to breathe. Still, she knew she must not let fear master her if she was to survive.

"Peace!" she said again. "I have no quarrel with you."

"Gant!" one of the dwarves shouted at her. His yellow eyes glared from beneath bushy brows, and his brown beard was atangle with twigs and bits of leaves. Nearly rigid with contempt and hatred, he jabbed his finger at her. "Gant!"

"I just escaped from there," she said. "I and my . . ."

Her voice trailed off, for the dwarf was still pointing at her in plain loathing. Glancing down at herself, she realized it must be her red chain mail that had upset them. Comprehension filled her. Of course. They obviously thought her a Believer.

"You don't understand," she said, although she wasn't sure how she was going to explain. "I'm not—"

An arrow whizzed past her face, missing her by such a close margin she felt the fletchings brush her cheek.

The spokesman shouted at her, gesturing in emphasis, but she could not understand what he was saying. Aware that at any moment they were likely to shoot an arrow through her throat, Alexeika pulled Severgard from its scabbard and held it up.

Several raised their war clubs in response, but when she made no effort to attack they hesitated.

Glaring at them, she raised Severgard higher so that they could all see it. Its huge sapphire glittered in the sunlight, and the blade gleamed. "Look at it!" she said. "A magicked blade, my ancestral sword, and dwarf-forged. It was mined from the Mountains of the Gods."

They understood that much, for some of them murmured and exchanged swift looks.

"Its name is Severgard. Do you know it? Was it made by an ancestor of your clan?"

They stared at her, but no one answered.

"Severgard!" she repeated. "Magicked and forged to fight Nonkind. No Believer from Gant could hold such a weapon."

"Gant!" the spokesman said angrily. "Gant!"

"Nay!" she shouted back. "I am Netheran! I took this armor from a foe I defeated. It is my war trophy. Do you understand?

I am not Gantese. Nor is he!" She pointed Severgard at Thum. "He's Mandrian. Netheran and Mandrian, *not* Gantese."

"Nether," the dwarf said slowly. His yellow eyes assessed the weapon she held. "Nether."

"Yes! I am from Nether." She bared her teeth at him. "No fangs, see? I am from Nether."

He looked at her teeth without coming closer, then pointed toward the forest. She stared at him a moment, but he stamped his feet and pointed with angry jabs, indicating that she should go in that direction. She slowly slid Severgard back into its scabbard, then bent over Thum in an effort to rouse him.

Dwarves surrounded her, and some pushed her hands away. They picked Thum up, draped his thin length across their shoulders, and marched away with him.

More dwarves crowded behind Alexeika, prodding her forward. She fought down her panicky feelings, assuring herself that all she needed was a way to communicate with them. If they could be made to understand that she was not Gantese, she did not think they would harm her. Even now, as she followed her captors into the forest of sweet-smelling pines, her feet silent on the fallen needles, she felt heartened because they had not sought to disarm her. She was not a prisoner yet. She must keep her wits about her, and not let fear overcome her good sense.

They walked deep into the forest. The pines grew thicker together, and were interspersed occasionally with stands of shtac and harlberries. Some of the latter bushes still had fruit clinging stubbornly to their branches. She grabbed what she could, but found the berries frost-burned and shriveled to tasteless knots. She ate them anyway, for she was nearly light-headed with hunger. Sometimes they had to push their way through the fragrant pine boughs in order to keep to the trail. Now and then a fallen log lay across it, but they climbed over it rather than go around. The dwarves seemed oddly loath to leave the trail. She wondered why.

Ahead she heard a drum pounding. Its steady, primitive sound filled her with unease. Now and then through spaces in the trees, she glimpsed a cleared expanse of white ground where no forest grew. She could not clearly see what it was, but she did not think it snow.

At midday, they reached a large clearing in the pines and an enormous dwarf camp. Countless tents were pitched very close together. On the far side of the clearing, a stand of thick-trunked oaks of tremendous age stood clumped together, bare-branched and massive against a backdrop of dark green pines. An ancient stone altar covered with small bronze offering bowls stood beneath the oaks.

A rope pen held a collection of short, shaggy ponies and donkeys. A grizzled oldster with his beard plaited in several sections sat on a stump, busily carving an ash quarterstaff with the faces of wood spirits while children watched him. There were wagons and carts holding peddler wares. Dwarves of all ages milled around. Some wore coarse linsey; others were garbed in furs and looked as wild as the Dark Forest they undoubtedly came from. Makeshift forges stood side by side in rows, and the air smelled of both heated metal and cooking. A young female dwarf emerged from a hole in the ground next to the surface roots of a large tree. After shaking the soil from her hair, she went running toward the crowd.

Startled, Alexeika realized the old tree must hold a burrow. She looked at it again in amazement, wondering what else its massive girth contained.

Such an air of excitement pervaded the camp that Alexeika's arrival was largely ignored. Laughter punctuated the chatter, and folk called out shrilly to each other, beckoning. Some went running to join the throng congregated around a blazing bonfire.

Halted by her escort, Alexeika waited while one of the dwarves hurried off and the others crowded close around her.

The drum was pounding louder than ever. Alexeika's head started pounding with it, and she was ready to sink to the ground in weariness when she heard a bugling snort.

Her head whipped around, and she stared at the spot where the crowd was clustered most thickly. Her heart was thudding. She told herself she was mistaken, but then the darsteed's head lifted into sight, its red eyes aglow.

Staring, she felt her throat choke with a hope she dared not admit even to herself.

It couldn't be, she told herself.

The Believers had outnumbered Faldain too greatly for him to escape. The darsteed's presence here meant only that it had been abandoned when Faldain was captured. Somehow it must have crossed the river, only to be captured by these dwarves.

And yet . . . and yet . . .

She stretched on tiptoe, trying to see. "Faldain!" she shouted. "King Faldain!"

Her captors gawked at her. People in the crowd fell quiet. Many turned to look at her, and as they did, the crowd parted between her and the darsteed. And there stood Faldain with his hauberk half-laced and a darkening bruise on his cheek. He held a stone jar of ointment in his hand, and had apparently been smearing the stuff on the darsteed where large patches of its black, scaly hide were peeling off.

He smiled at Alexeika, smiled with such warmth and obvious pleasure she felt it all the way across camp.

With a wordless cry, she went running to him. Her head was roaring. She could not feel the ground. All she could see was Faldain's face, his smile.

And with every step she thought joyously, *He is alive. He is alive.*

She did not know how he'd escaped the Believers. At the moment she did not care. His being here seemed like a complete miracle to her. Either he had more luck than any man alive, or the gods themselves were guarding his safety. Each time she believed him lost, he reappeared somehow.

But then she stumbled and came to a halt, breathless and afraid. The gods were giving her a second chance, but how could she confess now what she'd concealed and kept from him? He would hate her for it.

Faldain thrust his rag and jar of ointment into someone's hands, and beckoned to her. Sunlight shone into the clearing, bathing him in such brightness his chain mail glinted with every move he made. His black hair brushed his shoulders, and his pale gray eyes held all the future. He looked tall and hale and magnificent.

She dropped to her knees before him, and bowed her head.

"I don't believe it," she whispered. "I thought your majesty lost."

"Nay," he said, and his voice rang out deep and assured in the sudden hush about them. "I was able to get into deep water and thus escaped."

He made it sound so easy. Alexeika looked at the bruise on his face and knew it had not been.

The dwarves were watching avidly, nudging each other and whispering. Her yellow-eyed captor caught up with her and said something in the dwarf tongue.

Faldain replied fluently.

"Gant!" the dwarf said, pointing at her vehemently.

Faldain shook his head and explained. As he spoke, Alexeika slowly rose to her feet. She was shivering in her wet clothing and breathing hard in an effort to control herself.

All her emotions seemed to be overwhelming her at once. To be angry at him, then to think him lost, then to find him safe . . . it was too much. The Ring pressed against her skin, concealed beneath her clothing like a badge of guilt.

She realized she must give it to him, must tell him everything. And yet, if she did he would dismiss her from his service, for how could he ever trust her again? Although she knew she deserved such punishment, she could not bear to be driven from him now, not when she'd found him again.

His hand gripped her shoulder, startling her. "What's amiss?" he asked. "Are you hurt?"

"Nay, sire. I'm well."

But her voice quavered through her answer, fooling him not. She tried to pull back, but his fingers tightened with painful strength.

"Thank you for saving Thum's life," he said. "Maug tells me you did not let him drown, and I owe you much for—"

This time she did twist away from his touch, by rising to her feet. "Your majesty owes me *nothing*!" she said too vehemently. Then she made the mistake of meeting his gaze, and sudden tears filled her eyes. She was appalled by her weakness, yet there seemed to be nothing she could do about it.

"Forgive me, sire," she mumbled, pressing her hand to her face. "I thought . . . I was sure . . ." She could not go on.

Faldain took her hand, too brown and callused to be a lady's, and squeezed it in reassurance. He even brushed a wayward strand of hair from her face. He was so close she felt overwhelmed by his physical proximity. His kind concern shone in his eyes, and seeing it, she wept all the more.

For it was not his kindness she wanted as her body had craved water in the desert; it was his love.

"All is well now," he said gently. "Be at peace, my lady. These are dwarves of the Nega Clan. They will help us."

She sniffed, and nodded, but could not stop her tears.

Faldain stepped away from her and beckoned to two dwarf females in long tunics. Broad-faced, with large, perceptive eyes and hair the matted texture of moss, they came shyly forward. Faldain spoke rapidly to them in dwarf before turning back to her. "Go with these women, Alexeika. I have told them you are unwell. They will see that you're fed and are given a quiet place to rest."

She was horribly embarrassed by her weakness. She'd tried so hard to be as strong as any warrior, and now she'd broken down. "I'm sorry, sire," she whispered, wiping at her tears. "I'm sorry."

"No need to apologize," he said in concern. "Get some rest. When you are well again, we'll talk of our next strategy."

The women led her away to a tent that smelled of soil and moss. Tiny glowstones cast faint illumination in its shadowy interior. While one pulled off Alexeika's boots, the other brought her food and drink. Ravenous, Alexeika wolfed it down without heed for the unfamiliar spices and flavorings. They brought her a pail of water for washing, and dry clothes, then discreetly withdrew, lowering the flap behind them.

Alexeika found herself intensely grateful for the solitude. Aware that it was her exhaustion which had left her so vulnerable, she wept some more, then lay down to sleep.

It was not an easy slumber, for she dreamed of battles and blood. She dreamed of her father, striding along the battlefield in search of his soul, a soul she'd released. She ran after him, crying out, "I'm sorry, Papa! I'm sorry!"

But he ignored her, pacing back and forth in a desperate

search. "I must have my soul back!" he said. "I was not ready to die."

When at last she awoke, twilight had cast murky shadows in her tent, and the little glowstones shone more brightly. The air felt cold. Finding a comb, Alexeika used it, then washed the dried sticky tears from her face. Her eyes felt puffy and sore. She was hungry again, and finally ventured outside her tent.

A youth with square shoulders and short, bandy legs had obviously been waiting for her to appear. Giving her a shy smile, he beckoned for her to follow and escorted her across camp to a large fire where many were seated on the ground, eating roasted stag and jabbering nonstop.

Several in the company fell silent when she appeared, and eyed her with wary unease, but in anticipation of such a reaction Alexeika had removed her red mail hauberk and wore only her tunic and leggings, with her weapons belted around her lean middle. The dwarves made room for her, and soon the talk picked up again.

Faldain found her there soon after, sitting cross-legged on the cold ground and shivering a bit in the crisp night air while she gnawed on a meaty bone.

At the sound of his voice, she tossed her food aside and scrambled hastily to her feet.

"Forgive me for my unseemly display earlier, sire," she said, stammering a little in mortification. "I don't know what came over me."

He sent her a peculiar look. "Did your father force you to act like a son?"

His odd question surprised her. She frowned. "What? Nay, sire. Why?"

"It's just that you seem to hold yourself to a warrior's standard of conduct rather than a lady's."

Heat rushed up into her face, and she was mortified anew. "I—I just find it easier to fight if I hold myself—"

"Alexeika," he broke in gently, giving her a faint smile. "I do not criticize you. I just want you to know that you need not apologize for acting womanly today."

"For weeping like a gutless fool," she said bitterly.

He laughed at that. "You're far from gutless. Come. Put aside your dark mood and walk with me."

Happiness flared to life instantly inside her. Smiling back, she accompanied him to the edge of the clearing, well away from the others.

"'Tis their annual fair," Dain explained. "Cousins meet cousins. Family is reunited with family. Daughters see their parents again. 'Tis a special occasion for them. They have contests of skill at the forges and do much celebrating."

"Oh."

"Tomorrow they will begin conducting the worship ceremonies. Youths will be initiated into adulthood. Marriages will be performed."

She gazed at his profile, telling herself to find her courage now and give him the Ring. Instead she asked, "What is it your majesty wants to talk over with me?"

He pointed into the darkness. "Out there lies the Field of Skulls."

She gasped, and everything else fled her mind. "Thod's mercy, but it can't be. That's a legend, nothing more."

He gazed at her intently, his face half in shadow. "So even in Nether you have heard of it."

"Aye, of course, but it's just a tale, not reality."

"It exists," Faldain said grimly. "I have known about it all my life. Jorb, my dwarf guardian, told Thia and me many stories of the terrible battles that were fought in antiquity on that ground."

Thinking of the old legends she'd heard as a child, Alexeika felt chilled. "It's no place for men to walk," she whispered.

"Yet I must walk there," Faldain said. "Tonight."

"Why?" As soon as the question was out of her mouth, she grimaced and shook her head. "Forgive me, sire. I do not mean to question you."

"Of course you do," he said, but tolerantly. "Now come, and tell me how it is too dangerous and how I must not risk myself there."

He was teasing, but she remained serious as she answered: "If it's really the Field of Skulls, so many died on it that nothing grows there to this day. So many bones lie on the field that the ground is still white with them. It's supposed to still be laced with potent powers and spells. It is not safe."

"I know that, Alexeika."

"And still you are curious."

He snorted. "I'm no amulet hunter. My purpose is not to gawk and marvel."

A sense of dread seized her, and she reached out to him, though she dared not touch his arm. "Why must you go there? Why take the risk of disturbing the ghosts of long-dead warriors? It is no place for men."

"Alexeika, be quiet," he said in rebuke. "I go there to seek my father."

Astonished, she stared at him in silence.

"I have learned that the potency which lingers on the Field can still enhance anyone's powers. For that reason I believe I can summon Tobeszijian to me."

Shivering, she stared at Faldain in awe. "You could raise the ghosts of a thousand slain warriors with a summoning. Do you truly dare it?"

He screwed up his face in worry. "It is not as though I have never seen him in visions. But since I left Mandria he has not come to me. There is much I need to ask him, Alexeika."

"This is a terrible risk. What if you summon things you cannot withstand?"

He shrugged. "Truthseeker will guard me. Alexeika, there is a favor I seek from you."

"Yes?"

"As a *sorcerelle*—"

"Nay!" she said vehemently. "I am not!"

"But 'twas you who summoned me, long ago, in a spell."

She gasped, guilt and embarrassment flying through her. "Sire, I—I was foolish then. I hardly knew what I was doing. I could have harmed you."

"But you did not. Why did you seek me?"

She averted her face in shame. "I didn't. I mean, I wanted our priest to summon a vision of you to encourage the people after my father's terrible defeat, but Uzfan wouldn't do it."

"And so you did it instead. Why does this not surprise me?"

"Not by intention," she explained, wishing the ground would

swallow her. "I was grieving for my father, and I wanted to see him so, I tried to summon him. You came instead. My gift goes awry. No matter what I seek to do with it, something else happens. Something unexpected."

"Still, you are the only *sorcerelle* available to me."

"I'm not! Having a trace of eldin blood in my veins does not make me such a creature."

"You have more power than you will admit."

She frowned. "Uzfan said I could not be trained. I cannot control my gift as you do yours."

"Eldin females are always more adept than malefolk," he persisted. "Go forth with me, Alexeika, and part the veils of seeing. Show me Lady Pheresa, and whether she yet lives or lies dead."

Alexeika felt as though a pail of icy water had been dashed over her. Stiffening, she stood there and could not speak.

He gave her a strange look. "Must I plead with you?"

Rage burned her heart. How could he ask her to do such a thing for him? Desperately she sought an excuse, any excuse, to refuse. "Sire, I—I cannot!"

"Of course you can."

"No," she said, retreating from him. "I tell you, I cannot. Please!"

"Nonsense!" he snapped. "Is it only when you have a blade in your hand that you know courage?"

That hurt. Breathing hard, she whirled to leave him, but he seized her arm and held her fast.

"Nay, my warrior-maid," he said fiercely. "I must know her fate."

"You said all her guardians had been taken from her. You said she was dead."

"I believe she is," he replied raggedly. "But Cardo, the clan leader here, has heard that armies are massing on the Netheran border."

Her head snapped up. "Truly?"

"Aye. Now is the time for quick action, yet I will not proceed blindly. If she's alive, by some slim chance, she could be used as a pawn in negotiations, ransomed, threatened as a hostage, anything. I must know the truth with absolute certainty."

Alexeika nodded, forcing herself to calm down and listen. "Aye," she agreed reluctantly. "The usurper is not above using any tactic to his advantage. He has so little honor that he would even threaten a sick woman."

"Well?" Faldain demanded. "Will you part the veils?"

"And if my seeing goes awry?"

He gestured impatiently. "I've told you, the power lying across the Field of Skulls enhances every gift. Why should you fail?"

Because I love you too much, and I hate her more, Alexeika thought. Again she told herself to give him the Ring of Solder and flee, but she could not do it. Her will was too weak, her feelings too strong. She would do anything, sacrifice her own honor, to stay with him as long as she could. It shamed her, but even shame could not help her do the right thing.

"Alexeika! Damne, must I beg you?" he cried, then grimaced and made a gesture of apology. "Nay. I will not force you to do this. I ask it as a favor. But tell me now if you will do it or not."

She felt both cold and on fire. The lie kept spreading around her, and she could not break its hold now, for it had gone on too long, had grown too strong to rectify. But how was she to answer his request? Even if she did part the veils, what would her jealousy and secrets wring from the seeing? She was terrified to find out, yet to refuse him anything seemed beyond her ability. He had asked for her help, and her love would not let her say no.

"Aye, sire," she said woodenly, "I'll do it."

"Good!" Laughing, he clapped his hands together. "Run and fetch your cloak."

"Now?" she asked, appalled. "But is this the most propitious time?"

"We must act without delay," he said. "As soon as the dwarves go to their rest tonight, we'll venture forth."

——— PART FOUR ———

19

THEY WERE COMING again.

Propped up limply in the tall-backed chair like a child's rag doll waiting for its owner to return, Pheresa heard the sound of footsteps rapidly approaching.

Closer they came.

Closer.

She tried to rouse herself, tried to force herself to sit up straight, to receive them with dignity, but she could not move. Her limbs were leaden, lifeless. Her heart beat sluggishly inside her breast, and she could barely blink her eyes.

She sat in a long, empty gallery. On one side were a series of tall windows overlooking the snowy vista. Along the opposite wall were floor-to-ceiling mirrors, evidence of incredible past wealth, although many were now cracked and broken, begrimed, and fly-spotted. A few globes of king's glass hung suspended from the vaulted ceiling. Originally there must have been many such globes, but now their empty chains dangled. Long ago, someone had attempted to bind the remaining globes in protective cloth, but it had rotted away except for a few tattered strips.

Sometimes she dreamed of what this gallery had once looked like, with so much shining glass reflecting the candlelight while courtiers danced and made merry. Now it was a place of ghosts and broken dreams, eerie with shadows and cobwebs, with only rats dancing in the dead of night.

Megala, her serving woman, had vanished without explanation, and Pheresa feared the worst. A deaf-mute caretaker, terribly disfigured, and afraid of her, came limping in twice a day to build a meager fire in the tiled stove and to bring trays of food. Sometimes Gavril appeared to eat; often, however, he forgot and simply went on wandering aimlessly about the palace, prowling and talking to himself. If he did not come, there was no one to feed Pheresa. Unable to move more than her fingertips, unable to grasp a bowl of thin, greasy soup, much less lift it to her lips, she sometimes had to sit there with the food tantalizingly close yet impossible to reach. Hours would pass while the soup congealed and the bread grew stale. If the bold rats ate it in front of her, she would cry, averting her eyes and holding back her screams.

She knew instinctively that if she ever broke, if she ever let herself utter those internal screams, she would never stop.

The only brightness to her dreary days was when the potion was brought to her by Master Vlana, a court physician. Sometimes Count Mradvior came along. He would chat with her after the potion's effects took hold and she regained enough strength to converse. But on the days when the magician, the creature called a *sorcerel*, came to observe her condition, Pheresa's fear left her trembling and silent. She could barely bring herself to meet Tulvak Sahm's peculiar eyes, lest he enspell her. He always smelled of mysterious spices and something bitterly pungent. Ashes powdered his clothing, and when he bent over her to tap her fingernails or to peer into her eyes, his breath reeked of sulfur.

At the far end of the gallery, the door swung open. She heard the low murmur of voices and knew they were coming now to give her a new dose of the potion that kept her alive. Anticipation leaped inside her, yet at the same time she raged at her helplessness. What good was life of this kind, a half-life of immobility and dependence, chained perpetually to whatever degree of care and mercy these cruel individuals chose to give her?

What fools she and Gavril had been to come here. How naive, young, and trusting they'd been to believe the Netherans possessed either honor or compassion. Gavril had brought them right into a trap, despite all the warnings, and then he'd been so shocked, so surprised when their flag of pilgrimage was violated.

His reaction had made Pheresa, once she regained consciousness and understood the whole situation, reevaluate her opinion of him. Although previously she'd deplored his careless indifference, his arrogance, his conceit, his occasional cruelty, she'd never doubted his intelligence or courage. However, since reviving in this ruined palace and finding herself a prisoner, Pheresa had lost all confidence in him. At times he looked lost and afraid. Other times he boasted of bold plans to escape, plans which were ludicrous and impossible. She believed he had gone mad, and some days as she sat here in this chair, unable to move while he paced up and down the battered floor, his once-fine velvet doublet soiled, his golden hair uncombed, his dark blue eyes gleaming feverishly, she wondered why she did not go mad as well.

Count Mradvior's arrival ended her reverie. He walked up to her, then smiled and gave her a courtly bow. Of them all, she found him the least objectionable. Although he was not a kind man, he was at least civil. She understood that civility was a form of respect, and was grateful for it, but she never forgot that he was her enemy, one of her jailers.

There was no point in attempting to gain his sympathies.

Today, he gave her a searching look, frowned, and stepped aside for Master Vlana. Pheresa shifted her eyes so that she could watch the count gaze at her tray of untouched food. He wandered away, out of her range of sight, but she knew he would go to the opposite end of the room and feel the stove, which had grown cold. The deaf-mute had not come this morning, and Pheresa was nearly frozen.

"Bones of Tomias," Mradvior said in annoyance, striding back to them. "I can see my breath in here. Where is the fire? Where is that wretched half-wit?"

Clucking and mumbling to himself, Vlana stirred up the potion in a brass cup and pulled her erect, holding her firmly by the back of her skull while he put the cup to her lips.

She sipped weakly, shuddering at the bitter taste. It was so foul she thought she might spew it back up, but it always stayed down, lying queasily in her stomach for a few minutes until its effects spread renewed strength through her body.

When she finished the last swallow, she sighed and let her eyelids close for a moment. It was easier to breathe now. When she could curl her stiff fingers in her lap, she opened her eyes.

Everything looked brighter, more in focus. She could feel her mind sharpen, and she wanted to weep for having lost all in her young existence except this tiny fraction of life. She wished now that she'd spent her days at Savroix more gaily. Instead of hiding in her room and trying to keep both her dignity and reputation intact, she wished she'd gone to all the dances, flirted in the gardens, and banqueted like a glutton. She'd missed so much, and now . . . and now . . .

"Here, my lady, why do you weep?" Mradvior asked, standing by her chair. "This is a momentous day. Yes, yes, momentous."

"She must have some food," the physician murmured, gesturing at one of his minions. "And warmth. She is far too cold."

Pheresa let them fuss over her while she kept her gaze on Mradvior. His dark eyes were snapping with excitement, and she did not trust him.

"Well?" he asked her. "Will you not question me about the surprise I bring? Are you not curious?"

Impatience tightened inside her, but she held back the retort she wanted to make. The count always enjoyed these little games. Despising him, she said, "Of course I am curious."

He beamed, apparently satisfied with her answer. "Ah, then I will tell you. Look here what I have brought."

As he spoke he snapped his fingers at a page, and the boy brought forward a sword that Pheresa recognized with an unpleasant jolt.

"Tanengard!" she said in revulsion.

"A good surprise for his highness, eh?" Mradvior said, beaming from ear to ear. "Ah, yes, I think he will be very happy. Where is he?"

Thinking that Gavril's madness would only be intensified by the return of this evil sword, Pheresa gave her head a minute shake. "Somewhere, exploring."

Mradvior glanced at the page. "Find his highness and bring him here at once. We have little time to make him ready."

"For what?" Pheresa asked, then hope filled her. "Has the ransom come?"

"No," Mradvior replied flatly. "Today you will amuse the court."

"I don't understand."

But he didn't explain, for at that moment Gavril came striding in, haughty and defiant. "Mradvior!" he said in displeasure. "How dare you summon me like some lackey. I was—"

The count held out the sword, and Gavril stopped in midsentence. His blue eyes widened, and a smile slowly spread across his face.

"Tanengard!"

Clutching the weapon, he spun away and hurried over to the nearest window, where he examined every inch of it. As his fingers stroked the blade, he made little cooing sounds in his throat.

Feeling pity mingled with disgust, Pheresa shifted her gaze back to Mradvior. "What do you intend to do with us?" she asked.

His broad smile did not reach his dark eyes. "You will see. Look at this fine gown I have brought as a gift. Also, a lap robe of the softest fur. And here, jewels to make a lady's eyes sparkle."

As he spoke he tossed the necklace in her lap. She worked her fingers slowly until she was able to draw the chain and its bright sapphires into her hand.

The color was too garish, the weight of the jewels too light. She frowned. "Colored glass. Fakes!"

But Mradvior had strode over to cajole Gavril and paid her no heed. A group of servants came in. Some took Gavril away to don new clothes. The rest surrounded Pheresa. Handling her as though she were a life-sized doll, they peeled off her cheap gown and arrayed her in finery of heavy crimson silk. Once the color had been richly breathtaking, but it was now sun-faded to a pale coral. Pheresa saw the ripped seams that were pinned deftly to look mended. She even saw the bloodstains on the skirt that a maid folded out of sight.

Revulsion shivered through her. Who would save the clothing of a long-dead corpse? These people were mad.

The gown was too large for her, but the servants tucked and pinned it at the back and propped Pheresa up in her chair. Jeweled slippers were placed on her pale, slender feet, with rags stuffed into the toes to make them fit. The cheap, gaudy necklace was fastened about her throat.

Gavril returned, beaming in good humor and looking handsome in an old-fashioned tunic of rich green and a jaunty fur cap. Swaggering about with Tanengard on his hip, he flicked Pheresa's cheek with his fingertip while servants positioned a chair for him next to hers.

Seating himself, Gavril smiled as the servants unrolled a dusty red carpet across the battered floor. A dingy piece of needlework in a hoop was placed in Pheresa's lap. She glared at it, wishing she could fling it across the room.

His head cocked, Mradvior studied them before ordering the servants to add more props to the tableau he was creating.

Angered by the indignity of this situation, Pheresa turned her head fractionally to the side. "Gavril," she said with all the sharpness she possessed, "what is this about?"

"Why, my lady, at last we're to be paid the respect due us," Gavril said pleasantly. He smiled at her with a charm that once would have melted her heart. "The Netheran court comes to visit us today. Is this not a pretty reception we're going to provide? Over there will be refreshments. I asked Mradvior for musicians, but he said they will come later."

She frowned. "This isn't a reception. We're—"

"Ah, look! I hear the first guests arriving." Gavril patted her hand. "How pretty you look, my dear. That gown is much more becoming than what you've been wearing. As soon as we are wed, you must make an effort to keep up with fashions, even set them. Learn to do better, Pheresa. I consider attire important."

She wanted to scream at him, but he wouldn't have understood. The emptiness in his eyes made her despair. She had never felt more helpless or alone. With all her heart she wished she could turn back time to that night of the Harvest Ball at Savroix, when Dain had humbly offered her his heart. Enslaved to duty and responsibilities, she'd turned away from him to accept Gavril's offer instead. What a fine bargain she'd made. Gavril, so arrogant and heartless; Gavril, who hadn't given her a second's consideration until he saw that Dain wanted her; Gavril, who had told her he would marry her provided she kept her place and never interfered with his rule. She'd wanted a kingdom. She'd wanted everything but love, and now she had nothing but a madman and a nightmare.

At the door came the babble of voices. Titters of laughter rang out, for the Netheran courtiers had arrived. Swathed in furs and dusted with the snow that was falling outside, the queen and her companions entered the gallery while Mradvior bowed to them in welcome.

"My queen, lords, and ladies," he said cheerily. "For your amusement, I present a tableau . . . Behold the court of Savroix."

Little dogs costumed as courtiers came trotting out to surround Pheresa and Gavril. They yapped at her, and one of them urinated on the floor. The people laughed.

Gavril bowed to them grandly. "You are hereby made welcome," he proclaimed.

They laughed again, some applauding. Queen Neaglis—a lean, intense woman with black eyes set narrowly above a thin, pointed nose—gazed around at the tawdry, dirty room in disgust. When her eyes fell on Pheresa and Gavril, however, she smiled.

Dressed in magnificent brown velvet trimmed in lyng fur with tippets of islean, and carrying a matching muff over one arm, she walked forward with her ladies in waiting.

Embarrassment filled Pheresa and she wished she could do something, *anything* to drive these visitors away. Her helpless immobility so enraged her that she prayed to Thod for the ability to hurl this filthy piece of needlework at the nearest sneering face. Trapped and humiliated, she was forced to sit there while the queen approached her.

Still smiling with amused contempt, Queen Neaglis stared first at Gavril, then at Pheresa. One of her gloved hands made a little gesture, and her ladies in waiting gave mock curtsies to the Mandrian prince and his lady.

Mradvior hovered at her elbow. "Your majesty, I present Prince Gavril of Mandria."

Gavril stood up and bowed to the queen. "I am honored, your majesty. May I present my intended bride, Lady Pheresa du Lindier."

The queen's dark eyes were very cold. Stripping off her gloves and giving them to a companion to hold, she glanced at Mradvior. "Quite amusing, my lord."

He smiled back in gratification. "Thank you. 'Twas but a simple idea to while away a dreary afternoon. Yes, yes, a simple idea."

Giggling, the queen's ladies swarmed about Pheresa, touching her hair and fingering her fake jewels. "Lord Mradvior!" they called out. "Is it true she cannot move?"

"Very true," he replied.

A queer, tingling sensation swept over Pheresa. For an instant she felt peculiar, in a way she could not describe. The room, the staring people, all seemed to fade for a moment. She heard something, a murmur like song or voices. Her gaze shifted up toward the globes of king's glass, but it was not their song she heard.

The air overhead seemed to shimmer, and to her astonishment a hazy little cloud appeared. She saw a vapor forming itself into a girl's face, oval and lean with prominent cheekbones and blue-gray eyes. Amazed, Pheresa could not tear her gaze away. What was this vision? she wondered. What did it mean?

And then another face appeared next to the first one. Pheresa recognized Dain as clearly as though he were actually in the room. She grew faint, her temples pounding, and momentarily forgot how to breathe. Before she could cry out to him, the vision faded away. She went on staring upward, hoping he would reappear, but he did not. Tears welled in her eyes.

Dain, she thought, aching to be rescued. Where was he now? Why had he left? Gavril had said Dain's selfishness and impatience drove him away, but she did not believe Dain had willingly abandoned her, not after his promises to see her healed.

Unlike Gavril, Dain was no liar. She supposed that Gavril had driven him away.

Yet just now, she'd seen him. Was he searching for her? Was this vision some kind of message he was sending to her? A message of hope? A message to hang on?

If only Dain would come.

Or perhaps she was only hallucinating, going slowly mad in her despair. Sometimes Master Vlana's potions were too strong and played tricks on her mind.

"How queer and demented she looks," one of the ladies in waiting remarked. "Perhaps they are *both* insane."

Emboldened by Pheresa's silence, one of the women pulled her hair in a series of sharp tugs. The other one pushed her sideways in her chair, then pulled her upright again.

The queen laughed at these antics and reached out to pinch her quite hard.

It took every ounce of willpower Pheresa possessed not to wince or show the slightest flicker of pain. Nor was there any use in hoping Gavril would defend her. Oblivious to what the queen and her ladies were doing, or to how the other courtiers stared and pointed at him with snickers, Gavril had wandered off, caressing the hilt of Tanengard and mumbling to himself.

There had been a time, when they first embarked on the journey to Grov, when Gavril would have leaped to her defense. He'd been afire with zeal to save her. She'd delighted in his kindness, his brief visits, his apparent worry on her behalf. Like a fool, she'd told herself this illness was worthwhile if it made him love her.

But in truth she had no lover here, no defender, no champion. Gavril—always concerned most with himself—had stood over her encasement one night when she was suffering from fever and, thinking her unconscious, had sneered at her, revealing his true feelings of disgust and impatience. He'd spewed out how tired he was of caring for her. He could have gone home had it not been for her. He could have turned his armed forces against Klad and conquered it if not for her. He could have been out searching for the Chalice with Dain if not for her. She was a burden to him, and he wished he'd never offered her marriage. He wished she would die.

And now he'd gone mad; whether his wits could be restored she did not know. She hardly cared. At present he was of no use to her at all.

But if he chose to wander in his mind and thus evade the indignities heaped on them by their captors, Pheresa had no intention of doing the same. Seeing Dain again, even if it had been her own imagination at work, renewed her spirits. She believed that Dain, had he been imprisoned here, would have found a way to defy his tormentors. Well, then, why should she do less?

Her fingers moved slowly across the needlework in her lap, and pulled out the rusted needle that had been left in the stained cloth. Gripping the needle between thumb and forefinger, Pheresa managed to quirk her lips in a small, brief smile.

"Will your majesty take my hand and warm my fingers?" she asked sweetly.

The ladies in waiting giggled, and others—hearing Pheresa speak to their queen—clustered around.

"She can talk," a man said in amazement. "Did you hear her speak Netheran?"

"I didn't know she could talk," a woman said. "How is this so, count?"

Ignoring the comments, Pheresa kept her gaze on Queen Neaglis. The woman's cruel eyes made her shiver, but Pheresa did not back down. "Please, your majesty," she said softly. "Take my hand. Let a Netheran queen feel the clasp of one who will now never rule Mandria."

Laughter and approval rippled around the crowd. "This is better than a puppet show, Mradvior," someone said.

The queen, urged on by her companions, smirked and reached down to curl her perfumed hand around Pheresa's. Swiftly, with all the scant strength she possessed, Pheresa stabbed the needle in Neaglis's finger hard enough to draw blood.

The queen jerked back with a scream, and tiny drops of blood splattered on the floor while the costumed dogs yapped and milled around.

"Get out!" Pheresa said, her soft voice vehement with rage. "You Netheran swine have betrayed us, but you will not make us into puppets to play with. Get out!"

With her black eyes narrowed in rage, Queen Neaglis slapped Pheresa hard, knocking her from her chair. Pheresa could not catch her fall. Her head thudded on the floor so hard the world swam dizzily about her. In a haze she heard the queen screaming, then a jeweled slipper trod on Pheresa's hand, bringing sharp pain.

"Mandrian cow!" the queen choked out. "Your defiance will cost you dearly."

Pheresa could not pull away, and the queen's foot grated on the delicate bones in her hand. Clamping her lips shut, Pheresa refused to cry out in pain.

"Mradvior, you fool!" Neaglis was shouting. "She has attacked my royal person. She should die for it. Your sword, man! Your sword!"

"But the king—"

"Must I run her through myself? Where are my guards? They'll take care of her."

"Your majesty, please!" Mradvior was saying in a horrified voice. "I never dreamed she could do anything to harm you. Some idiot servant put the needlework in her lap. I assure your majesty that we did not—"

"Stop babbling and kill her. I command it!"

Pheresa shut her eyes. *Yes, death,* she thought with longing. *Anything to escape this horrible place.*

"The king, majesty," Mradvior protested, "has ordered me to keep her alive. I regret—"

"You spineless fool! She has insulted me, and I want her death!"

"Let me punish her, majesty. There are ways to make her suffer."

"Then punish her hard, my lord," the queen said ruthlessly, taking her foot off Pheresa's hand at last. "Punish her very hard. For if you are merciful, I shall see that you are slaughtered in her place."

Furiously the queen swept out with her courtiers while Mradvior bobbed in their wake, still apologizing.

"Pheresa," Gavril said, wandering back from the window, "why are you lying on the floor? 'Tis most unseemly behavior in one of your station. Really, must you act like a peasant?"

Lying there, Pheresa did not even attempt to reply. How long, she wondered in despair, was she to go on enduring this? And she wept.

With a little gasp of exhaustion, Alexeika tipped the bowl of god-steel in her lap and poured out the water it held. The misty vapor that had formed above the water's surface shimmered a moment in the cold night air and vanished. Weariness pressed all the way to Alexeika's bones. She realized with surprise that she'd parted the veils of seeing as Dain had asked her to, and that the results she'd feared had not come to pass.

Indeed, it had gone well. For the first time in her attempts to use her gifts, she'd been able to focus her mind correctly. She'd felt the power center itself inside her body, then radiate forth to do her bidding. The vision she'd sought had come.

But right now, she felt too exhausted to take the slightest amount of satisfaction in a job well done. Around her, the Field of Skulls spread out, the ancient bones gleaming pale white under the moonlight. Old magic crisscrossed the ground and quivered in the air. If she sat very still, she seemed to hear muted whispers and moanings, battle cries and death cries, the clang of steel and the clash of shields. There was an unsettled aspect to the place that prickled uneasiness through her. Yet never had she been more in command of herself, or more able to focus the powers of her mind.

Faldain's hand gripped her shoulder without warning, and she jumped violently.

"I saw her," he said excitedly, ignoring Alexeika's reaction. "There at the last, I saw her. I—I think she saw me."

Alexeika's heart burned with misery, but she forced herself to look up. She even fought off the temptation to lie. "Yes, you saw her," she said in a dull, tired voice. "You've been wrong to think her dead."

"Aye," he said, sounding amazed. In the moonlight she could see him quite clearly. A lock of his black hair fell in his eyes, and he brushed it back impatiently. "Pheresa is alive. Alive, by Thod!"

"Not only alive, but well," Alexeika forced herself to say. She might as well tell the truth about everything she saw. Her father had not raised her to lie. "Your fair lady is well enough to be sitting in a pale red gown, with a necklace of sapphires around her throat, and her hair combed into a simple knot at the back of her neck. She's beautiful."

He nodded, drinking in the details, although he'd seen them for himself. "Aye, she is."

"I saw people coming up to her, the Nethcran court perhaps. Queen Neaglis spoke to her."

Faldain grinned. "To think Pheresa is at Grov, being paid deference at Muncel's court. I am amazed by the miracle of it. My suppositions have all been wrong."

Huddled in her cloak, Alexeika felt a hundred years old. Her heart ached, yet she was so tired she no longer cared.

"Rejoice in her good fortune, sire," she said. "The Chief Believer told you lies."

"The Netherans must have given her a cure," he said, and laughed. "Oh, Alexeika, well done! This more than makes up for my having failed to summon Tobeszijian."

She stood up, but she could not smile in return. "And now your way is clear. Tomorrow you'll ride to get the Chalice and—"

"Nay!" he said in good humor, gripping her hand and squeezing hard. "She has no need of a cure. Though not safe in my uncle's hands, she is well at present. And what of the prince?"

"I saw no one else in the vision," Alexeika said.

Faldain grunted. "I fear Muncel's trickery against her and Gavril, yet I will not be held back. At first light, we ride for the border. I've already sent a messenger, one of Cardo's nephews, off to find General Matkevskiet. If we can rendezvous quickly with the Agya warriors, there will be time perhaps to prepare for battle."

Alexeika blinked, not certain she'd heard aright. "Battle?"

"Aye, 'tis what you've been arguing for. If I can assemble an army in time, I'd like to strike Grov on Selwinmas. Let Muncel choke on my sword for his celebratory feast!"

"But—"

He gripped her shoulder, forcing her to move. "Well, come on! We've done all we can here. Let us get what rest we can before daybreak."

Alexeika had the uneasy feeling that Faldain was rushing ahead too heedlessly and that there was something he'd overlooked, but she was too tired to think of what it might be.

"What of the Chalice?" she asked again.

"It will wait."

She stared at him, seeing the battle light in his eyes, and wondered if this place was not somehow affecting him. "But you said the Chalice should be returned to Nether first, before you sought your throne."

"And you argued the opposite just a day ago," he countered. "What's come over you, Alexeika? Where is my warrior-maiden?"

Unsure how to answer him, she asked another question instead. "And if Thum cannot ride?"

"He's better. I checked on him not two hours past," Faldain said blithely. She had never before seen him in such high spirits. "The dwarves have tended him well. He'll ride, all right."

"Well, what of—"

"Oh, hush," he said. "Let us go!"

He strode away briskly. Alexeika picked her way after him much more slowly. Treading over the bones unnerved her, for she felt as though she was desecrating them. She couldn't help but think of that mountain valley up near the World's Rim where her father's bones lay unburied in the winter grass.

What would the general say about Faldain's sudden charge to battle? She could not guess. Faldain's eagerness to fight was exactly what she'd hoped for all along, yet it worried her. Because despite the high principles he'd spouted yesterday, Faldain was still thinking of Lady Pheresa first. Although she wanted Muncel defeated, Alexeika wished Faldain would fight for a reason other than his Mandrian lady.

But, alas, the maiden was beautiful indeed, even with her slender face drawn from illness. Graceful and completely feminine, her reddish-gold hair bright about her face, Pheresa was everything Alexeika would never be.

Tripping over a skull, which went rolling away from her foot with a clatter, Alexeika faced the fact that she'd lost her only chance of winning his heart.

Oh, if only the vision had shown Pheresa dead instead of alive and well.

But as soon as she thought that, Alexeika felt ashamed of herself. If he wanted Pheresa, then he would have Pheresa. Alexeika vowed to wish no more harm against the lady.

Her heart ached, and she felt eaten alive inside.

She thought of victory in Grov and how Pheresa would have his love. His eyes would go to her first, before any other. His voice would soften for her alone. His hand would take her slender one and hold it. His embrace would hold her safe.

Alexeika's tears burned past her control. When she reached the edge of the Field of Skulls, she ducked into the pine forest and halted, gripping a fragrant, low-hanging bough to hold herself up. Faldain strode on ahead of her, heedless that she'd fallen so far behind. She wished he would at least glance back. *Dear Thod, husband of Riva,* she prayed, *please let him see me as a woman just once. Just once.*

She sank to her knees in the pine needles, wrapped her arms tightly about herself, and wept.

20

THREE MORNINGS LATER, Dain waited impatiently outside Alexeika's tent, stamping his feet against the cold and hugging himself beneath his cloak. He did not understand what was taking her so long. Usually she was up and going at daybreak. But while they'd been staying here in the dwarf camp, she'd acted subdued and unlike herself. Perhaps she was simply very tired from all the ordeals they'd endured. Still, they were rested now and well-fed, thanks to the generous hospitality of the dwarves. At times Dain couldn't help but compare the dwarves' treatment of them to that of the eldin, his actual kinfolk. Of course, the kindness was due to Dain's guardian Jorb having been Cardo's cousin. Last night, round the fire, Dain and the clan leader had talked late.

"War is a bad thing," Cardo had said solemnly. "Because of clan war, Jorb's artistry has been forever lost."

Dain frowned at the crackling fire, turning over old memories of grief and hatred. He remembered the day when he'd led Lord Odfrey's men against the dwarves who'd killed Jorb and Thia. Revenge had been exacted that day, but it did not bring his family back.

He sighed. "Sometimes war is necessary, whether we want it or not."

Cardo nodded. His gray beard hung down his chest, marking his great age. "All the news of late is war talk. Man-war. Mandria has taken arms, it is said."

"Against Nether?"

Cardo shrugged. "Oth be thanked, not against Nold."

Troubled, Dain squinted at the crackling fire. He knew Muncel had taken Gavril and Pheresa hostage before handing over their church soldiers and priests to Gant. Small wonder even a man as peace-loving as King Verence had been provoked to war.

Of course, Verence's ire was all to Dain's advantage. Perhaps he would be able to join forces with the Mandrian king against Muncel.

It was time to fight, Dain told himself with resolve. Ever since the night he'd walked the Field of Skulls, he'd felt a growing sense of urgency. The only reason he was not already on his road was Thum, who'd needed more time for mending than Dain had anticipated. He would not leave his friend behind.

"Aye, war," Cardo repeated gloomily, sipping from his cup. His square face, leathered and wrinkled like a piece of dried-out wood, was thrown partially into shadow by the firelight. "I hear the rebels are rising again in Nether. Sanfor's family have talked of nothing but that since they first arrived for this gathering. They've been delivering goods to Count Votnikt's hold for years, but this time there were king's soldiers crawling every-where, ready to think Sanfor a spy for the rebels."

Dain half-smiled. "Isn't he?"

"Aye, of course!" Cardo replied with a hearty laugh. "He's built up a great treasure for his burrow over the years, trading information for gold."

" 'Tis late in the year for armies to march," Dain remarked.

"It's fight or let Gant rule us all," Cardo said. "I will share a secret with you, because once you were Jorb's boy. This week, the clan elders have discussed uniting all the dwarf clans to-gether to keep Nold strong against Gant. We fear those devils will turn against us too. Our sages warn us of terrible trouble in the future."

"Take heed of such warnings," Dain said, his voice low and serious. "The Chief Believer means to consume every kingdom he can. He would have used me for the purpose, had I not es-caped."

"The gods were kind to you."

"Aye," Dain said worriedly, "but I fear that in my flight, I have provoked the Gantese into full-scale war."

Cardo shrugged. "If there must be war, then let it be fought with hearts brave and true. And let it be fought hard and fierce, with no holding back."

"Aye," Dain agreed with a nod. "No holding back."

Now he stood outside Alexeika's tent in the crisp morning air, blowing on his hands to keep them warm, and wished she would hurry. There was much to be done before they could leave. He was anxious to get at it.

Maug, the yellow-eyed dwarf who'd first brought Alexeika and Thum here from the river, came by with a bundle on his shoulder. He squinted up at Dain. "You will not wait one more day and share the final ceremonies?" he asked in his gruff way.

Dain shook his head. "I respect them, but they are not for me."

Maug grunted in satisfaction. "You understand our ways well."

"Have you brought it?" Dain asked.

Maug shifted the bundle off his shoulder and held it in his

arms as though it was heavy. "All here. My brother thanks you for the purchase, but he says the sizing—"

"Never mind that," Dain broke in impatiently. He handed Maug the gold pieces they'd agreed on earlier in sharp bargaining, and shook the tent flap. "Alexeika, come! Hurry!"

The flap twitched aside, and she stepped out. Garbed in her red mail hauberk, she wore her hair braided for battle. From head to toe, she was clean and polished. Even the tears in her cloak had been mended, and Dain could smell the honing oil she'd used on her sword and daggers. He'd seen her yesterday bargaining for whetstone and oil from one of the swordmakers. Apparently she'd been able to strike a deal, and she must have been up half the night taking care of her gear. The dark smudges beneath her stormy eyes confirmed his guess.

With a smile of greeting, Dain gestured for her to take the bundle from Maug. When she did so, she looked startled by its weight.

"Too heavy?" Dain asked.

At once her head snapped up, and her mouth tightened with determination. "Nay, sire."

Amused, he let her shoulder the burden and led her across the camp to one of the forges. The sun had not yet risen above the treetops. Light filtered into the clearing in lateral beams, dancing golden among the pines. The air was very cold and still, with scents of the forest overlaying the smells of the camp.

Old memories of dwarf mead, of burrows fragrant with soil, moss, and live wood filled Dain's mind. His childhood had been secure and happy, busy with chores, and always marked by the steady *plinking* of Jorb's hammer in the background.

Stopping at one of the portable forges now, its fire still banked in ashes, and the anvil cold and idle at present, Dain glanced back at Alexeika as she trudged up beside him. She was puffing a little with exertion, her breath misting white. Puzzlement filled her eyes, but Dain only smiled and swung around to face the dwarf who appeared.

"A well morn to you," he said cheerfully.

This dwarf looked secretive and unfriendly, the way many of the armorers were. Dwelling too much with fire and metal, they sometimes lost the ease of dealing with other folk.

"You pay," he said sharply.

"You hand over the goods," Dain replied with equal sharpness.

Distrust puckered the dwarf's bearded face. "Show me your coin."

Dain fished out his last gold dreit and held it up in his fingers so that it glinted in the rosy sunlight.

Greed filled the dwarf's eyes. He produced the sword he had wrapped up in an old cloth, then shook open the folds to reveal a splendid weapon with a hilt wrapped in silver wire and beautiful carvings down the scabbard.

Behind Dain, Alexeika gasped. "How beautiful."

Scowling at her, the dwarf wrapped the sword up hastily as though fearful she would grab it. Clutching it tightly, he handed over a smaller bundle to Dain.

Dain glanced inside, nodded, and tucked it into his pocket. Then he held out the coin. The armorer held out the sword. They exchanged goods and money at the same time, then stepped back from each other.

The dwarf bit the coin and examined it with a grunt of satisfaction before hurrying away.

"What is all this?" Alexeika asked. "Have you need of another sword?"

"At present, aye," Dain replied, and grinned at her, refusing to say more. "Come."

They went to the far edge of camp, stirring now as folk roused themselves and began to light fires under the cooking pots. Located well away from the dwarves' ponies and crosstethered inside a flimsy pen of wattle, the darsteed snorted at their approach, watching them with its fierce red eyes.

Its mind reached out to Dain's: *Food/food/food/food!*

He took a half-frozen, unskinned hare from a pouch hanging in a nearby tree and tossed it at the darsteed. One lunging snap and the hare vanished down the darsteed's throat. Immediately the beast trained its fierce gaze on Dain again.

Dain laid aside the wrapped sword he'd just purchased and tossed another hare. Although hampered by its tethers, the darsteed managed to catch it. One gulp, and it was gone.

"It's showing better appetite," Alexeika said.

Dain nodded as he busily eyed the darsteed for other signs of improving health. No flames as yet burned in its nostrils, but the patches of missing hide which had peeled off after its immersion in water had scabbed over and were already healing. Stamping and lashing its barbed tail, the darsteed tugged impatiently at its tethers.

"Aye, it'll do," he said in approval. "Another day and this flimsy pen won't hold it. Time to travel."

"Can it carry the three of us again?" she asked.

"Nay. I won't ask that of it."

"Then—"

A halloo from the forest caught Dain's attention as Thum and two dwarf children emerged from the trees. The boys were leading two shaggy ponies, and Thum limped ahead of them. He looked gaunt and pale, but his hazel-green eyes were bright with eagerness.

The darsteed turned its attention on the ponies, who abruptly balked, refusing to come closer. One of them began backing up, nearly dragging the bandy-legged child who held grimly to its rope shouting dwarf curses at it.

"I pray to Thod these brutes don't run off again," Thum said, puffing heavily as he limped up to Dain. "Good morn, sire. I ask your pardon for not being ready, but they bolted the moment they saw our monster. Would you please thank these young sprouts for helping me get them back?"

Dain smiled at the children. "Don't try to force the ponies closer," he said in rapid dwarf. "They're too frightened. It will take them time to grow used to the darsteed."

The larger of the two lads clamped his arm over the neck of his pony and stared at Dain with open curiosity. "It wants to eat them."

"Aye."

"You won't let it?"

"Nay, that I swear."

"On dwarf honor or Netheran honor?"

Hearing the child's mistrust, Dain walked over to him. "On dwarf honor, by ash and salt, I do swear." He spat in his hand and held it out.

Looking impressed, the boy spat on his own hand and gripped Dain's hard. "I accept your oath, King Faldain."

"Good. Now tie the ponies securely over there where they can get used to the darsteed's scent but not feel too threatened. Have you boys any duties to perform this morning?"

The boys looked at each other. Square-headed with wide-set eyes, they were clearly related. One nodded, but the other shook his head and dug his elbow sharply into his brother's ribs.

"Speak truly now," Dain said sternly.

The sulky one answered him: "I wanted to help with the blood oaths to Vannor, but, nay, we're assigned to light Element candles for the weddings. Pah!"

"Will you witness a ceremony here? A Mandrian ceremony?" Dain asked. " 'Twill not take long."

"Oh, aye!" they chorused.

"Good." He pointed. "Stand over there."

"Sire?" Alexeika said quietly. She'd shifted the coarse linsey sack off her shoulder to the ground. "The sun is climbing. I thought you meant to take the road by now."

"I did," Dain replied, squinting at the angle of sunlight and selecting a spot to stand. "But this has importance too."

"I have our provisions packed in the saddlebags," Thum said. "All we need is to fill waterskins and—"

"Aye, Thum. Over here to me."

Thum obediently limped up. His dark red hair had grown shaggy of late, and his beard needed trimming as well. He'd managed to procure a new cloak for himself, but it was too short for his lanky height. The knees of his leggings were patched and stained, and he was clearly starting to outgrow them. Dain had never seen him look so ragged, but his friend was still the capable, industrious, hardworking loyal companion he'd always been. Still a thinker more than a warrior, but with a brave heart all the same.

Dain glanced at Alexeika. "Would you come here? Nay, leave the bundle where it is."

Looking as puzzled and impatient as Thum, she obeyed.

Dain pointed at Thum. "Help him to kneel without hurting that leg."

A look of stunned comprehension flashed across Thum's

face, and he turned white. Although his mouth fell open, and his throat apple jerked up and down, he said nothing.

Though delighted by his reaction, Dain remained outwardly stern. While Thum shakily knelt, Dain drew Truthseeker and held it aloft in the sunlight.

Alexeika's blue-gray eyes were alight now with approval. Glancing at where the new sword lay in its wrappings, she smiled.

"Thum du Maltie," Dain said, speaking Mandrian, and wishing he could have done this before the entire company of Thirst knights, before an entire army, with heralds and trumpets to make fanfare, "I do now call forth the announcement that you are a courageous and worthy man, valiant and true."

Kneeling before him, Thum gulped again. His eyes were shining like stars.

"You have shown prowess with arms, faithfulness to your oaths and duties, and courage in the face of danger. I, Faldain, Chevard of Thirst and rightful, though uncrowned, King of Nether, do hereby knight you."

As he spoke, he touched Thum on either shoulder with the flat of Truthseeker's blade. Thum bowed his head, praying beneath his breath. When he finished, Dain extended the hilt of Truthseeker to him, and Thum kissed it reverently. No longer did he seem afraid of the weapon, as once he'd been. He'd seen enough in Gant to make him understand the difference between rightful magic and wrong.

"Arise, Sir Thum," Dain said, beaming at him, "and count yourself a warrior."

A grin flashed across Thum's face, but it vanished just as quickly. He remained kneeling. "I, Sir Thum du Maltie, do hereby give my oath of fealty to Faldain of Nether," he said in an unsteady voice. "I vow to devote myself and my arm to seeing your majesty rightfully crowned."

Proud gratitude swelled Dain's heart. He held out his hand as Thum struggled to rise, and their clasp was hard with all the feelings they could not openly express.

Then Thum took a step back, blinking as though he could still not believe all that had happened.

Dain sheathed Truthseeker and reached into his pocket to

pull forth a set of spurs, silver and well-wrought. "It is customary for a new knight to receive gifts, either from his father or friends. Here is my gift, as one former foster of Thirst to another."

Thum took the spurs with obvious delight. "Dain, I—I mean, your grace, I—"

"And as your chevard," Dain continued, striding over to the sack that Alexeika had carried, "I am obligated to outfit you properly."

He pulled out a hauberk of shining new mail and held it up so the sunlight glinted off the metal links.

Thum limped forward. "Great Thod above," he said in astonishment. "How did you get such a fine—"

"It should have been fitted to you, but perhaps in the future you can acquire custom-made armor. In the meantime," Dain told him, "never again will you be expected to join combat without proper protection. I would not have seen you wounded so grievously for the world, my friend."

Thum took the hauberk and held it up against his chest. Alexeika came over and helped him check the length of the sleeves against his arms. "A bit short, but 'twill do," she announced, smiling. "My congratulations on this honor done you, Sir Thum. 'Tis well-deserved."

"Thank you," he said, looking stunned. "But I—I didn't even help with the escape from Gant. More like I was a burden—"

"A true friend is never a burden," Dain said fiercely. "*Never.* You were worthy of being knighted long ere we were taken to Gant."

Thum kept stroking the hauberk, and even laughed. "Now I suppose this is something else for me to polish."

"Aye, you've no squire to do for you," Dain said merrily. "For that matter, nor do I. We shall have to do our polishing together, provided we can persuade Alexeika to share her honing oil."

Alexeika blushed.

"Well," Thum said, grinning as he went back to examining his gifts. *"Well!"*

"It is a Netheran custom," Dain said now, "for the king to

bestow his notice on a knight in particular favor. I wear no crown, Sir Thum, but I would keep that custom."

Thum stared at him, and Dain picked up the sword he'd bought. Leaving it wrapped, he handed it to Thum.

"Nay," Thum said, sounding overwhelmed. "What is this?" He draped his hauberk over his arm, unwrapped the sword, and held it by its carved scabbard with hands that trembled visibly.

"Draw it," Dain said quietly. "See if its balance fits you. The dwarf who made the weapon can adjust it if necessary, or fit you to another."

Thum bowed his head, busily blinking back the moisture that shimmered in his eyes. Collecting himself, he fitted his hand around the hilt and slowly drew the blade, which flashed in the sunlight as only virgin steel can.

" 'Tis plain," Dain said, "but worthy of your rank. Better than that dull piece you used to wear on your belt."

Without being told, Alexeika unbuckled his belt and threaded it through the scabbard straps, then knelt and fitted the spurs onto his boots.

"Put on your hauberk, Sir Thum," Dain said.

Thum's eyes were shining. "I have done nothing to deserve such high honor. No valiant act have I performed, no shining bravery have I shown."

"Nonsense," Dain said gruffly. "You have been my most loyal friend. You have served me well, better than I deserved. 'Tis I who must ask your pardon yet again for having taken you into battle as a squire, with no armor and no—"

"My pardon is given freely," Thum told him. "Think of it never again. I would fight for you again without armor or sword, if necessary. I just regret that I could not serve you while we were in Gant."

Dain's brows shot up. "Not serve me? And who took the arrow meant for me? Put on your hauberk, sir, and get ready to ride. Your feet may drag the ground on yon pony, but by Thod, you'll go forth mounted and spurred. As for your shield, you will have to provide that for yourself someday."

Thum's laughter rang out.

A female dwarf came hurrying up, a look of exasperation

on her face, and began to scold the boys, who'd been watching solemnly all this time.

Dain had forgotten about them, but now he turned and hurried over to intervene. "They are here by my request," he said to her in dwarf. "I bade them wait."

"They have sacred duties this day," she said impatiently. "This is no time for them to fall idle."

"But they are witnesses to the knighting of this man," he explained. "Let them bide here a few minutes more. I shall not keep them long."

"Our ceremonies—"

"I know. I honor and respect your ceremonies. Please honor and respect mine. I shall release them shortly."

She frowned, looking indecisive, and glared at her sons. "Well, then, see that they hurry. You are a guest here, and welcome, but you must not interfere with us."

"My word is given," Dain told her.

As soon as she left, he nudged the boys forward to Sir Thum, who now had donned his hauberk gingerly over his wounded shoulder. It was short in the sleeves and too loose in the girth, but once his sword belt was buckled, he looked well enough. The pride shining in his face rivaled the sun, and Dain could not have been more pleased with the outcome of his surprise.

The dwarf boys, encouraged by his wink and nod, stepped up to Thum and in unison intoned, "Steel and brass. Brass and steel. May your sword hold strong. May no arrow pierce your armor. Let the breath of the war gods Fim and Rod protect you in battle."

Sir Thum listened to this benediction with bewilderment. When they were finished, he glanced at Dain. "What did they say?"

Dain translated. "It's an ancient dwarf blessing for warriors. The same blessings have been said over your sword and mail as they were made."

"Oh." Gripping the hilt of his new sword, Sir Thum turned to the boys and bowed with his best courtly flourish.

Grinning, they retreated and looked at Dain. "Now do we go?"

"Not just yet," he said in dwarf, and turned around. "Alex-eika."

She was still eying the fit of Thum's hauberk with a criti-cal eye, but at the sound of her name she glanced up and gave Dain a quick nod. "Aye, sire. If you're ready to depart, I'll get the ponies."

"Nay," he said before she could stride away. As usual she was still trying to anticipate him, and half the time getting things wrong. "There's something else to do first."

She frowned. "No disrespect to Sir Thum, but the day is get-ting on."

"Alexeika, come here," Dain said.

She hesitated, then obeyed him. She was still frowning and would not meet his eyes. He'd sensed disquiet in her for days, but whatever was troubling her would have to wait.

"I will not let you ride forth in that red armor," he said. "Take it off."

Her eyes widened and an angry flush crept up her cheeks. "Sire?"

"You heard me. Take it off."

"But—"

"It nearly got you killed by the dwarf patrol at the river," he reminded her. "Maug told me how he first mistook you for a Believer. You cannot continue wearing it. What if the next time a Mandrian knight on patrol puts an arrow into you and asks questions later, or dwarves attack, or the Netherans—"

"Your majesty makes his point," she said with acerbity. "But 'tis my war trophy."

"Then put it in a saddlebag and use it to adorn the walls of your ancestral hold. But wear it no longer."

She scowled, stubbornly defying him. Dain swallowed a sigh. In truth, she was about as easy to handle as the darsteed.

Finally she asked, "Am I then to ride no more into battle? Stripped of my armor, am I to fold my hands and retire, of no further use to your majesty?"

Her voice was rough with appeal, and now even Sir Thum was frowning at Dain. "Sire," he said, "would you—"

Dain shot him a look that silenced him, then glared at Alex-eika until the red in her face intensified.

She pulled off her cloak and jerked at the lacings of her gorget and hauberk. Thum started to help her, but Dain gave him a quick head shake and he backed off.

Alexeika flung the red mail on the ground and stood there in her tunic, her eyes flashing defiance.

Involuntary admiration touched Dain, and he could not help but smile at her temper. "Better," he said. "Now kneel before me."

Her eyes flared wide, and in an instant all the color drained from her face. "No," she whispered.

"My lady, you seem determined to defy your king today at every opportunity," Dain said harshly.

Tears swam in her eyes. She dropped to her knees and bowed her head.

"A warrior you are already," Dain said, drawing Truthseeker once more while Sir Thum and the dwarf boys looked on in awe. Dain noticed that a few other dwarves had come up to stand in a curious cluster. "Your valor is proven in combat."

She shook her head. "I am unworthy of honor, sire," she whispered.

He frowned, unsure why she'd become so feminine and moody of late. But he wasn't going to be thwarted. "Let your king determine that," he said in rebuke, wishing she would learn to be silent. "Now, I do grant and bestow knighthood on this lady, Princess Alexeika Volvn, a true and worthy servant of her king."

He touched her shoulders with the flat of Truthseeker's blade, then extended the hilt to her as he had done with Thum.

She knelt there a moment as though she would refuse.

Exasperation filled Dain. He did not understand her at all. "Alexeika," he said sharply.

When she tipped back her head to look at him, tear tracks shone on her cheeks. "A maiden cannot be a knight," she whispered.

"She can if I make her so."

More tears spilled from her eyes. He frowned, wondering what was wrong. He'd believed this would please her.

Struggling to explain, he said, "I—I thought this would honor you. 'Tis a fitting tribute to your father as well. You are indeed a worthy and courageous heir to his name and sword."

Many emotions filled her eyes. In silence she kissed the hilt of Truthseeker, then drew Severgard. Its huge sapphire gleamed in the sunlight as she held it aloft by sword tip and hilt, balanced thus on her fingertips. "This great sword was pledged to the faithful service of King Tobeszijian and to his father before him," she said gruffly. "Now do I pledge it anew to the service of Faldain, son of Tobeszijian."

She proffered it to Dain, and he touched it lightly. The black blade flashed with dazzling brilliance, radiating a white light.

Dain felt the tingle of its energy pass through his fingers, and in that moment he absorbed a hint of the weapon's incredible magic, a magic vastly different from Truthseeker's power. Then Severgard's radiance vanished, and it looked like an ordinary sword once more.

He stepped back, clenching his tingling hand. "Rise, Sir—" He halted and laughed a bit self-consciously. "Forgive me. This is a time when a herald would be invaluable. By what title shall I call you?"

She said nothing, busying herself instead with sheathing Severgard as she rose to her feet.

He glanced at Sir Thum, whose eyebrows were still high.

"Um, er, well," Sir Thum said, blinking rapidly. "To my knowledge there has never been a lady knighted before. At least not in Mandria—I know not the history of Nether. But would she not use her higher title? After all, sire, *you* are a knight, but it is your highest rank that—"

"Ah," Dain said, feeling foolish for not having worked this out for himself. "Of course. Thank you. Come, princess, and accept this gift."

She looked startled and tense, like a doe ready to leap out of sight into a forest thicket. "But I—"

He'd already pulled the second set of spurs from his pocket and was holding them out. "Fellow comrades were we in the desert," he said with a smile. "Accept these with my wishes of friendship."

She went to him and took them shyly, but her eyes would not meet his. "I thank your majesty," she said.

"And as custom dictates—"

Her eyes snapped up to his. "But I have a sword already!"

He had to laugh ruefully. "Ah, Alexeika, my lady, you indeed will never change. Sir Thum?"

His friend had already guessed his intentions and was pulling a second hauberk from the sack. Its brass links gleamed in the sun, and Alexeika gasped with her first genuine smile of the day.

She ran to take it from Thum's hands, then spun around to face Dain with a new frown. "And you made me carry my own gift across the camp? You—"

Dain laughed, and after a moment so did she.

"Forgive me a small joke," he said. "Let us see if it fits you."

He and Thum started to hold it up against her, but she looked suddenly shy and retreated from them.

Gripping Severgard, she ran out of sight into the trees, and was gone a very long time indeed.

Dain glanced at his friend, who was preening and examining his sleeves with a very satisfied smirk. "What is taking her so long? Do you suppose it doesn't fit? What is she doing?"

"Crying," Sir Thum replied.

Dain was startled. "Crying? Again? But why?"

Sir Thum shrugged. "Who knows? My sisters do it at the strangest times."

"But I don't understand her," Dain said, genuinely puzzled. "All the time we were prisoners, she never faltered. We crossed the desert, starving for water and food, and she was stalwart the whole time. Not a complaint. Never a flinch from anything we faced. But ever since we came here, she's been so odd. Why should she cry now?"

"Women cry sometimes because they are happy."

"I *know* that," Dain said impatiently. "But she isn't happy."

"Does your majesty want my advice?"

"Of course!"

"Leave her be."

"But—"

"Leave her be, sire. I vow that soon enough she'll be herself again. The less you fuss over her, the quicker she'll be the Alexeika we know."

Dain frowned. " 'Tis strange advice."

"Well, I do have sisters."

"So did I," Dain reminded him. "Thia never acted this way."

"Oh? But your sister was eldin."

"Alexeika has some eldin blood," Dain said.

"Not as much as—"

"Hush! She's coming."

Alexeika returned wearing the hauberk, which fit her perfectly. She walked with her head high and her shoulders erect. Her face was now perfectly composed, and only some redness in her eyes betrayed the fact that she had indeed been crying.

Dain eyed her warily, but she seemed all right now. She rolled up her red hauberk into a bundle, stuck it under her arm, and put her cloak back on. Her new spurs jingled faintly with every step.

"Thank you, sire," she said in a clear, calm voice. "Your majesty has been most kind in granting me this honor. I vow to serve you with—with less argument."

He smiled, and she gave him a wan smile in return.

When he beckoned to the dwarf boys, they came, though with obvious reluctance.

"A woman?" they asked in disbelief. "You make a warrior of a woman?"

"Look at the sword and daggers she carries. See how her hair is braided. She is a very brave fighter."

"Cannot be so," one of the boys scoffed.

"Give her the blessing just the same."

But the two boys exchanged looks and ran off without a backward glance.

Sighing, Dain gave Alexeika an apologetic shrug. "I will speak the dwarf blessing myself."

She held up her hand. "Please don't. 'Tis unnecessary. Your gesture and gifts are generous enough."

"Alexeika, what is wrong?"

Her brows lifted, and he felt the lie even before she spoke it. "Nothing, sire. Will you give us the order now to saddle up?"

He still did not know what had gone awry, or why this had

upset her. But if she did not choose to tell him, he was not going to force her. "Aye," he said with a sigh. "Let us be gone. We have a hard journey ahead of us. By Maug's reckoning, we've at least a week's travel to cut through the forest and reach the border. Then we'll have to find the Agyas."

Alexeika blinked, and in an instant the clear-thinking, cool-headed warrior he knew and valued was back. "We'll find them," she said. "As soon as we reach the border we'll be able to send a messenger to them."

He snorted dubiously. "A Netheran we can trust?"

"Horse thieves make the best couriers," she said with a grin. "Give them enough gold, and they'll do anything to bring Muncel down."

"Is that all I can count on?" he asked in dismay. "Horse thieves?"

"Perhaps a few others. Remember, majesty, that I'm a thief as well."

He disliked the brittle, mocking way in which she said that, but let it pass. "Were a thief," he corrected, already striding toward his darsteed to saddle it. "You *were* a thief, but you're one no longer."

"So you think, majesty."

He swung around and looked at her very hard. "So I *know,* Alexeika. Now, let's ride."

21

EIGHT DAYS OF hard riding through forest that grew increasingly thick and in places nearly impenetrable brought them head-on into a snowstorm. Lashed as they were by howling winds, and with the swirling snow nearly blinding them, even Dain could no longer be sure of the correct direction.

He called a halt, and his weary darsteed pawed the ground. Beside him, Alexeika and Thum were barely recognizable shapes huddled inside their snow-covered cloaks and hoods. Alexeika's eyebrows and lashes were coated with snow. Thum's beard was crusted over. Dain himself felt frozen to the marrow. He'd long ago lost any feeling in his fingers or toes, and he knew they were in mortal danger of freezing to death.

"Must find shelter!" he shouted over the howling wind. His lips were so stiff he could barely speak.

"How?" Thum shouted back. "Where?"

Dain frowned. He was so cold and tired he couldn't think clearly. They needed a cave or a burrow, but neither were at hand. And if they tried to make camp here among these trees, they would surely perish.

Alexeika lifted her head bleakly. "Do we kill the animals?"

Slaughtering their mounts and disemboweling them so that they could shelter inside each animal's body cavity seemed a last resort, one Dain found himself reluctant to act on. Most important, if they survived, they would be afoot. Then too, he was not eager to see the innards of a darsteed.

The snow blew harder, all but obliterating the nearby trees and wrapping the world in a cocoon of white. Dain's usual landmarks of sun angles, slanted growth of trees, and moss on tree bark and stones were of course gone. He could not follow scent, for the snow had covered even that. For all he knew, they'd been traveling in circles for hours.

Alexeika drew one of her daggers. "We'd better slash their throats at the same time. Otherwise, the smell of blood will make the darsteed—"

Something reached him, a faint glimmer of instinct perhaps, or the touch of a mind far distant. "Nay, not yet," Dain said.

"Why? It's our only chance."

He could not answer why. Whatever he'd sensed was too indistinct for him to identify. But he gestured for her to put away her weapon. "Bide a while. Let's keep going if we can."

"We can't!" she shouted harshly. " 'Tis futile to keep on in this."

"Come on!" He kicked the darsteed forward.

The creature balked, no longer possessing the strength to rear in protest. Dain finally managed to urge it forward, one struggling step at a time.

The ponies, short-legged and stalwart, actually fared better through the deep snowdrifts. Tireless and bred to this cold country, they lowered their heads against the wind and shouldered forward.

Dain lost track of time again. He focused everything he had left on seeking that one instant of contact. Friend or foe, it no longer mattered. He simply kept urging the darsteed toward it and hoped numbly that Thum and Alexeika were able to follow. His mind was swimming, and he could no longer concentrate. He felt a strange roaring in his ears beneath the shriek of the wind, and had found himself swaying in the saddle when suddenly a glimmer of light appeared ahead.

It took a moment for his brain to absorb what he was seeing, then he blinked and came back to awareness. A pale, ghostly light shone just ahead of his struggling darsteed, and as Dain stared the light grew more distinct and clear. A cloaked figure clad in a breastplate embossed with hammer and lightning bolt was blocking his path. It was Tobeszijian, his ghostly form so thin Dain could see snow blowing through him. Astride his ethereal darsteed, whose red eyes glowed through the swirling snowfall, Tobeszijian stared at Dain without speaking. His black hair blew back from his stern and handsome face, and in silence he pointed at Alexeika, who drew rein beside Dain and squinted.

"Why do you stop?" she asked. "Are you—oh!"

"Do you see him?" Dain asked in wonder, and she nodded without taking her eyes off Tobeszijian.

She stared a moment, then seemed to collect herself. Deeply she bowed. "The king who was," she whispered.

Tobeszijian stared at Alexeika a long time. He was still pointing at her, but at last he lowered his gloved hand. She uttered a little gasp, shuddering. Her hands clenched and unclenched on her reins.

Dain turned his gaze back to his father. For an instant their eyes met, and he felt his father's sadness pierce him. Forever lost, forever caught between worlds, neither dead nor alive. Yet despite his compassion for Tobeszijian's, Dain was filled with an overwhelming sense of relief. "Father!" he called out. "Guide me before we perish!"

Tobeszijian turned his darsteed around and walked it away. Hurriedly Dain reined his darsteed in that direction and followed. "Stay close!" he shouted to Alexeika and Thum.

Alexeika turned her head and shouted to Thum, who seemed to wake up and spurred his pony closer. But soon he was lagging behind, and then Alexeika also fell back. The sturdy ponies had stamina, but their short legs could not keep up with the longer strides of the darsteeds.

Sleepily Dain recalled that he had several questions to ask his father, yet he was so cold he could not rouse himself enough to remember what they were. *War,* he thought hazily. *Strategy and —*

Abruptly his darsteed went plunging and skidding down an unseen bank into a snow-filled ravine. Scrambling desperately to keep its footing, the animal snorted flame and lashed its tail, just managing not to tumble before it landed at the bottom. The jolt snapped Dain's teeth together.

Barely able to comprehend what had happened, he glanced around, but Tobeszijian had vanished. Dismayed, Dain had opened his mouth to call out when figures erupted from the snow on all sides, popping up from snowdrifts to surround him. Clad in heavy furs, their eyebrows and mustaches coated white, they hardly seemed like men at all. But there was no mistaking the swords and javelins in their hands.

Up at the top of the shallow ravine, Thum's voice called out faintly through the howling wind. "Dain! Sire, where are you?"

Dain looked up, but the snow was blowing so thickly he couldn't see his friends. Meanwhile, his circle of captors had closed in around him. Their dark eyes glittered with hostility, and Dain knew he'd be dead with a javelin through his throat before he could draw Truthseeker.

Anger warmed Dain. He'd trusted Tobeszijian to lead them to safety; instead, the ghost king had led him into a trap. Why?

"Halloo!" Thum called again, his voice even fainter than before.

One of the men pointed. "You and you, go get that one. Hey,

Believer!" he said sharply to Dain. "How many of your filthy kind ride with you?" He spoke Netheran with an accent that seemed vaguely familiar to Dain. "How many?" he repeated.

Praying that Thum and Alexeika would wander on into the snowstorm and escape capture, but fearing luck had run out for all of them, Dain found himself too cold and weary to answer.

One of the men gripped his arm and jerked him off the darsteed, which squealed and snapped viciously. It was too weary to have much fight left in it, however, and as he thudded into the snow, Dain was conscious only of how slow everything seemed to be happening. He felt warmer than before. The bottom of the ravine must be sheltered a bit from the wind, he thought vaguely. His eyes drifted shut.

They jerked him up to a sitting position, and a javelin tip tapped his shoulder for attention.

"No point in questioning this one," someone said. "He's frozen."

"Take his weapons. We'll let him and his monster freeze together."

Rough hands grabbed at Dain's cloak to pull it open, but with his last ounce of willpower, he drew his sword with fingers too stiff and clumsy to hold it firmly. "In the name of Tobeszijian, I defy you," he mumbled.

Silence fell over the men surrounding him. The javelin resting on his shoulder slid off.

"What did he say?" someone finally asked.

"Tobeszijian. *Tobeszijian!* He invoked the lost king's name."

"Aychi!" breathed another as he squatted down in front of Dain. "Look at this sword. It's not—"

"Take care, Chesil! The Believers poison their weapons."

"He's not Gantese," Chesil said gruffly, and pushed back Dain's hood. Roughly he scrubbed the frost and caked snow off Dain's brows and peered into his eyes. He jerked aside a lock of Dain's hair and ran his gloved fingers over the tips of Dain's ears. "Eldin! Or partly so. He's—"

"He's Tobeszijian!" someone else said in awe.

"He's not!" another voice protested. "Where's his crown? This sword ain't Mirengard. It ain't magicked."

" 'Tis! And I did hear him say his name."

They all started talking at once. "The darsteed!" "The sword!"
"His eyes and—gods save us! It must be!"

Dain was sinking deeper into the warmth, so welcome after
his having been cold for so long, yet he thought them fools to
mistake him for his father. He would never be half the man
Tobeszijian was. "Not . . . ," he mumbled, and thought of Thum
and Alexeika. "Find . . ."

His mind was full of fragments, like chips of ice that could
not be fitted together. He heard the men talking around him,
felt them shaking him, but their voices were now just a buzzing
inside his head. He sank into darkness, and left them.

When he awakened, it was to a sensation of true warmth and
the cozy comfort of a crackling fire. He found himself lying
in a low-pitched tent made of hides, with heavy furs lying atop
him and a fire burning merrily in an iron cresset. He had no
idea of how long he'd lain unconscious, but through a slit in
the tent flap he glimpsed darkness outside. The shadows inside
his tent were deep except where the fire threw them back.

Slowly his mind pulled memories together until he remembered his capture in the snowstorm. Well, they hadn't killed
him as they'd first meant to. He checked, but his wrists and ankles
weren't bound under the furs.

Sitting up, he frowned, wondering if they still actually believed he was his father. If so, he thought, they must be rebels,
and he must speak to them.

As he pushed off his furs, the tent flap opened, sending a
gust of icy air whistling inside. A man ducked in with it, paused
as his gaze met Dain's, then dropped to one knee and bowed
his head. He was a giant of a man, with muscular shoulders
and a neck like a bull's. A luxuriant brown mustache drooped
down either side of his mouth past his chin. He was red-cheeked
and brisk, with brown eyes that twinkled in the firelight.

"Your majesty," he said, his voice deep and rich. "It is good
that you are awake. With your leave I will tell the others."

"Wait!" Dain said quickly before the man could rise. "Who
are you? What camp is this?"

"Ah. Forgive me, sire. I am Count Omas. My father served
yours in the old days."

Dain blinked at him and slowly smiled. "Then you don't think I am Tobeszijian, Lord Omas?"

The count laughed, his voice booming strongly. "Nay! But it made a good sport for us when the scouts came in with you, bleating in panic at what they'd captured."

"I'm glad they thought it," Dain admitted wryly. "Otherwise, I think they would have slain me for a Believer."

"That darsteed would make anyone think you were Gantese, except for your armor. No fire-cater, eh?" He laughed again, slapping his knee.

Dain realized he'd been so concerned that Alexeika would be mistaken for Gantese that he'd never considered the effect his own mount might have on folk. "I thought the beast might be useful," he said.

"Eh? Well, perhaps." Omas pursed his lips. "It's already eaten a camp dog and injured two grooms. We've got it staked with as many ropes as we can spare, and a man is standing guard with a crossbow to kill it should it break loose."

"Is this a rebel camp?" Dain asked.

"One of them. We've been on the march nigh twenty days, held up thrice with this blighted weather. But that's the fate of men bent on waging war in winter."

"You got my message, then?" Dain asked, only to frown immediately. If these men had been on the move for twenty days, they'd started out well before he'd even been taken to Gant. "Nay, of course not. Forget I asked that question, my lord."

"No message from any courier of yours, sire," Lord Omas said with puzzlement. "Not since you sent acceptance of Lord Romsalkin's pledge."

"Are these Romsalkin's men?" Dain asked.

"Aye, we are," Omas said proudly. "When we heard that you'd been captured and taken by those heathen devils, Lord Romsalkin vowed to strike at Grov though we all died for it. And so here we are, and it's Thod's grace that brought you into our scout trap. Aye, Thod's grace indeed."

It was Tobeszijian's mercy, Dain thought, but he said nothing.

"Hungry, your majesty?"

"Aye," Dain replied, but as Lord Omas jumped to his feet

and started out, Dain called after him, "And what word of my friends?"

The giant's hearty face creased into a look of disquiet. "Why, your majesty, two of 'em is all we managed to find in the storm. Come daylight we'll search again—"

"Two!" Dain said in astonishment, not understanding. "But of course you mean Sir Thum and the Princess Volvn? There are no others."

Lord Omas stared at Dain in astonishment of his own. "So the wench in chain mail claimed, but we could not believe her. Your majesty would not travel with so small a party."

"They are all that is left," Dain said in a voice of flint.

"Forgive me, sire! I meant no offense." Lord Omas's heavy brows drew together. "A princess, you say? That piece is—I— I mean—a lady?"

"General Ilymir Volvn's daughter," Dain said, annoyed to hear they'd not been treating her with proper respect. "She's no drab, no wench, no camp follower. If I learn any have treated her as such, those men will answer to me!"

Omas tucked in his chin, and although he could not stand at his full height in the low tent, he gave the impression of a man coming to attention. "I'll see to it at once, your majesty. And now, if I may have leave to order your supper and see that Lord Romsalkin is notified that you're awake?"

Dain nodded dismissal, and the count vanished through the tent flap with another gust of icy wind. Fuming a little, Dain tossed off his fur covers and found himself clad only in his tunic and leggings. His boots and hauberk were nowhere to be found, but Truthseeker was hanging by its sword belt on a tent pole hook.

He belted on the weapon, and his dagger too, wondering what they'd done with his boots. He knew instinctively that Lord Omas was an honest man, but allies or not, the men in this camp were strangers, and Dain had no intention of remaining long in this tent when the situation required closer examination.

Shivering as the cold ground numbed his feet through his stockings, he stepped onto one of the fur robes and wrapped another around his shoulders.

"Sire!" called Lord Omas from without. "Permission to enter?"

"Come," Dain said impatiently.

The man ducked inside, bringing with him another draft of freezing air and snow. Dain ignored the servant following with a tray of food, and scowled at the count.

"Where are my boots?" he demanded. "My hauberk? My cloak?"

Omas blinked as though taken by surprise. He turned on the servant, and pelted him with rapid-fire questions in a dialect that Dain did not understand.

The servant—short, old, and wearing a collar of slavery—replied in the same language.

"Ah, yes," Lord Omas said, turning back to Dain. "Your cloak is being dried. The rust on your hauberk is being polished by my youngest squire. Your boots are being cleaned as well."

"I want them," Dain said. "And I want to speak to Lord Romsalkin as soon as possible."

Lord Omas bowed. "At once, majesty. I shall inform his lordship of your summons—"

"Nay!" Dain broke in. "I'll go to him."

"But that's not—" Omas choked off his protest. "As your majesty wishes."

"Get my boots and a cloak I can use," Dain said. "Have them here by the time I finish my supper."

Omas started out, but Dain gripped his sleeve. "And tell my companions I wish to see them."

"Yes, your majesty."

"Have they eaten? Are they well?"

"I believe so, your majesty."

Dain was aware he had this man of high rank and perhaps some authority jumping like a squire, but he gave Omas a curt nod. "That's all for now."

"Yes, your majesty." Omas bowed, then rushed out.

The servant remained behind. He had brought not only food, which was plain fare but steaming hot, but a pail of warm water to wash in.

Grateful for these civilized amenities, Dain cleaned up and

then, with a ravenous appetite, applied a wooden spoon to the contents of his bowl. It did not take him long to eat, but by the time he finished, his boots—hardly recognizable for their gleam—had been delivered, along with his hauberk. The latter was freshly oiled, and mended where the sleeve had hung in tatters before. The servant helped him put on these articles, and by then someone was outside, handing over a cloak of magnificent lyng fur, pale cream with variant shades of gray stripes.

Awed by its beauty, Dain could not help running his palms over the soft, silky fur. He wondered who had surrendered such a fine, warm garment to his use.

The servant threw it around his shoulders before Dain ducked outside, into a bitter night indeed. The storm had abated, but the breeze was still brisk enough to feel knife-sharp. Snowflakes continued to fall, dusting his hair and collecting on the long tips of lyng fur.

He found both Thum and Alexeika standing out there, waiting for him and jigging up and down to keep themselves warm.

Both of them bowed to him, but Dain wasn't willing to stand on formal ceremony. Grinning in relief to see that both of them were well, he strode forward with his hands outstretched, but then noticed a crowd of knights gathered in the shadowy background, staring at him in awed silence. Dain realized he must now act like a true monarch. No longer could he rush about informally as just another knight and comrade-at-arms.

Recalling all he'd ever learned from King Verence, he beckoned Thum and Alexeika to him. "You are well?" he asked quietly.

"Yes, sire," Alexeika replied with dignity.

"I shall never feel warm again," Thum complained, "but, aye, sire, we've been well treated here."

Dain gave him a fleeting smile, but his gaze shot again to Alexeika. Although she was acting subdued, he saw fury flash in her eyes before she averted them from his. There had been insults indeed given to her, he knew, and his own ire came up protectively.

"Alexeika?" he asked again.

She was tight-lipped and stiff. "Your majesty might as well

know there's been trouble. I had to stab an oaf for giving me insult and—"

"Did you kill him?" Dain asked swiftly.

Her eyes flashed again. "Nay, but I wish I had."

"We can't afford to lose a single man for the battle to come," he told her, but gently to let her know he didn't disapprove of what she'd done. "If you must stab others, make sure you avoid their vitals."

A smile tugged at the corners of her mouth, and suddenly there was muted laughter in her eyes instead of rage. "I'll remember that, sire."

Lord Omas approached them. Glancing his way, Dain stepped close to Thum and Alexeika. "Stay near," he said quietly. "These are Romsalkin's men. They are friends by their former pledge, but let us take care until we know how things truly lie."

At once Thum's eyes grew serious and wary. Alexeika nodded her understanding. With them at his back, Dain faced the count.

"Lord Omas," he said, "please escort me to your liege commander."

There was no mistaking Romsalkin's tent. A wondrous relic from an earlier age, it was huge enough to be divided into three rooms by walls of hard-woven cloth. The whole edifice creaked and shifted with every gust of wind, the ropes creaking and snapping taut against the poles. Beyar skins and worn, motheaten carpets covered the frozen ground. Torches on stakes provided illumination. A campaign table spread with a faded map, a miscellaneous collection of stools, and a table holding a paneatha with icons of the gods dangling from its bronze branches all served to furnish the central room of the tent, which is where Dain, Thum, and Alexeika were escorted to meet Lord Romsalkin.

The latter proved to be a short, barrel-chested man with sparse tufts of white hair standing up on his head and a short white beard trimmed to an emphatic point. Wearing an old, rather battered breastplate buckled on over his hauberk and a sword of ancient design, Romsalkin threw down his pen with such enthusiasm he overset an inkpot and blotted the entire page of vellum he'd been writing on.

"Damne, what a mess!" he said in disgust. Snapping his fingers at a page, he pointed at the dripping ink and went to greet Dain with hardly a pause. "Your majesty!" he said with gruff pleasure, and dropped to one knee. "I have looked forward to this day for lo these many years. Thod be praised that I have lived to see you."

"Lord Romsalkin," Dain said formally, "your friendship and loyalty is much appreciated. This is Sir Thum du Maltie, my adviser. And this is Princess Alexeika Volvn, daughter of General Volvn."

Romsalkin gave Thum a nod of his head and a glance of swift appraisal, but at Alexeika's introduction, his brows shot up and he looked stunned.

"Ilymir's daughter?" he said. Tears shimmered in his eyes, and he reached out his hands to clasp hers. "My dear, dear child. What a blow we suffered when he died."

"Yes," she said with perfect composure. Watching her, Dain realized that she had indeed been trained in courtly manners, her rough ways notwithstanding. At the moment she was as formal, indeed as regal, as any fine lady of high breeding. He could not help but mentally contrast her dignified behavior tonight with those times when she'd been spitting mad and cursing like a knight, her hair falling out of its braid and dirt streaked across her face. No doubt Alexeika had more surprises up her sleeves for them all. He wished he'd seen her stab the man who'd dared offend her earlier tonight.

"I realize your lordship and my father did not always agree on strategy," she went on calmly, "but I heard him speak much of you at times."

Romsalkin released her hand and barked out a laugh. "Cursed me, more like. Aye, my dear. We used to fight like vixlets after the same prey round King Tobeszijian's wardroom."

Stiff and hostile no longer, she grinned back at him.

Dain sensed no deceit in the man, and stepped forward, eager to get on with the matters at hand. "Forgive my haste, but there is much to be done. I've heard from Lord Omas that you're marching on Grov."

"Aye!" Romsalkin growled, punching the air with his fists. "No force to speak of, just my two hundred men and a small company of Grethori riders I've enticed along by promising 'em free looting afterwards. But, by Thod, I intend to give the usurper a sharp lick before I go down. Aye, so I do!"

"I would rather see Muncel licked than you," Dain said. "Can your men wait here while word is sent to Matkevskiet?"

"Word's already gone to him, the sly dog. All these years, holding his men back, never helping us strike against the usurper. Depend on his help? Pah! I'd as soon wait for a pack of Believers to come and join our cause."

"I have his pledge of four thousand men," Dain said. "I've sent a messenger to him, but can another go forth?"

"Enough messages have gone forth," Romsalkin said. His shrewd eyes glanced from Dain to Omas and back again. "So you would have us fight together, eh?"

Dain smelled a trick, and grew tense. "If all the little rebel factions do not unite into one force, then they are fools who deserve no change in their government," he said harshly.

"And your majesty thinks that of me," Romsalkin said. He was serious now, his gaze intent. Rocking up and down on his toes with his hands clasped at his back, he never let his eyes stray from Dain's face. "Leader of a little faction."

"Nay, leader of two hundred knights pledged to my cause," Dain replied, and drew Truthseeker. Slamming the blade atop the map with a crash that made Romsalkin's aides jump, he said, "Exactly what size is this Grethori company, and can any more be coaxed into joining us? Can they be trusted? How many other men have been levied? Prince Spirin notified all the rebel leaders of my discovery at Savroix. You've had plenty of time to assemble and contact each other. Stop trying to test me, my lord, and give me a blunt report of exactly where I stand."

"Hardly the ill-trained boy described in those dispatches to Muncel we intercepted," a new voice said.

Dain turned his head and saw a tall, broad-shouldered man with long, iron-gray hair tied in a multitude of tiny braids. Tawny-skinned, he had an old, deeply puckered scar running across his forehead and down through his left eye. White with blindness, it made a stark contrast to his dark, sighted eye.

Garbed in vivid blue with a crimson sash across his chest

and a curved scimitar hanging at his side, this individual strode in from the rear room of the tent and stood surveying Dain with frank appraisal.

Dain stared right back, not exactly pleased with this trick. "You are General Ingor Matkevskiet," he said.

The Agya leader bowed with a haughty, fierce expression. "I am."

"And is Samderaudin the *sorcerel* also here?" Dain asked. "With the weapons and armor he promised?"

Matkevskiet's lips curved in a fleeting smile while his gaze went on stabbing into Dain. "Yes," he said. "But he is busy casting your horoscope to see what fate will grant us."

"Fate will grant us what we're willing to fight for," Dain said impatiently. "How many more men besides your four thousand?" His gaze shifted to Romsalkin. "And your two hundred–plus?"

"The Grethori can't be trusted, sire," Alexeika said softly behind him. "Don't count them."

Dain accepted her warning, but his gaze remained on his allies. "How many more?"

"Seven hundred," Matkevskiet answered, then admitted, "Most are farmers and rabble, untrained and worthless except to rush to the front line. I believe even a few thieves and bandits have volunteered. We would be better off without such men. They will be in our way."

Romsalkin turned on him, white beard bristling. "And I still say they can be used."

Matkevskiet frowned back, but before they could argue, Dain interrupted. "Then our numbers are sufficiently equal." He met their surprised glances coolly. "My intelligence reports state that Muncel has a standing army of five thousand. Unless he can send for additional troops from Gant, and get them quickly, we have enough to give him a scare."

"Aye, that's so," Romsalkin agreed with a nod.

Matkevskiet sneered. "To scare the usurper is not enough. We must crush him!"

Dain gave him a steely look. "I will fight to the death to bring down the man who murdered my mother. Can we set forth at dawn?"

"If the weather clears enough, aye," Romsalkin said eagerly. He grinned at Dain and gave Matkevskiet a nod. "I like the boy's spirit. Aye, that I do."

But the general was still eying Dain with distrust. "A fearless boy is a battle-green boy. *I* will lead the men, but only if Samderaudin himself fends off the Nonkind that will be sent against us."

"Perhaps his majesty will be able to persuade Samderaudin to—"

"I do not come here as a diplomat," Dain said in disbelief and rising anger. "I come here to lead an army."

"No," Matkevskiet said. "The fighting is ours to do."

Romsalkin bristled. "And what makes you think *my* men will follow an arrogant Agya dog like you—"

"So this is why Nether perishes under the heel of a sniveling, despicable, half-mad tyrant," Dain said. Anger cracked through his voice with so much vehemence and contempt that the torches in the tent flickered and nearly went out.

Both Romsalkin and Matkevskiet dropped their argument and faced him in startlement.

"You deserve what has befallen you," Dain went on harshly. "This petty bickering, this *stupidity*! Why have you waited eighteen years to depose the man, letting him build an army of Nonkind and filth, letting him pillage the land and sicken it until it won't feed the people? Why did you not join forces and fight?"

Matkevskiet narrowed his good eye and said nothing, but Romsalkin lifted his head defensively.

"We had no king to lead us," he said. "Tobeszijian vanished, and we waited for him to come back."

"Aye, waited," Dain said scathingly. "Waited and plotted, but *did nothing*! How many battles have your men fought against Muncel's forces, Lord Romsalkin?"

"Now see here—"

"How many? Open, declared battles?"

"Why—why—a few," Romsalkin said uneasily. His gaze flicked at Alexeika, then fell away. Her face, Dain saw, was set and grim. "Better to hit targets and sprint away, doing what harm we could on the run."

"Volvn took five hundred men forth," Dain said.

"And died in a futile gesture, wasting himself and his men," Matkevskiet said coldly.

Alexeika stiffened. Her eyes were aflame, and her hand was on her sword hilt, but she did nothing, said nothing, much to Dain's relief. He did not want her interference now.

"Volvn was my father's best general," Dain said. It was the truth, by all accounts that he'd heard, but to say so to these men was a deliberate affront. He saw both stiffen. "Why did you not join with him, follow his leadership in overthrowing Muncel?"

"And do what, crown Volvn our next king?" Romsalkin blustered. "A preposterous notion."

"Better that, than to roll over tamely beneath Muncel's domination."

Romsalkin turned bright red. Matkevskiet glared at Dain, as intent on him as an eagle sighting its prey.

"And where was Tobeszijian, our rightful king, all this time?" he asked now, his voice thin with contempt. "Why did he desert us?"

"He did not," Dain said, just as sharply. "He hid the Chalice and myself and my sister, then he rode back into Nether to begin civil war."

"Easy to say. He ran. Took the Chalice and *ran*," Matkevskiet said, years of pent-up resentment spilling forth. "Why did he not come to his Agyas? We would have protected the royal children *and* the Chalice!"

Dain frowned. "So that's what this is about. Old insults. Old resentments. My father's reasons are not yours to question."

"They are if he deserted his duty. He deserted us!" Matkevskiet said fiercely.

"If he'd deserted you, he would be living in exile at his ease," Dain retorted. "He did all he could, and now he is lost in the second world forever, trapped there in a fate more wretched than death."

Matkevskiet actually blinked, and Romsalkin's mouth fell open.

"By Thod!" the latter cried. "Is this true?"

"Would I say it were it not?" Dain retorted.

"Merciful gods, we must have prayers said for his soul at once," Romsalkin said. Catching Lord Omas's eye, he said, "Inform the priests. Damne, what a terrible thing."

Matkevskiet went on staring at Dain. "Your father is accounted for, but what of you, young king-to-be? Where have you been all these years?"

"Growing up, so I could come here today and lead your men," Dain said icily. "You're wrong to think me green, general, but I'll not fault you for it now. Hear me. If I do not lead the battle and the men you've promised me, then I say break your pledge and take your men home."

Someone in the tent gasped. Matkevskiet's single eye bored into Dain without even a blink. "A bold bluff," he said.

"Think you so?"

"Aye. Tell me this. Have you the Ring of Solder?"

Dain knew where these questions were going. His heart sank, but he did not hesitate to give his answer. "Nay. It is gone forever."

"Have you the Chalice?"

"I know where my father hid it."

"Have you Mirengard, which the son of our king must carry?"

"It remains in the second world with my father," Dain answered.

Matkevskiet's gaze shot scornfully to Romsalkin, who was frowning. "And this boy would lead us into the field, my lord. Brave bluster means nothing in combat. If the gods are merciful and we should prevail, I will see him crowned, because I loved his father. But no Agya warrior will follow him into battle. I do not squander men with an untried boy."

"Alas," Romsalkin said, turning to Dain with regret. "It seems we must listen to the general, sire. Really, the fact that you are present and awaiting the outcome of the battle will hearten the men—"

"Morde a day!" Dain exclaimed in disbelief. "I tell you I will not sit in a tent like some court daisy. Would any Agya warrior fight for such a fool, fight with all his heart and soul? I think not."

"The Agyas fight as I tell them to fight," Matkevskiet said darkly.

"Then send them home," Dain replied. "I thank you for your offer, general, but I decline your pledge."

Matkevskiet laughed. "He's mad, Romsalkin. Send my warriors home and leave himself but two hundred trained men and assorted rabble? Such foolishness only confirms my doubts."

"You dare judge me," Dain said harshly, blowing out his breath in an effort to keep his fraying temper. "I come here more seasoned than you know, but you dare to find me wanting. My sword is not Mirengard, general. Nay, it's not a magicked blade, not like Severgard, which Alexeika here carries." He held out Truthseeker. "Look at it! Or do you know god-steel when you see it!"

"God-steel!" Romsalkin echoed, his eyes bulging. "Thod's bones, it can't be. Why, that's—"

"Impossible," Matkevskiet said, refusing to look at Truthseeker. Contempt and disbelief shone in his one eye. "This lie will not impress me more, sire."

"Is that scimitar of yours magicked?" Dain asked.

"Nay."

Romsalkin raised his hands and made patting motions. "Now, now, your majesty, pray calm yourself. There's no need for this. No need at all. Let us share wine and cool our heads."

Dain ignored him, never taking his eyes off Matkevskiet. "Draw your weapon."

The Agya general lifted his head, his nostrils flaring at the challenge. From the rear room suddenly appeared two youths about Dain's age. One of them he recognized as Matkevskiet's son, the courier named Chesil who'd come to Dain at Thirst. The other looked enough like him to be a brother. Both wore expressions of horror.

"Father, do not!" Chesil said. "To raise arms against the king is mortal sin."

"Perhaps outside would be better for combat," Lord Omas suggested.

Alexeika had her hands on her weapons. Thum crowded closer to Dain.

"Sire, I like this not," he whispered on Dain's left. "Have a care."

Dain glanced at him, but said nothing. His gaze went back

to Matkevskiet, whose temper was clearly battling his common sense.

"Quiet yourselves," Dain said to the room at large. "I do not intend to fight the general. Sir, draw your weapon."

"He will be very fast," Alexeika whispered in Dain's right ear. "Agyas move quicker than thought. He will catch you by surprise, if you are not careful."

Grateful for the warning, Dain flicked her a tiny smile. But he was very serious indeed as he returned his gaze to Matkevskiet.

"I gave you an order," he said. "Will you defy me in this as well?"

The general shrugged, then slowly drew his scimitar, despite his sons' protests. After silencing them with a gesture, he faced Dain. "A fool will be a fool. Who am I to disobey the order of my unproven king?"

"One engagement only," Dain said, shrugging off his fur cloak. He hefted Truthseeker in his hands, flexing his shoulders to loosen them. As the others moved back to give them room and servants hastily shoved aside Romsalkin's desk and the precious paneatha, Dain was well-aware that his challenge could fail. It was risky to take on an opponent he did not know—moreover, an opponent he had seriously provoked.

"I have a point to make," Dain said. "One engagement, general, but do not hold back."

Matkevskiet smiled a cold, dangerous smile, revealing his filed teeth. The light of battle shone in his single eye, and Dain felt the menace in him like a tangible force. Civilization was a thin garment this man wore.

Swiftly Dain shoved aside his momentary qualms and moved into a crouch. He never took his gaze off his opponent and pulled all of his concentration into play. "Thod, strengthen me," he prayed beneath his breath.

At that moment Matkevskiet loosed a blood-curdling yell and sprang. He was a blur of motion, his scimitar whirling in his hands. And he did not simply charge at Dain in a straightforward run. Instead, he danced and kicked with complicated footwork that enabled him to leap into the air at exactly the same moment he swung his blade down at Dain's unprotected head.

Had he hit, he would have cleaved Dain's skull in twain.

But Dain's special senses were guiding him. Without watching Matkevskiet, he began to counter the moves he sensed Matkevskiet would make. As a result, as the general leaped, Dain was already in motion, ducking beneath him and turning as the general spun in midair.

And when Matkevskiet landed, Dain was not where the general had obviously expected him to be. Instead, Dain was still facing him, off to the side, and already swinging Truthseeker.

The scimitar flashed in the torchlight, but as the two blades came together with all the strength both men possessed, it was the scimitar which shattered into dozens of razor-sharp pieces.

At once, Dain stepped back. Pale with astonishment, Matkevskiet stared at him. Dain swept him a salute and sheathed Truthseeker with satisfaction.

"Ho!" Lord Omas boomed out, clapping loudly. "Well done, sire! Well done!"

Not even with the merest glimmer of a smile did Dain acknowledge the applause. He'd just defeated and shocked a proud warrior because he was lucky enough to possess a superior weapon. The last thing he wanted was to make an enemy of Matkevskiet by dealing him humiliation.

"God-steel," he said quietly, "has its advantages, as you can see."

The general went on staring at him, his expression quite impassive. Then he dropped to one knee and pressed his fingertips to his forehead and out in salute. When he looked up, he was beaming.

"So would your father have fought me for the cruel things I said," he announced with pride. "Exactly like the father is the son. Tobeszijian's son. *Aychi!* I give thanks to the gods that I have lived to serve my king again."

Now it was Dain's turn to stare with astonishment. "That was a test? All that argument? All those doubts and insults?"

"They were real enough," Matkevskiet said, rising to his feet. "You have proven your courage, young king. Now it remains to be seen whether you can prevail against the usurper. Can you lead an army?"

Dain's gaze grew steely. "Can you follow my leadership?"

"To the death," Matkevskiet said simply. "As I swore to follow your father."

A sense of relief swept over Dain then. He grinned for a moment, feeling almost light-headed, and everyone crowded around him. Romsalkin called for wine, and Lord Omas asked questions about Dain's sword. Matkevskiet's sons, looking awed, hung on every word.

"Celebration is too soon!" announced a voice that sent a chill up Dain's spine.

The hubbub fell silent immediately, and men stepped back to give Dain a clear sight of the individual now entering the tent. Snow blew in behind him, ruffling the beyar furs he wore as clothing.

His eyes were tilted, his face curiously smooth-skinned, although Dain sensed at once that he was extremely old. He glided forward as though his feet barely moved, yet suddenly he was standing very close to Dain.

He smelled of something bitter and acrid. His gaze held secrets no mortal should know.

Dain's heart was beating fast. This had to be the *sorcerel* Samderaudin, yet although he was supposed to be an ally, Dain could not help but instinctively distrust him, as he did all enchanters of this kind.

The *sorcerel's* gaze burned into Dain. He lifted a bony, taloned finger in admonition. "Celebrate not yet," he said, his voice crackling and humming with a resonance that spoke of spells and powers.

It was almost like listening to the tainted sword Tanengard, Dain thought. He frowned, forcing himself not to be distracted, and said, "You are—"

"Much danger lies ahead," Samderaudin interrupted curtly. "I have cast the future, yet it remains unclear. There is betrayal to come. You have been warned of this by Tobeszijian. Do you heed it?"

"Aye," Dain replied with a frown, conscious of the others

exchanging swift looks behind him. "But I've been betrayed already."

"More is to come. More danger. More trials." Samderaudin leaned toward him, and Dain had to fight himself not to draw back. "Death lies heavy along your path, Faldain."

"Thank you for this warning," Dain forced himself to say courteously. "I hope your foretelling means that I will deal much death to others, and not find it myself."

Alexeika gasped, but he did not glance at her.

The *sorcerel*'s expression did not change. His eyes were yellow and intensely compelling. Dain felt the power emanating from them and found himself wanting to babble all his secrets. Gritting his teeth, he resisted, and after a moment the pressure eased.

"There is more," Samderaudin said. He pointed at Truthseeker. "It protects you with the power of the ancients. But you will face a choice, Faldain. Count the risks before you decide. The reach of Ashnod can be very long."

Dain frowned, trying to fathom what the *sorcerel* meant. He opened his mouth to ask questions, but without another word Samderaudin turned and glided out.

Dain hurried after him, ignoring those who called to him. But when he stepped outside into the falling snow, the camp lay quiet and dark, and Samderaudin was nowhere to be seen.

22

AT DAWN, THE army marched forth. Romsalkin's banner of crimson and white unfurled in the frosty air. Matkevskiet's banner of sky blue and green flew beside it. The skulls tied to a pole draped with islean pelts represented the tribe of Grethori, whom

Alexeika cursed and avoided at all times. Even the rabble carried streamers of different colors to signify their regions. And above them all flew the burgundy and gold pennon of the royal house of Nether.

When its heavy folds, creased and worn from long years of storage, shook free and billowed forth in the wind, Romsalkin was visibly moved. "Ah, to see it fly again," he said to Dain, wiping his eyes. "This does stir my heart."

Dain stared at it, seeing the hammer and lightning bolt depicted in gold across a field of burgundy, and his heart was stirred too. Before him stretched his army, a vast sea of faces cheering his name.

He lifted his arm in response and glanced at his generals. "Let us ride to war."

They marched to Grov, struggling against the obstacles of harsh weather and inadequate provisions. This was the wrong time of year to wage war, yet now that their course was set, none of them was willing to wait for spring—Dain because he was anxious to rescue Pheresa, and the others because they had already waited too many years to strike at the tyrant they hated.

They made no contact with the Mandrian army rumored to be on the march. The scouts found no evidence of it. Romsalkin dismissed the rumor as a falsehood.

The journey became a sort of king's progress, for every pathetic village they passed by turned out to stare at them, sometimes in terror and sometimes in hope. Dain would not let the Agyas loot such places, for clearly the people were starving already. Instead, they plundered the royal storehouses in larger towns.

"I am the king," Dain declared. "And I take what is mine!"

Sometimes Muncel's soldiers put up token resistance; often they fled their posts at the granaries. Meanwhile, word of Dain's coming flashed from town to town, spreading across the land with every woodcutter, every fur trapper, every merchant or peddler who had not yet denned up for the long cold.

"No help for it," Romsalkin would mutter, fretting at night when Dain and his advisers met in the huge tent to plan strategies. "Muncel has plenty of time to prepare for us. We can lay siege to the city fortress or Belrad, if he chooses to meet us there. He can defend it better."

"Ought to take Belrad first," Matkevskiet suggested. "Give him no bolt-hole."

"Split off a detachment to see to that," Dain said. "But I must take Grov first. 'Tis the capital that must be claimed for my own."

Muttering, they would peer at the map again. The Nonkind worried both old strategists terribly, for they claimed that Muncel had an entire auxiliary force of soulless warriors, dead men who would fight without tiring or stopping. And the cache of magicked armor and swords that Samderaudin had indeed provided was insufficient to supply every man in Dain's force.

"We need more *sorcerels*," Matkevskiet kept saying glumly, squinting his one eye. "Without them we'll be outmatched."

Dain frowned at such pessimism. "If Mandrians can fight Nonkind without magic or even salt, who are we to bemoan what we have?"

Romsalkin's white beard bristled. "Mandrians, pah!" he said, forgetting that Thum stood at Dain's back. "What do they ever face but little raids from time to time? Nay, your majesty, I'm talking about a vast Nonkind force to be reckoned with."

Eventually they agreed on a plan. Grov was bordered on one side by the Velga River, but to the southwest lay a sweep of rolling meadows and a bit of valley where the city sprawled. There they would meet Muncel's forces. It was by far the best ground available.

For Dain, used to fighting when and where the emergency struck, such advance planning was very interesting. He wondered, however, if Muncel would adhere to the formal rules of battle or if he would instead pour Nonkind at them from all directions.

"Of course he will," Alexeika muttered one night when she and Thum gathered with Dain inside his tent. It was larger than the first one he'd slept in, but nothing like Romsalkin's magnificent dwelling. Although he'd been offered the use of Romsalkin's quarters, Dain was content to use this plain tent of ordinary size. It gave him privacy for these quiet talks with his friends.

Restless and clearly on edge, Alexeika got up from her stool and began to pace back and forth in the limited confines. The fire in the cresset cast shadows and highlights across her face. "Muncel did not hesitate to use deceit and trickery against my father. He will do the same to you, sire."

"Then we must prepare some tricks of our own," Dain said thoughtfully. "Romsalkin intends to put all the men with magicked swords and armor at the front, but I think we had better deploy them at our rear and sides."

"You mean, make a ring of such protected men?" Thum asked.

"Aye."

Chesil Matkevskiet twitched aside the tent flap and peered in. "Forgive me for interrupting, sire, but Lord Omas is here to see you."

Dain glanced up. "Ah, yes, admit him."

He had servants assigned to his use now, and a squire to oversee his weapons and mail. Young Chesil, hero worship shining in his dark face, short braided hair swinging energetically, served as Dain's aide, running messages back and forth for him daily. Sir Thum stayed close by, ready to give Dain counsel whenever he was confronted by something he did not instantly understand. There was much to learn and much to do. He received dispatches and letters daily, many of them from Prince Spirin and other notable exiles of the old Netheran court. There were petitions to join Dain's court, blessings, pleas to grant the return of lands confiscated by Muncel, and a barrage of other matters that left Dain feeling overwhelmed whenever he tried at night to cope with them. Although his command of the Netheran language had improved swiftly, he still found it difficult to read and even harder to write. He needed clerks to handle the paperwork, and at last he ordered Thum to simply sack up all the letters, reports, and requests, to be dealt with later, if and when they took Grov.

This evening, although the hour grew late, Lord Omas came ducking through the tent flap with his usual massive briskness. Little icicles had formed on his long mustache. Icy beads of moisture glistened on his cloak from the sleet falling outside. The wind moaned and thumped against the sides of the tent.

"Your majesty!" Lord Omas boomed, bowing low. He stripped off his gloves, then slapped them against his palm. "I stand ready to serve."

Dain gestured at the warmed wine they'd been drinking, and Lord Omas took a cup with a grateful sigh.

"Ah, that does warm the insides. Thank you, sire."

"I have made inquiries," Dain said, gazing up at the giant. "I'm informed you have your own hold."

"Aye, 'tis so small and so unimportant and so out of the way that even the usurper didn't want it," Omas replied cheerfully. "I have a standing army of twenty knights, all of whom are now here among your majesty's forces. The original warrant granted to my ancestor was for the hold to guard a mountain pass for an old trade route up near the World's Rim."

"Guard against what?"

"Grethori devils mostly. Even the Nonkind don't venture that far." Omas grinned. "Sometimes we see boat raiders from the Sea of Vvord, but not often."

"And Romsalkin is your liege?"

"Aye, majesty. But only in the levying of armed men and an annual tribute."

"I ask these questions because I have a request of you," Dain said carefully. "But I do not wish to offend you by discounting any obligations you may have elsewhere."

"No offense can be given by my king," Omas said, his twinkling brown eyes looking serious for once. He was plainly intelligent, despite his size, muscle, and cheerful manner. Dain had been observing him for days, and at no time had that instant sense of trust and liking he'd felt for the man in their first meeting left him. "Please tell me your majesty's request," Omas said now, "and I will—"

"Make no promise until you hear it," Dain interrupted swiftly. He leaned forward on his stool. "I would have you serve me as my lord protector. But only if you have no obligation elsewhere, and if such service would please you. Speak freely if you wish it not, and I will hold nothing against you."

A tide of red flooded Lord Omas's face, spreading up from his throat to burn his cheeks. He seemed, for once, at a loss for words. Then he dropped to his knees and bowed low.

"Your majesty," he said hoarsely. "This honor is profound. I . . . But how can you trust me so? Your majesty hardly knows me."

"You are a good man," Dain told him. "Clearly your heart is honest and brave. And you are big enough to make two protectors," he added with a wry smile. "Would such service please you?"

Lord Omas was blinking hard. He looked both stunned and overwhelmed. "Aye," he said in a choked voice.

"Would your duties take you too much away from your family?"

"Nay." Something bleak and transitory crossed Omas's face. "My lady wife is dead. I have twin sons, presently fostered for training."

Dain rose to his feet. "Then it is settled. You are my protector, and my life is entrusted to you."

Lord Omas put his hand atop Dain's foot and bowed even lower. "I pledge myself to your majesty's service, to the death and beyond."

"Good." Dain smiled at him. "Go without for a moment and make what preparations are necessary. You will begin your duties immediately."

Lord Omas climbed to his feet with a radiant smile, almost knocked his head on the top of the tent, and hurried out.

"At last!" Alexeika said as soon as he was gone. "I was beginning to think your majesty would never choose someone. It's been a worry to us all, seeing you go about without a protector."

Dain gave her a nod, but his gaze went to Thum, who was looking pensive and sour. He knew Thum had secretly hoped to be named his protector, but it would not do.

"A good choice, sire," Thum said without enthusiasm. "He's twice the size of Sir Terent."

"There will never be another Sir Terent," Dain said quietly. "As for you—"

"Ah, yes," Thum said too quickly. "Too much a scholar to make a good knight."

"Too good a knight and adviser to make a protector," Dain corrected him. "Why should I waste your talents in such a post?

I would rather have you at my side, my friend, than at my back."

Thum turned red, and he seemed placated. "Destined to be your chancellor someday, no doubt," he said lightly.

He spoke in jest, but Dain remained serious. "Exactly."

While Thum's eyes widened and he choked in astonishment, Dain picked up his cup and raised it high. "A toast to my protector," he said. "And now the two of you can stop fretting over me."

Alexeika drank the toast, but her gaze remained uneasy. "As long as there are enemies to be faced, we will continue to worry. Do not forget Samderaudin's warning."

But on the morning they finally reached Grov, the *sorcerel*'s mysterious foretelling was the last thing on Dain's mind. Geared for battle in breastplate, mail, spurs, and helmet, his fur cloak warm and heavy on his shoulders and the darsteed he rode spitting fire, Dain drew rein on a gentle rise and found himself gazing at his father's city.

This was a cold, cheerless day, as gray and bleak as mist. The air smelled of snow, though as yet none had started to fall.

Down in the city proper, there seemed to be little or no activity. A church bell was ringing, but without urgency. Across the city where the river was half-frozen and dotted with small ice floes, a long team of kine struggled to pull a floating barge laden with logs. On the hill rising steeply behind the city jutted the spires and towers of the palace, the place where Dain had been born.

He stared, drinking in the sight of this place he had not seen since he was two years old. Nothing looked familiar to him, but as he drew in a long breath, the myriad scents of the land, the river, and the city came to him, and vague memories stirred deep in his mind. He recalled sitting in a room bright with shades of yellow, green, and blue as sunshine poured in through enormous windows. He was sitting on a stool so high his legs dangled, drinking from a silver cup that had tiny animals carved on the handle. He remembered playing with them, imagining them to be alive and his playmates. And from somewhere in the next room came the murmur of feminine voices, then the sound of his mother's laughter, light and full of song.

He heard it clearly, and with a gasp of surprise, he reached inside his hauberk and pulled forth his pendant of bard crystal. Swiftly he rubbed his fingers across its faceted sides, and its song came forth, in exactly the same musical key as his mother's laughter.

Only then, for the first time in his life, did he understand how this small part of her had always been with him. He had not, had never, lost all of her as he'd thought.

Emotions rushed him, and his eyes stung a moment with tears. Then he tucked the bard crystal away, and firmed his mouth and blinked his eyes dry. She had died there, in that palace. And he had come to avenge her.

"Where is my uncle?" he asked, pointing at the empty meadow.

"Morde a day!" Romsalkin said, puffing through his beard. "I thought their army would be here to meet us."

General Matkevskiet came galloping up on his stallion. He was not wearing his helmet, and his long gray braids flew out behind his head as he rode. "More trickery!" he said furiously. "He knew we were coming with a force nearly equal to his. Why is he not here? Does he expect us to send him an invitation?"

Dain's head came up, and he gazed at the right-hand side of the city a long moment, gazed at a small fortress of gray stone perched near the river. His senses were sweeping forth, but he already knew the answer he sought.

"Muncel is not here," he said.

"What?" Romsalkin exploded. "What does your majesty say? Not here? How can this be?"

"The army lies hidden in that pesthole of squalor and filth they call a city," Matkevskiet said angrily. "They will spring out and ambush us the moment we ride into the streets."

"No," Dain said.

Sitting nearby on his horse, his strange eyes on fire and his fur clothing bundled shapelessly about him, Samderaudin swept forth his hands in a gesture that made the air crackle and pop. "They are not there," he said. "It is as the king says."

Dain was already spurring the darsteed forward, ignoring

calls for him to come back. Alexeika and Lord Omas plunged after him, their horses kicking up sprays of snow.

The others had no choice but to follow. Thus did Dain lead his army into Grov unchallenged. It was hardly a triumph. On all sides he saw the signs of hasty flight and damage, belongings strewn about and dropped as people had fled, signs of looting as though Muncel's army had pillaged as it left. The few inhabitants remaining were in hiding.

Dain glimpsed faces peering at him from broken windows and sensed others, concealed and terrified. As for Grov itself, he saw at once how glorious its past had been. The architecture of its buildings made him marvel. He admired the broad central avenue that led through the heart of the city. There were streets of enormous palaces that must have belonged to the noble families. But past glory was nearly obscured by the squalor of the present. Dain rode past smashed and torn-down statues, saw how the palaces had been damaged and burned. Entire wings stood roofless and windowless. Some buildings had trees growing up through them. The ones still lived in were shabby and unkempt.

The lesser sections of the city appalled him. Narrow streets of mud twisted in all directions through a maze of wooden buildings. Nonkind stench lingered here, keeping everyone alert and on edge. But no attacks came, no ambushes, no traps. There were only a few pitiable individuals in rags fleeing from sight, stinking piles of refuse and filth, starving dogs skulking for what they could find in the garbage, and vermin too bold to run.

Dain's face grew stony as he struggled to hide his shock. He'd heard all the stories, of course, but never had he believed a city could be as terrible as this. Muncel lived here, kept his court here. Had he no pride in what he'd stolen? Was he truly so insane, so indifferent to everyone except himself that he was willing to let his city look like this?

"Sire," Thum whispered as he rode up alongside Dain. His hazel-green eyes were wide and disbelieving. "This is a dreadful place. It's ruined. There's nothing left."

"Aye," Alexeika said, pointing at a section of the city which had been burned. "They tried to destroy it before they fled."

Dain sighed. "Small wonder Muncel deserted this."

"Nothing to fight for," Thum said with scorn.

"Wrong," Dain said, pulling himself back together. He lifted his chin and squared his shoulders. "This is *my* city, the city of Netheran kings. Lord Tamski!"

An officer riding near Dain came alert. "Yes, sire?"

"Organize patrols. I want every section swept, to make sure no pockets of resistance remain."

"Yes, sire!" Tamski wheeled his horse and galloped away.

"Lord Romsalkin," Dain said, "please see that the church bells are set ringing."

Tears had dried on Romsalkin's cheeks, but he scowled fiercely at Dain's order. "Aye, sire. I will! Does your majesty want the *Glorias* rung?"

Dain had no idea what he referred to, but nodded. "Whatever is appropriate."

Romsalkin galloped off, shouting to the men he wanted with him.

"And you, majesty?" Matkevskict asked, watching Dain closely with his one eye. "Where do you go now?"

"Muncel's fortress must be secured," Dain said.

"Aye, but where do *you* go now?"

Dain drew a deep breath, thinking of Pheresa and his past. "I go to my father's palace," he said.

Runtha's Folly, some had called it. Dain—heavily surrounded by a guard of Agya warriors, Thum and Alexeika at his side, and Lord Omas at his back—rode across the wooded grounds of the sprawling palace compound. Although it had been allowed to become overgrown, and woolly thickets now choked the place, he saw signs of old cultivation, plantings that were not wild varieties, and occasional traceries of the last few blooms of some delicate shrub now frozen by winter's blast.

Today was Selwinmas, celebrated in Mandria as the day the monk Selwin became the first convert to Tomias's reformed teachings. Here in Nether, Dain had learned, Selwinmas was more commonly referred to as wintertide, the first official day of the deep cold and the shortest day of the year.

So far, there was nothing to celebrate.

He kicked the darsteed and galloped right up to the broad

steps of the palace. The building's surfaces were carved into fantastic creatures or twining vines or twisting branches or cavorting beasts. There was too much to look at, too much to see.

Dain did not try. He could feel his mother's bones somewhere near, somewhere out in the gardens beneath the snow. There were memories here, perhaps not all of them his own. He sensed old emotions, lingering like ghosts: emotions of fear, anger, hatred, and love all jumbled and mixed together in something he was not yet ready to deal with.

Just now, he was not interested in ghosts. He sought the living.

"Sir Thum!" he said crisply, dismounting even as the Agya commander in charge of his guards protested that he must wait until they secured the palace. "We must look for Pheresa."

Thum seemed startled. "They wouldn't leave her here. Surely they took her and Prince Gavril with them."

"Hostages would be in the fortress, sire," the commander said.

Dain met Alexeika's eyes, and he wondered for a moment why she remained silent. "Nay," he insisted. "They were kept here. Come!"

He strode inside, forcing the swearing Agyas to leap off their horses and hurry after him. Lord Omas was almost treading on his heels, saying with every step, "Let me go first, sire. Let me go first."

But Dain wouldn't listen. The place was eerie and silent, full of shadows, and empty in a way that chilled his bones.

He hurried through one enormous stateroom after another, barely registering the faded or destroyed magnificence, the rotted hangings, the broken windows that let in icy drafts. His boots echoed loudly on the floors as he searched. Later, much later, he would have to explore every inch of it for himself, but not now.

There was no sense of Pheresa, nor of Gavril. He knew that, and yet he steeled his heart against the truth, telling himself they must be here. The alternative was too heartbreaking.

"They are not here!" Alexeika finally said, as they halted partway up the broad staircase. It had once been painted in the most fantastic mixture of colors, but all was faded now. As a rat went scrambling out of sight above them, its red eyes looking vicious, Alexeika planted herself in front of Dain. Her blue-gray eyes were wide and pleading. "Please! Abandon this search. They are gone. Everyone is gone. In Belrad, perhaps, they will be found."

A part of him wanted to agree with her, but he'd come so far, had endured so much. He couldn't accept it, refused to believe that once more he'd failed the lady he loved.

Gently he pushed Alexeika out of his way and continued up the staircase. "We haven't found the room I saw yet," he said.

She turned as he passed her and reached out as though tempted to grip his arm. "Don't!" she cried out. "Please don't!"

Ignoring her, he went up to the next story. There, through a set of tall, heavily gouged and battered doors, he found the room of mirrors and bard crystal that he'd sought. For a moment, as he entered, reflections seemed to come at him from all sides. He remembered a day in his childhood when sunshine had poured in through the tall row of windows, only to be reflected back again by the mirrors. The bard crystal globes overhead had spun in the summer breezes, singing and refracting light in glorious colors. He remembered, too, the vision of Pheresa as he'd last seen her, sitting in a gown of pale red, with candles blazing, and people in jewels and velvet surrounding her.

And then all the memories and overlapping impressions faded, allowing his mind to clear. He looked down the length of the gallery and saw Gavril and Pheresa sitting in tall chairs, just as Thum's hand clamped on his elbow.

"Great mercy of Thod!" Thum exclaimed hoarsely. "They *are* here!"

Dain stared at the pair, sitting at the far end of the gallery. Neither of them moved or spoke; perhaps they were dead.

Swallowing hard, Dain slowly peeled Thum's hand off his arm. His ears were roaring, and he paid no heed to anything that was said. When he walked forward, his footsteps thudded loudly on the boards. Lord Omas hastened ahead of him to reach the royal couple first.

Gavril sat there, clad in dirty velvet. His blond hair was long and unkempt, his beard untrimmed, his eyes reddened and staring fixedly. He clutched Tanengard in his begrimed hands, and only an occasional blink showed any life in him.

Shocked, Dain stared at his old enemy, unable to reconcile this Gavril with the one he'd always known. So arrogant and sure of himself, so favored, so handsome, so falsely pious, Gavril had many faults, but he'd always been strong, vigorous, and full of zest. Now, it seemed the Netherans had broken him. He was a wreck, a shadow of himself, so deeply withdrawn into the ruin of his mind that he seemed completely unaware that they were here.

"Gavril," Dain said. "Prince Gavril!"

The prince did not respond. It was as though he did not hear Dain, did not see him standing there. His dark blue eyes stared emptily.

Frowning, Dain turned to Pheresa. She sat slumped in her chair, clad in a filthy, torn gown of faded silk, a necklace of tawdry glass around her throat. Pale and sweating, she was unconscious. The moment he touched her hand and felt its fever heat, he knew the eld-poison still consumed her. She was very near her end.

"Oh, Thod," he said in despair, kneeling before her. "And I thought you well."

"Sire, don't touch her," Thum said uneasily. "You might contract the poison yourself."

"Poison?" the Agya commander asked in alarm. "What poison? Or is it a spell that's been cast here?"

"Sire," Alexeika said in a hollow voice. "Nonkind are nearby."

He smelled nothing, sensed nothing. "No."

"I say they are!" Alexeika shouted. She drew Severgard, and the blade was glowing white with power. "The sword does not lie!"

The Agya commander shouted orders, and his warriors ran to the doors and all corners of the room, their weapons drawn and ready.

Dain looked around swiftly. "Sir Thum, we must get Pheresa out of here. Find a blanket, a tapestry, anything to wrap her in. Quickly!"

Thum hurried away to do Dain's bidding.

Alexeika circled around behind the chairs, alert and brandishing Severgard in her hands. "I like this not. Something is wrong here. It's a trap, and these two are the bait."

"Perhaps," Dain said, intent on Pheresa. How drawn and thin she looked. Her bones were pushing through her skin, as though the Netherans had starved her.

And Gavril looked hardly better. Dain thought of what King Verence would say were he to see his fine son in such a state.

"Where is Sir Thum?" he asked impatiently. "Lord Omas, do you see aught we can use to wrap her in? 'Tis freezing in here. I wonder she has not already perished of such cold."

"Faldain!" Alexeika screamed in warning.

It was the only warning Dain had as Gavril came suddenly to life, rising from his chair and swinging Tanengard with deadly intent.

Bent as he was over Pheresa, Dain had no chance to draw his weapon before Tanengard clanged across the back of his breastplate and bit deep into his shoulder. The blow drove him down across her unconscious body.

He tumbled to the floor, awash in a sea of incredible pain. The magicked blade had sliced through his armor like a hot blade through butter, and it filled him with an agony beyond anything an ordinary wound might have caused. Unable to move, he was conscious of nothing except this all-consuming pain. He cried out, his body wanting only to flee the pain, to escape it, but there was no getting away. It hurt so horribly he wondered if his arm had been hacked off. Then at last, the pain eased enough for him to draw in a breath. He felt blood gushing down his back, and shuddered.

"Faldain!" Alexeika shouted again, her voice distorted by the roaring in his ears.

From the corner of his eye he glimpsed Gavril looming over him. Then Tanengard's blade came flashing down once more.

With all his strength, Dain forced himself to reach past the agony and *move*. He managed to roll over, and Tanengard thudded into the floor where his head had been just a second before. The sword caught there, and Gavril—his expression still empty—tugged at it, to no avail.

Dain scrambled away from him, hampered by his injury and

all but pinned against the chairs. Gavril could have turned on him, could have plunged his dagger through Dain's heart in those few seconds, but he continued to tug at his sword with mindless intensity.

Scooting frantically to get away, Dain saw a gaping hole in Gavril's neck just beneath the back curve of his skull. Horror flashed through Dain at the sight of it. Despite his long dislike, and even occasional hatred, of Gavril, no enemy deserved this fate.

Gavril's soul had been eaten. He was Nonkind.

The smell reached Dain then, a foul, putrid wave of decay that burned his nostrils and left him gasping.

Desperately he grabbed for Truthseeker, missed, and grabbed again. Although the pain had now localized itself in the back of his left shoulder, his whole body had become strangely weak. He felt his head swimming, and tried again to draw his sword. But Alexeika gripped him by his cloak and dragged him away from Gavril.

"Dear Thod," she was gasping. "Dear Thod!"

And time, which had seemed frozen since Gavril had struck the first blow, flowed forward again. Now everything seemed to be happening at once, with men shouting and running. Omas was bellowing, and only Dain seemed unable to flow with time or to hear what anyone was saying or to move as he wanted to.

He knew he had to warn them, but he lacked the breath.

Gavril pulled Tanengard free. Lifting it, he turned and came at Dain again, moving like a jerky puppet.

Lord Omas charged between them, and alarm gave Dain the strength and breath he'd been reaching for.

"Get back!" he shouted in warning. "He's—"

Lord Omas's sword plunged through Gavril's midsection, but to little effect. Gavril stood there, impaled on the weapon, and merely blinked at Omas, who turned white and uttered a terrible curse.

Omas jerked out his sword, and Gavril swayed, then focused on Dain and tried to attack him once more.

Alexeika growled something and sprang up. With a mighty swing of Severgard, she hacked off Gavril's sword arm. Tanengard, still gripped by Gavril's severed hand, dropped to the floor. Dain weakly kicked it as far away as he could.

Gavril, his stump leaking blood that was black and foul-smelling, swayed from side to side. His empty eyes stared at Dain and his remaining hand clenched and unclenched.

By then the Agyas had surrounded them. Dain was pulled even farther back, and the warriors closed in on Gavril.

"No!" Dain said, then winced as he seemed to lose his breath. Blood was still running freely down his back. Little dots swam in front of his vision, but through sheer willpower he refused to pass out. "Don't hack him to bits. He's soultaken. It will avail nothing. Alexeika!"

She nodded, and plunged Severgard through Gavril's chest.

His mouth opened in a soundless scream, and his dark blue eyes fastened on Dain. For a moment they almost regained their sanity, then he crumpled to the floor and moved no more. A terrible stench of burned flesh filled the air.

Silence fell over the room, broken only by Dain's hoarse breathing. The pain swept over him in waves now, and he struggled anew to stay conscious.

The commander issued orders as he threw salt on Gavril's body with curses and the warriors crowded around Dain.

"My lady," the commander said, dropping to his knees beside Alexeika, who was now cradling Dain in her arms. "How is he?"

She was weeping, some of her tears dripping on Dain's face, and did not answer. When Lord Omas gently unbuckled Dain's breastplate and cut open the back of his hauberk to expose the wound, their faces grew grave indeed.

"We must bind him quickly," Lord Omas said. He gave Dain a stricken look. "My first test, and I failed your majesty. May Thod forgive me."

Dain wanted to tell him he'd not failed, but he couldn't find the breath. The commander, his braid beads clacking as he worked, swiftly pulled off his surcoat and cut it into strips, which he used to bind the wound tightly.

Crying out, Dain felt himself sucked to the very precipice of unconsciousness, but he held on and did not completely pass out. A moment later, when he dragged open his eyes, feeling shaky and drenched with sweat, the men were arguing about how to best move him. Thum appeared, white-lipped and horrified, still holding a tattered length of tapestry in his hands.

"Dain!" he said, kneeling down to grip Dain's bloodstained fingers. "Sweet Tomias, how came this to happen?"

Dain tried to smile at him. "Gavril always hated me," he whispered, while Alexeika pressed her hand to his cheek.

"Do not talk," she said, tears shimmering in her blue-gray eyes. "Please, *please* rest."

Dain ignored her. "Now he's finally struck down his . . . hated pagan." A shudder passed through his body, and he gritted his teeth again the pain it aroused.

Chesil Matkevskiet came running in. "Majesty!" he called out. "Bad news! The usurper's—"

Breaking off in mid-sentence, he stumbled to a halt and stared at Dain aghast. *"Aychi, nin a myt!"* he cried. "This cannot be!"

"What news?" Dain whispered.

Alexeika tried to shield him and gestured for Chesil to go away. "Do not worry about it now. You must rest until a physician is found."

But Dain shook his head, his gaze remaining on Chesil. "What news?"

The youth had turned pale; his eyes were enormous. "The general sends word that we must flee Grov at once. It's a trap. The usurper's army is coming."

More commotion ensued. Dain felt a cold sweat break out over his body. At last, here was the battle he'd vowed to take on, and now he was unable to do more than lift his head. A terrible feeling of doom sank through his bones, and he realized that he was on the brink of failing completely. Failing his father. Failing Pheresa. Failing these men, who'd trusted him and followed him into this trap.

Anger ran through him like fire, and he tried to sit up, gripping Alexeika's sleeve and hanging on with desperation while she tried to push him down.

"No," she was saying. "No, you will only make yourself bleed more."

"Our forces are scattered across the city," Lord Omas said in dismay.

By my order, Dain thought with fresh guilt. "If they are caught in the city, they'll be massacred," he gasped out.

Bleak silence fell over them all.

Dain sighed. "Should have known it was . . . too easy. Chesil, dispatch messengers . . . give the word. Must . . . retreat." He winced, knowing it meant defeat even if most of the men escaped alive.

"They are coming to Grov from three sides," Chesil reported. "But I'll do my best to—"

"Wait!" Alexeika said. Her eyes were dark with emotions, and she was trembling. "Majesty, I have a confession to make. I—"

"Not *now,* Alexeika," Thum said impatiently.

Ignoring him, she took Dain's hand between hers. "Sire, I am the betrayer."

Dain blinked at her. Looking shocked, the others started asking questions, but he gestured for quiet. "Explain."

Fresh tears spilled down her face. "I'm sorry. I'm sorry!" she cried, and drew forth a cord from beneath her clothing. On it swung a ring, and as she pulled the cord over her head and held it out, Dain gasped sharply.

"What miracle is this?" he whispered.

"Nay, I kept it from you. Even when I knew what it was, I kept it!" she said in anguish. "All that you needed most, I withheld."

"How did you come by this? How did you find it?"

"In Gant," she said. "When that man—"

"Sulein."

"Aye. When he fell down dead, I saw the Ring fall off his finger. I picked it up, knowing what it must be, but I kept it hidden from you." She bowed her head as Dain turned the Ring of Solder over and over in his fingers. "I was a jealous fool. I thought only of myself. I know I cannot be forgiven, but let me use it now to get the Chalice for you." Her eyes bored into his pleadingly. "Let me do this last act in retribution before I am executed."

"What!" Thum said, outraged. "Trust her, after this? Let me get it for you, sire!"

Dain glanced up at his friend, so serious, so ready to serve although he did not understand what his offer entailed.

"Nay, sire," Lord Omas said. "Let—"

" 'Tis *my* responsibility," Dain broke in, closing his fingers tightly around the Ring. Inside, he was awash with a tangle of emotions. Why had Alexeika kept it from him all this time? Why?

But there was not time to ask her reasons. He had one last chance to save his kingdom, to save them all. He knew he must take it.

"Chesil," he said, trying to make his voice sound stronger. "Tell your father . . . tell Romsalkin . . . they must hold off Muncel's men as . . . as long as they can."

"Majesty, I—"

Dain glared at the distraught youth. "Do as I command. Then tell Samderaudin that I've gone to get the Chalice. Go."

Gulping, the youth ran.

Dain gathered all his determination together. "Sir Thum, I entrust Lady Pheresa to your care. Keep her safe. Give your life for hers, if you must."

Thum looked as though he wanted to protest, but he bowed his head. "I swear it," he said harshly.

"Lord Omas."

"Sire?"

"Get me . . . get me to my darsteed."

The giant's face sagged with worry, but in silence he gently picked Dain up, then carried him downstairs and outside into the freezing air. The cold revived Dain a little. He was still sweating, still subject to trembling fits he could not control, but his left arm was starting to feel numb now, and the previous blinding agony had diminished. He slid the Ring on his right forefinger, and it began to glow immediately. He felt the band grow warm against his flesh, and its presence heartened him.

At the foot of the steps, Lord Omas set Dain tenderly on his feet and steadied him as he swayed. Dain's head was spinning, and he did not think he could keep his balance.

But he had to do it. After blowing out several forceful breaths, he finally mastered his weakness and braced his feet.

The darsteed was led up, bugling and slashing at anyone within reach. Seeing Dain, obviously sensing his weakness, it lunged at him with a vicious snap of its jaws, but Dain struck it with his mind.

The darsteed reared in surprise. Abruptly docile, it dropped to all four feet and stood motionless with its head lowered. Only the rumbling in its nostrils betrayed its pent-up anger.

Lord Omas lifted him into the saddle and held him there while Dain struggled to keep from tumbling off. His brief spurt of energy seemed to have failed him, and he could feel himself bleeding again inside his bindings.

His courage sagged inside him, and he felt very, very tired. *I cannot do this,* he thought.

But there was no one else to do it. Slowly he pulled himself erect in the saddle.

"Sire, I must go with you," Lord Omas said worriedly.

"Nay, you cannot accompany me on this journey. It will be quick, that I promise," Dain said to him. "Swear to me that you will all hold fast."

At that moment General Matkevskiet came galloping up on a lathered horse, his gray braids flying about his head as he reined up hard. "Leaving us, sire?" he called out scornfully.

Lord Omas turned to glare at him. "He's going after the Chalice."

The general did not look appeased. "Perhaps the son is more like the father than we would wish for. Look yon!" He pointed across the city.

Through a gap in the trees, Dain saw a spiral of smoke in the distant sky.

"They're coming!" the general shouted breathlessly. "Not just the usurper's troops, but half of Gant by the looks of 'em. And our leader is leaving."

"I'll be back," Dain said, knowing how this looked, how it sounded. "You must hold only a short while."

"Thod's bones! Why should we? We—"

"Because you must!" Dain said harshly, cutting him off. He glared at the old man. "You must! In the name of all that remains good, you must fight as you've never fought before. Gant means to invade Nether, and Mandria, and the world if it can. It means to destroy us all. We will stop it here. We must!"

"They are twice, three times our number," Matkevskiet argued. "We are trapped, doomed, unless we flee."

"If you take the coward's road," Dain said, "then we are all surely lost to Ashnod's dominion."

"I will stand," Lord Omas said.

"And I!" called out the commander of the guards.

"And I!" shouted another man, then more joined in, and more, until they were all shouting it.

A lump filled Dain's throat. He met Matkevskiet's one good eye, waiting for the answer he had to have.

Frustrated fury reddened the general's face. "Then by Thod, see that you're quick. Bring us the miracle we need!"

Dain gathered his reins, braced himself, and gazed down at the Ring, which glowed brightly on his hand. He thought of the Chalice and the place in Nold where it was hidden. *Please Thod, let no one have moved it during all these years,* he prayed.

"Stand back," he said to the men trying to hold the darsteed.

As soon as the men jumped away, the beast whirled around so fast it nearly knocked Lord Omas off his feet. Hanging on by sheer determination, Dain gritted his teeth and spurred the animal into a gallop. As it bounded across the gardens, he sent all the force of his mind into the center of the Ring's power.

Chalice! he thought.

And with a flash of golden light, he vanished into thin air, leaving only a trail of golden sparks behind him.

23

A LIGHT DRIZZLE was falling in the ravine where Dain materialized. Reeling in the saddle, flooded with waves of pain and nausea, he barely noticed that he was once again in the first world, until the darsteed tried to drag him off under a branch.

Coming to with a jolt, Dain blinked and squinted, gasping for breath. This was not much of a ravine, being shallow and choked with tree saplings and brambles. A tiny stream trickled through mossy rocks at the base of the hillside. With effort, Dain focused his mind on the task at hand. How long did it take to journey through the second world? Days? Hours? Minutes? He was now in Nold, perhaps a half-day's ride from Thirst Hold by his rough reckoning, and far, far away from the brave souls presently fighting the Gant invasion in Grov.

How easy it would be to just remain here, Dain mused, safe and far away from that danger. But he discarded the temptation in an instant. Wiping clammy perspiration from his forehead, he forced himself to get on with what he'd come here to do.

Gazing up at the hillside, he saw the ancient stone carving, blurred with the erosion of time and an overgrowth of lichen, that marked an old shrine. His heart leaped in his chest, and suddenly he was able to push his pain aside.

He dismounted awkwardly, then met the darsteed's snapping jaws with a strong slam of his gloved fist and staggered away from the brute.

The simple act of walking a few steps brought on fresh weakness. His head started swimming, and he could not seem to hold himself upright. Yet he struggled to keep planting one foot in front of the other, and thus splashed his way across a stream that ordinarily he could have jumped lightly over.

Climbing the hillside was nearly impossible, even when he grabbed onto shtac saplings to pull himself forward. He could manage only one or two steps at a time without having to sit down to rest, breathing heavily all the while.

The mouth of the shrine was only a few feet distant, but it looked far away. He could feel himself sinking into unconsciousness, and desperately fought to stay awake. If he swooned now, he would likely die, and so would his friends, and all the Netherans fighting in his name.

"I . . . will not . . . let Gavril kill . . . me!" he vowed through gritted teeth.

He crawled awkwardly forward, using his knees and one hand, his left arm clamped to his body to keep from moving his shoulder. Panting and sweating, he paused once to be sick, then forced himself onward.

The hillside canted on him as though it would spill him off. Moaning, he clung tightly to some brambles—which scratched his hands—clenching shut his eyes until the wave of vertigo passed. Then he drew in several breaths and inched his way forward.

Eventually the musty old smell of a trolk den reached his nostrils. Revived a little by the stink, he lifted his head and squinted, and was surprised to find himself almost in the very mouth of the cave.

By force of habit, he picked up a small stick and hurled it weakly into the cave. If anything lurked in there, that would provoke it into coming out. Trolk he did not fear, for his keen sense of smell told him the scent was a false one. No doubt used in a protection spell long ago, its effect was fading with the passage of time.

Hurting, he half-crawled, half-scooted himself inside the cave, rested a moment, then ventured deeper.

It was a shallow place. He'd expected to find it running deep into the hillside, but instead it formed a small, roughly circular room. The ceiling was tall enough to allow him to stand, had he been capable of doing so.

Pausing on the cold, slightly damp ground, Dain looked around through the gloom. Almost no light filtered inside, yet it seemed as though the shadows were dissipating a bit. Glancing down, he saw the Ring glowing white on his finger. It cast about the same amount of light as a glowstone, and when he lifted his hand its radiance strengthened enough to dimly illuminate the cave.

Near the back wall, he saw a V-shaped fissure about halfway up. He frowned, remembering how his father had once stood there. That's where the Chalice had been left.

Only it wasn't there now.

Disappointment crashed through him. Gone, he thought dully. Someone had found it, taken it. Who? Where was it now? Why had the finder not proclaimed it?

He felt his strength and determination trickling from him like the blood seeping down his back. "No," he moaned. "Great Thod, no."

He sank onto his side on the cold ground. He was so tired. He'd come so far, tried his best. How cruel fate was to cheat him now.

Yet something inside him would not let him wallow in this self-pity. He thought of his father, who'd destroyed himself trying to keep the Chalice safe. He thought of his mother, poisoned by villains. He thought of Thia, born a royal princess but raised in a dwarf's burrow. He thought of Lord Odfrey, who'd been the first man to show him kindness. He thought of King Verence, who'd taught him how to be a king. He thought of Sir Terent, a Mandrian who had sworn fealty to him and followed him unto death. He thought of Thum and Alexeika, both friends on whom he'd come to rely so heavily.

And the anger in his heart against Alexeika faded. Lying there, he simply let it go. Had she given him the Ring the day she found it, the Chalice would still have not been here.

Of course, now her moods made sense. He understood why she'd been so upset the day he'd knighted her and given her a hauberk and spurs. Her tears and prickly temper sprang from guilt, festering in her heart all that time. Why she'd done it did not matter; her change of heart had redeemed her.

He thought of Gavril, who'd come into the Dark Forest on a quest to find the Chalice. Gavril, who'd lost first his faith and then his soul and finally his life, because of too much arrogant pride and a tainted sword he could not relinquish.

As for Pheresa, Dain regretted he could not save her. He'd wanted to make her grateful to him, to turn her love from Gavril to him. He'd thought that if he could bring her a cure he would win her heart. But it was no good to force love from gratitude.

Besides, he hadn't saved her, hadn't been the big hero he'd longed to be.

Nay, he'd done what his father had done—abandoned his people and vanished. Were they cursing his name now, while they were dying?

He would go back to them, he vowed. Although he returned without the Chalice, he would stand with them to meet his death in combat. In some ways, he'd been just as arrogant, foolish, and overconfident as Gavril. But he would go back to his people, empty-handed, and stand with them to the last.

Sighing, he forced himself to sit up. As he waited for the cave to stop spinning, he noticed a few scattered stones on the ground, as well as some sticks propped against the wall.

Another dim memory came to him. His father had knelt there once on the moist soil and placed those stones just so. Thia had helped him. Then they'd prayed together.

For his family's honor, Dain decided to do the same before he left.

Gasping, he crawled forward and slowly, one by one, placed the stones in a circle. The sticks had been peeled of their bark long ago. They had darkened with age and no longer gleamed white, but they were ash and therefore sacred. He ran his hand up and down their lengths, cleaning dirt and cobwebs off them, before he crossed them carefully. He had no Element candles to light, no bronze knives of ritual, no bell, and no green vines, but he did have salt. He took out a small handful from his salt purse and poured it carefully in a thin white line just inside the stone circle. When that was done, he knelt, feeling clammy and weak and very tired, and uttered the simple prayer that Thia had taught him when he was little. He even said the nonsense words they used to say afterwards, nonsense words that he now recognized as Netheran and sacred.

Then he lifted his gaze upward. "Forgive me, O Thod," he prayed simply, his heart pouring out its trouble. "Forgive me for the sin of pride. I wanted to prove to all men that I could do better than my father. I was angry with him for deserting us, and I meant to prove myself his superior. I am not. I am merely a man who tried but could not do all that I meant to . . . just like my father."

Closing his eyes, he bowed his head and let the silence soak through him.

Turn around.

The voice echoed through his mind, and made his heart jump in fear. He opened his eyes with a gasp, not certain he'd heard rightly. Yet the voice had been clear.

Not yet willing to think that Thod might have actually spoken to him, Dain turned his head and looked behind him.

The cave was suddenly filled with radiant white light. His heart started pounding rapidly in his chest. He looked around, then stared at the rough rock wall and decided the light seemed to be brightest there.

Dain crawled to it on his knees, and there, lying on its side between some small boulders and the wall, was a tall, flared vessel of white metal, glowing with a power that seemed to reach out and enfold him.

Trembling with the shock of his discovery, he stared at it in disbelief. Then he reached out an unsteady hand, and let his fingers brush along the vessel's side. The metal felt warm to his touch, as though it were alive.

He heard the Chalice's song chiming inside the metal. It was a song of hope, peace, and purity. A song of healing and strength. Awed, he reached down and reverently picked it up.

As he held it aloft, its light streamed down over him in rivers of brightness until his head and body glowed with it. He felt his wound close, the festering evil left by Tanengard cleansed away. Strength returned to his limbs, and his exhaustion faded.

"My son," a deep voice said quietly from behind him.

Startled, Dain turned around, and found himself staring at Tobeszijian. The ghost king looked almost solid in the light cast by the Chalice. Standing in his armor and spurs, his sword belted at his hip, he stood tall and somber, staring at his son.

Dain swallowed hard. "Father."

"You have done well in all that has been set before you."

Dain frowned, feeling as though he did not deserve such praise. "My reasons were wrong," he confessed. "I—"

"You have done well," Tobeszijian said. "Now you must face the greatest task of all."

"Yes," Dain agreed. "I must go back to them quickly."

Tobeszijian's pale eyes bored into Dain. "When we talked before, I told you that a king's sword should be passed to his son. Now the time has come."

"But you can't do that," Dain said.

Tobeszijian frowned. "God-steel does not belong in the first world. It was never meant to be left there, or to be used by mortals."

Dain thought of the bowl he'd stolen from the Chief Believer and lost when he was submerged in the Charva River. Now he glanced down at Truthseeker hanging at his hip. It had become a part of him. He could not imagine life without it. Or battle. "I couldn't have escaped Gant without this sword."

"It has served you well. But it is wrong to keep it past its purpose."

"But Lord Odfrey told me his ancestor was given the weapon as a reward."

"So was he told, but 'tis untrue. Many tales change and grow false through centuries of retelling. Truthseeker was taken as plunder by Odfrey's ancestor."

Dain frowned. "But Lord Odfrey told me this sword was holy and to be kept with honor."

"Was it honorable for Lord Odfrey to hide it from all?"

"He brought it out at my trial," Dain argued.

"Concealed beneath a cloth. He kept it hidden, spoke little of it, feared it. This is not honorable, my son."

Dain swallowed more protests. "Have I been dishonorable with it?" he asked humbly.

"Only once."

And Dain knew instantly that his father referred to his showing off by breaking Matkevskiet's scimitar. Ashamed, he walked silently to the rear of the cave and placed the Chalice in the fissure. Then he slowly unbuckled his sword belt.

Reluctance filled him, and he thought of Samderaudin's warning about having to choose between Truthseeker and something else. He did not want to relinquish this magnificent sword. He'd bonded with it in combat. He knew its song well.

Yet with a sudden chill he thought of Gavril, and remembered how the prince's obsession with Tanengard had led him to tragedy. No possession should ever become that precious, he thought.

And he laid Truthseeker in its scabbard on the ground inside the circle of stones and salt.

"Truly you have learned wisdom," Tobeszijian said.

Dain turned back to him and saw his father grown smaller and dimmer as though fading away. But Mirengard lay on the ground, gleaming with life and beauty.

Once before, for a moment only, Dain had been able to reach into the second world and touch its hilt. Now he stared at his father's sword in amazement.

"Pick it up," Tobeszijian told him.

When he obeyed, the sword felt solid in his hands. He lifted it, marveling at how this could happen, yet suddenly anything seemed possible under the power of the Chalice. He curled his fingers around the hilt, and felt it ply itself to fit his hand. Warmth flashed between it and his palm, and the sword sang to him, sweet and high. Unlike the dwarf-made swords Dain had known all his life, this weapon was eldin-forged. It sang of truth and justice and nobility of spirit. It felt light and perfectly balanced in his hand. Instantly he understood what his father had been trying to tell him. Although he'd adapted to Truthseeker and learned to use it boldly, he remembered back to the first few days when handling it had been almost frightening.

"God-steel really isn't for mortals to own," he said now. "Is it?"

"Nay. It can come to possess you, give you false confidence, lead you down paths you should not follow. Mirengard will never possess you, never fail you, never tempt you wrongly. Use it well, my son. Use it for justice and right."

"I shall," Dain promised, his throat suddenly choked.

"There is more," Tobeszijian said. He pointed behind Dain.

Dain turned around, but saw nothing. Then light seemed to flash, dazzling his eyes. He squinted and blinked and suddenly there lay at his feet the breastplate of embossed gold, its hammer and lightning bolt gleaming brightly. Dain gasped in amazement at such a gift, and as soon as he picked it up he felt its power go tingling through his hands, for like Mirengard, it was magicked.

Dain buckled it on with excitement, hung Mirengard on his belt, and faced Tobeszijian, feeling for the first time that he truly was a king.

"Father!" he said with a smile, then stopped in dismay, for Tobeszijian looked dimmer and mistier than ever. He was fading away, and Dain was not yet ready to let him go.

"I can do no more for you," Tobeszijian said softly. "I can do no more. Farewell."

"Wait!" Dain called out to him. "Please . . . what can I do for you, Father? How can I help you?"

"Go to your army. Help Nether, for it needs you sorely now."

"Aye," Dain agreed. "But are *you* not Nether also?"

Tobeszijian was barely visible now, but Dain saw him smile. His pale, stern face was transformed completely, and he came closer once more.

"Would you do this?" he asked eagerly.

Dain spread out his hands. "Ask whatever you wish."

"Let me ride into battle one last time . . . with you," Tobeszijian said. "Let me be inside you, a part of you, guiding you. Let me take my revenge on Muncel. Let me return also to my people, as I once promised to do."

Tears burned Dain's eyes. He thought of the long years Tobeszijian had existed in his terrible, lonely limbo, and how much pain lay in that request. Although he did not understand how it could be done, he could not refuse.

"Of course, Father," he said. "How is it to be done?"

Tobeszijian walked forward and silently stepped into him. Dain felt himself sway, then there was Tobeszijian's mind wrapped around his. His body felt strange—still strong, but not like his at all. Yet when Dain glanced down at his hands he recognized them for his own, down to the old scars on his knuckles and the new callus on his thumb.

They shared no thoughts. There was no internal discussion, yet Dain felt as though his spirit and Tobeszijian's had somehow become one.

He took the Chalice from its niche and tucked it beneath his cloak to protect it from the drizzle outside. Then he walked away from the cave, and did not let himself look back.

Outside, the leafless trees with their rain-darkened bark seemed in sharper focus than ever before. The gloomy clouds overhead dragged their bellies on the topmost branches, and the drizzle quickly became a downpour.

The darsteed stood where he'd left it. As Dain came down the hillside, it flung up its narrow head and glared at him with red eyes, snorting uncertainly. It backed up a step as though it did not recognize him, yet the merest touch of his mind forced it to obey.

Dain mounted, secured the Chalice well, and stared at the Ring, glowing brighter than ever on his hand.

"Home," he said, and in a flash he was there.

The transition was too abrupt, too sudden to comprehend at once. In one blink he had left the rain-soaked forest of Nold behind and was suddenly in the snow-covered meadow outside Grov, surrounded on all sides by men shrieking and fighting with all their might.

Dain's arrival in a golden shower of sparks caused the men fighting close by to break off and stagger back. Even the Believers paused to stare.

He sat there astride the flame-snorting darsteed, clad in the gold breastplate and shimmering with a bright radiance that streamed from him to puddle momentarily on the ground, melting the snow wherever it touched down. As Dain drew his new sword, it flashed blinding white, and its radiance obviously dazzled the closest Believers, who groaned and flinched away, some even shielding their eyes with their hands. The darsteed reared high, bugling for battle, and Dain spied his royal banner flying next to a solitary tree of massive and ancient girth.

Fearlessly, Dain aimed the darsteed in that direction and went galloping through the midst of the men, forcing them to break off their fighting and jump out of his way. A few Believers who weren't frozen with astonishment tried to stop him, but their weapons seemed unable to touch him.

It was the Chalice's presence, he knew.

Boldly he galloped right through the heart of the battlefield, with man after man stumbling out of his way. Then cheering came in his wake, a rousing wave in the distance that swelled ever louder behind him. The Netheran knights and Agya warriors shouted and brandished their weapons.

"Faldain! Faldain!" they shouted with new hearts and restored courage.

Reaching the tree and the banners streaming from their poles, Dain saw Romsalkin and Matkevskiet, protected within a spell circle cast by Samderaudin. They stared at him in astonishment.

Without a word, Dain wheeled the darsteed around and let it rear again. As it did so, he pulled out the Chalice from beneath his cloak and held it aloft for all the army to see.

The cheering swelled to new heights, rising to a frenzy now.

Dain looked over his shoulder, knowing that all the encouragement this gave his men would more than be matched by the furious determination of the Gantese to capture it.

"A priest!" he shouted. "Here. Take it with reverence." He leaned down to hand the Chalice to a bearded old man who'd come running forth to take it. The priest was crying openly, and his hands trembled so that Dain feared he might drop the sacred vessel. "Fill it with water, and see that the Lady Pheresa drinks from it at once," he commanded.

"Yes, your majesty," the priest answered, sinking to his knees.

"Romsalkin," Dain said. "Go with him. Guard the Chalice with your life."

The old lord drew himself to his fullest height. His eyes were shining, even as Lord Omas came galloping up wild-eyed.

"Your majesty!" he shouted in disbelief. "You are whole again, but how—"

"Never mind," Dain snapped, seeing the Gantese forces charging anew. Their war cries rang in his ears. "Stay with me."

"Aye, sire."

"Matkevskiet!" Dain said to the general. "Stop hiding here under spells and get out your trumpet. I want your warriors redeployed."

Matkevskiet was staring at him in openmouthed wonder. He looked as though he'd never seen Dain before, and yet as though he knew him well but could not believe his eyes.

"Divide them," Dain said, certain something in his voice or manner was now like Tobeszijian's. "Send a wedge charging straight into the heart of their right flank. That's where the Nonkind are, and that is their weakness."

"Surely that is their strength."

"Their strength lies in the *magemons* surrounding Muncel," Dain said crisply. "The rest of your warriors I want with me. I intend to cut a path to Muncel. Get to it!"

Matkevskiet wheeled his charger around and raised his horn to his lips in a series of sharp blats that only the Agyas understood.

Dain turned to Samderaudin. "Is protection all you can do?" he asked. "Or can you hurl fire spells and cyclones at them? To confuse them, to keep the worst of the Nonkind off the men?"

But the *sorcerel* was staring at him. Instead of answering Dain's question, he said, "So this is the choice you've made. This is the path you've chosen. The riskiest one of all. Welcome home, my liege."

Dain could see a company of Gantese fire-knights closing in. He had no time to discuss anything philosophical now. "If you can spell-fight, do so!" he ordered, and charged his darsteed straight at the oncoming foes.

Lord Omas rode with him, shouting defiance at the top of his considerable lungs. Together they met the foremost Believers, and were soon surrounded and fighting with all their strength and prowess. They were outnumbered far too greatly to prevail, and Dain had a tricky time at first in adjusting to the balance and heft of Mirengard, much less its failure to hack through the fire-knights' obsidian armor.

"Stop fighting the sword," came a voice in his mind. *"Let it fight for you."*

And then he got the knack of it and settled himself into the song and rhythm of a magicked sword untainted and pure.

Moments later, more Netherans joined him and Lord Omas, helping to drive the fire-knights back. During a moment of respite, Dain glanced around and saw the Agyas coming at a full gallop toward him, with the general at their head. Grethori, screaming at the top of their lungs over a dreadful screech of war pipes, rode behind them.

Dain did not wait for them to catch up, but spurred the darsteed forward. "We go to Muncel!" he shouted.

At first they cut through the thin Gantese defenses easily, but the Believers rallied and began to concentrate in front of them, holding them away from Muncel. Dain's charge slowed, and then practically stopped. They fought their way through, one foot at a time, trampling over the bodies of the fallen and driving their foes slowly back. And now Dain found himself fighting Netheran knights as often as he fought Believers. There was a terrible desperation in their faces as they saw him and forced themselves to attack. They had sold themselves to the wrong side in this civil war, and they knew it. Although they fought, often they had little heart in it. As some were quickly slain, others began to throw down their arms and flee.

It was a trickle of desertion at first, then a stream. More and more of Muncel's knights fled the field. Dain was close enough now to see his uncle standing beneath an awning, shaking his fist and screaming at the deserters. Hurlhounds chased after them, bringing many down.

But the Believers did not flee. They grew fiercer than ever, and now they were joined by Nonkind troops, shambling, dead-eyed men, some with lolling heads, all mindlessly stabbing and chopping under the direction of the Believers who controlled them.

Mirengard cut them down so easily it was sickening. As quickly as he could, Dain broke through their line, and suddenly there were no more knights ahead of him. The darsteed raced right up to the very boundaries of the protection spell shimmering around Muncel and his generals.

For the first time in his life, Dain came face-to-face with his uncle. He saw a sour-faced man with a coward's eyes, stooped in posture, and filled with hatred.

A rage not his own filled Dain. He wanted to seize this man by the throat and throttle the life from him. Realizing that these were his father's feelings rather than his, Dain pointed his gory sword at Muncel.

"'Tis over!" he shouted. "Surrender now or—"

"Nay, pretender!" Muncel shouted back. "You have lost by coming here."

"My men are defeating your monsters," Dain said. "Your Netheran knights have already deserted you. Soon you'll be—"

"You have lost!" Muncel shouted, shaking his fists and laughing wildly. "They said you would come to the trap, and so you have. You always do, foolish boy."

Dain frowned, staring at the man in puzzlement, for he saw no trap. Lord Omas caught up with him, and the rest of his men were breaking through now. But a cyclone suddenly spun into existence between Dain and his men, cutting off the Agyas. The trap he had not seen sprang shut.

Muncel stepped aside, and as the protection spell dropped, three *magemons* with rounded shoulders and moon-shaped faces stood revealed. Their mouths were bloodstained and they stank of rotten meat. Standing shoulder to shoulder, they stared at Dain with their weird, compelling eyes, and an involuntary shudder went through him. He felt suddenly light-headed and cold.

In a flash, he remembered the two previous times he'd felt this way, as though he were sinking into a place where all the life was being drained from him.

"The Chief Believer has no need for you now," Muncel said with glee, rubbing his hands together. "When I give him the Chalice you have brought from hiding, his Great Plan will be accomplished without you. And now these *magemons* can complete their spell, as they promised me. You are dead, pretender! Dead!"

At last Dain understood what Samderaudin had meant by the last part of his prophecy, about the reach of Ashnod being long, about the consequences of exchanging Truthseeker— which had protected him from this spell—for Mirengard, which could not.

The terrible coldness sank through his limbs. It slowed his heart, smothered his lungs. Gritting his teeth, he spurred the darsteed forward, intending to strike Muncel down, but the darsteed took no more than a couple of steps before it stopped and would not budge.

"Sire!" Lord Omas yelled in alarm. "What's amiss? What are they doing to you?"

"Attack," Dain commanded.

Lord Omas charged the *magemons,* only to be knocked from his saddle by an invisible force.

Despite his efforts to resist, Dain felt his life being stolen bit by bit. His energy drained from him until he could no longer stay astride the darsteed. He felt himself sway, then the next thing he knew was the jolt of impact as he hit the snow-trampled ground. Lying there, certain this was the end, he used all he had left to keep his grip on Mirengard.

Muncel walked up to him, the hem of his long, fur-trimmed robes dragging on the snow. He wore red leather slippers with long pointed toes. The man was not even dressed for war, Dain thought in disgust. Chances were he'd never fought in a battle in his life.

"And now you die, spawn of my half-brother and his blasphemous slut. You are the last of the mixed blood tainting my ancestral line. Nether is finally free of you, as it will soon be free of all eldin." He kicked Dain in the head. "Now die!"

But although the coldness still dragged through Dain's limbs, rendering him weak and sluggish, he didn't die as he was supposed to. He reached out, gripped Muncel's foot, and hung on for dear life.

Muncel jerked his foot, but was unable to pull free of Dain's grasp. "Kill him!" he shouted at the *magemons.* "Tulvak Sahm, why does he not die?"

The *sorcerel,* hovering nearby, craned his neck to peer at Dain without coming closer. "He is not what he appears to be. The fates have changed."

"What?" Muncel glared at him. "What do you mean?"

But the *sorcerel* simply pressed his long hands together and vanished into thin air.

Muncel's mouth fell open, and he shook his fist. "Come back! Damne! You there!" he said, beckoning to his protector. "Give me your sword. I'll deal with this puppy myself."

But the man's eyes were bulging with terror. He turned and ran away.

Cursing him, Muncel tried again to twist his foot from Dain's grasp, but Dain could feel his strength seeping back. He tightened his fingers and would not let go.

Muncel reached down and grabbed Mirengard from Dain's

hand. "This should have been mine as well," he muttered, then a scream burst from his throat, and he dropped the sword in the snow. His hands were on fire, the skin blistering and charring as the flames burned higher. Frantically he beat them against himself, but only set his clothing on fire. Dain released his foot, and he flung himself to the ground, rolling over and over and screaming horribly. The flames would not go out.

His generals and protector stared openmouthed, then fled.

Dain knew this was his chance. He scrambled clumsily to his feet, still hampered by the spell, which could not kill him but held him weak. Although lifting Mirengard seemed to take more strength than he had, he staggered over to the *magemons* and plunged his sword into the nearest of the three.

A high-pitched scream hurt his ears, and then they were all three screaming. A terrible stink filled the air, and the *magemon* Dain had stabbed began to burn. The others caught fire from him, but Dain stabbed them all in swift succession just to make sure.

As they went up like kindling, still screaming, the last vestiges of their spell dropped away so suddenly he staggered.

Lord Omas caught him with a steadying arm. "Sire! Great Thod, are you all right?"

Dain grinned at him, blinking as he realized Tobeszijian's presence had saved his life. "Aye," he said. "Let's get back to the rest of this battle."

The cyclone which had fended off the Agyas vanished, and they came rushing up to stare, hard-faced and unsympathetic, at Muncel, who was still burning alive.

It was a horrible death, but Dain knew of no way to hasten the end for him. He looked at that agonized face, still visible through the flames, and thought of how his mother must have died, suffering in agony, deserted by her court and friends, as the eld-poison ate her alive.

"Majesty, the battle is turning against us!" one of the Agyas shouted.

Dain looked where he pointed and saw the rebel forces falling back beneath another onslaught of Believers. Cursing, Dain sprang onto his darsteed and wrenched the animal around.

"Let's to it!" he shouted.

But even as he spurred his mount forward, he did not know whether they could prevail. His forces were tiring. Many lay dead. Despite the desertions, there were still plenty of Believers, far too many.

Then there came the loud wailing of horns in the distance, horns Dain had not heard in a long time. He looked around, refusing to believe his ears, as suddenly a new army appeared at the edge of the meadow.

Reining up hard, Dain stared with his heart pounding. He did not want to hope, did not want to believe falsely.

Beside him, Lord Omas stood up in his stirrups. "Thod's mercy," he said in despair. "What is this come against us?"

The new army seemed to fill the horizon. With drums pounding and banners flying proudly, they marched forward, emerging from the forest and heading for the rear lines of the Gantese forces.

Dain kept staring. Snow had begun to fall in tiny spits of ice. He couldn't see clearly. Couldn't be sure.

Sir Thum, spattered with gore from head to foot, came galloping up with a wild yell that startled Lord Omas.

"Uplanders!" he shouted, grinning at Dain. "Mandrians! Look yon, sire! I see Thirst's banner flying, and Lunt's, and Carcel's, and lowland banners as well. And there! *There!* Do you see it?"

Dain looked, and at last saw the royal, purple and gold pennon of Mandria flying proudly above the others. And there, at the head of the army, rode an upright figure, broad-shouldered and breastplated in gold.

"King Verence," Dain said in wonder. "He has brought his army."

Thum whooped like a crazed man while the Agyas stared in astonishment. "Now see some real knights in action!" he shouted just as the distant orders rang out. The Mandrians began their charge.

Shaking off his amazement, Dain called out orders to his men. "Now is the time to strike hard, while these fiends are caught between us. For Nether!" he shouted, making his darsteed rear.

At that moment the clouds parted and a pale shaft of sunlight came down. It shone over Mirengard as Dain held it aloft, and the blade flashed brightly for all to see.

They rejoined the battle, chanting their war cries as they charged the rattled Believers. Soon thereafter, the combat finally ended. The air hung heavy with the stench of burned and salted Nonkind. The last of the Believers had either galloped out of sight or been taken prisoner and lined up in long rows, where grim-faced Netherans executed them one by one.

Twilight began to draw shadows across the meadow. The air lay still and very cold. Dain, weary to the bone and sticky with dried blood and gore, made his way back to the massive tree. He dismounted, his legs feeling wooden, his mind numb. Romsalkin, beaming from ear to ear, bellowed orders, and a chair and a cup of wine were brought for Dain. He quaffed down the liquid without tasting it, sighed, and pulled off his gloves. But he knew he could not rest yet. There was still something else to be done.

"My lord," he said to Omas, who bent over him at once. "Is this the Tree of Life?"

Omas looked blank. "Indeed, I know not, sire." He turned and called out, "Lord Romsalkin, is this the Tree of Life?"

Dain's mind was spinning with a hundred details. Muncel, his flames put out at last by Samderaudin, lay salted among the dead, his slain officers beside him. Dain had no idea if Pheresa had been attended to properly. He hadn't seen Alexeika during the entire battle and was worried about what had become of her. There was still King Verence to find and thank properly, before Dain delivered the terrible news about Gavril.

Yet before he could do anything else, he had one task that overrode them all. He could feel a terrible sense of urgency beginning to burn inside him. "I must know," he said.

Romsalkin stared at him, then the old tree. Its branches were gnarled and stunted. At one time part of it had split, leaving a gaping hole high in the upper part of the trunk. When Dain put his bare hand on the rough bark, he felt no life in it, not even dormancy.

"The eldin told me the Tree of Life was dead," he said. "Does no one know if this is it?"

"Aye, majesty," said an old, quavery voice. It belonged to

one of the priests. Stooped and white-headed, he limped forward. "So says the legend. 'Twas under these branches that the eldin worshiped long ago, before the First Circle was made by men and eld-folk. All kings of Nether, save the usurper, did vow to protect this tree."

Dain drew a deep breath, listening to what spoke inside him. "Then I must be alone," he said, and swept them all with his gaze. "Leave me for a few minutes."

They stood there, staring at him with concern. It was Lord Omas who finally began to shoo them away. "You heard his majesty. Withdraw. Give him the privacy he needs."

Muttering and uncertain, they backed away, Romsalkin included. Lord Omas would not even let a squire come up to light the cressets. And he himself retreated a short distance from Dain, close enough to help if wanted, but not intruding.

In the distance came a stir and the noise of several voices. Pages ran through the crowd of Netherans, crying out, "Make way for King Verence!"

Dain ignored the approach of the Mandrian party. Tobeszijian had to be attended to first.

He knelt at the base of the old tree, not yet fully understanding what he was to do. Despite the noise and commotion behind him as Lord Omas held the Mandrians back, Dain bowed his head.

Tobeszijian's spirit slipped from him, and for a moment Dain saw his father's ghostly visage shimmering at him in the gloom.

"I came back," he whispered. "The people will never know it, but thanks to your help, my son, I came back to them."

"Father—"

"You have done well," Tobeszijian said. "I am proud of you."

"Wait," Dain said quickly. "Let the people see you—"

"You will make a good king." And with that, Tobeszijian sank into the soil.

A feeling of peace swept through Dain, and he understood that his father was finally at rest.

There was no need to grieve, but still Dain bowed his head and placed his hands on the bark of the gnarled roots atop the ground. He knew that he would never again see visions of his father. He understood that Tobeszijian's spirit wandered no longer between worlds. He had gone to the third world now, perhaps to be reunited with his wife and daughter. And Dain was left alone to build his own life anew.

"Look!" someone shouted. "What is that? Look!"

Torchlight suddenly flared from behind Dain, shining on him.

Frowning, he rose to his feet and turned around. But the people were not looking at him now. Instead they were staring at the branches above his head, pointing and shouting in amazement.

Tipping back his head, Dain stared at one of the lower branches, for it had leafed out despite the cold and snow. Suddenly it was green with renewed life. Astonished, he pressed his hand to the bark. He could now feel the low, quiet, slumberous life of a tree in dormancy.

"Thod's bones," he said, laughing a little. "It lives again."

The old priest came up beside him, and even Samderaudin drew near as though to listen. "It is the way of all eldin, your majesty," the priest said with shining eyes. "Where they dwell, so do all things know life and renewal. The eldin can bring even dead wood back to life. 'Tis their gift."

Dain frowned at him, his momentary joy sobered. He looked past the priest to the crowd of men standing a short distance away. Even the Mandrians had fallen quiet, content to stare, many of them drawing the sign of the Circle on their breasts.

"I am more eldin than man," Dain said, and his voice rang out loudly enough for all to hear. "My birth caused a great division in our land. There were many then who did not want to serve an eldin king. What say you now?"

They burst into cheers, roaring his name, and Dain had his answer.

.

24

SEVERAL DAYS LATER, Dain stood in one of his palace's state chambers. Although the room was minimally furnished, it was warmed by a fire burning in a colorful tile stove. Dain wore a tunic of burgundy and a narrow gold circlet adorned his brow. Before him stood Lady Pheresa, still very thin and pale, but recovered fully.

She wore a borrowed gown of hard-spun wool and a fur cloak of sables tipped with ermine. Her reddish-gold hair was pulled back neatly. A dainty gold Circle hung at her throat. Her brown eyes were grave, for King Verence planned to leave Nether this day. Gavril's body, wrapped in a shroud, and carefully frozen so that it could make the long journey, was being taken home for state burial in a tomb at Savroix.

It seemed there had been one interruption after another, but at last this morning Dain had won a few minutes in private with the lady. Now that she was here, and they were alone, with even Lord Omas standing outside at the door, Dain found himself with little to say.

She watched him, her eyes brimming with many emotions. Gratitude was perhaps the most evident, and the one he least wanted to see.

"Thank you for saving my life," she said. Her quiet, melodic voice, once able to send desire racing through his veins, now sounded too compliant, too quiet. "Words seem inadequate to express what I feel. I owe you everything."

"No," he said stiffly, finding himself tongue-tied and awkward. "There is no debt, my lady. From the bottom of my heart I regret every day that you suffered."

"My suffering was not your fault," she said. She tilted her head to one side and studied him for a long moment. "You came to me once, with your heart in your hands, and I treated you ill. I regret that now."

Heat stole into his face, and he swiftly averted his gaze from hers. He felt choked. How many times had he dreamed of such a moment, when she would turn to him this way? And now . . . and now, he did not want her. Suddenly, as though chains had dropped from him, he knew the truth. He no longer loved her, if he ever had. A boy's infatuation was a far cry from a man's love. She'd been a dream for him, but now he was awake.

"I'm sorry, my lady," he replied, anxious to end this embarrassing interview. "We seem always to be at cross-purposes. Your gratitude will pass quickly enough. Do not mistake it for some other emotion."

She frowned, drawing in her breath sharply. "You no longer love me."

Her bluntness surprised him. Before her illness, she would have never spoken so plainly. Yet the only thing to do was to offer her the same directness. "Nay, my lady, except in friendship."

"Oh." Tears shimmered briefly in her eyes, and she half-turned away from him. " 'Tis a pity," she said with bravado. "We could have united Mandria and Nether in an invincible alliance, two great kingdoms joined against—"

"Nether is not great at present," he said swiftly. "There is much to rebuild."

"And you do not want my help," she replied softly, her brown eyes lifting to his.

He returned her gaze steadily but said nothing.

She blushed. "I was a fool that night of the Harvest Ball, so ambitious and stupid. I wanted to be queen, and Gavril was my means to that. Alas, although Gavril is gone, I still want to be queen."

"Are you not heir now?" Dain asked.

She stared at him wide-eyed before she sighed. "No one believes I am capable. The court despises me. The king used to pay me little heed. And now with Gavril gone, he hardly notices me at all."

Taking her delicate hands in his, Dain felt as though he could crush her fragile bones if he were not careful. Yet despite her apparent frailty, there was a new fire and purpose in her gaze that he'd never seen before.

Very gently he kissed her on the cheek. "Make Verence notice you. Take hold of what is due you and do not relinquish it. You are wise and good, far more clever than anyone at Savroix has given you credit for. And were you not very tough and courageous, you could not have survived this."

She gave him a tremulous smile.

"Stop hiding your true self, Pheresa," he said, "and show people your steel."

"I will," she said softly, and withdrew her hands from his. Her chin lifted. "I will."

"Then we part as friends?" he asked.

Her smile brightened as she curtsied. "Friends. I will never forget you, Faldain of Nether."

He bowed in return. "Nor I you, Pheresa of Mandria."

Soon thereafter, he met with King Verence. Grief-stricken, his eyes reddened and sad, Verence was departing Nether today while there was a favorable break in the weather.

Because of Dain's tremendous liking and admiration for Verence, he deeply felt his suffering now. Verence had genuinely loved his son, loved and spoiled him, loved and forgiven too many faults.

Quietly Dain said, "I owe you a tremendous debt which I can never fully repay. But tell me how I may try."

Verence frowned. His graying blond hair fell softly to his shoulders, held back by a narrow crown. His coat of arms, embroidered in gold thread, glittered on the front of his purple surcoat. "Nay," he said gruffly, withdrawing his hand. "Do not speak to me of debts. You owe none."

"But you saved the battle."

"You owe none!" Verence said sharply. "I came to pay Muncel's ransom demand with my sword, and by Thod, I did so. My only regret is that I could not finish him myself."

"That duty was mine," Dain said simply. "I am sorry you must depart in such sorrow."

Verence frowned. "I came to bring my son home. That will I do."

"I wish it did not end this way," Dain said.

"You are kindhearted as always," Verence told him, summoning a wan smile. "We both know how Gavril treated you. What he was. What he was becoming. He would have made a bad king. Alas, Dain, I feel old today. I should have sired more sons."

"You still have a successor," Dain said quietly, "if you will but see her qualities."

Verence looked at him in startlement. "Pheresa?" he asked.

"She's your niece, a member of the royal house. Do you think Mandria would not accept a queen in her own right?"

"By Thod," Verence said softly, thinking it over. But then he frowned. "Meddling in my affairs of state already, are you?"

"Well—"

"Come, come! I thought you might offer to marry the girl. Now that your way is clear."

Dain drew a deep breath, desirous of casting no offense. " 'Tis Mandria she wants to rule, not Nether."

"Damne! What's this?" Verence stared at him. "Has she rejected you?"

"We have talked. Our mutual decision is no."

"Nonsense!" She can be wooed if you will but try—"

"Let her rule Mandria after you," Dain interrupted firmly. "Train her well for the task."

"That soft girl? Nay! She hasn't the spirit."

Dain raised her brows. "No spirit? And who stabbed Queen Neaglis with a needle? By Thod, your grace, there's more to her than you think."

Verence barked out a laugh, which seemed to surprise him. "I'll give her nothing, unless she proves her mettle to me. It takes more than a woman's needle to rule a kingdom."

"Aye, that's true enough."

"Well, Dain," Verence said with a shrug. "I can't fault her for not wanting this blighted mess you've won. Heed me and execute that pair in your dungeons."

Dain frowned, thinking of Neaglis and her sickly child Jonan whose fate he still had to decide.

"Exile them," Verence said, "and civil war will drag on endlessly. You must show strength now if you're to keep your throne."

"Rebuilding this kingdom will not be easy," Dain admitted.

" 'Twill keep you busy. As for Thirst, I'll have to find a new chevard to—"

"You will not," Dain said fiercely. "It's mine, by inheritance and charter. The men are sworn to me, and I'll keep my hand on it. And them."

Stiffening, Verence sent Dain a sharp look indeed. "You would not dare . . . you cannot! I refuse to have such a Netheran inroad to my lands. No!"

Dain glared back. "'Tis done, and by your own signature."

"I'll not have it!"

"You can't stop it. The law supports me."

"That charter will be taken apart, analyzed word by word."

"Do it," Dain said boldly. "And let your diplomats meet with mine."

"Done, by Thod! You're a rascal and a devil, Dain. Indeed you are."

But Verence was grinning as he spoke, and they parted on good terms. Dain saw the Mandrians off, glad to see him and his entourage depart at last. Entertaining someone like Verence, who'd been frankly appalled by the condition of both the palace and the city, was a considerable strain when the treasury was depleted and the larder less than well-stocked. Someday, Dain promised himself, Grov would again rival Savroix for its beauty and culture.

"I hear, your majesty," Lord Omas remarked, "that a delegation of the eld-folk is on its way here."

"Aye," Dain said absently.

"They should have fought with us, and not hidden like cowards," Lord Omas went on. "Still, if your majesty can make a treaty with them, that will be quite a change for the kingdom."

"There are many changes to be made in this kingdom," Dain said with determination. Snapping his fingers, he summoned a page. "Bring the Princess Alexeika to me in the Gallery of Glass."

When she came, he was standing at one of the tall windows overlooking what had been his mother's private garden. Overgrown into a thicket, its paths could barely be determined, yet from this height he could see traces of the original design. Sea hollies and old roses, their canes bare and encased in ice from last night's sleet, could still be spied among the weeds and brambles. He would restore the garden, he vowed. He would restore all he could.

"Lady Alexeika!" announced a page.

Dain had heard them coming. Lord Omas, stationed at the door, boomed a few words to her in what he believed was a murmur. Her reply was brief and quiet.

When she entered, her footsteps echoed quick and light on the floor. The few sticks of tawdry furniture had been removed, leaving the room empty of all furnishings. The broken globes and mirrors had been taken away. The burned outline of Gavril's corpse on the floor had been sanded down and obliterated. Cobwebs and years of grime had all been cleaned away, and similar work had started slowly on other inhabitable parts of the palace. Below ground, in the sacred vault of the original shrine and the First Circle, the Chalice glowed its pure light over the altar. The paneatha, with its icons of the gods—slightly mismatched at present—had been restored to its rightful place.

There was much to do, an overwhelming amount to do, but right now Dain's attention was centered on the lady advancing toward him. She was no Alexeika he recognized.

She halted before him and curtsied low, while he stared at her. She was completely transformed. Attired in a gown of long, dark gray velvet trimmed with fur at sleeves and hem, she displayed a shapely figure indeed. She wore her dark chestnut hair loose and full, allowing it to spill down her back in a wealth of shining curls. Little jewels hung from her ears, winking and glittering in the sunshine.

Her beauty stunned him, and Dain did not know what to think of this new Alexeika.

As the silence between them lengthened, defiance filled her blue-gray eyes. Lifting her chin, she started to speak, but he was quicker.

"You're wearing a gown," he said, then instantly realized how inane his remark sounded.

Her nostrils flared. "Aye, sire, I am. Since I'm female, I have the right."

"No, no!" He held out his hand, laughing a little. "Forgive my clumsiness. I meant to compliment you on how well it suits you, but did so poorly. You look charming."

"Thank you, sire."

"I just didn't expect to see you dressed this way."

"And how would your majesty prefer me to dress at court? In leggings?"

Her voice was as sharp and satirical as ever. Suddenly he felt on solid ground again. Beneath all this beauty and femininity could still be found his Alexeika, the sharp-tongued, swearing, tough little knight and comrade he'd grown to like so much. She wasn't wearing her daggers, he noted, and wondered if she'd sold them to buy this finery.

"What does your majesty wish to discuss with me?"

His brows rose at her impatience. She was as prickly today as a hedge thorn, but he answered her question with good humor. "I summoned you to discuss the matter of your court duties."

She stiffened. "I deserve no such favor."

"That is—"

"Nay!" she said sharply. "Please, sire, grant me leave to depart your court . . . and Grov."

"You want to leave?" he said in surprise, far from pleased. "But why?"

Her cheeks burned. "I seek to reclaim my ancestral home from the upstarts who seized it when my father was exiled. With your majesty's permission, I will—"

"No," Dain said.

She fell silent, her brows knotting together. Anger glinted in her eyes.

"In good time we shall deal with all the legal claims and tangled properties," Dain said, "but not today. Sir Thum has told me that you did not join the battle, that instead you stood guard over Pheresa, you alone, and that you killed two hurlhounds to protect her."

Alexeika's face grew redder. Her eyes would not meet his. "The task had to be done," she said gruffly.

"I thank you for your kindness toward the lady," he said.

She shook her head. "Give me no thanks, majesty. I deserve none. Punish me. Cast me out, but don't be kind."

"Why should I punish you?" he asked gently.

Although her mouth trembled, her eyes flashed angrily. "Now you make sport of me."

"I do not. Why should I punish you?"

Her gaze fell from his. "Your majesty knows why. I b-betrayed you."

"Nothing of the kind."

"But—"

"Alexeika, you did not. Whatever wrong you think you committed is forgiven."

"No!" she said sharply. "I don't want forgiveness. I know what I am, sire. A petty, cruel barbarian of the mountains. I tried to keep you from saving her."

He stared at her gravely. "Why?"

"It doesn't matter why!" she cried. "Not now. Please give me leave to go."

"You will stay," he commanded, "until you tell me why you acted as you did."

She whirled around and began to walk in a small circle, her back rigid and stiff.

"Tell me," he insisted.

"Because I hate her!" she cried as though goaded too far. "I am jealous of her, and each time your majesty's gaze goes to her, I feel sick inside."

"If you truly hated her you would not have fought to protect her during the battle. You would not have held the Chalice to her lips and coaxed her to drink the waters that healed her." He met her eyes with compassion. "In fact, you could not have even held the Chalice at all, had you been guilty of all that you claim. It would have burned you."

"I—"

"Alexeika, forgive yourself. No one blames you for concealing the Ring as long as you did. I do not."

She frowned. "Your majesty is too kind. Too softhearted. Everyone here will take advantage of you—"

"Nay," he said, stepping closer. "There is only one person at court who can do that."

Her head jerked up, and she grew visibly flustered. "You flirt with me now only because *she* has gone! If you love her, go after her."

"Do you mean that?"

Biting her lip, she turned away. "I care nothing about Lady Pheresa, but I would see your grace happy no matter the cost."

"Ah," he said with a smile. "Then my happiness is here, for I do not love the lady."

Her eyes flashed to his. "Of course you do. You said so many times."

He shrugged. "Things that once seemed very important to me now appear less so. Others that I failed to value at first have become quite precious."

Her gaze penetrated his, as though desperate to know the truth. "How could your majesty change heart so suddenly? You are not a whimsical or capricious man."

"No, I am not. But I looked at her this morning, and knew she was not the one I want forever with me. I think the change has been taking root in me for several weeks."

"But why, sire? She's all you've ever dreamed about. She's your first love, your ideal of all that's best in a woman. Sir Thum told me—" She broke off suddenly and blushed red. "Forgive me," she said in apology. "I have no business questioning your majesty about anything."

"But I like your questions. And your honesty. Not always your scolding or meddling or arguing, mind, but I like a good, rousing discussion."

"And for this reason you rejected the niece of King Verence?" Alexeika asked in astonishment. "Does your majesty not understand how tremendous an alliance this would be, the union of Nether and Mandria? You could use her dowry to rebuild your treasury. Think of the opportunity."

"Hush," he said. "I've heard that before. The opportunity I want is right here." Without warning, he pulled her into his arms. Ah, he thought in satisfaction. Here was a woman sturdy enough to hold tight. Alexeika might be slender in the right places, but there was nothing fragile or delicate about her.

She yelped in surprise, and her face flamed red as she pushed with all her might against his chest. "What are you doing! King or not, you've no right to take liberties!"

"I haven't taken them yet," he said. "But I shall if you don't grant me any."

She stamped down hard on his foot, making him flinch, and

twisted free. She whirled around in a billow of skirts and hurried away toward the door.

Laughing, Dain hobbled after her. "Alexeika!" he called. "Wait!"

She halted in the center of the room with her back to him.

"You little she-cat," he said, catching up to her, "don't you understand anything? I love you."

"You can't. You don't!"

"Ah, but I do." He put his arms around her gently, not to startle or capture her, but to caress her.

She turned to face him, pushing again at his chest, but this time without much determination. "I'm a knight," she said with loathing. "A comrade-at-arms. A horse thief. A warrior-maid."

"All those things," he agreed, smiling at her. "Although you must promise to stop thieving horses. I cannot permit my queen to do that."

Her eyes flew open wide, and she gasped. "Your queen?"

"My queen," he said. "To rule at my side. To give me dispute rather than gentle compliance. To have courage equal to my own. Alexeika, I would rather love a woman who has the passion to make mistakes, just as I make them, and the honesty to admit them afterwards, as I hope I will always do, than to spend my life with someone docile and dull."

A wicked little light gleamed in her eyes. "Dull?" she echoed. "You think Lady Pheresa is *dull*?"

"Compared to you, aye," he said with conviction. "Do you love me, Alexeika?"

She trembled in his arms, looking shy, and nodded as though her voice had left her. All her heart shone in her eyes.

And he kissed her.